SOARING EAGLES

WES FOLSOM

ISBN 978-1-0980-1836-8 (paperback)
ISBN 978-1-0980-1837-5 (digital)

Christian Faith Publishing, Inc.
832 Park Avenue
Meadville, PA 16335
www.christianfaithpublishing.com

Except for recognized historical figures, all characters are figments of my imagination, real to me, but never having lived. Any resemblance to persons living or dead is strictly coincidental.

Printed in the United States of America

Wounds untreated can deform a person, a family, or a town.
If true healing is given a chance to do its work,
Wounds can scab over and flake away,
Hope can rise and be restored,
And a new beginning can set us free,
Lifting us upward like soaring eagles!

The Author with Jim Ryun

ACKNOWLEDGMENTS

Many people played a part in the creation of "Soaring Eagles." Doc Hensley helped in editing and creating a cohesive story. Ed Bryson, David Hull, and Rick Garside were sounding boards, giving great advice. Dr. Ted Baehr and his clinics were inspiring.

Al Cecere was instrumental in everything to do with eagles. As President of the American Eagle Foundation and the brain trust behind flying the eagle "Challenger" at football games and important functions, his expertise with eagles still dazzles me.

Matt Kinne, a great compatriot, passed too early. Jerry B. Jenkins, Bart Gavigan, Cristobal Krusen, James Hiatt, Rob Stroup, Evan Atwood, Dave Ezell, and the many athletes I trained with and those I coached all contributed to developing inspiration for the story.

My granddaughter, Elizabeth, who read the first draft at age 10 in twelve days, kept me going. She circled several parts she said were boring! But she ended up saying it was the best book she ever read. Granddaughters are great!

My wife Susan deserves more praise than I can give. Her patience and devotion to the story and to me was constant. She pulled me out of many rabbit trails. Our four children, Katrina, Ryan, Kristen, and Eric and their spouses were loving and patient, always believing.

Contents

PROLOGUE

Growing up in a southern mountain town is great until it's awful. I, Billy Cline, understood little of our family history in the Smoky Mountains of Tennessee until Saturday, a week before my twelfth birthday. On that last day of April 1978, my folks drove to Rockside from our Ruby Lake cabin with my two brothers for Jake's baseball game. I opted to stay home and out of curiosity, climbed into our attic. I found a key hidden on a corner hook that opened a locked trunk. Inside, I discovered Pa's high school journals, letters from his deceased brother Jacob, old newspaper clippings, Ma's diaries, and three pair of worn-out running shoes.

Placing the papers in my knapsack, I began reading at Ruby Lake. It changed me. The newspaper article said my Grampa Cline outbid the Clausen-Cowler clan by one dollar for the prized Ruby Lake land, cabin, and its dock, making it the most contested auction in town history. I learned how my Ma, Lily, turned a tragic loss into a life of opportunity with my Pa, Ned, and how testimonies proved the Clausen-Cowler clan had sabotaged Pa's championship race his senior year. What they proved against his running rivals made me want to fight to restore my Pa's lost honor. It became my mission.

After returning from Jake's pitching performance, Ma quoted from Proverbs at bedtime: "A man's steps are directed by the Lord." From my bunk, I brushed back my wavy brown hair in a silent rage, remembering the ragged look of Pa's worn-out running shoes in the trunk. He had taken thousands of steps, but who could believe God would direct the hateful steps the Clausens and Cowlers had chosen to take against my Pa? Newspaper articles confirmed the truth of my folks' writings.

I vowed someday to write about Ma and Pa's journey, using the newspaper information and their own written words. As each year of high school passed, I learned life offered me two choices: right or wrong, fight or flight, love or hate, blame or forgive. Could shades of truth inhabit both sides? Which should I follow? Which should I shun?

If I didn't choose sides, my existence would imitate wind-blown sand, scattered until vanishing; an empty life without purpose. How could I live that way, with something seething inside me called a conscience?

I realized to understand my parents' heart-rending story, I first had to experience my own. So I accepted the opportunity to write about both our journeys in one book, a family history. I'm doing it now.

What started in my attic has taken wings. After graduating, I've written about my dawn run up the mountain at age twelve to save my eagle Victory, and then I've covered Ma and Pa's tragic life journey before I was born. Am I living in a parallel universe?

Questions still haunt me. Why did the eagle bond with me? Would Pa's failures bleed into mine? Would Jenny desire Jimmy Jack over me? Could an old coach with a tragic past teach me anything about life with a group of broken-up teens? Could anyone break the stranglehold of generational persecution still thriving in Rockside? That journey would be an upward climb on an uncharted trail.

Chapter 1

Billy's Dawn Run and Big Storm

May 6, 1978

At 4:32 a.m. I slipped out of the covers and into my clothes, tip-toeing down the wooden stairs and out the cabin door into the shrouded mist of the Smoky Mountains. Knapsack secured, I hit the dirt running.

My brothers slept in on Saturdays. I was awake. Why wait?

The moist summer air glistened in the moonlight. I squinted through fogged glasses as I scampered up the rugged trail. *Am I doing the right thing?*

Groans from aging trees grew louder as if it was their duty to scare away trespassers. *Is that who they think I am? Can't they tell I'm only twelve?* The wind whined, a twirling leaf flicked my ear, and a branch skimmed my hair. I turned full circle, knowing they knew. Fear stalked me. To wait was to be a target. To run was freedom.

I bolted forward, burrowing between two strange walls of trees—not the original path Pa had taught me. I pulled on a limb and peeked through an opening, spying the upper ridge.

Climbing, I tripped, skidding into a bush. I adjusted wet glasses only to bring into focus menacing arms of trees hovering over me, reaching downward, propelled by morning breezes.

Inside my head, I heard Ma reading from her Bible. "Fear not…" Had I outrun my fear? No! I rolled to my knees, wiped my glasses, and jerked up. Hunched over, cautious, eyes darting, I heard Ma's voice speak out again: "For I am with you." I turned to the trees.

"I'm Billy Cline, and I'm not alone! God is with me!" The wind stirred up a violent spiral of debris. My knees shook, but I stood my ground and let out another barrage. "I belong here! Just like all of you!" The wind dwindled, ceasing to nothing. I circled a bush and waited. Had I grown up? I wasn't sure, but I felt taller.

The forest sweated inside the groves. Trudging up the slopes, droplets splashed as I nudged a bush. Jarring a leafy limb overhead, a dew shower doused me, my surprise replaced by a grin.

A glint of color laced the horizon. I reset my bearings to the lookout, spotting the waterfall, a landmark Pa said was crucial. In the dark, I had panicked and lost my way—a lesson learned.

At the waterfall, my excitement matched the bubbling spring spilling over rocks. In May's heat, fresh drinking water was welcome. I climbed up a ledge and sipped near the top of the falls before filling my canteen. A side pool created a shallow reservoir where Pa and I had seen deer drinking. Beyond that, the falls plunged into a section of Ruby Lake where centuries of pounding water had created a fifteen-foot-deep pool, safe enough to survive a leap from the falls after the rains. Grampa Cline had done it years before. The sun peeked from the horizon as I left the top of the waterfall and completed the climb to my boulder cliff lookout.

How can I share this experience with my brothers? Impressing Chester is easy, but Jake would demand dramatics, or he'd wrestle me to the ground and give me an Indian rope burn.

My shelter buttressed against two boulders, covered by tarps Pa had secured with rope. He had looped rope ends through a tarp to the base of a sapling with metal stakes pounded into the rock. I scaled one of them and gazed at the glorious sunrise, its vibrant colors brightening.

The sheer cliffs allowed me to spit more than a hundred feet when the wind was right. When it wasn't, I learned not to spit. I peeked over the edge and saw the tips of trees below appear as bushy toothpicks stuck in the valley floor. The summer's warmth dried the forest dew while my perspiration tried to replace it.

Pa demanded the shelter be well-stocked: two sleeping bags, a blanket, jacket, some rope, a knife, two canteens, binoculars, a flashlight and batteries, a knapsack, and my fishing pole. I slid down the boulder, ducked under the tarps, and grabbed my fishing gear. I strode to the cliff's edge and stared to the west at darkening skies. *Would I have time to fish?*

I watched my Pa's bald eagle fly over the lookout and land in a huge nest on a stately tree near the cliff's edge. Pa and I had seen the heads of two eagles and an eaglet for several weeks, but I had only twice seen that eagle fly.

I grabbed my binoculars, spying what I assumed to be the male eagle with no fish in his talons. The female pecked at him, forcing him to the edge of the nest. *Wow! Don't show up without a fish!* Chuckling, I wondered if I might suffer the same fate if I showed up empty-handed at the cabin. I ditched the binoculars, grabbed my fishing pole and a few supplies, and ran upward toward bowl-shaped Misty Lake to complete my mission.

My classmates would ask, "Why does running fascinate you if it just makes you tired?"

My answer: "I like the power to propel myself and the freedom to decide where and how soon I want to get there. I enjoy the journey as much as reaching the destination. In our Smokies, each peak you scale and each meadow you cross brings something new."

Pa understood, but Ma couldn't wrap her fingers around it. She was into baseball. She told stories how her Pa and Ned's big brother Jacob had taught her and six younger brothers to pitch. But, just once could I recall hearing Pa talk about running. He shared how my Grampa Cline had let him run wild over the Ruby Lake land when he'd trained for the championship race his senior year. Pa's face had lit up and it proved magical to me. But, just as fast, Pa's smile faded.

The steady run up to Misty Lake was challenging, but the thrill of conquering it brought joy. To the west billowy storm clouds collided, forming a band of darkness. It scared me. My parents had lectured me on the "volatility of summer storms." Regardless, I was here. I had succeeded in the trek up and now stared at calm lake waters. I prepared my gear.

That same bald eagle soared over the lake and braced his wings to slow. He dipped and snagged a fish and flew into the fleeting mist.

How can he spot those fish from so far away? I don't know, and I don't…well, I would care if I could learn how to do it myself. I laughed. *At least he'll enjoy better terms with his eagle family. Now it's my turn.*

I dug up some worms on the muddy banks and balanced a walk on a fallen tree jutting into the lake. I tied my hook to the line, set the bait, and cast. I found a protruding branch and eased down. My thoughts wandered to family.

Jake was completing his eighth-grade pitching season. A reporter from the *Rockside Bugle* said he was the most promising pitcher to come through our school system since his real Pa, Jacob Cline. It was due to Ma's upbringing. Ma had a rifle for an arm. Jake, too, but he didn't share the love of God like Ma. He had a few "rough edges," as Ma called them.

He didn't care much for school, and school didn't care much for him, until he beat the Haybury Hogs. Even the teachers loved him then. Jake was a regular in the principal's office, receiving a detention notice one day and a trophy the next.

Chester was nearing fourth grade, and a "handful." Somehow, we got along, but Ma was always on his case to develop a fastball like Jake.

When my vision grew blurry and my glasses prescription strengthened, Ma let me off the hook, baseball-wise. That was the only break I'd had growing up. They penalized me to make up for it—like doing Jake's chores when he had a game or a long practice. I wondered if Chester envied my release from Ma's watchful eye. She didn't have to critique my pitching as she did with Chester. My choice was to run the forest trails like Pa when he was young.

Whenever I brought up running to Pa, he'd pause to reflect before redirecting the conversation. I knew he loved it, but his smile soon bent downward. When I'd press him, I learned it didn't pay to rile Pa. He'd give me another chore to keep me from asking again.

During my reminiscing, I took in my first catch of the day, a largemouth bass—two to three pounds of him. Unhooking it, I placed it in my knapsack. I wanted to celebrate at the lake while trees waved in the wind, but everything surrounding me was still: the lake, the trees, and the air. I felt an eerie sense of danger wafting through the forest as I listened for a sound of life—a bird chirping or a squirrel scampering through leaves. I heard nothing. In the stillness, the sky to the west moved, washing away patches of blue for a shadowy gray.

Twigs snapped. The brush shook violently as a snarling beast sprang from its hiding place onto its prey, teeth ripping into flesh. Fear stabbed me as I crouched, grabbed my knapsack, and hot-stepped along the log to firm ground.

A throated growl! Halted, stone-still, I saw the unmistakable head of a mountain lion that had plunged onto a white-tailed deer. After a short-lived skirmish beyond a corner of the lake, two bulging eyes met mine. I looked down submissively and retreated sideways, vanishing behind some trees. My mind ordered flight, but my body stiffened as if squeezed in a vice. *Am I the next victim?* There were no mountain lions in Tennessee, they had told me!

In the distance, dark skies sparked with lightning. Clouds like luminous juggernauts sped my way, as if some cruel magnetic force beneath my feet beckoned them. Leaves swayed gently. A dance of sunlight sparkled off twisting leaves and doubled its reflection on rippling lake waters.

A thunder blast released me. I hoisted the knapsack and turned my fishing pole into a lance. Circling the lake perimeter, I charged down the rock-strewn trail toward my shelter.

The gentle rhythm of leaves changed, no longer smooth as in a lackadaisical ballad, but with the cadence of a military march. Tree limbs struck like drum sticks, pounding out staccato beats on adjacent branches. Lower limbs doubled as brooms, ready to sweep me off my feet.

This brazen trail was a misstep nightmare. Razor-edged rocks lined the path, a prelude to huge cliffs shorn centuries before by forces of nature.

I wove around twisting turns and pushed off rocks to steady my footing. Doubts welled up, but I smothered them, focusing on two jaunts made with Pa from Misty Lake to my lookout.

Wind gusts wrecked my progress and slammed me into a sweeping branch. I dropped my pole and gripped the branch, riding it like a playground swing, setting myself down on its return.

I high-stepped over obstacles, hid my face with my arm, and crouched behind a tree for protection from flying debris. Pa's teaching spun in my mind that nature, like life, had two sides, and the darker side might be a monster.

The trail opened onto my boulder-cliff lookout. I ran to the edge of the cliff walls and gazed into the valley. A fast-moving funnel cloud whirled destruction like a giant drill, leaving behind trees tattered into wood chips. *And it's coming my way!* Blackness blanketed the hillside.

Whoosh! A blast of wind blew me sideways. I hopscotched over rocks, but slipped, skidding to a stop, lying face down between my shelter and the tree that housed the eagles' nest.

I pulled my knapsack off, shielding my face. *Crack!* A limb-splitting sound echoed, followed by a *thud.* I looked up to see the eagles' tree rip apart and half the nest plunge to the ground. *It must have weighed a ton!*

"No! No!" I yelled as two adult eagles slammed onto the ledge beneath the fractured limb. Through a torrent of winds, an eaglet's whimpering cry pierced through the swirling storm. The eaglet in the nest was alive!

I glanced at the security of my lookout, stared in awe at the approaching funnel cloud, then dashed to the fallen nest. Staying afoot, I hovered over the tangled mess of sticks and mud with its treasure inside: a terrified squawking eaglet! I yanked a towel from my knapsack and picked up the battered bird, placing it inside.

Zipping it up, I ran to my lookout. Knocked off my feet, I twisted in the air so I wouldn't crush the eaglet. After failing to regain my footing, I crawled the last yards to my shelter, slipping under the tarp tied by thick ropes and buttressed up against the two boulders.

Crackity crack! Smack! Whack! Inside, I lifted the tarp's edge and peeked underneath at marble-sized hail bouncing off the rocks. I slumped inside my shrinking tarp chamber, each hail strike a bullet fired by an angry cloud. Then I heard it—the strident sound of a roaring train careening around a corner of steel tracks. But there were no tracks and no train, only a super-spinning, murderous twister!

Squawk! Squawk! The eaglet whimpered, trapped inside my knapsack.

In minutes, the thud of hail pellets changed to a pounding rain. Edges of the tarp waved a wild goodbye to the departing twister. The tarp chamber Pa had insisted I maintain held up.

My body lay stiff from the strain. I changed positions but found little relief. I braced my flashlight so its beam shone on the knapsack. I opened a pocketknife, unzipped another compartment, and stabbed the lone bass, slicing off several pieces. The hungry eaglet whimpered above the din of rain and extended his beak outside the knapsack's opening and gulped his meal.

When the storm subsided, I climbed from my cocoon. The eaglet's head peeked out of the knapsack's opening. *Am I to take ownership of an orphan eaglet? How bad are his injuries?*

At the cabin, I imagined a different storm was brewing. *What determines the power of a mother's love? Can it equal the intensity of a tornado? Can it be dangerously protective? Can it act as a weapon?* Oh, yes! Ma threw her fear for my safety like a lightning bolt toward Pa. Wasn't it yesterday morning I'd overheard Ma and Pa talking?

*****

Pa arrived home after working night shift at the railroad in Rockside. I stood in the hallway, thinking about the things I'd found and read a week ago from the trunk in the attic. I listened for Pa's reaction when Ma told him what I wanted to do on my twelfth birthday. He sat on the couch, hearing her fears while my brothers ate breakfast. Soon Ma would drive us to school. I kept thinking it had been fourteen years since Pa's race as a senior at Rockside.

"Oh, Ned, you stopped at Skeeter's place." Ma waved her hand at the stench.

"Come on, Lily, we deserve a drink for spendin' our lives workin' in the dark."

Ma rose and gave Pa a hug. "I had the 'big eye' last night."

"Couldn't sleep?"

"Yeah. Billy insists his first venture to the cliffs alone in the dark be on his twelfth birthday tomorrow. He wants to train to win the cross-country championship they cheated from you. Our Billy's a dreamer!"

Pa's eyes glazed over from a distant memory. "Some dreams can become nightmares. Look, Jacob and I did our early dawn run at age twelve. Jake did it two years ago, and Chester will, too when he's twelve. 'It's the Cline way,' as my Pa used to say."

I slipped into my bedroom as Pa got up and Ma followed him into their bedroom. I was sure Pa would let me run tomorrow!"

*****

That night before Pa left our cabin for the railroad, Ma and Pa came to our room to say good night. "Okay, Billy, tomorrow is Saturday, May 6, your birthday. It's time to earn your right to manhood. Set your alarm." Lily squirmed, but Ned's smile of pride matched mine. "You can run up in the morning to the boulder cliff lookout—alone. Make sure you've got what you need when you fish up at Misty Lake. Bring back fish for us and do what I taught you."

Ma put her arm around me, showing her dutiful support for the Cline family tradition. My half-brother Jake, fourteen, sat on the top bunk, working a baseball in his hands. "Just keep your head, Billy—you'll be okay."

Chester, my nine-year-old brother, whined from his cot. "I could drop dead before I ever turn twelve!" That brought a few laughs before Pa walked out to drive away, dressed as usual in his railroad overalls.

*****

Back at the boulder cliff lookout, I dismissed thoughts of yesterday and rallied my strength for the downward journey back to the cabin. I knew this storm had hit our cabin and most of Rockside. I also knew Pa's love was as strong as Ma's but shrouded within tradition. Pa believed overcoming danger, even if life-threatening, was a rite of passage his boys had to face and survive to reach the celebrated status of manhood.

Before the storm subsided, I knew Pa would be out the door, maintaining the virtues of fatherhood by responding to Ma's pleadings. I knew he would follow the path to the cliffs. Sure enough, on my long descent, I rounded a stand of trees and our eyes met. Pa's face beamed, seeing my rite of passage had left me unscathed.

"Billy! You're alive!" We hugged. "Never forget this day, son. You've now made this land your own."

"The cliff lookout! I never would have—never could have..." Feelings got the best of me. "I could only save your eagle's eaglet." After an intense pause, Pa gave me another fatherly hug I will never forget. It sealed my arrival into manhood. Ma might require an answer in detail, but with Pa, survival secured my position. He lifted the knapsack from my shoulders but withdrew when the eaglet's head stuck out again. Pa tousled my hair, realizing the rescue involved me from the beginning. Among the trees, rocks, and wildlife, our conversation echoed the events I'd endured.

Pa summed it up: "Surviving a mountain lion, a tornado, and saving an eaglet all in one day! Not bad!" He extended a playful fist to my shoulder.

I approached the cabin and saw Ma reading her large study Bible while rocking at high speed below her crucifixion-stained-glass window. Jake and Chester were sprawled on the porch beside her, rolling a baseball back and forth through a makeshift maze.

Ma saw us first and quoted from Psalm 91:1: "He that dwelleth in the secret place of the Most High shall abide under the shadow of the Almighty."

She and my brothers sprang to greet us. Chester charged me, but when I extended my arms, he stopped. Surprised, I noticed him staring at my knapsack. The eaglet's head had popped out, followed by a squawk.

"What's that?" he said. My mind whirled, and I never answered him. Chester hugged me anyway though his eyes never strayed from the eaglet.

Jake's hug followed. "Thought you were a goner," he said. After Ma's hug, we walked inside. I set the knapsack in the middle of the floor.

"Let me help!" Chester said, reaching for the bird. I jerked my head toward him, my steely stare stopping him in his tracks.

Ma grabbed hold of Chester's shoulders and pulled him close. "Billy can do it, honey." Her instincts matched mine. I found fish scraps and snatched them to begin another feeding.

"I'll call the US Fish and Wildlife Service," Pa said, heading to the phone. After a muffled conversation, I heard Pa's final words: "Just past Ruby Lake dock...the last cabin up the dirt road."

After I cleaned up, we all downed Ma's vegetable soup. Pa transferred the eaglet to my Grampa Cline's old green dog carrier and joined us, sitting on our porch rockers. Dusk came and nearly ebbed away before we heard the engine of a US Fish and Wildlife Service vehicle drive up. Two officers slammed their truck doors. One grabbed a dog carrier. As they approached, the cabin's overhead fans flickered shafts of light, resembling that of old silent movies. Brilliant bands of colored light shone through Ma's special window and onto her face, her expression on the porch more profound than I had ever seen.

Pa spoke to the officers as they transferred the eaglet. "Before the storm, my son Billy encountered a mountain lion at Misty Lake."

"Really?" an officer said. He hesitated, his eyes of concern aimed at Pa. He turned and smiled at me. "You're a lucky boy. It's been three years since we last had a sighting. We'll want a full report first thing in the morning. Can you do that?"

I looked at Pa. "We can. Right, Pa?"

"We'll head there when I get home from night shift."

The officers carried the eaglet to their truck. *Will I ever see him again?* That thought rattled in my mind as Ma tucked us boys in that night.

"Don't forget to say your prayers. We all have much to be thankful for," she said, turning off the bedroom light.

I adjusted the bed covers, lost in thought about my scary day. Recalling Ma's words, I slid out to kneel at the side of my bottom bunk. I folded my hands and prayed out loud. "O, Lord, thank you for saving me and the little eaglet. I wish you could have saved the ma and pa eagle, too."

Hesitating, I gathered my courage, knowing Jake on the top bunk and Chester on his cot were listening. "Thank you that the mountain lion wasn't hungry anymore. Thank you I wasn't busted up by those trees and rocks and wild winds or sent over the cliffs and smashed like I almost did! God, you are great, and I am still alive. Thank you for my brothers and Ma and Pa. I love you, and so do all of us. Thank you for the cliff lookout. It saved my life, or my brothers would be crying and going to my funeral! Amen."

Big brother Jake never made a sound or said a word. Little brother Chester had to blow his nose. As I crawled back into bed, I knew it was my greatest prayer.

CHAPTER 2

Becoming the "Eagle Boy"

When Pa and I arrived at the rehabilitation center, a US Fish and Wildlife officer greeted us. "Hey, everybody, here he is, the bravest boy on the mountain! Saved an eaglet in the storm, stared down a mountain lion, and lived to laugh about it!" Everybody applauded. A photographer snapped a picture for the *Rockside Bugle* front page.

The photograph embarrassed me. The picture showed me with the eaglet beside cheering employees. The caption read, "Billy Cline, the Eagle Boy!"

The officers agreed to give me the opportunity to name the eaglet. They gave me a week, but I didn't need it. I thought about what Pa desired when he raced in 1964. He ran for victory, but they denied him that. The more I thought, the more I wanted to run that race to honor Pa with the victory he deserved. It was that moment my decision became the driving force of my future. "I'll name him 'Victory!'" The main headlines for our weekly newspaper on Thursday, May 11, 1978, read: "Pete Rose Gets 3,000 Hits" and "Affirmed Wins Kentucky Derby." But one phrase seemed to stick, calling me the "Eagle Boy."

When hailed a hero, I flashed a red face, but Pa patted me on the back. The officer recorded my encounter with the mountain lion. I admit I left out a few details, never telling him how I froze at first, probably miscalculated, saying the mountain lion was a little closer than he was, but, besides that, I was pretty much a straight shooter.

"It's good to know your Pa made that cliff lookout strong enough to survive the storm," said an officer. "And you showed great courage. If there is something up there, we'll clear him out or capture him—you can count on it."

"I'm proud of you, son."

The officer smiled, leading us to a room where the eaglet was treated. "This is how we feed an eaglet—excuse me—how we feed Victory. This puppet looks like his mama. See that? When we use the puppet eagle, he'll think he's with his mama. He's learning to take his food like an eaglet. We'll also treat his injuries, and later, when stronger, he'll learn to take short flights in our outdoor enclosure."

"What about his injuries? How bad is he hurt?"

"His wing got a little hurt. There's a big process in keeping an eagle wild so he can survive in his natural habitat. If he thinks humans are feeding him, when we release him back into his world, he won't know how to hunt for food. That's called 'imprinting,' and that's bad. We rehabilitate, or fix up the eaglet, just as a doctor fixes up injured people."

For days thoughts about Victory's future haunted me. "Pa, I'm so thankful my eagle survived…and I want to watch out for him when he's released."

Pa scratched his head at my words. "You mean Victory?"

"Yes, Pa, I want to make a place where Victory can land and feel safe."

Pa's eyes questioned my motives. "An eagle makes his own place." My head dropped. To appease me, he drove me to the rehab center twice a week to follow Victory's healing process.

*****

One Friday evening several months later, Pa was light-hearted and grinning. "Billy, get to bed early tonight. We've got a job tomorrow when I return from the railroad."

"What is it, Pa?"

"Never mind, just get to bed." When Ma smiled, I knew tomorrow would be special.

I rose early on Saturday. Pa arrived home, and we started. "Grab an ax and a hatchet from the barn!" We packed our mule, attached a sled with tools, and hiked toward the cliff lookout.

That's how a landing place first materialized. We used a fallen tree from the storm that blocked the trail. Pa raised his heavy ax and cut a thirteen-foot length from the trunk. He whacked off a smaller five-foot limb, and I used the hatchet to cut off small chutes. It took several weeks on Pa's days off for him to finish carving a half circle atop the thinner top-end trunk. We placed the smaller cross limb perpendicular onto it.

I was full of questions each day. Pa listened and kept me working. "How did you know what to do, Pa? Are those US Fish and Wildlife officers gonna think this is okay? We're not supposed to *improve* him, are we?" Pa laughed.

"Is that the right word?"

"*Imprint!*" said Pa.

"Oh, right. We don't want to *imprint* him. An eagle needs to know how to hunt and stay wild. But I want him to know me. How will he know me, Pa?"

"Come on, son. Keep those hands workin' while your jaws are flappin'! Those officers know Victory wouldn't be alive if it wasn't for you. But know this—he needs to be free, to soar. He needs to be an eagle—to be everything he's meant to be."

With the help of our mule and several retired lumbermen Pa knew at "Skeeters," we hauled the limbs up to the cliff lookout on a sled. We continued to seat and secure the crossbeam atop the main beam with rope, wire, and special screws, its shape now like a capital *T*.

Using a fence post digger on a small portion of dirt at the side of the boulders, we lowered the heavy T-Cross into its new home beside my lookout. Pa attached smaller supporting limbs from the center trunk, protruding into the ground or braced against a buried boulder. That gave it stability when strong winds blew. We added supporting cable and pounded hooks into the cleft of the rock. By connecting cable to the anchored hooks, we secured the T-Cross implant. We smiled as we guzzled down a drink, gazing at our creation, what we called our "T-Cross."

*****

During the next few months, we learned the US Fish and Wildlife officers were working on a special report about my eagle. They had taken great care of him, using his training and their facility in a wildlife study on eagles. Pa and I had visited the facility many times. Pa often dropped me off for an hour or two while he met friends at Skeeter's Bar.

I raced Victory outside his fenced-in enclosure to the other side. Victory showed patience waiting for me before flying across to meet me on his special landing limb. He was a coach using interval training on me, and I never realized it. Sometimes I did thirty of those half-lap oval-like sprints back and forth. Exhaustion had set in when Pa returned, but my eagle never looked tired.

Once, I twisted my ankle while racing Victory. Al, the head of the facility, ordered workers to maintain a smooth running trail beside the fenced enclosure for "our Eagle Boy."

Later, my eagle flew first, waiting for me to catch up to him. Whenever I was slow, Victory gave a shriek to speed up my sprinting beside the enclosure. Soon, I gave him my version of a cry, "Wooo-eee." That became his signal to start his next soaring maneuver again. Now, I was training him the same way he had trained me!

Several US Fish and Wildlife officers congregated on coffee breaks, enjoying a good laugh when Pa picked me up. "Hey, Ned, who's winning? I think the eagle may outlast Billy!" They jotted down notes, argued, and made bets. Some called it a game. Others thought it was a training session for us both. One officer told Pa my newfound endurance impressed them.

The officers couldn't explain why our routine continued. They seemed embarrassed to put it in their journals, fearing their superiors would ridicule their reports in DC. Nobody had ever known such a bonding between an eagle and a human. I didn't care. I believed we had adopted each other.

The *Rockside Bugle* updated our story every few weeks. That's when I'd hear my nickname of Eagle Boy repeated around town.

I couldn't wait to enjoy the release of Victory into the wild. Our T-Cross was ready. But authorities in DC wanted to witness my eagle bond to one of their trainers. After a delay in completing the red tape, it was time to release Victory. The DC people gave up and chose instead to chastise Al, the trainer who had first come up with the idea for me to race Victory beside the outdoor enclosure.

Al knew racing benefited Victory. He flew faster in the enclosure each week. Al proved it. I returned three times a week to race my eagle beside the enclosure and Al video-taped it, comparing it with earlier tapes made by staff workers.

I had no doubts. Al taught me that an eagle mates with one eagle for life. That meant they understood loyalty. I figured loyalty could carry over to a bonding with a human. Since I had saved the eaglet from certain death in that wild storm, I was the perfect candidate to achieve it.

Al joked, "They don't call you the Eagle Boy for nothin'!"

New eagle arrivals for rehabilitation needed to use the enclosure, so Al scheduled Victory's release at a strong section of his old nesting tree near the boulder cliff lookout. Pa and I made sure the T-Cross was ready.

On release day, I cut school as three US Fish and Wildlife officers brought Victory to place him high in his old split tree for release. For this time only, Pa lifted me up so I could place a small fish on top of the T-Cross beam sixty yards away from his future nest.

"Will Victory land this close to the lookout and eat the fish? Will he land on the T-Cross?"

"I don't know, son. I'm hopin' so."

Pa and I sat atop the boulder cliff lookout to observe the release. Thirty minutes later, I shouted "Wooo-eee!" The eagle swooped down, shrieked, and landed on the T-Cross. He turned to us and must have seen our wide grins because he sank his talons in and ate the small fish in a hurry. I wondered if he thought Pa and I might want the fish for ourselves.

I was in awe as my eagle perched on the T-Cross and teared up as I recalled the memories of the storm. My eagle swooped toward Ruby Lake to develop his skill as a hunter from the sky.

I noticed the shape of his wings—flapping, extending upward over his body in a "V." I whirled to Pa at that moment. "I'm really proud I named him Victory."

Pa nodded. "Victory is the perfect name."

Pa understood me—my need to be on the mountain and my desire to run. Why shouldn't he? Running brought balance and challenge to my young life, and Pa had experienced it, too. In high school, Pa trained on the Ruby Lake land and loved his "childhood cabin," plus the land that stretched to the cliffs and beyond.

*****

Years before Pa's championship race, Grampa Cline outbid the Clausen and Cowler clans by a dollar in the most disputed auction in Rockside history. Threats were made against us, but lawmen failed to prove it. However, Ned ended up bloodied in his championship race.

Now, Ned's calm but authoritative manner reinforced the urgency of keeping my supplies up to date. Pa, like Grampa Cline, was old-school. If I followed his rules, I could sleep there, warm and protected from the elements, tucked in a sleeping bag underneath the rock overhang.

The month after my fifteenth birthday, my running friend, Tom Pryor, helped me rough out a wider trail. We hung five-foot-long yellow streamers from tree limbs to mark the route from my homestead. The streamers helped me find my way since my eyesight had worsened.

*****

My blurred eyesight carried a fancy name—keratoconus. My cornea was cone-shaped and thin, blurring my vision, like looking through a hand-blown glass jar. As the problem progressed, they strengthened my prescription, enabling me to read and maintain the trips to my boulder lookout, the place where I discovered inner strength, where Victory was only a call away.

My eagle's continued existence there remained a mystery. Since the rescue, I had grown fascinated by his elegance as he soared along the cliffs. His shrieks proclaimed the power of his presence. Nearly an adult, Victory's appearance became proud and stately. He levitated over me when strong winds caught his wings and feasted on fish, both from Misty Lake far above the cliffs and from Ruby Lake below our cabin. Victory was the best fisherman on the mountain.

Running up my trail to the lookout brought me pure joy; I had fashioned an original path into the wilderness. In my mind, the cliffs were mine—a site where I could ponder my place in the world.

That was when I realized the acceptance; it was not imprinting, not the eagle's dependence on me to provide his food. After a shaky beginning, he'd learned the craft of hunting well. It was his choice to fly over and seek one human—me. He seemed to be living a life born from necessity. Unable to find a mate from the eagles' dwindling numbers, he allowed a human to enter a distant but purposeful alliance. This bald eagle directed a serious intensity toward me, yet only the US Fish and Wildlife officers who knew of our game at the enclosure could offer a reason why he favored me. Once he made his appearance, I was imprinted for life.

This uneasy connection transformed into one of continued acceptance. The boulder cliff lookout was my place to be. When he was not fishing, exploring, or resting in his old nest tree, the T-Cross was often Victory's place to be. For two great years, I treasured the times he swooped in, spread his wings, and gripped his talons onto the T-cross. He'd give his familiar shriek so I knew of his presence. When I ran through the forest, I often gave my "Wooo-eee" cry to him. I would see him soaring above me like an angelic protector. His presence was my food and drink: food that nourished my acceptance and drink that watered my imagination.

Ideas flowed into my teenage mind as I conversed with Victory on his T-Cross. The sense of ownership I felt regarding this rich visual landscape was born from more than a youthful dream. It was hallowed ground, where my vision of running powerfully across the rough Tennessee terrain would match the ease with which Victory soared over the same beautiful vistas. The working out of that dream was to change Victory and me forever.

CHAPTER 3

Pa's Championship Race

October 1964

Standing dead center in the heart of Tennessee's Rockside Park, my Pa, then seventeen-year-old Ned Cline, brushed back his brown curly hair and heard the town clock chime three times. He leaned over the water fountain, wrestling with his looming four o'clock decision.

It was a lose-lose situation. He'd trained all year to win the Rockside 5K championship. But, could he keep his mind on the competition when his heart was at the train station where Lily stood alone, waiting for his brother Jacob's coffined body?

Ned turned to his right as runners from seven high schools prepared for the race in one hour. Family cars and pickups were parking beside military recruitment signs that hung on chain-link fences. Kids sold popcorn, candy, and hot chocolate as parents spread blankets in the park.

A cheerleader held a sign: "CALE CLAUSEN Is #1!" Cale, a well-built senior at Rockside and undefeated in cross country, stood beside her, exuding bravado, giving a "thumbs-up" to a crowd of unabashed supporters. Rawley Cowler, his tough-guy cousin, walked in his shadow wearing a letterman's jacket, army boots, and a rope belt.

Ned stared left at the station where activity on the platform nagged at his conscience. Confusion reigned over his brother Jacob's death and what he should do about it now.

In a letter from the US Army to Grampa Cline, the father of a young woman killed Jacob over a simple purchase, twisted from a cultural misunderstanding. Jacob was serving a US Army post in Italy and knew his young wife Lily loved stained glass. He paid many lira to a poor local woman who sold him her crucifixion stained-glass-window, salvaged twenty years ago by her father from a bombed-out church in WWII. The money Jacob paid must not have equaled the loss her father felt. The woman's father fired the shot that took out Jacob. Ned had questions.

How long can hatred build until it expresses itself in revenge? If true love leads to new life, what does true hatred lead to? Permanent death? Did Jacob's death prove hatred can bleed from one generation to the next? Does hatred always have to be deadly? And last forever?

Ned, undecided about whether to run, jogged out a half mile past a row of trees to a small lake at the edge of town. Patches of melting snow softened the landscape beside the elevated train tracks that led into Rockside. He dropped to his knees, mourning the loss of his brother.

Looking up, Ned spied a bald eagle soaring over the rocky ridges and colorful pristine forests of autumn's Smoky Mountains. *What elegance!* He knew the eagle from his runs up the steep trail from his cabin near Ruby Lake to his boulder cliff lookout.

That vantage point remained secure between two large boulders that formed a shelter, complete with a rock overhang and tied-down tarps, which protected his supplies. Climbing atop the boulders and gazing over the sheer cliffs, the view of Rockside below and the rising nearby mountainsides had always drawn delighted sighs from Ned. The eagle's huge nest lay within easy eyesight, cradled on a giant limb along the same cliffs. This created a connection with wildlife he held special. Ned's view, now blurred by tears, ended his thoughts about nature.

Pa's words reflected his feelings in his personal journal dated November 6, 1964, two weeks after his race and the return of his brother Jacob's body.

I've always loved and respected Jacob as a brother, a champion pitcher, and a soldier. He was a great role model. But I've loved Lily ever since being in fifth grade with her. I never told Jacob about it, but I didn't need to. It frustrated me when Jacob swooped in and wooed her with his pitching mastery during the last few years. Lily's father conducted the wedding before Jacob deployed overseas. She was only sixteen!

It shocked me at their spring wedding last year when Jacob was on leave. I don't deny feeling sorry for myself. I knew Lily had faced grief before, losing her mother during the childbirth of her youngest brother. When Rev. Moore got sick, instead of canceling the wedding, Jacob offered to send money back and allow Lily to stay behind to help her father rear her six brothers. I realized it was a classy and loving move by Jacob to honor Lily's father and help her brothers. I saw Lily nearly every day until she dropped out of school. It was always a struggle for me to hold back my true feelings for her.

This was another entry I found in Ned's journal.

I went to Jacob's grave last weekend. Even though I know Lily is now free to marry again, I hate myself for feeling joy over having a second chance at winning my one true love.

In looking back at the championship race, I faced tough questions that drove my actions. First, how could Lily ever respect or love me if I showed no respect for my dead brother and her grief? Likewise, what would my teammates think if at the last moment I became a no-show and abandoned them to join Lily at the train station? Either way, when that clock tower chimed four times, I would be a loser. I had to figure a way to honor Lily, my brother, my teammates, and the expectations of my town.

On October 18, 1964, five days before Pa's race, he had heard a thrilling radio recap of Americans Bob Schul and Bill Dellinger winning a gold and bronze medal in Tokyo's Olympic five-thousand-meter run. That gave Pa the idea he wrote about in his personal narrative:

If I win October's 5K cross country championship on the twenty-third, I'll not only strike a blow against the Clausens and Cowlers, but I'll show Lily I'm as worthy an athlete as Jacob was. So I will run and win it to honor her and my brother Jacob!

Pa wrote,

I'm nervous over the battle of challenging Cale Clausen, knowing his kin's grudges flame red with passion and green with jealousy if we Clines are involved. How long will the Clausens and Cowlers hate us over losing their bid for the Ruby Lake land and cabin they desired? Is it true my Pa snookered them in a rigged auction? And, if I win this race, what will the Clausens and Cowlers do next to retaliate against us?

Those questions sent shivers through his body, not caused by the coolness of late October breezes or the speckled snow lining the forest paths he might soon run on, or even the thin Rockside running uniform he was wearing. The clock was ticking, and Ned had to make the most difficult decision of his young life.

The prognosticators favored Cale Clausen in the race, and Ned knew Rawley Cowler would back his play to secure the win. That's how they operated. And Lily? *She would want me to be with her at the train station.* Another shiver sent Ned springing to his feet, *I can't win no matter what I do!*

Gazing into the sky, Ned fixed his eyes on the bald eagle he'd seen for years as it skimmed the lake, looking for a meal. The eagle missed the fish this time, but Ned knew he would never quit on his journey. Ned rose, his decision made as he watched the eagle soar into the heart of Rockside Park. *That eagle will never give up, and neither will I.*

*****

Back near the starting line, a trusted teammate later told Ned what happened when Cale and Rawley stepped up to Cale's Pa, Cory Clausen. Cory was a single above-the-knee amputee, wearing his old Pearl Harbor vet jacket. Cory gagged a sickly cough before pointing a bent finger at Cale's chest. *"Those Clines stole the Ruby Lake land in that phony auction. It's payback time! Got it, son? Make sure, Rawley."* Cale and Rawley nodded.

Cale glanced at his Rockside Raven teammates, knowing they heard every word Cory spoke. Only Ned was missing, the runner Cale feared, the one who trained on the Ruby Lake land. The Ravens waited for Cale to lead them in their run-outs. However, he must have had no intention of dividing his focus as he jogged off saying, "The people came to see me win!"

At the score table near the finish line, Ned's same teammate stretched near his Rockside Ravens cross country coach, Pop O'Reilly, who held his five-year-old daughter, Rachel. Pop gave Rachel a hug and a peck on the cheek before sitting her next to his friend, Principal Stamper. Pop pulled out his starter pistol and spun the barrel to confirm the chamber was full of blanks.

Cale looked up, spying the dazzling Lily (Moore) Cline, seventeen since January, who walked from the train station, past the drinking fountain, and approached the starting line with her six younger brothers in tow. Her auburn hair spilled from under a baseball cap. She wore a black gingham dress, holding nine-month-old Jake Jr. in her arms. Her six brothers all wore baseball gloves, tossing a ball back and forth. Lily handed Jake Jr. to one of them and stepped up to Cale as her brothers stopped short to give her space.

Little Rachel ran up to greet Lily, but seeing her red eyes, Rachel stopped as her own eyes teared up.

"Where's Ned?" Lily demanded of Cale.

"Lily, you look so fine dressed in black. Ned doesn't care about you or his brother. Right, Rawley?"

Little Rachel shed a tear and whimpered as she gazed back at Lily's brothers. She ran to Pop O'Reilly, stomping her foot and pouting. "Daddy, Cale and Rawley are mean!"

Pop hugged Rachel, trying to quiet and comfort her. He checked his watch and turned to Principal Stamper. "Ned's running out of time."

Lily looked up as her brothers' heads turned to the side. She spun and saw Ned jogging toward her. She rushed Ned, who stopped to absorb her charge. Lily pounded her fists on his chest before sinking into his arms in tears. Voices in the crowd grew silent. The only sounds were clicks from a reporter's camera, documenting her anguish for the newspaper.

"He's my husband and your brother! Why won't you join me at the train?"

Ned's arms enveloped Lily as words from her fury sank in. With his hands on the sides of her shoulders, Ned pushed her back to arm's length, "My brother Jacob never missed a baseball game, did he?"

Ned paused for a rebuke but got none. "I won't quit a race before it starts! It's the Cline way!"

Lily appeared subdued by Ned's response when coupled by her emotional outburst witnessed by the crowd. She jerked herself loose from Ned before leading her brothers across the park and back to the train station. All eyes followed her. Lily signaled for a baseball from one of her little brothers. She glanced back and saw Ned still staring, so she fired her baseball at a popular recruitment sign that read, "Look Sharp, Be Sharp, Go Army!" Her pitch split the wooden sign in half—one section dangling from the fence before falling to the grass.

All eyes turned to Ned, who jogged toward his coach as runners continued their warm-ups. The crowd murmured.

Ned approached Pop O'Reilly and little Rachel, hearing Pop's words. "I'll support your decision, Ned, either way."

Rachel forced a smile. "Are you gonna win?"

Her question hung heavy for an interminable time until a train whistle, like a death knell, pierced the atmosphere. Ned's heart directed his pain-filled eyes to gaze back at the train station, where his brother lay entombed in a casket within a slowing railroad car. With a sigh, he forced a determined stride toward the starting line. All knew the decision: Ned would run.

*****

At the train station, Lily and her brothers witnessed puffs of steam wheeze from the lumbering steel, braking to a stop beside her family, church friends, and servicemen in dress uniforms. The town clock chimed four times, and Lily placed a dark veil over her baseball cap. She twisted her wedding ring, clutched Jake Jr. into her arms, and muttered, "Little Jake."

She turned to her pastor-father, "Daddy, I miss my Mama." Her father's lips trembled. A trumpeter from Jacob's high school days held his instrument, ready to play on the removal of Jacob's casket.

Two workers slid open the train's cargo door. An American flag covered a military casket. Lily bit her lip as she gazed at the bitter symbol of stark reality.

*****

At the starting line, Ned's eagle soared over the race banner and the runners while the eager crowd pointed upward and gazed in awe. Ned struggled to reign in his emotions. The stakes were rising.

Standing alone twenty yards behind the starting line, Ned repeated his goal out loud to help him believe it. "I will win this race and honor Lily and my brother Jacob at the same time." Ned moved back to the starting line.

Pop spoke into his bullhorn and held his starter pistol. "On your marks!" Ned saw little Rachel press her thumbs over her ears, blinking her eyes. Runners grew tense, organizing their team's seven runners within seven starting zones. Spectators shifted to gain the best view.

*****

Beside the open cargo door, two of six veterans in dress uniforms climbed into the train, joining the two railroad workers. A veteran lifted part of the flag draped over the casket, confirming the name: Pfc. Jacob P. Cline, US Army. That veteran, Jacob's former classmate, turned to Lily and pounded his chest twice before pointing to her. Tears welled as she kissed her son's head.

*****

Pop raised his bullhorn. "Get set!" The words carried over to Lily's ears. After a pause, Pop discharged the starter gun—*bang!* Lily's head jerked as if hearing Jacob's kill shot. She broke into tears as the enthusiastic roar from the race crowd became a painful reminder that life goes on for those left behind.

*****

Forty-nine runners circled the spectators on the flat portion of the park as cheers and shouts of encouragement followed. The back side of the single lap took the runners past the train station. *My eyes took in Lily's laser-like stare which devastated my plan to resist my feelings for her to save energy. I've got to stay focused or I'll sap my strength.* After completing the lap, the runners disappeared into a narrow, forested trail leading up the side of the mountain, the toughest climb on the course.

Cale was first to enter and Ned was fourth. Once on the upward trail, Ned caught a glimpse to his left of a large figure, camouflaged behind thick brush. *Is that Rawley Cowler?*

The runners followed the rising twists and turns on the mountain trail. Ned quickened his run, passing two runners and gaining on the leader. On the dangerous descent, Ned stormed down with reckless abandon, closing in on Cale's lead. Dense brush and trees on this forested section were unforgiving to runners who failed to complete the tight turns. Centrifugal force could drive a runner face-first into disaster.

*****

The trumpeter played a dirge. Six servicemen carried Jacob's casket, placing it into the hearse. Four of Lily's brothers carried a wooden crate that accompanied Jacob's body on the train. The crate read, "Fragile—Stained Glass—Italy." They placed it in the back of her father's pickup.

*****

Nearing the end of the dense trail before a repeat of the final park loop around the spectators, Cale looked back and slowed, allowing

Ned to catch up and position himself right behind him. Surprised, Ned thought, *Is he weak? Does he have a side ache? Go for it!* The trail was narrow, but Cale was running on the left side, as if inviting him to pass. Ned sped up, but Cale timed it to perfection. Leaning into Ned with a heavy shoulder, Cale thrust out his right elbow, knocking Ned off the trail and smack into a tree.

Thump! Ned was down, and he wouldn't be getting up soon. Rawley Cowler emerged from the brush, gazing at Ned lying bloody on the ground. Ned looked up as he thought, *Rawley's services won't be necessary.* Within seconds, a Haybury Hog runner sprinted by gazing at Rawley, who ducked beside Ned's battered body before leaving the area.

*****

At the finish line, Cale was honored as the last runner announced. He accepted the huge first-place trophy from Principal Stamper. Cale raised it as the crowd applauded and Didi screamed with delight, waving her sign for the photographers.

That's when Ned limped in, covered with wicked-looking bruises, multiple scrapes, and deep cuts bleeding through his shredded uniform. Few noticed Ned's approach until he stumbled by Rawley, shouting, "Cale! You cheated!"

Spectators turned as Rawley grabbed Ned and swung him around before punching him in the jaw. Ned crashed into Cale, which broke his trophy and knocked his Pa, Cory, to the ground.

Moments before, medics had approached to treat Ned but now turned to assist Cory, who struggled to breathe. They moved to support his efforts. Cale locked eyes with his cousin Rawley. For Cory Clausen, it was the bitter end of a long battle that had begun at Pearl Harbor. Cale moaned as he and Rawley followed the ambulance rushing Cory to the hospital.

When the dust settled and order was restored, Ned's testimony that Cale had knocked him into a tree agreed with the second-place Haybury runner's testimony.

Pop O'Reilly, the meet director, disqualified Cale Clausen for cheating, declaring the second-place Haybury Hog runner as champion. The score sheet marked Ned as "did not finish." Principal Stamper suspended Rawley Cowler from school for fighting, and the emergency room doctor declared Cory Clausen "dead on arrival" at Gorman Hospital. Nobody could recall an award's presentation like what they witnessed that Friday, October 23, 1964.

CHAPTER 4

Ned and Winter's Fiery Fury

December 30, 1964

Christmas lights still shone on the snowy porch of Pastor Moore's parsonage. Pa had received an invitation to share an evening meal Lily would prepare for her family. Pa had convinced my Grandpa Cline to give him a ride down from their Ruby Lake cabin and pick him up at the church ball field by 10:00 p.m.

After her brothers gobbled up most of the food, Ned and Lily put on their winter jackets and bundled-up Jake Jr. before stepping onto the porch. Lily's diary and Ned's journal gave precise information from both perspectives.

I [Lily] carried a serious disposition as I sat with Ned on the porch swing. "Ned, I want to share something with you."

"Sure, Lily."

"Pa's health is doing much better now, and the church is growing. Good news? True, but I'm still caring for six brothers and Jake Jr., too. I've wondered, who would show interest in a woman like me who has carried so much grief in her life? A woman with so much baggage?"

"Do you want out?"

"I can't leave without a future. Pa told me 'God works in mysterious ways' and I believe him."

"What else did he say?"

"That's all. He believes God will take care of me."

"Pastors must have faith."

"*There is something else.*" I reached for the edge of the baby blanket and adjusted it to better protect Jake Jr. from the cold. "*Cale just asked me out.*"

Ned sprang from the swing, sending Lily and Jake Jr. sliding sideways. "*What? Don't be stupid! Cale cares only for himself!*"

"*I told him I'd think about it.*"

Ned's arms flew up in anger. "*Think about it? Are you ready to say God allowed Jake to take a bullet over a twenty-year-old stained-glass window so you could date a jerk like Cale? Get serious!*"

"*I am serious. Are you, Ned?*"

"*Meaning?*"

"*Just what I said.*" I paused, taking in Ned's intense glare. A tear from each eye coursed down my cheeks as I gazed back at Ned hyperventilating. "*I don't want Cale.*"

Pa was mind-deaf and caught flat-footed, his anger boiling over with such ferocity he bounded off the porch and down the street. All he could think about was his past heartbreak when Lily married his brother Jacob. He wouldn't admit he had no way of supporting her while still in school. He felt this disappointment was not to be relived especially with Cale on the opposing side!

Pa muttered as he staggered down the street, "*You could have waited for me! God have mercy! I want her so bad!*" But he was walking away, leaving Lily holding her baby, alone.

Lily's father stepped onto the porch, putting his arms around Lily and little Jake as she sobbed in his arms.

Pa continued down the street, lit by occasional streetlights and a full moon. He stopped at a telephone pole and pounded his fists on it, trying to recover from his anger. As he pushed away from the pole, he read an advertisement, "Discounted Fireworks." Another read "Railroad hiring!" with an address. He studied that sign.

Pa sought advice from Pop O'Reilly. *My coach will listen and give good advice.*

It was then Pa's mind replayed the scene on the porch. *What had Lily said?* Embarrassment and guilt replaced feelings of anger and frustration. *Maybe I got it wrong!*

Arriving beside Pop's mailbox, Pa stopped, trying to build up his courage and find the words to explain himself. He turned around, wondering if he should go back to Lily's place and apologize. Two figures running down the street flashed in silhouette by a neighbor's porch light. Pa knew those strides belonged to Cale and Rawley.

Knowing he was unseen, Pa darted down the driveway into Pop's backyard, circling behind a large oak tree. Within a minute, Cale and Rawley sneaked down the driveway themselves, stopping on the front side of the same large oak. Pa hugged the back side of the tree, trying to blend in with the bark, while opening his mouth wide to lessen the sound of his nervous breathing. He wrote about the event.

In a low quiet voice, Cale spoke first. "Like my Pa said before the race, 'It's payback time for them land-grabbin' Clines.' Since coach never invited me to the team's New Year's Eve fireworks' party, we'll enjoy our own celebration with their fireworks."

Rawley responded, "Yeah. Coach O'Reilly will pay first for disqualifying you. I've got two large match boxes to spark our celebration. Ned, the snitch, will pay another way. They chuckled. As Cale and Rawley walked toward the back of Pop's house, I peeked around the tree and saw Rawley carrying the arson tools in his hands.

The two ruffians tiptoed up the outside stairs to the second floor. Cale cut out a hole in the screen with a knife, unlatched the hook, and they entered the open-aired screened-in back porch.

Days earlier, Pa had accompanied Pop O'Reilly as he purchased a large box of fireworks for the New Year's Eve team party at the church ball field. But Pa now worried about the old WWII four-gallon gas can marked "Gas Rations A" that sat next to the fireworks. The bent metal lid on the gas can could not screw onto the top, so Pop had covered the spout with cellophane wrap, held in place by rubber bands.

Cale flipped on the inside porch light as Rawley bent over and appeared to rip open the cardboard box. I saw him hold up two large boxes of matches, one in each hand, and dump them over the fireworks. Pa's fear grew as he realized he may be too late to change anything. Rawley struck a match and raised the volume of his unrestrained words,

"To honor your Pa's passing!" Rawley lit it and tossed it in the box onto the other matches.

Cale pushed open the screen door and ran down the steps as Rawley tripped over something and fell. Rawley limped out and leaped off the porch, rolling to a sprawled position on the grass, muttering, "That gas can!" The matches caught fire, igniting the fireworks. A huge explosion blew out a second-floor door, setting fire to an upstairs bedroom.

"What was that?" Cale yelled.

"A house warming!" said Rawley, looking back at his handiwork.

From behind the backyard tree, my Pa leaped onto Rawley, who recovered and slammed Pa to his back. Cale jumped onto him and shoved his forearm across his neck, gagging him.

"You cost me a championship!" said Cale in a fierce voice. "But I didn't expect this."

Rawley took over. "Ned, you say one word and we'll burn you Clines off that Ruby Lake land your Pa stole in that phony auction! And Lily won't find safety, either!" Cale and Rawley slugged Pa in the gut before they ran off.

Pa gasped, finally taking in air after they knocked out his wind. He moved toward a neighbor's back hedge and hid behind it, trying to cope with the pain. He lifted his eyes and stared at growing flames while hearing a child's screams.

I heard Pop yell, "Rachel! Rachel!" Through the fiery fury, I saw Pop's image flash by a bedroom window. Pop's shouts turned into cries of terror as he followed her screams and found her. "Awww!"

Outside, Ned tried to stand but failed as he lay moaning and mourning.

Voices echoed in the firelight. *Two neighbors arrived carrying a tall ladder. Pop threw a chair through the window as flames and smoke billowed to the stars. Two neighbor ladies stood beside Mrs. O'Reilly as their husbands raised a ladder to Rachel's bedroom window. With Pop's shirt sleeves smoldering, he climbed down carrying his lifeless daughter's burn-charred body. Mrs. O'Reilly screamed, and her legs buckled as she fell in a heap.*

Hidden behind the hedge, Ned was curled into a fetal position, silent and frozen in shock. Broken and battered, Ned later disappeared into the darkness, circling the edge of town before showing up alone at the bleachers of the ball field.

When Pa showed up to take me back to the cabin, I had my jacket zipped and my hood pulled down to cover my face. "I'm feeling sick. It's so cold, Pa. Let me sleep up the mountain." He agreed, and I leaned over to sleep, saying nothing.

*****

Ned walked into little Rachel's funeral the next weekend. His tears spent, shame smothered him. It hurt doubly when he overheard an old man say, "You know, it's hard, but tragedies and funerals are a part of life."

After Ned sat, Cale and Rawley walked in. Ned walked out, throwing up in the bushes. He missed a week of school. Ned's only solace was on the mountain.

I read part of Pilgrim's Progress, feeling like John Bunyan's character, who kept trying to unload the burden bound onto his back.

Ned reasoned with himself. *If I tell what happened, I'll put Lily in danger and cause the destruction of our Ruby Lake land by fire. I can't bring Rachel back. Maybe I can bury this hideous guilt so deep, I'll remember it no more. Who would believe what I saw, anyway?* That's when Ned sneaked liquor to the lookout to drink away his sorrow.

*****

After being cheated out of the championship race in October of 1964 and losing his older brother Jacob the same year, my Pa graduated from high school in '65. The *Rockside Bugle* reported on the marriage between Ned Cline and Lily Cline in mid-June, reminding the community of the tragic loss of Lily's former spouse, Ned's brother, Jacob, in Italy. Now with Jake Jr. in the family, my Grampa Cline invited them to live at the Ruby Lake cabin while he built an extra-large room to provide space for them. With Ned's help, Grampa Cline and several friends completed the addition that summer. *Lily congratulated me for getting the railroad job, and I worked hard to make a comfortable home for my true love since fifth grade.*

Grampa Cline, knowing he faced physical issues and declining health, deeded the land to Ned for one dollar before he passed. That fired up the Clausens and Cowlers again, reinvigorating the feud. Grampa Cline had made good on his vow to keep it in the Cline family, even after receiving additional offers from the Clausen-Cowler clans. This action gave my Pa the opportunity to begin a new life. It also brought anger and rising hatred from both rival clans.

Ned loved the freedom the cabin location offered—enough to drive my Grampa Cline's old beat-up pickup all the way into town to work his night-shift railroad job in Rockside.

CHAPTER 5

Billy and Victory Bond

May 1983

A warm halo hovered over Rockside and the Smoky Mountains. The hazy summer day of May 28, 1983, ascended to the horizon. My junior year was ending. Arising early, I read a chapter from the Bible aloud to Ma and completed my early morning chores with Pa.

After I downed Ma's amazing biscuits and gravy, Pa gave me the free time I cherished to enjoy what I loved. Grampa Cline, rest his soul, had done the same for Pa when he was a teen. Pa smiled, saying those summer-like hours in the forest were the only free time he knew.

The afternoon baseball game created the biggest challenge of Jake's budding Minor League career. As a member of the Rookie Johnson City Cardinals and reinstated by his coach from an earlier incident, Jake prepared to pitch against the two-time defending Tennessee State High School Baseball Champions. Jake was the only pitcher to defeat the Haybury Hogs in his senior year. Refusing a ride to Rockside High, I opted to run down the mountain later and join my family there.

Ignoring the heat and its thick humidity, I powered up the mountainside, my legs churning like pistons. I wove between trees and skidded through patches of forest debris that resembled our shredded hall carpet. Trickles of water from a dwindling brook cooled my feet.

Along the rugged mountain cliffs, Victory pierced through a steady breeze. I heard the familiar sound of wind whisking across his feathered wings. I imagined myself like an eagle coming into my own, on the edge of adulthood, just like him. Feeling the strength of my seventeen years, I brushed back my wavy brown hair, adjusted my thick glasses, and leaped onto the flat portion of my boulder-cliff lookout. My confidence was high for my senior year since I had grown three inches.

"Wooo-eee!" I yelled. Victory soared in a half circle and swooped with wings spread wide, landing on the T-Cross. His white head, neck, and tail showcased his splendor. I smiled. I had carved his name onto his T-Cross.

With Victory, I felt no restraints on the mountain. Whether I suppressed my spirit in sadness or expressed my joy with gladness, I was free. Thick glasses confirmed my failing eyesight, but I wouldn't consider myself handicapped. I had dreams to achieve and life to live! If poor vision gave me trouble, I applied grit and creative problem-solving to overcome it.

"Magnificent!" I shouted. "Another perfect landing for Victory!" I drew close, relishing the thought the T-Cross was the bird's favorite perch. "If I can run like you soar and see the way you see, I can be free, free, free!" I never held back anything from Victory, speaking what I believed, convinced he understood what emotions I felt.

Turning from the mountaintop Victory had descended, I knew why he carried no fish. "Did ya strike out on Misty Lake?" Victory's doleful chirp answered that question. "I know, I know. The pickin's are gettin' thin."

Backing away, I slid under the rock overhang and its rainproof tarp that protected my supplies. With binoculars in hand, I stepped out and climbed high onto the tallest boulder and gazed toward town.

"There she is—Jenny," I said, aiming at the distant, fuzzy form of a shapely female mowing her lawn near the railroad tracks. Sighing, I refocused the binoculars. "Victory, my future girlfriend is a knockout. My problem is that I can't see her well from here—you know—blurry eyes." Victory shrieked.

I pulled the binoculars back. "Tough luck, you say? I suppose you can see her with your eyes?" Victory turned, locking his view straight down the mountain in her direction. His beak appeared to turn up in a grin.

Shocked, I rubbed my eyes, forgetting to heed the doctor's warning. "Don't rub your eyes or it will worsen your condition." It was too late again.

"So, if I had your eyes, I could see Jenny clearly? Is that it?" I asked with a laugh, wondering if Victory felt the guilt trip I put on him for having the best eyes on the mountain.

Grabbing the canteen, I soaked a washcloth, reclining as water streamed over my eyes to cool them. The summer sun and a wet washcloth relaxed me as if pulling down shades for a nap.

Life at our homestead would be normal. Pa would pound nails onto new roof shingles to repair the gaps causing water leaks from summer showers. Ma would stand in the cabin clearing, catching a rubber baseball pitched by Chester, her current protégé, now four-teen years old.

I imagined hearing her words of correction—the same words I'd heard when Jake practiced with Ma years before. *Don't short-arm the pitch, Chester! Smack it into my glove!* Ma would be on the warpath about Chester's slow fastball, or his breaking ball, which barely bent.

She'd grip the seams and emphasize what pitch was coming with a warning. *Keep your eye on this one. It's gonna drop!* Chester could read Ma like a book, especially when she curled up the side of her mouth in her windup. He'd best be on full alert.

Chester hated a continuous dose of Ma's high-speed breaking balls. Her pitches would often glance off his glove and zip past the plywood backstop, forcing him to fetch the ball in the woods. Other times he'd get hit on the shin and ice the bruises at night.

When Chester had enough of Ma's breaking balls, he'd chal-lenge her to throw the fastball. Big mistake! He couldn't handle her fastball, either. One time he fell backward off balance and rolled to the side onto a mound of red fire ants. The red welts on his posterior matched his red face of embarrassment. I laughed through the wet washcloth.

Other thoughts came to mind as the sun baked my body on the boulder. Jake's suspension for two weeks before this game came to light under a vow of secrecy. Ma told me, but not Pa. Ma wanted to warn me against following Jake's "bad example."

In a late-night hand of poker after a clinic in Georgia, two con artists worked Jake like "soft dough in a baker's hands." Those were her words. Jake believed a winning hand in a deck would find its way into his hands. It seemed true earlier, but by midnight, he saw nothing like it. Humiliated by his loss, Jake later created a ruckus in the clubhouse the next day and arrived home penniless, not yet ready or able to drop his gambling or drinking habit. It was a wake-up call for Jake.

It was tough to see him change from a cocky, top-of-the-mountain pitcher to a bitter, down-in-the-dumps brother. A week later, he was scratching out drinking money from a few friends in Rockside. He promised to pay back his buddies, but they knew it would never happen. Their gifts were more like a tip for his old high-school MVP season.

That's when Jimmy Jack Clausen set up a low-down plan with the Cowlers. Jimmy Jack convinced Jake to help him knock over the pharmacy and split the money. He said the pharmacist had swindled the townsfolk and deserved it. *What a lie!*

Jimmy Jack became more than my running competitor that day. He was already the top cross-country runner at Rockside last year, just like his Pa had been. Nobody had beaten him, and Jimmy Jack said I wouldn't be the first.

Soon, a Scottish beauty named Jenny Hart moved into town next door to her cousin, Tom Pryor, my running buddy. *Wow! She was somethin'! Her smile could light up the outdoors at midnight.* Before I could whistle with delight, Jimmy Jack asked her out one night. The next day he claimed he was her boyfriend. He didn't understand Jenny at all. Soon, his one date of egotistical behavior led to Jenny's decision to dump him. And it went deeper, always deeper in these mountains. Jimmy Jack was a Cowler cousin. His Pa was Coach Cale Clausen, my Pa's former rival, who always rendered payback.

I never knew what started our family's dislike for the Clausens and Cowlers. I recognized the threats over the auction with Grampa Cline, but there was more. Pa wouldn't talk about it. Someone said it was Pa's teachers, who insisted on alphabetical seating. The order of Clausen, Cline, and Cowler placed my Pa between two volatile characters. I re-learned it when faced with the same situation; sitting between Jimmy Jack Clausen and Cletus Cowler.

Pa was tight-lipped about Cale Clausen getting the coaching job two years before at Rockside. Even though I needed experience in races, I held off running for Rockside until my senior year. Suspecting my goal to win the championship would be in jeopardy with Clausen at the helm, I chose to surprise them and win it in one bold race my senior year.

*****

Jake's trouble reignited when Jenny and I were talking on her porch as she played her guitar and sang. A teenager rode up on his bicycle and tricked us into calling in a pharmacy burglary. *My stomach churns—we thought we were doing our duty as good citizens. What a setup!*

During Jimmy Jack and Jake's so-called burglary, head Deputy Rawley Cowler and his brother trainee, Blimp, arrived as if by personal invitation. Jimmy Jack and Jake had just broken a side window and crawled through. Their crime, besides breaking and entering, was stealing a candy bar. Jimmy Jack was arrested and placed in a jail cell. People in the know said it elated him with his early release for good behavior. Those same people had no clue why my brother Jake had a black eye, a swollen jaw, sore ribs, and a resisting arrest charge when the Cowler lawmen flung him onto the jailhouse floor for the same crime.

Editorials in the *Rockside Bugle* criticized Sheriff Bart Logan for keeping Jake in the local Rockside jail to await his "resisting arrest" sentence. Editorials said Sheriff Logan was biased since Pa had rescued him from a hiking accident a decade before. Logan argued the Haybury jail was overcrowded with undesirables, and Judge Jasper agreed until town politics, fueled by the Cowlers, reversed the decision. Jasper then ordered Jake to be transferred to Haybury. I knew the treatment he'd get there since Jake had destroyed their perfect season with a one-hitter last year.

My biggest issue was family. Jake was our blood. The judge's decision to transfer him to Haybury sent a blast of bitter air through us of Jake's sinking reputation when up against the powerful Cowler clan. Most people thought it pure luck when Judge Jasper found grounds to block his transfer and suspend his jail time as time served. This allowed Jake to pay a fine and return to his minor league team. But I knew better. Jasper's decision relieved the Cowler lawmen from explaining their violence in the jail cell.

*****

There I go again! I hate thinking about the past. I ripped off the wet washcloth from my face and stood on the boulder. I looked up at Victory and saw him perched regally on the T-Cross. That brought me back to the present.

"Make ya a deal," I challenged Victory with a sly grin. "There's a new Scottish beauty in town—Jenny. I wanna spend time with her. Race me to Ruby Lake, and I promise you a fish!" My eyes cooled, I was ready. "Wooo-eee," I yelled and ran down the ribbon-marked trail.

Teasing myself, I thought I could beat Victory in a race to Ruby Lake with a head start. But Victory took off, shrieking when I glanced back. His powerful wings flapped, lifting him skyward for another match race against me. *He's one game eagle!* I had surprised Victory and put distance between us.

As usual, though, he caught up, his shadow cast on treetops, soaring left to right to left, staying above my rapid descent. I hung onto a glimmer of hope. *I can still win!*

My eagle never argued. If he didn't like something, he ignored me. But he seemed to love my challenges. Racing Victory was a game I had never won, but, oh, how I loved to play. Grinning with the joy of competition, I wove a path through trees, avoiding rocky boulders, and raced down my maze-like mountain trail. I tripped on a root but did a perfect somersault, springing up and continuing the pace. *Cool—things are going my way.*

"Wooo-eee!" I yelled. Victory shrieked from above. Barreling by the spring, I spooked several deer from their leisurely drink. The thump, thump, thump of their hooves pounded the hard earth as they departed.

I dashed around thick underbrush and leaped over several logs. My confidence grew as I bounded through the forest.

Rays flickered through leaves and flashed strobe-like as I peered upward at Victory. Brightness irritated my eyes, and I realized I was doing it again, rubbing them, causing all I saw to be blurrier.

"Faster, huh?" I hollered. I followed the path of streamers Tom and I had hung. Victory shrieked as I neared the waterfall. In pure exhilaration, I leaped high off a boulder above the falls, holding my arms outstretched eagle-like. For the slightest instant, I was no earthbound boy restricted by gravity but a majestic, soaring eagle! I covered my glasses and eyes just before I splashed feet-first into the lake.

*****

I swam to the edge, stepping on smooth stones until I continued our competition up the rise on the mountain trail. I sped past more yellow ribbons as water dripped from my body. The stand of trees grew thinner as I neared the clearing by our cabin.

Sure enough, there was Chester, walking out of the trees and into the clearing from what I suspected was a trip to retrieve one of Ma's rubber baseball pitches he'd mishandled. It was no coincidence my running trail passed straight through Chester's pitching zone.

"Hey, Ma!" I heard Chester yell. "I found Jake's missing Honus Wagner card in my shirt pocket! And here comes Billy! Watch this!"

I had suspicions about Chester's tendency for tomfoolery, but I wasn't about to let him spoil my tight contest with Victory. As I sprinted by, Chester uncorked a doozy of a fastball, aimed at my legs. The rubber baseball whizzed between them.

"Awww!" Chester groaned, knowing he would have to fetch it again in the woods. He knew Jake would rub his head raw if he saw him miss that badly from close range.

Ma was at the top of the ladder, delivering a bucket of nails to Pa on the roof. "Can't hit a movin' target, either!" I heard Ma complain. I never slowed as I zipped past the cabin and into the trees below. Victory shrieked. This was the break I needed. Victory often circled the cabin in a wide arc before continuing toward Ruby Lake. Pa called it "the eagle's gesture of respect." I could only imagine Pa's big smile and his roof-side "toast."

My last two-hundred-yard dash to the lake wouldn't take long, and I now had a good lead. I dodged a few trees and prepared to leap onto the short dock and end my losing streak.

I long-jumped onto it, shouting, "Wooo-eee!" Victory shrieked as he swooped past me. Momentum carried me to the end of the dock where I leaped into the rowboat, preventing me from plunging headlong into Ruby Lake. I landed on two life jackets. Between heaving breaths, I screamed, "Tie goes to the runner!" Victory soared majestically over the crystal-blue lake, unconcerned with such trivialities as winning or losing a match race with me.

Recovering, I sat in the rowboat, enjoying nature at its finest while wallowing in my first hard-earned win. I looked back to see if anyone witnessed my magical triumph over Victory. Glancing up from the dock, I saw Tom Pryor standing beside his grandfather's refurbished 1952 Buick Roadmaster, the words *Blue Beauty* scripted on its side. He grinned, shaking his head.

I pulled my glasses off and yanked out the washcloth tucked in the side waistband of my running shorts. Blinking, I poured more water from the rowboat canteen and closed my irritated eyes, placing the dripping washcloth over them. "Ahhh!" I exhaled. Cool relief.

Tom watched Victory snag a fish. "He must love Ruby Lake!"

"I promised him a fish, Tom."

"Look, Billy, if you wanna see my cousin Jenny before Jake's game, let's go!"

Chapter 6

Dating Jenny

Seeing the Blue Beauty arrive in Tom's driveway next door, Jenny cased her guitar, slid it under the swing, and jogged over.

"Hey, cuz," Tom greeted through his open window.

I smiled and jumped out of my "shotgun" seat, holding the door open for Jenny. She slid in and I hopped in next to her. We were off to Jake's exhibition baseball game.

"Thank you, Billy, but...you're all wet!"

"I'm drying as we speak."

"Billy's Ma knows more about baseball than anybody in these mountains."

"How come you don't play ball, Billy?"

"Look at his glasses, Jenny."

"Everything is a little blurry," I said.

Jenny sparked a curious smile. "Am I blurry?"

My long gaze at her was hypnotic. "Your face is like a spring rainbow."

"Good grief! Billy can't see squat! I hung yellow ribbons on tree limbs or he'd get lost."

Jenny's eyes twinkled. "So the yellow ribbons are enough?"

"Funny how Victory guides me, too."

Jenny grinned. "The first thing Tom shoved through our U-Haul window when we moved here was that old newspaper article of how you saved an eagle. You were very brave."

"Billy was very lucky," Tom said, turning into the parking lot at the ball field.

*****

Walking to the pay booth, two men and their young sons received permission to bring in two birthday cakes to celebrate later during the game. Jenny sang "Happy Birthday" until the boys blushed. She stopped, but her smile left them grinning as they walked in. Tom paid his way in as I pulled a wet five-dollar bill from my sock and bought tickets for Jenny and me.

Over the public-address system, an organist in the announcer's booth played sing-along songs before the game. Several older couples hummed the tunes and swayed back and forth, enjoying the songs of their youth. As we entered the stands, I named the title while delighting in Jenny's presence.

"Let Me Call You Sweetheart."

"What?" Jenny said, turning with a sheepish grin.

"Uh, the song, the song. Mr. Stubblemeister plays organ at church and donated his old organ for the ballgames. He loves baseball."

"So, what are you saying, Billy? The name of the song or that… you want me…to let you…call me…sweetheart?" Jenny's dramatic body language emboldened me.

"Both…if it's okay to call you sweetheart on a first date."

"Is that what this is? Sounds like you expect more when numbering them."

"Does it?"

We continued walking, then leaned against a fence, viewing the baseball diamond. "Jenny, when I was seven, our church bought a new organ. The next Sunday, old Mr. Stubblemeister set up a prank and chose me to help pull it off. He signaled me to demonstrate the organ's technical excellence. I marched up and slid onto the organ seat. They all laughed as I raised both hands high, ready to pounce my fingers onto the keys. When Mr. Stubblemeister gave me the sign, my fingers came down fast and furious, followed by the masterly music he had recorded on his professional tape recorder beside a dynamic microphone. I faked a difficult arrangement of *A Mighty Fortress is our God.* No one could see my fingers."

Jenny laughed with fascination at my story.

"After the clapping died down, the pastor approached me with his microphone. 'Amazing rendition, Billy. Did you know Martin Luther wrote that music just after the middle ages? What do you think about Martin Luther now?'"

"'He must be really old,' I said. 'Perhaps over forty.' Hearing laughter put me in unknown territory, a popular showman, if only for a moment."

Jenny laughed and put her hand on my shoulder as Tom leaned over the rail, realizing he was a third wheel.

"Hey, Jake!" I yelled, grabbing his attention between warm-up pitches. "It's up to you!" He tipped his cap, smiled, and threw a fastball. Chester and I always laughed when Jake complained about his old coach saying those same words before each game he pitched.

We stepped to my folks and Chester, who sat in the front bleacher row beside the birthday boys and their boxed cakes. As I walked up, a group of French Club students sitting behind us shouted in French while waving a sign that read HAYBURY THE DAMN YANKEES!

The sign hit Chester in the head several times as they waved it. Ma rose and turned to them, speaking with authority. "Wise up, Frenchies! The Yankees left Johnson City three years ago! It's the Rookie Johnson City Cardinals now!" When Ma turned back to sit, we could hear a female voice respond in French. The French Club kids laughed in ridicule.

"This is Jenny," I said. My family greeted her, looking her over from head to toe.

"Nice to meet you all," Jenny said.

I glanced at the massive umpire, Blimp Cowler, as he studied the lineup card. Blimp was retiring as an umpire in the minors. He would become the newest deputy in Rockside, joining his older brother, Deputy Rawley Cowler, a classmate my Pa knew too well. The only Rockside deputy we trusted was Chappy Smith, a former catcher on Rockside's baseball team. Years before, Chappy had encouraged Jake to dream big.

When the tunes ended, the Haybury Hogs' cross-country coach grabbed the microphone and imitated his championship hog call that rumbled through the bleachers—a Haybury tradition. Blimp's huge frame bounced up and down as he laughed with the crowd.

"Blimp better put aside family history," said Ma. She turned from staring at Blimp and spat over the rail. "Jake's ready for his best pitching performance—I can feel it."

"Lily, relax," Pa said. "You taught him since he could grip a baseball. He's roasted the Hogs in the past. He'll smoke 'em today. Those two guys on the front row are Major League scouts."

"It won't be long till Jake shows his stuff!" Ma said. "He's lookin' strong in warm-ups—got zip on that fastball! That'll set up his breaking ball, you watch! It's exciting, but I'm nervous about Blimp's calls. There's a reason Blimp got downsized from the minors."

"Blimp downsized? Really?" questioned Chester. When the sign waved again, he leaned defensively over his bleacher seat. "Ma, you always said God invented baseball. Do they play baseball in heaven?"

"Sure. Can't you imagine Moses coming to bat with that big staff? A pure power hitter, batting cleanup! And the Green Monster in Boston? By the eighth inning, it would crumble like the walls of Jericho from his line drives!"

"Wow!" said Chester. "Even New York's Yankees can't do that."

"Well, they try, Chester. Try this. If you needed a pinch runner, and you were Tom Lasorda of the Dodgers, which apostle would you bring in, John or Simon Peter?"

"As a pinch runner? That's a tough call, Ma. Who would the Dodgers have drafted first?"

"It doesn't matter who they would have drafted first. They'd bring in the apostle John! He outran Simon Peter to the tomb, remember?"

"Oh, yeah. Is that why you carry your big Bible? Because of the stories?"

Pa interrupted, "If she didn't carry her Bible, she'd be carryin' a baseball and a bat, lookin' to start a pickup game."

Ma laughed, patted her Bible, and nudged Pa.

Just then, Pa took a small flask from his pocket and sneaked a drink. Jenny learned firsthand of my Pa's problem. Pa stood and walked to another bleacher section, helping Pop O'Reilly seat a paraplegic boy.

"Who's that man your Pa's with?" Jenny asked.

"Pop O'Reilly, head of a boys' home and school that includes a wing for handicapped boys. He was Pa's cross-country coach in high school."

Chester tossed his rubber baseball high in the air, but it landed a row behind in an up-do of Mademoiselle Juliet Dubois. She wore avant garde high-fashion clothes, red high heels, and flashed blood-red nail polish. She and her French club students were appalled.

"Vous garcon stupide!" Mademoiselle Dubois screamed at Chester.

Lily whirled around and plucked the rubber baseball from her fancy up-do, which caused her hair to uncoil in a tangled mess. Dubois hissed, flashing sharp nails at Lily's aggression before muttering a French rebuke. The students laughed.

Lily stood steady as a rock. "Next time, catch the ball, Frenchie!" Lily turned back and sat as Mademoiselle Dubois made a hand gesture Lily never saw. Lily put the rubber baseball and Jake's special "Honus" baseball card Chester held into her purse for safekeeping.

"Come on, Chester, let's get closer and wave to our brother." Tom and Jenny joined us.

Chester needed to vent after the Dubois put-down. "If Jake wins, everybody in town will remember who Jake Cline is...and maybe someday they'll know my name, too. Huh, Billy?"

"Chester, I already know your name. Your day will come. Here's a dollar. Go buy yourself something. I've gotta talk to some friends."

I noticed two varsity runners on the Rockside team, the Cowler boys. Cletus was to be a senior and Gopher a year younger with a smaller frame. They stood staring at Tom and me and Tom's beautiful next-door neighbor, the new-in-town Scottish beauty, Jenny Hart.

Jenny saw tension on my face. "So, Billy, how's the brother of the star pitcher doing?"

"Better, since my kid brother headed for the snack shack."

As we approached the Cowler boys, Gopher hollered out a question. "Hey, Billy, did ya think 'cause your brother was pitchin', they'd honor you as bat boy? Look at your glasses. Blind as a bat! Get it? Blind as a bat!" Gopher cackled like a goose.

"No, I guess not, Gopher."

"Guess nothin'! Cletus got to be bat boy," Gopher said, "not you. And they voted for me as ball boy. And Jimmy Jack Clausen, our undefeated cross-country champ, will throw out the ceremonial first pitch. They will always choose us Cowlers over you sorry Clines."

"Wait a minute, Gopher," said Jenny. "Isn't Jimmy Jack Coach Clausen's son?"

Cletus butted in. "Technically, but Jimmy Jack's ma was Didi Cowler, from our kin! He may run like his Pa, but Jimmy Jack's a Cowler through and through. And he gets mighty provoked if anybody questions his duel clanship."

"Duel clanship?" I said. "Thanks for clearing that up, Cletus."

Cletus continued, "And Jenny, Jimmy Jack wants you to visit him at the batting cage."

"Sorry, I'm sort of with Billy and Tom. They gave me a ride here."

I stepped toward Cletus. "So, Cletus, you're the bat boy, huh, instead of me?"

"That's right," Cletus said, putting his hands on his hips. "The vote was unanimous."

A boy's distant voice shouted, "Hey, Cletus, Jimmy Jack said to get down here...now!"

"Well...congratulations," I said. "We don't want to hold you up. We know you have important bat-boy activities to perform."

"I'll take this up with you later," Cletus said, pointing a finger at my chest. "You Clines better watch yourselves. Blimp just got sworn in as deputy, so we Cowlers are the law in this town!" Cletus grinned, nodded to Gopher, and jogged away.

Gopher smacked his hands. "Cletus just gave you a warning, and Jimmy Jack'll back his play. You'd best remember that," said Gopher.

"Hey, Gopher," I called, "since you're the ball boy, help out your brother. Go shag some flies. There's plenty buzzin' around the dumpster!"

Jenny stifled a laugh before playing peacemaker. "Just drop it, boys. We're all from Rockside. Let's root for the home team."

"Root for Jake Cline? Forget it!" Gopher said.

The PA announcer spoke, "This exhibition features the Minor League rookies of the Johnson City Cardinals against the two-time defending Tennessee State Baseball Champions, the Haybury Hogs! Rockside's pitcher from last year, Jake Cline, starts for the Cards. He was the only pitcher to defeat Haybury last year."

Tom, Jenny, and I clapped, irritating Gopher.

The PA announcer continued, "Throwing the ceremonial first pitch is Rockside's undefeated cross-country champ, Jimmy Jack Clausen!"

Gopher clapped. He left as I led Tom and Jenny to our seats.

Jimmy Jack Clausen was tall, lean, and sinewy. He personified charisma as he threw the ceremonial pitch to applause. Jogging in to retrieve the baseball from the catcher, he spied Jenny in the stands. He winked and tossed the ball up to her. Jenny blushed. "I'll autograph it for you later," Jimmy Jack said with a smile.

Before Jimmy Jack could leave, Ace Makowski, another senior, wearing a #1 Haybury Hog running jersey, accosted Jimmy Jack. "Undefeated?" Ace shouted. "Not this year, 'cause I, Ace Makowski, and Deucey here say so!" His girlfriend, Deucey, wore a special #2 Haybury Hog jersey. All of us heard Ace's prediction. He was a serious competitor, a close second behind Jimmy Jack at last year's cross-country championships.

Chapter 7

Jake's Exhibition Baseball Game

"Play ball!" Blimp thundered.

Ma was in her usual hyper-baseball mode. On the first pitch, Jake threw a fastball down the pipe. The Haybury batter swung at nothing but air. Blimp thrust out his right hand.

Ma let out a whoop that drew stares. "That's my boy!" she shouted. "Pitch him tight!" The next pitch was a strike on the inside corner, handcuffing the batter.

"Strike!" Blimp grunted.

"All right! Yeah!" Ma yelled. "Think, now, Jake. Throw the right pitch." Ma turned to us and muttered, "Breaking ball—down and away—just off his shoe tops." Sure enough, that was the pitch and the leadoff hitter reached for it, swinging like a golfer.

"Stee-rike three!" Blimp shouted. We stared at Ma, smiling.

By the top of the sixth inning, the Minor League Rookie Cardinals had scored seven runs, including a grand slam, and Jake had struck out five batters, giving up zero runs. Ma thumped her Bible on the bleacher rail in time with her chant. "Hey, batter, batter, batter! Swing, batter, batter, batter!" The Rockside fans were joining in.

Jake was setting them up with blazing fastballs on the outside corner or hard breaking balls at their ankles. Haybury's right-handed batters couldn't get around on his fastball and hit line drives foul outside the first base line, nearly decapitating their first base coach. On Jake's breaking balls and sinker, left-handers were pounding the ball into the dirt on the first base side.

The outs came on strike-outs or batters who leaned over the plate and hit weak high hoppers back to the pitcher on the first base side. Each time, Jake sprang off the mound as if on a pogo stick and held it, grinning like a Cheshire cat as each batsman tried to beat the throw to first. On the last occasion, the bang-bang call got the first base coach tossed out.

Ma's "whoop" followed that event. The Haybury fans, at first impatient, were now fightin' mad. One Haybury mom yelled, "Tell that Bible-thumpin' lady to shut her mouth!"

Lily turned, grinning at Mademoiselle Dubois while enjoying Jake's dominance over this year's defending conference champs.

Mademoiselle Dubois rose and hovered over Lily from behind, shouting, "Ferme la grande bouche!" Her words drew stares from the stands. Lily rose, but Deputy Rawley Cowler stepped up, causing Mademoiselle Dubois to back off and walk down to the Haybury dugout to confer with the Hogs' manager.

"Ned," Rawley shouted to him in the stands, "control your woman or I will!" After a pause, "You heard me!" Rawley shouted again.

Ma looked at Pa, who finally responded, "Is there a law against cheering?"

"Yes, against excessive cheering that berates an opponent!"

Ma fired back, "When they can't hit a ball out of the infield, it's their own play that berates them—not us!"

"One more outburst and I'll run you both in!"

"Where's the code for that?" Pa said.

"Hezekiah 3:4!" Rawley answered.

"Yeah!" said a few illiterate Haybury fans. Rawley waited for a reaction, but it never came. Pa sank to his seat as Rawley grinned and nodded to the Haybury fans. I was humiliated.

The announcer spoke again, "Next up is Max 'the Moose' Michaels, the Tennessee state home run champion. Ladies and gentlemen, we are honored to have Mademoiselle Juliet Dubois with us from Paris, France. She's had a celebrated career as a high-end Parisian fashion model while dabbling with a second career in education. Mademoiselle Dubois served as an exchange vice-principal for

Haybury High before her next modeling tour in New York. Housed by the gracious Moose Michaels' family, she concludes her Tennessee experience today."

As soon as the Moose stepped into the batter's box with two outs, Jake quick-pitched him, giving him a shave with a chin-high fastball. That seemed to rattle the Moose and Haybury fans as he spun out of the batter's box, staring at the umpire, but getting no sympathy.

Before stepping in again, the Moose held his hand up, signifying to the umpire to let him settle into the batter's box before allowing Jake to release the next pitch. He pounded his heavy bat on home plate with ferocity, displaying his bulging muscles that rippled through his baseball uniform. On Jake's next pitch, the Moose did not get the blazing fastball he expected, but a lollipop curve. He swung and topped an easy come-backer to Jake. The Haybury slugger was already slow of foot, but he exhibited Academy Award-type humiliation for another weak performance at bat as he jogged toward first base.

Jake snagged the ball and mocked him with a comment, "Gonna hustle, Moosie?"

Moose sprinted all-out to first base until he pulled a hamstring and fell onto the base path, writhing in pain. Jake waited and waited, ball in hand, before walking to the Moose with a proud grin etched on his face. *What would Blimp call?*

Lily called it first from the stands. "It's baseball Scripture! The Moose is crawling to the dugout! He's exceeded the boundaries of the baseline!"

"Out of the baseline!" Blimp bellowed, making an emphatic gesture with his right thumb.

Moose turned first to Jake and then to the umpire, making a gesture of his own with both hands before throwing his batting helmet at Jake.

Blimp, with a sweeping arm motion, a rugged voice, and a protruding right thumb, repeated his own gesture, "You're outta here!" Blimp's words had a double meaning.

"That's right, Blimp! Send him to the showers!" said Lily.

That brought shouts of derision from the Haybury team. The Hogs' manager, "Skinny" McKinney, sprinted away from his conversation with Mademoiselle Dubois toward home plate to get into Blimp's face, but he underestimated his speed. He tripped and slammed into Blimp's chest protector and slumped to the ground like a gnat hitting a semi-truck's windshield. Blimp threw him out, too.

Hog fans had bragged how their manager ate burgers with double onions smeared in Limburger cheese for arguing with the umpire. He was skilled at saying it and spraying it! When Skinny stood and began his full-fledged routine, Blimp could take no more. He not only threw the manager out of the game but off the premises. Sheriff Bart Logan intervened, escorting the irate Haybury manager off school grounds while holding a handkerchief over his nose. That left Mademoiselle Dubois as the highest ranked school official for the Haybury Hogs.

I looked at Jenny and Tom and shrugged.

Jenny surprised me by reaching her hand to mine and giving a squeeze before shouting, "That-a-way, Jake!"

We'd heard the head of the Rockside grounds crew had cooked up a scheme with the PA announcer. Though nobody could prove it, we knew it must be true. During the ruckus and departure of the manager and the Moose, Mr. Stubblemeister played a tune while the grounds crew came out with a wheelbarrow of dirt, filling in the divots near home plate and on the first-base side of the foul line. The ground was beaten up.

Two things angered Haybury beside losing. First, Jake was up to bat, standing near Blimp, enjoying the shenanigans of the grounds crew as he waited to hit in the bottom of the inning. Second, during the delay the PA announcer delivered another dig.

"Folks," he said, "we're sorry for the delay, but the Haybury batters are creating divots the size of gopher holes by pounding the ball into the dirt along the right field line. It's not safe to run to first base." That explanation brought laughter and hoots from Rockside and Cardinals' fans but a chorus of boos and more than a few flying objects from the Haybury faithful.

Mademoiselle Dubois strutted onto the field in her tight-fitting European-style high-fashioned outfit to object to the umpire. She sported a sparkling pair of maroon-colored high heels and a refurbished fancy up-do from her recent encounter with Ma. Her body language signaled disgust since preparations for a post-game victory party appeared in jeopardy.

Mr. Stubblemeister couldn't resist. During her rickety high-heeled walk to home plate, he played *Pop Goes the Weasel* in time with her model-like steps. And the home crowd howled! The PA announcer added, "The Statue of Liberty is not the only gift France gave America! Presenting Mademoiselle Dubois!"

If that wasn't embarrassment enough, she waved her arms in a French-laden verbal tirade against Blimp, who stared back with a clueless expression. Mr. Stubblemeister repeated his dynamic organ challenge three times as the raucous crowd shouted, "Charge!" Before returning, she stomped one high-heeled shoe into the dirt, making a divot of her own, but broke off a heel. During her extra-rickety-walk back, she pointed at Jake, who was unsuccessful in toning down his laughing spree as he stepped to the plate. When she hoisted her red thumbnail at Jake in a "you're out" sign, Ma sprang from her seat and leaped over the railing onto the field.

Pa held his head in his hands. I followed Ma, vaulting over the railing.

I glanced at Jake, who turned to see Ma and Mademoiselle Dubois on a collision course. Jake looked back just in time as the pitcher sneaked a beanball pitch at him. He back-pedaled, avoiding it by an inch, doing a back roll out of the batter's box.

Mademoiselle Dubois slashed Ma with spiked fingernails, drawing blood. Ma did a 360-degree spin, swinging her large-print study Bible like a thirty-ounce Louisville Slugger bat. The PA announcer wasted no time explaining the outcome.

"Down goes Dubois! Frenchie's down! Struck down by the Word of God!"

The truth, or as later reported, was that Mademoiselle Dubois fell back awkwardly, the victim of imbalance caused by a gust of wind from Lily's Bible and her damaged high heels. That view was squashed by eyewitnesses who finally settled on one for the Rockside Bugle: "If Lily had fully connected, it would have been 'lights out' for Mademoiselle Dubois!"

The catcher and pitcher piled onto Jake. The benches emptied as the Hogs followed the Moose, who hobbled badly. I ran into the fray doing all I could. Rawley tried to pen me to the ground, but I escaped as Blimp tried to restore order. When enough officials entered, I landed one great punch at the opposing pitcher who had tried to bean Jake. That got me arrested.

Special deputies, Carson and Blake, helped by cuffing Ma and Mademoiselle Dubois as Pa and Chester followed them to a police cruiser.

In the stands, raucous French club students waved their signs as "cake" fathers retaliated by stuffing their son's birthday delights into the sign carriers' faces in a stand-off.

"By order of the superintendent, this game is suspended. The score counts because they played five innings! Please exit the stadium!" Mr. Stubblemeister played "When the Saints Go Marching In" as the crowd dispersed.

Jenny looked at Tom as she reached the bottom of the steps. "Tom, is this typical of Tennessee baseball games?"

Jimmy Jack stepped up and interrupted before he responded. "Hey, Tom, I can give her a ride home so you can check on Billy. I need to sign Jenny's baseball, anyway. Is that okay?"

Tom looked at Jenny, who nodded. Tom walked toward Billy, and Jimmy Jack gave a grin of confidence to Jenny, saying, "We should let the fans clear the area first. Do you have a pen?"

I heard whistles from disgruntled fans while Sheriff Logan and Deputy Smith restored order. The officers took Ma and Ms. Dubois from the Haybury deputies and led them into their separate cruisers, transporting them to the Rockside police station.

Deputy Rawley Cowler and brother Blimp stayed at the school for the present time to maintain order. The events rekindled our bad history with the Cowlers.

I knew Ma and Pa's relationship would become strained again. Ma feared that Pa would go on a drinking binge the following week. It always happened to Pa when life turned dicey.

*****

Jimmy Jack walked Jenny to Cletus's '57 red Chevy convertible to take her home. Jenny held her ceremonial baseball, the autograph by Jimmy Jack visible below the insignia.

When they arrived at the Chevy, I glanced up from the parking lot and saw her standing with Jimmy Jack, beside Cletus and Gopher, who laughed inside their convertible. I knew they laughed at Jake and me since we stood gazing at Jake's car with two flat tires and a cracked front windshield. Four Haybury ballplayers plus the Moose surrounded us, jeering. Tom stood alone a safe distance away, beside his Blue Beauty.

I wondered whose side Jenny was on. She turned to Jimmy Jack and conversed with him while pointing to us. Jimmy Jack laughed as Cletus and Gopher cackled inside the Chevy!

Jimmy Jack left Jenny at the convertible and walked straight toward Jake and me. My first inclination was they now outnumbered us more than before until Cletus slapped his car door hard and yelled, "Jimmy Jack! No!" But he kept walking toward us.

At that moment Jake charged the Moose, landing a wicked right cross to his jaw. Four Haybury players responded, pounding Jake. I pulled away two until a barrage of punches slammed me to the ground.

Jimmy Jack yanked two more Haybury players from Jake before he received a glancing blow to the face. I thought, *Perhaps Jimmy Jack is making up for Jake's jailing over the pharmacy debacle.* Cletus and Gopher hopped out of their convertible to protect Jimmy Jack as Rawley and Blimp skidded to a stop in their police cruiser and charged in.

"Break it up! Break it up!" Rawley shouted.

Jake threw another round of blows to the Moose as I fought off the last two Haybury players, who ran to their vehicles and peeled out.

"Break it up, I said!" Rawley yanked Jake off the Moose as I yielded to Blimp, who cuffed me. Jake tried to flee, but Rawley took him down with a hold on Jake's pitching hand.

"Calm down or your wrist may break!" Rawley shouted.

Jake moaned in severe pain as the Haybury players escaped. "You lettin' 'em go? You Cowlers!"

Rawley cuffed Jake and joined Blimp as they jerked both of us Cline brothers spread-eagled, bent over the back of their cruiser.

Jimmy Jack and the Cowler boys led a bloodied Moose to their convertible. Passing by the cruiser, Rawley barked orders. "Cletus! You, Gopher, and Jimmy Jack drop off Moose at the hospital! We'll take care of the Clines! And no side trips!"

Jimmy Jack, his lip still bleeding from a punch, walked up to Jenny beside the Chevy. I heard his words. "Jenny, I helped them… since you asked me." She seemed concerned as if responsible for his injury. Just then, Rawley and Blimp shoved us into the backseat of the cruiser. From the back seat, I saw Jenny take out a handkerchief and lean in on Jimmy Jack, braced against the Chevy. He held on to Jenny's waist while she wiped blood from his lips, their faces too close for my liking. I glared at them unseen through the window from the departing cruiser. Jake and I were accompanied by the Cowler lawmen to the Rockside Police Station.

Tom told me later he had seen everything, and after we left handcuffed in the cruiser, he tried to protect Jenny. Approaching his cousin, Tom spoke, "Jenny, I'll take you home."

It startled Jenny, not realizing Tom was there. She turned and stared at Tom, then at Jimmy Jack, followed by the Cowler boys and the Moose waiting in the convertible. Each of the others had suffered multiple injuries. She paused, then pushed away from Jimmy Jack and walked to Tom as the two angled toward the Blue Beauty for the ride home.

*****

Inside the Rockside Jail lobby the Duty Officer switched off the auto door-lock as Rawley shoved Jake inside and Blimp followed in with me.

"What happened to my Ma?" shouted Jake as he entered. Surprised, we saw Ma, Pa, and Chester look up at us.

Ma answered. "I'm here, Jake! They booked me and Frenchie, but I'm going home. She's on her way back to France."

Pa was more than curious why Rawley and Blimp were man-handling two of his sons. "Rawley, what trouble did my boys get into?"

"Enough to file charges on Jake! And we're keeping Billy over-night!" Rawley passed his paperwork to the duty officer. "Ned, sign the paperwork and we're done! It's been a long day!"

Ma saw Jake favoring his sore pitching wrist as Rawley and Blimp took them through a steel door to the cells. Pa sighed, then signed the papers, slamming the pen on the counter.

Lily looked at the duty officer. "Sir, your deputy hurt my son's pitching wrist." Ma pulled out the rubber baseball from her purse and handed it to him. "Squeezing this will help loosen up his wrist. Your son was on his team, remember?" The officer was quiet, squeez-ing the rubber baseball himself as he nodded.

Chester added, "And he'll calm down knowing I found his favorite baseball card. You'll thank me for a quiet night." Before a response, Chester reached in Ma's purse and pulled out the Honus Wagner card, placing it on the counter.

The duty officer again nodded, taking both without a second thought.

Pa added one more suggestion. "Ice would be nice, not only for Jake's pitching wrist but on both their facial bruises, too. Thank you, sir, for your gracious help with our wayward sons. My signature here will let you release Billy in the morning. Right?" The officer concurred.

Inside the Rockside hall of jail cells, Rawley slung Jake into a cell while Blimp shoved me into an adjoining one. The Cowler law-men jerked the steel doors shut and rattled them. Rawley threatened

Jake. "I've got you for assaulting a minor and resisting arrest! You're in a heap o' trouble, boy!"

Blimp added his two cents. "Billy, this overnight is a warning! Keep your nose out of other people's business!"

Rawley and Blimp left in a huff as the duty officer entered and dropped off an orange jump suit for Jake, ice bags, a rubber baseball, and the baseball card. Both Jake and I grabbed an ice bag and sat on our bunks, holding it to our jaws. Jake stared at the "Honus" card tossed onto the floor. He rose and placed it on the bunk before gripping the jail bars, jerking them violently. He'd have pulled them apart if he could.

"We got a bum rap!"

"What do you mean?" I asked.

"Those Cowlers strong-armed us!" Jake paced in his cell, his face red and flushed. "Pa didn't even try to get us out!"

"How? He's trying to calm Ma."

"He should 'a stood up for us. My real Pa would'a stood up to 'em!"

I paused. "You mean Jacob? Don't say that. He and Jacob were blood brothers."

"Ya know, Billy, sometimes you sound just like your pa...takin' the weak side."

"Pa's not weak, Jake. He's protecting Ma." I turned away.

Jake stepped closer, gripping onto his jail bars and staring at my back. "Your pa's a drunk! So he lost a race! I'm sick of that story!" Turning, I faced Jake, who continued, "What's crazy is, you'll get off because you give in. I stand up for myself! You and your pa never figured out how!" Sitting, Jake grimaced, lifting the ice pack to his face with one hand, then squirming as he squeezed the rubber baseball with the other, and moaned as he stared at the bent baseball card.

CHAPTER 8

Jailbreak

Ma's return to off-season normalcy was standard, at least for her. On this Saturday morning, she drove to her church friends' knitting circle without me. Usually, I went with her, but I was in the Rockside Jail with Jake. I missed the lemonade they always offered me before I ran to Tom's house. Ma walked the wraparound porch of the rambling Rockside home where the ladies were knitting.

"Well, girls, guess I won't make it back for a few weeks," said Ma.

"Yeah, we heard," said Margaret, the organizer of the knitting group. "How long this time?"

"Same," said Ma. "Start next week."

"Same sentence?"

"Yep."

"Community service again?"

"Yep."

"Don't you ever tire of cleaning latrines at the park and community center for the same offense every year?"

"Yep."

"What can we do, Lily? How should we pray?" asked Margaret.

"Don't know…just pray. I get riled up—so riled up!"

"We're sorry. How ya doin' on those socks?"

"Had to rip 'em out."

"What happened?"

"Well, I kept thinkin' about the game—just got so…"

"Riled up? Oh, Lily, we all love you."

"Yep, I know." She gave a look of appreciation to her friends and sat to knit, moving her fingers with aggressive perfection.

*****

That same Saturday morning, I woke up and sat on the edge of my jail bunk. In the adjoining cell, Jake stood in his orange jumpsuit and stretched his upper body between pitches. My well-muscled brother stood at one end of his cell and threw the rubber baseball into his pillow. *Whack!* Jake lunged forward, picked up the rubber baseball, stepped back, and repeated his throw. *Whack!*

Deputy Blimp Cowler, forty, entered and sat at his desk in the jailhouse, watching. He grinned at Jake's senseless pitching into his pillow. Blimp bellowed, "And pitching his last game for the Rockside Jailbirds is...Jake Cline! How does it feel being released by the Minor League Cardinals? Oh, yeah! I heard! Stick a fork in ya, you're done!"

"You shouldn't talk, Blimp! Both of us are out of baseball. At least, I've still got passion for this game!"

Blimp chuckled. "Passion or not, those Johnson City boys cut you faster than green grass through a goose. You're spoiling their image!"

"Hey, Blimp," I complained, "when are you gonna let me outta here? I'm starving!"

The duty officer walked in through the steel door, talking about the Little League game. "Okay, Blimp, I'll take your ten bucks against my team in blue. You'll be so sorry."

"Why?" Blimp said. "My team in orange is a cinch to win. I wonder if they'd let Jake play in his orange jumpsuit?" Both laughed.

Jake walked over to my bars and held a finger to his lips. "Shhhh," he whispered, "I've got a plan. Pete Rose is gonna break me out. Take your time at Dooley's Doughnuts."

"What are you talking about? Doughnuts?" I said, not understanding.

"I'll tell you later how it works with doughnuts," said Jake in a normal voice.

The duty officer got the ten bucks from Blimp and laughed at what he thought was Jake's conversation. "You wanna know how doughnuts work? Look at Blimp! You eat too many, you grow up the size of Blimp!" He laughed.

"Get lost, man," said Blimp. "Your money will be mine before the sun sets!"

Blimp unlocked my cell. "Your Pa signed a release last night. Your buddy Tom and a gal are waitin' out front. If it's doughnuts you want, try Dooley's. It's just up the street. Tom may hang down his head at Dooley's, but you won't!" Blimp laughed at his own joke.

"Give me a few minutes," I said to the duty officer. "I'm hungry but I need to get my senses back." *What is Jake up to?*

"I could count to three before those pitches crossed to the pillow!" said Blimp.

"Oh, yeah, I bet you I could split this pillow open with a real baseball!"

"Wow, Blimp, tryin' to make money off Jake?" asked the duty officer.

Blimp laughed while munching on a leftover doughnut. White sugar dusted his chin, the front of his uniform, and his paperwork. "We shouldn't have let you have a rubber baseball in the cell. Some would think we're keepin' your baseball dreams alive! But I doubt your pitchin' will improve since you've been released from the minors and can't stop gamblin'."

"What about Jimmy Jack?" Jake argued. "He got a pass to a troubled teens resort and gets out of camp chores to run the trails because he's your nephew! What a racket! At least he got away from your cousin, Cale Clausen! Too bad your sister couldn't do the same!"

Blimp slammed his hand, snapping his pencil. "As an umpire, I've learned how to take insults and toss 'em aside," he said, standing. "You wouldn't like it if I forgot what I've learned. We should have hung you out to dry after the pharmacy break in! So, what if Jimmy Jack tricked your brother Billy here to call in your burglary! It worked, didn't it? You broke in! You got arrested, and now you've resisted arrest. You Clines are the laughingstock of this town!"

Jake slumped to his bed in shameful silence as Blimp pivoted back to his paperwork. I saw Jake's eyes come alive with a devious grin, which confused me.

His eyes now focused on the wall above Blimp. He gazed at the impressive Hall of Fame trophy shelf filled with pictures and a dusty plaque honoring Blimp Cowler as a former Rookie Triple-A Umpire of the Year recipient. Beside the plaque was Blimp's favorite baseball, autographed by the 1963 National League Rookie of the Year, Pete Rose.

Personality-wise, Blimp was the nicest of the Cowlers. But Blimp's umpire honors brought no praise from Jake. I remembered when Blimp umpired Jake's final playoff game of high school because the lead school umpire was sick.

Ma couldn't forget it, either. She asked her churchgoing knitting friends to pray for her since she struggled to forgive Blimp for his calls. Jake told me that was reason enough to hold a grudge, even if he'd had a game when he couldn't pitch his way out of a paper bag.

One of Jake's friends had verbally bludgeoned his pitching performance after that game, saying, "You couldn't get your breaking ball over the plate, so you resorted to aiming your fastball! The result: you pitched a game of homerun derby!" Jake cut ties with that friend.

Jake must have known how he would break out of jail. Jake glanced at his own baseball card. "Hey, Blimp! I know ya like baseball cards. I got somethin' here better than all your hall-of-shame awards on your shelf!"

"Whoa...boy!" Blimp slid his chair and stood. He circled his desk area before turning defensive, shaking his head. Blimp couldn't disguise his curiosity as he glared at the card Jake now held out.

I knew Jake had rattled him. "Collectors know this baseball card as one of the most treasured in big league history. Some collectors would sign over their homes or their firstborn to own this card." Blimp salivated, but Jake and I knew this one was a fake, a sweet pickup from a poker game in Atlanta.

"Hohhh-nusss Waaag-neeer, 1910!" announced Jake, as if Honus himself was looking from heaven. "I'll show it to ya, if you'll let me see the Pete Rose."

Blimp hesitated at first, but would he bite? Blimp turned to his award shelf, unlocked his Pete Rose autographed baseball off its mount, and trudged to Jake's cell, still holding it.

The duty officer spoke up. "Take a bet, Blimp. Winner take all!"

"It's real…look," Jake said, showing no interest in the Pete Rose. "Won it from a poker stiff in Georgia. The guy was sure I was bluffin' him. A card hound from the Braves organization authenticated it." Jake backed up and held Honus just out of Blimp's reach. Blimp squinted, adjusted his glasses, trying to read the card. He reached in, his fingers mere inches from the prize.

"Oh-oh! A squinting ex-umpire! Oh, yeah, so that's why they put you out to pasture…to graze!" Jake later told me that put-down felt good to him, but it didn't rattle Blimp. Maybe Blimp had his own plan.

Blimp surprised Jake and intoned a reply as if he were standing before a national treasure: "Honus Wagner, 1910? Priceless!"

"Precisely! And I'll show it to ya up close if you'll let me get a look-see at your Pete Rose…and if you'll let me pitch with it…you know…into the pillow."

"Not so fast," Blimp retorted. "We told ya, you're done. For assaulting a minor and resisting arrest, you've got two strikes already. And who's saying that Atlanta fella knew anything about baseball cards."

Jake must not have counted on Blimp's deductive skills. "Whatever ya say, Blimp, for we know you're the gatekeeper of *aaall*…baseball!"

"Okay, that's enough" said the duty officer. "Come on, Billy, let's get you out of here since you're so hungry." I got up, but the drama between these baseball fanatics fascinated me.

The duty officer seemed that way, too. He settled in, paying attention to the dynamics between the two. Jake held up the Honus card even closer, wooing Blimp. But Jake soon realized he couldn't win a stare down with a seasoned umpire, especially one with Blimp's dimensions.

"Blimp?" Jake asked again, using the politest tone I'd ever heard since he begged for candy from his fourth-grade teacher. "May I just try out the Pete Rose…you know…as a gesture of kindness for a washed-up minor league pitcher? I just want to feel a real baseball. I'll give it right back, I promise. Please?" That was a mouthful for Jake, and Blimp knew it.

"See you later, Blimp," said the duty officer. "I'll be in the lunchroom, but if I were you, I'd take him for everything he's got. Kim will call for your lunch order." He unlocked my cell and led me out and shut the steel door.

*****

In the lobby, I glanced at Tom as Jenny gave me a brief hug before I signed the papers. We took the Blue Beauty up the street to Dooley's Doughnuts.

*****

We found out from Jake later what happened. Blimp, holding the Pete Rose for Jake to take, reached for his keys, unlocked the cell door, and swung the squeaking metal bars wide open. *Clang!* The entire jail vibrated. He took a step inside and stared in full umpire face. If this was a game, Jake knew he dare not blink or he'd get tossed. Since he was already in jail and might be transferred to the Haybury facility, Jake retreated to his bunk.

"Okay, Blimp, you win. You can take the 1910 Honus Wagner card if I can't split open my pillow with that Pete Rose in your hand." After that comment, Jake gave a sorrowful sigh he'd learned from Ma.

Blimp licked his chops and grabbed "Honus," flashing a sly grin for his own plan. "So you've got a gambling heart yourself, huh? Just like me?" Without a second thought, Blimp was magnanimous and underhanded the baseball to Jake. "Here…feel a real Major-League baseball…one you could'a thrown past hitters like Pete Rose." Then Blimp shamed him with a victorious smile. "This card better not be fake or I'll remind those Haybury jailers how you offered more than chin music to their baseball-playing sons."

That caused Jake to boil inside. But, like a splash from spring water, he cooled himself on the exterior and accepted the rebuke, shrinking onto his bunk. Blimp advanced inside Jake's cell and stood like a mountain, enjoying his dominance.

"Here we go," Blimp demanded. "Ya got two strikes on ya already, big mouth! Split this pillow open right now or it's goodbye Honus Wagner!"

Just then the phone on Blimp's desk rang. Blimp shoved his hand at Jake with authority, motioning him to stay. Blimp moved out of the cell to his desk and answered the phone, still studying the card.

"Hi, Kim. No, there's no trouble. I just got a little energetic with the jail bars. Everything is fine. Sure, Kim, I'll watch the lobby. Yeah, take my cruiser and get a dozen glazed and an extra-large 'Tom Dooley,' the one with the hangman's noose!" Blimp laughed, glancing back as Jake sat on his bunk with the Pete Rose in his pitching hand. Blimp hung up the phone and turned on his desk lamp for a clear view of the Honus card.

Jake rose, rolling the baseball in his fingers, the seams and the Pete Rose autograph spinning in his hand. He viewed a tight but clear aerial path from the cell to Blimp, who was lost in study and vulnerable, bent over the end of his desk. Jake raised a leg and hurled a fireball. Sensing danger, Blimp turned, his eyes huge. He spun to duck away, but it was too late. The Pete Rose ricocheted off the back of Blimp's head and into his trophy shelf. Blimp dropped face-first to the floor, out cold, as trophies tumbled upon him.

"Strike three...I'm out!" Jake pounded his fist into his gloveless hand and slipped out of the cell. With Kim gone out front and the others in the lunch room, Jake pushed the button and entered the lobby, then slipped out the front door, feeling like a free man.

*****

Tom and Jenny sat watching me munch on an extra-large "Tom Dooley" doughnut, listening to the song about a hanging, "Tom

Dooley." And why not? We were in Dooley's Doughnuts, where the song played at the top of every hour.

I saw Kim step out of a police cruiser and enter Dooley's to order.

"Billy, you are hungry," said Jenny. "And what's up with the 'hangman's noose?'"

Tom hung his head after he gazed at the Tom Dooley poster. All Tom had eaten was a glazed doughnut. He licked his fingers. Downcast, he spoke with a forced drawl. "I should'a got a Tom Dooley." Tom turned his head, staring outside. He poked me and pointed to Jake running like a wildman wearing orange. We saw him stop at Tom's Blue Beauty, open the back door and jump inside.

"He broke out!"

"Who?" asked Jenny.

"Jake!" said Tom.

Every patron turned toward Tom. Jenny and I were stunned. When Tom spotted the uniformed lady officer staring, he tried a diversion.

"But Barney Fife saved the day for Opie!" Tom continued. "Oh, yes, he did! Andy was so grateful, he promised to take them fishing where they could snack on Aunt Bee's special pie!"

Officer Kim and the patrons appeared satisfied and turned back to their previous activities.

"Whew!" said Tom, whispering. "I almost blew it." Tom leaned to look again. "His head just popped up inside the Blue Beauty and disappeared onto the backseat floor. Oh, oh, it's parked right beside the police cruiser."

Kim grabbed her large bag and exited Dooley's. All three of us rose and saw Jake's head rise and dip inside the Blue Beauty before Kim climbed into the cruiser.

"What now?" Jenny asked.

"Let's go, everybody!" I said. As we ran through Dooley's, I asked, "Anybody want a hangman's noose?" A kid raised his hand, so I tossed him the noose. We dashed to the Blue Beauty, seeing Jake shake on the backseat floor, as nervous as a race horse on derby day.

"Tom, take me up the mountain, now!" Jake said.

Tom looked like a still-life painting, staring at Jake. He stepped out, grabbing his keys, but they fell, jingling onto the pavement. Tom snatched them and we piled in.

"I thought she saw me," said Jake.

"How on earth did you get out?" I asked.

"I beaned the Blimp! Remember? I had a plan!"

"You what?" Jenny asked.

"Beaned the Blimp!"

"Great balls of fire!" Tom said, as he pulled out of the lot to a red light. "Now I've become the get-away driver! Won't this make me an accessory, Billy?"

I looked to Jenny for help.

"No, not really, Tom. An accessory is a necklace or a set of earrings."

Tom gulped. "Oh, well, my grandpa bought this Buick in May of 1953, the same day Dark Star upset the great Native Dancer in the Kentucky Derby!"

A light turned green. "Then make like Dark Star and gitty-up outta here!" Jake shouted. Tom's tires squealed.

Through Jenny's demanding words, Tom slowed to his normal boring speed, keeping city cops at bay. That's when Jake told us how he broke out of jail.

*****

Blimp's older brother, Deputy Rawley Cowler, was by nature surly. He had a personality as if kidney stones were knifing their way through his body. Always short-tempered, he'd turned impossible after he lost a run-off election for sheriff against Bart Logan. Instead, he'd become the number-one deputy in Rockside, a position he thought beneath him.

No one doubted he was tough, including the lawbreakers who tested him. After the election, a drifter had blown into town and caused a ruckus at Skeeter's Bar. When Rawley came to arrest him, the drifter threw a bottle and cracked the side window of his police cruiser. None too pleased, Rawley manhandled him into the backseat, but the drifter put up such a fight, he bent the rear door so it wouldn't close.

Rawley didn't horse around. He immobilized the troublemaker and used two cuffs and a rope to tie him spread-eagle onto his hood, the drifter's legs spread to the front bumper, his hands to the side door jambs. Rawley drove past the bars, honking his horn with that poor drunk strung out, staring at the sky, crying for mercy! When the bars emptied, customers witnessed country justice in action. Word spread not to put up a stink if Rawley arrested you.

At least, that was the story Rawley's two sons, Cletus and Gopher, told. They lived in a middle-class home on a dead-end street. Mrs. Cowler had left long ago. Rawley insisted Cletus and Gopher run cross-country and not play football. I never understood why since they had a mean streak like their Pa. However, Rawley demanded they keep engaged year-round.

*****

On that same Saturday morning of Jake's jailbreak, Mikey Millhouse, a teen neighbor of the Cowlers' and a friend of mine, told me later what happened. He saw Cletus and Gopher complete a long morning run and cool off in the front yard. Mikey walked across the street to ask the Cowler boys about the upcoming cross-country season.

"Do you boys think you can keep up with your cousin Jimmy Jack if he comes back? Most of my friends say, 'No way!'" Mikey told me the Cowler boys seemed irritated by the question. Cletus doused his head with water from a hose while Gopher leaned against the Chevy before grabbing a lighter and a firecracker from the dash. He walked to a gopher hole and lit the firecracker, tossing it in. After the pop, Gopher sat in the shotgun seat of his brother's red '57 Chevy Bel Air convertible, guzzling a drink he had pulled from the backseat cooler. Cletus grabbed a rag and a half-used can of Turtle Wax to wipe off a smudge he noticed on the hood.

"Hey, Mikey, can ya finish the other side for me?"

"Sure, Cletus." Mikey picked up the rag and the Turtle Wax.

"What ya drinkin', Gopher?" Mikey asked.

Gopher giggled and wiped his mouth. "Jimmy Jack says, 'a little suds after a run'll make ya hum...' but I got me a sodee-pop." He held up an RC Cola and finished the final gulp.

A screen door slammed on the front porch as their dad stepped out, adjusted his gun belt, and surveyed the front yard littered with gopher holes. He frowned, seeing several gophers peek from their holes. He walked to his son's convertible, parked beside his Rockside Police Cruiser. "Did you boys get your run in?"

"Yes, sir, both of us...the entire run."

"I want you runnin' with Jimmy Jack, ahead of that Cline kid if he's got the guts to run."

"We ain't worried about him, Pa," said Cletus.

Rawley paused a moment, then rubbed his finger over the Chevy, examining the waxing Mikey had just completed. "You two stay out of trouble, hear?"

"We're too tired for trouble," Gopher complained. It was no surprise to Mikey that Gopher answered to the word *trouble*. He'd gotten his nickname for trying to capture gophers by digging holes in the front yard. After his erratic shovel work, the yard had three times as many holes as before, giving their gopher residents new passage-ways to explore.

Rawley stepped to his cruiser and looked at Mikey, who was still waxing. "Hey, Mikey, you wax my cruiser when I get back, and I'll take you and my boys for a cruise through town and finish with an ice cream cone."

"Well...I don't know. I shouldn't interfere in police business," Mikey said, his voice as weak as the subdued snickers from Cletus and Gopher.

"Well, I still need my cruiser waxed tonight, don't I?"

"Oh, well, uh, sure," Mikey added.

"Much obliged, Mikey. Gopher will help you."

Buckling himself in, Rawley roared his engine. Gopher rose in the convertible's shotgun seat, smiling, leaning on its headrest. He urged his Pa to increase the RPMs even more. Rawley roared it once more before he chuckled and opened the windows, allowing the trapped summer heat to escape before switching on his police radio.

Gripping the microphone, he spoke, "Deputy Rawley Cowler reporting in."

Deputy Chappy Smith's high-pitched voice at police dispatch blared. "Rawley! Jake's escaped! Blimp's out cold on the jail floor!"

Rawley stomped on the accelerator, his tires screeching down the driveway onto the street, preceding the piercing sound of his siren.

"I hate those Clines!" shouted Gopher.

"Let's find that snake Jake! Come on!" Cletus scissor-kicked his legs over the driver's door and slid into the front seat. He fired up the engine and copied his Pa's screeching-tire routine as they fishtailed onto the street.

*****

Tom was still nervous and turned into his own driveway and stopped.

"No, Tom," I said. "Take Jake to the cabin so Pa can figure out his next move."

"That'll be the day when your pa does something positive for me," said Jake.

"Come on, get real! We're blood! Are you afraid to give Pa a chance?" All stared at Jake.

"Okay," Jake said after a long pause. "Sorry, Tom. Billy might be right. Please, take me up to my homestead. It's better than sittin' here."

Tom added, "And you'll all testify I didn't volunteer to be the get-away driver. Right?"

"We know you didn't volunteer," said Jake.

"You just did it, Tom," I said.

"You did," Jenny added. "And I'm proud of you. Here, have a Hubba Bubba."

"Good grief!" Tom said, accepting the gum.

Tom backed down his driveway, then faced the railroad tracks, accidentally bumping on his wipers. Up the street screeching tires slid over the railroad tracks, causing us to look up.

"It's the Cowler boys!" Jenny yelled.

Cletus skidded to a stop five feet from the side of Tom's open car window. The aroma of burnt rubber wafted into our nostrils as Cletus sneered at Tom's waving wiper blades.

Tom twisted on the window spray as thin streams of wiper fluid shot over the front window onto the roof. Tom gulped and turned off the wipers.

Cletus slapped his hand viciously on the side of his car door, glaring at Tom. "Ya seen Jake?" It reminded me of outlaws in old western movies who'd ask citizens for the location of someone they would gun down on sight.

Tom's eyes narrowed. "Jake who?"

"Billy's brother, you retard!" Cletus said, adding another hand slap to his car door.

Jenny chewed faster, trying not to give away Jake. "Of course, we saw him on his way to jail!" Jenny's upbeat voice surprised herself. She blew the largest bubble of the morning, barely able to see as she took in air to expand the bubble. The Blue Beauty rocked as Jake squirmed.

"Where is he now?" Cletus said, showing his teeth. Jenny's enormous bubble burst across her face, hanging from her lips. Tom gagged a nervous laugh.

Gopher rose like a jack-in-the-box, sitting on the shotgun seat headrest. "You laughin', Tom? Teammate or not, I'll turn that crooked grin to a bloody pulp!"

Jenny wiped the bubble from her face. "Simmer down, Gopher! I saw him at the ballgame yesterday, same as you!"

"And I saw him in jail this morning before they released me," I added.

"Not anymore," said Cletus. "He's a wanted man!" Gopher dropped into his seat as Cletus spun his tires again and drove off to look for Jake elsewhere.

Jenny peeked over the seat and held out a piece of gum. "Hubba Bubba?" Jake's hand reached up and took the gum as a train whistle sounded in the distance.

"Floor it, Tom!" Jenny said. Tom stomped on the gas, using all the horses of his straight-eight "Fireball" engine to propel them down the street and over the tracks, beating the descending railroad arms as he headed for the Cline cabin.

*****

It's a good thing Deputy Chappy Smith was on duty that day, or we might never have known what happened. He'd been a senior baseball catcher when Jake was in fifth grade. Later, when Jake pitched for the high school team, Chappy offered advice and friendship.

Arriving at the police station, Rawley flung open the station door, yelling, "Blimp!" He reached the jail room and saw Blimp with an ice pack strapped to his head, lying on a bench seat between two paramedics. Blimp raised a hand to acknowledge Rawley's presence.

"Got a big lump on the noggin—from this," Sheriff Logan said, tossing the Pete Rose autographed baseball into the air.

"How'd Jake bean him from the cell?" Rawley demanded.

"Distracted somehow—we found this fake card." Logan held up the replica of the rare 1910 Honus Wagner baseball card. "The cell doors were wide open!"

"So Jake wants to play baseball, huh? Well, batter up! I've got just the bat!"

"Hold it!" Logan warned. "We'll bring him in my way!"

Rawley didn't wait. "All I know is that my brother, who is also my fellow deputy, was knocked out by that no-good Jake Cline kid you said would be safer if he stayed in our Rockside jail instead of at Haybury. So I'm waitin', Sheriff. Just what is your way?"

"We'll look for Jake's buddies first…where he might hang out! If we don't find him, then we'll go up to the Cline homestead! Is that clear?" Sheriff Logan had the badge, the office, and was Rawley's equal in determination. Rawley nodded, but everyone knew his heart said no.

CHAPTER 9

Homestead Hideout

I was relieved when Jenny stepped out of the vehicle first. Tom, a master of politeness, spoke. "Good morning, Mrs. Cline. It truly sparkles." His usual calm voice displayed tension as Ma cleaned her most prized earthly possession, her crucifixion stained-glass window.

"I love how the morning light makes the front room glow with splashes of color. I don't dwell on the image of the cross but imagine the story's next image because the cross happened."

Tom nodded and looked to Pa and Chester repairing the roof again. Tom fired a queston. "Guess who flagged me for a lift?" Neither could think of any names except Jenny, who stood beside the car.

The back door flew open, and out sprang Jake. "Surprise!" Jake shouted. "I broke out!" Ma, Pa, and Chester gasped, speechless. Chester gripped his own rubber baseball from the nail bucket and threw a strike from the roof that Jake barehanded in one smooth motion, returning a cocky grin.

Pa hollered from the roof, "Out of jail? How?"

"A baseball," Jake said, holding up the rubber baseball. "I beaned Blimp Cowler, the worst umpire in Tennessee!"

Ma and Pa stood like mute statues.

"I let him have a look-see at my fake 1910 Honus Wagner card—the one Chester found the other day. I got it from Ma in the slammer and bargained with Blimp to let me pitch his Pete Rose autographed baseball for a chance to get Honus!"

"Blimp fell for that?" Ma said, knowing the answer as she slung down her cleaning towel.

"Yeah…umpires must like baseball cards, Ma. I fingered the Pete Rose as if I had to strike out the most prolific hitter in baseball history! Instead, I nailed Blimp on the back of the noggin with that split-fingered Blimpball you taught me!"

"Blimpball?" Ma moved closer to her oldest son. Jake's shenanigans had often driven Ma to her knees. "Jake, why are you always gettin' into mischief?" She held her arms wide as Pa scrambled down the ladder, followed by Chester. Ma hugged Jake, kissed him, and ruffled his hair before she grabbed hold of Jake's ears and yanked!

"Ouch! Ma! Owww!"

"You're not showin' a lick of sense! You don't go boppin' deputies!" She calmed. "I love ya, Jake, but there ain't no furlough from jail time!"

Jake grimaced as he massaged his ears. Ma knew tenderness, but in her book of ethics, doing something with false motives cost the wrongdoer a painful price.

Jake hesitated before giving an excuse to Ma, his ultimate fan. He looked deep into her eyes, a technique he used before throwing an ankle-busting change-up instead of a fastball. Jake's voice quivered. "Blimp said…my pitchin' days…were over!"

Ma sighed.

"Jimmy Jack set up that burglary to get away for the summer from Cale Clausen, his coach and ol' man! My arrest and the treatment they gave me was a bonus for the Cowlers! Now they want me socked away!"

A slight tear gathered and slid down his cheek—a rare event for Jake. "I ain't rottin' over at Haybury! Those boys ain't forgot how I clocked two of 'em in the playoffs!"

In high school, it wasn't unusual for Jake to act first and think second. I hoped he had changed, realizing his future, whether bright or grim, hung in the balance.

Pa went to the core. "Good behavior from you at the jail could'a cut the sentence! Now, the Cowlers'll be comin' for ya, lookin' for blood, and the law is on their side!"

"Good behavior? Could'a cut the sentence? The Cowlers have stomped their boots on us for years! When will you stand up to 'em, Pa?"

Pa softened, "We want to live our lives without…"

"Trouble?" Jake said. "Living with your head tucked in a shell is not living!"

I interceded. "Jake, the Cowlers don't bother us up here."

"That's what you think, Billy? They got to me, didn't they? You're a Cline, and you're their next target!" Chester looked at me with a fearful stare.

"That's enough, Jake!" said Pa. "What kind of damage did you do to Blimp?"

"I flushed him, Pa…to the floor, out cold," Jake said matter-of-factly.

Pa liked to figure things out, but he seemed to struggle with this tangled mess. "Billy, since lower sections of the road are within sight, take Chester up, and when he spots the law, hightail it back and warn us!"

"What if I'm not fast enough?"

"Fast enough?" Veins in Pa's neck bulged as he sauntered up, ready to mete out mountain discipline. "You practice runnin' down that mountain every day!" Pa wanted straight obedience.

"Pretend it's October's big race," suggested Jake.

I nodded to Pa as Chester hugged Jake. I carried guilt over Jake's first arrest, and Chester felt it now. It was the baseball card he brought to the game that had sparked this morning's jailbreak.

We knew Jake had a mind of his own, but Jake was blood, and we loved him deeply. Before I left, words spilled out. "When I fell for that setup and called the sheriff's office, Jimmy Jack's lyin' buddy laughed at me! I figured somethin' wasn't right. I ran to the pharmacy as fast as I could. You gotta believe me, Jake! My lungs were aching! I saw the lawmen arrive. I…I…"

My lame reasoning tortured me with shame. My words were meaningless now—seeming more like a confession than an explanation.

Jake peered into my eyes. "Don't blame yourself, Billy. That's between me and Jimmy Jack. Now I've committed a second crime." His voice grew louder by the word: "But I'm out, and I'm stayin' out!"

Ma wasted no time stating her intentions. "We got enough fire-power up here to..."

"Lily! Settle down!" Pa demanded. We stood stone still. We knew if Pa couldn't maintain family discipline, things could go side-ways faster than you could say "Jackie Robinson."

I turned to Chester. "Follow the yellow streamers. I'll catch up." Chester nodded and ran.

I connected with Jenny in a brief glance. She was frightened, as much for me as for Jake.

"We're countin' on ya!" Pa said. Those words brought no comfort. I was separating myself from Jake. I felt paralyzed, unable to influence what might happen. *Will I be floundering on the mountain when the law comes?*

"Tom, you and Jenny better skedaddle," Pa said. "That older Cowler deputy has a chip."

Tom and Jenny recognized their cue and climbed into the Blue Beauty. I walked over as Jenny vented to Tom. "We've gotta delay Rawley and the lawmen to give Billy more time!"

"I'm knee-deep in Cowlers as it is!" Tom said. Jenny turned and gripped my arm through the open window.

Spinning back around, Jenny handed another piece of Hubba Bubba to Tom. "For courage, Tom! Let's go! I've got a plan." Tom added the gum and drove away.

*****

Jake paced in front of the cabin, wondering what to do. "Should I load my rifle?"

"No, I'll use your rifle for backup only," said Pa. "There'll be no weapon for you. I ain't given 'em a reason to plug ya! Pack up! Its bear cave for you till I work this out with Sheriff Logan. I want no Cowlers involved! Hurry!"

Jake walked to the cabin, shaking his head, and handed the rubber baseball to Ma. I knew Pa wouldn't give Jake a loaded rifle with a Cowler deputy thirsty for blood. But I also knew Jake didn't always follow orders.

Ma matched the intensity of her husband's voice. "Jake, toss a pair of your old jeans in the basket for washin'. No son of mine will wear those Halloween jail clothes on our land! You're free as long as you're here, and nobody better say otherwise."

CHAPTER 10

Gunplay at the Homestead

From our homestead, I sprinted up the mountain to join Chester. I caught and passed him while dodging trees, logs, and rocks, climbing to the small waterfall where the water pooled. A buck bolted as I arrived.

"Ah! It's okay, we can share." At the waterfall, I laid my glasses aside and leaned in, letting the cool mountain water run over my head.

When Chester caught up, he doubled over from exhaustion. "Lean over the falls and cool yourself," I said. "Feels good."

Chester pulled his head out, looking as if he'd been in one of those county-fair dunk tanks. We continued our trek together.

At the lookout, I ducked under the tarp, grabbing the binoculars for Chester. He sat on a boulder, scanning the length of dirt road. "No sheriff, no cruisers. Nothing,"

"Wooo-eee!" I yelled, signaling Victory to the T-Cross. He swooped down from the twisted section of his old nest tree and locked his talons onto the T-Cross. Thoughts of Jake whirled in my mind—from his younger days to the present. His current predicament came from the choices he made. Jake needed help, so I turned to Victory.

"Jake broke outta jail. I gotta warn him, 'cause trouble's a comin'. A Cowler is comin', and it may get ugly." I paused, resolve flowing from me. My guilt seemed to connect with Victory. Thoughts tumbled out of emotion—almost as a prayer. "Wish ya could fly over the road and keep those eagle eyes open...and give us a warnin'!"

Victory's head pivoted as he stared at Chester holding the binoculars, then stared at the distant dirt road below.

I waved my arm, sweeping it over the valley, and shouted, "Off! Off!" Victory shrieked, soaring downward.

*****

"The sheriff and his deputies will come after Jake," I said. I knew Deputy Rawley Cowler would be the one to fear. Deputy Chappy Smith would accompany him, and we heard his take on the action later.

According to Deputy Smith, Sheriff Logan turned onto the long dirt road that led past Ruby Lake for two hundred yards to our cabin. He led Rawley Cowler's cruiser and turned into a cow pasture where they could talk and plan their final preparations to raid our Cline homestead.

"I stepped out from my shotgun seat in Cowler's cruiser," Chappy said, "and plunked my foot deep into a fresh cow pie." He skirted the cruiser to meet with Sheriff Logan and Deputy Rawley.

"He'll have a spotter up there," the Sheriff said. "Goin' up, we're not sparin' the horses. I'll lead!" Logan paused for reaction, but none came. "Rawley, you and Smith follow, but I'll be the one to arrest Jake. Got that?" The sheriff's words were granite.

Rawley asked, "What if Blimp had sustained serious injuries?"

"Can you handle this?" Logan said. "I ain't packin' along a revengeful deputy! Decide."

"Okay, okay, I'll handle it," said Rawley. Deputy Smith knew Rawley didn't want to miss this arrest. They hopped back into their cruiser and followed the sheriff up the dirt road.

*****

Pa sipped on a bowl of vegetable soup, waiting on a porch rocker till Jake joined him. "You're packed now, so eat up, son. One sign of a lawman or a warning from Billy, and you're outta here to bear cave!" Pa finished and found his guitar.

"How can you play guitar at a time like this?" Jake asked between sips.

"It eases my mind…and I've got a lot of easing to do." Pa picked out a slow blues piece.

"Does Billy help around here?"

"Sure…but all he thinks about is that big footrace in October. You and I know what he needs, but who's got the money?" Pa's head dipped in disappointment.

While listening to Pa's music, Jake lowered his head, appearing to be reliving events that ended his minor league career and led to his botched burglary job and fight at the exhibition. "Pa, I gotta tell ya somethin'." Pa continued playing. "One night in the minors, I got in a high-stakes poker game. By midnight, I had won enough money to pay for Billy's corneal transplant."

Pa stroked a major chord not found in his blues tune and stopped, waiting, staring at his own fingers. "But, within an hour, I lost it all."

A tear flowed down Pa's cheek as he strummed a discordant chord. "That's why they call it gamblin'!"

Ma walked past them to hang a pair of Jake's jeans to dry on her taut forty-two-inch-high clothesline. She used it to teach Chester control of his fastball, just as she'd done with Jake. She would stand several steps behind it. Sometimes she hung two pair of jeans to represent a left-handed or a right-handed batter. The baseball would zip between the jeans.

One thing she wouldn't permit was for a pitch to rise too far above or dip too far below the clothesline. I heard it a thousand times: "You will not bounce up a wild pitch! That will show me a weak arm! You will not throw it too far inside or outside! A pitch off line will knock the clean clothes in the dirt! Guess who will rewash them?" She would clarify her teaching until she was blue in the face. It didn't pay to argue with her about baseball. Even Pa didn't do that.

After Ma hung up the jeans, she walked back, voicing another tirade against Blimp. "Them baseball scouts knew you could throw a ninety-plus-mile-per-hour fastball! But Blimp wouldn't call a strike. Couldn't see ya whittle the corners!" As she stepped on the porch,

Pa's guitar playing stopped. Ma was ready to blow. Jake set down his bowl. Ma picked up one baseball from the metal porch bucket. She stared long and hard at the jeans hanging on the clothesline.

"It's best Blimp's not here," she said as she turned and fired a bullet ball, hitting the crotch of the hanging jeans.

"Ooo!" Jake and Pa moaned. The impact jerked one edge of the jeans off its clothes pin.

"Ohhh!" Jake and Pa groaned as the other side of the jeans slid loose and fell in the dirt.

Ma shook her head. "I need more prayer."

I knew police cruisers would soon speed up the dirt road, creating a spiral of dust with their lights flashing. But their sirens would remain silent. They dared not announce their presence. According to Deputy Smith's rendition later, Sheriff Logan was being decisive: "You should have seen the scowl on Rawley's face as he followed the sheriff!"

Victory flew high when he left the T-Cross, and with his eagle eyes, he must have seen the cruisers. I imagined him circling over them as if they were his meal and he their predator.

*****

Inside his cruiser, Rawley was irate, giving Deputy Smith a foul look before rolling down his window. "Jake's gonna rot in jail for what he did to Blimp! He's gonna pay!"

"You know what the sheriff said," warned Smith.

"I know! But Jake's not goin' easy. You know it. I know it! You better be ready!"

The sheriff slid around the dirt corners with deft precision, sending a shower of pebbles into the air. Wheeling sideways from a sharp turn, Sheriff Logan approached the narrow "Y" turn at high speed. In front of him sat Tom and Jenny inside the Blue Beauty, its hood up, blocking access through the narrow passage between two thick stands of trees.

Sheriff Logan swerved off the road, just missing a collision, skidding into the brush. Rawley slammed on his brakes, halting five feet from the Blue Beauty.

"That's Billy's friend!" Rawley said to Smith. Rawley jerked himself out and stomped to Tom's open car window. Sheriff Logan was already spinning his tires in reverse.

"Move this bucket of bolts!" shouted Rawley through Tom's car window.

A speechless Tom heard Jenny's reaction: "The Blue Beauty is not a bucket of bolts! It's a 1952 Buick Roadmaster with a straight-eight Fireball engine! Hubba Bubba?" Jenny offered gum, leaning across Tom to Rawley.

Rawley reached through the window, knocked the gum from her hand, and shifted Tom's Buick into neutral. "You ain't road-blockin' me!" Rawley pushed hard on the door frame, shoving the Buick off the road and against a tree.

"How rude!" Jenny shouted as she honked the horn over and over in protest.

As Rawley returned to his cruiser, Tom sat motionless, muttering, "You're killin' me."

Sheriff Logan was already on his radio and ordered the duty officer to send an ambulance up to the Cline place. "I expect gunplay!" He then revved his engine, spun his tires, and kicked up more roadside debris, cracking Rawley's front cruiser window with an errant rock. Rawley floored his throttle, now even more determined as they powered up the dirt road to, in the sheriff's words, "arrest Jake."

Unseen, but circling above, Victory shrieked. Jenny stepped out and saw him flap his powerful wings, turning toward the cliffs.

*****

Back on the lookout, I poured cool canteen water on my washcloth and reclined, placing it over my eyes. "I will not let my brother down. I will warn him in time by running all-out!"

"Seen anything yet?" I asked Chester, staring through the binoculars.

"Nothing yet," Chester affirmed.

*****

Inside the cabin, Jake lay on a couch below Ma's stained-glass window, resting. The crucifixion image from the sun's rays passed through the window and lay across his face. He knew having to imitate hibernation in the old bear cave for days would be no picnic. Packed, Jake prepared to dash off. Below him, his jail clothes lay on the floor. Ma and Pa entered. Ma sat beside him, rubbing his hair across the image.

"Sleep, Jake...Billy'll warn us. You'll make it to the bigs someday." Jake turned over, away from her, his unbelieving eyes still open.

Ma saw Pa walk to the closet and grab Jake's rifle, loading the chamber with bullets. "Why?" Ma asked.

"Insurance," Pa said. "No one will bully me on my land!" He pointed to the jail clothes. "Bury 'em!" Ma took the clothes out, looking back as Ned leaned Jake's rifle against the wall.

*****

At the cliffs, Victory shrieked as he landed on the T-Cross. I sat up, surprised, as Chester yelled, "Here they come! They're halfway up! I must have missed 'em!"

"No!" I shouted.

Tucking in my washcloth, I leaped to my feet and began my sprint. Though Victory followed, a sickening fear replaced the normal thrill of the run.

*****

At the cabin, Pa rocked on the porch as Ma peeked inside through the stained glass. "Still resting," she muttered, seeing her firstborn lying motionless on the couch.

"Stop worryin', Lily…Chester and Billy are watchin'. They'll warn us."

*****

Sprinting by the waterfall, I missed colliding with a young buck, then slipped and rammed a tree, gashing my shoulder. I fought off the pain and continued, not with a smooth stride, but with an awkward limp.

*****

Police cruisers circled the edge of the lake below our cabin. The roar of their engines was unmistakable. Ma screamed as her worst fears became a reality. "Jake! Jake!"

"Get him up! Where's Billy?" Pa yelled. He dropped his guitar and grabbed his loaded shotgun on the porch railing. Ma ran into the cabin and saw Jake standing, white-faced.

"Jake, they're comin'! No rifle!" she said. Jake had already thrown on his backpack as he cocked his rifle. Ma stepped toward him, clutching her oldest son, trying to yank away his rifle.

Jake pulled loose, causing the rifle to fire. The bullet hit the center window frame, blowing out Ma's prized stained-glass window. Shattered glass peppered Pa. The door burst open. Wham! Out came Jake with a cry, "Pa!"

With minor cuts, Pa motioned Jake to the trees. "Bear cave! Leave your weapon!" But Jake ran to the trees, still gripping his rifle. Hiding behind the first large tree, Jake stopped and looked back. Ma sobbed as she stooped, trying to pick up pieces of her stained-glass shards on the porch. Jake pounded the tree with his fist, angrier than Pa had ever seen him.

"Sit on your rocker!" There was nothing gentle about Pa's command. Ma, trembling with frustration, sat beside Pa as both police cruisers skidded to a dusty stop. The lawmen pushed open their doors and crouched behind them, weapons drawn.

Behind the tree, Jake raised his rifle, looking through the scope at Deputy Rawley Cowler, caught in a hazy cloud of cruiser dust. "Ker pow," Jake whispered.

In silence, Sheriff Bart Logan stared at Pa, the man who had saved his life ten years earlier in a hiking mishap. Now that the dust had cleared, Logan greeted him. "Good afternoon, Ned!"

"Is it?" Pa said in a huff. "You boys in a hurry?"

"Now, Ned," the sheriff continued, "I heard a rifle blast!"

"Target practice! Sometimes we get skunks up here!" Pa said, staring at Deputy Cowler.

*****

As I labored down the trail following the yellow streamers, a grim sickness spread through my body. The sound of that unmistakable rifle blast echoed through the forest, dominating my thinking. *Am I too late?* The only comfort I had was that Victory soared above me, urging me on.

*****

Pa stood beside his rocker. "This is my land, my homestead, and my family! Nobody can come here and dictate our destruction." He stepped off the porch, gripping his shotgun.

Ma stopped rocking. The sheriff responded. "What's it gonna be, Ned, a guitar or a shotgun?" She understood her husband as well as Ned understood the sheriff.

"Depends on the tune ya dance to!"

"I don't dance. You know that," confirmed Logan. "You saved my life, remember? Our families go way back. My Pa and yours used to play music together at the fair. Remember? I don't want trouble—just talk a spell."

Pa hesitated. "Ya got feet?"

"Sure do," the sheriff said. Pa waved him to the porch. "Comin' up…nice and easy." Sheriff Logan ordered his two deputies to stay at their cruiser.

"You seem nervous, Bart," said Pa.

Ma rose and stepped toward Pa, showing a united and imposing duo. It was her nature to defend—her six brothers in the past, her son now.

"You know Jake broke out," Logan said. "Knocked Blimp unconscious with a baseball."

"He should'a ducked!" Ma said.

Jake, from the tree, repositioned his rifle, this time aiming at the sheriff.

Sheriff Logan knew southern protocol and tipped his hat. "Good afternoon, Lily." Pa noticed Logan staring at the blown-out window and the shattered shards on the porch. The sheriff knew he had trespassed into the emotional center of the Clines's turbulent world.

"Now, Ned, I don't know where Jake is, but if he will just turn himself in…"

"In to who? The Cowlers?" demanded Ma, gazing at Rawley, who was now swaggering up behind the sheriff a la "Billy the Kid," wearing only a sidearm placed loosely in his holster.

Pa knew Sheriff Logan could see his angry eyes fall upon the advancing deputy. Pa also knew flexing his trigger finger was a telltale sign of trouble.

Rawley spoke, "Sheriff, wherever Billy is, Jake is!"

"Cowler, what did I say about skunks? Get off my land!" Pa warned.

"It's Deputy Cowler…and that's my brother Jake hit!"

"Back off, Deputy!" Sheriff Logan ordered.

When Pa fingered his shotgun, responding to Deputy Cowler's bravado, Rawley, like gunfighters of old, drew his pistol, challenging him.

Jake took aim at Cowler.

Deputy Smith, crouched behind a cruiser door below, took aim at Pa.

"Ned…" The sheriff spoke with a steady voice.

"I'll plumb shoot your hand off!" said Cowler.

Pa released his trigger finger and placed his shotgun butt down, fingers circling the barrel.

"Try the holster, Rawley?" the sheriff said. Deputy Cowler hesitated but complied.

A gust of wind swirled as Victory and I, free of the trees, powered into the cabin clearing, catching them by surprise. Victory shrieked, flapping his wings, and swooped over the officers.

Cowler spun sideways and re-drew his pistol, firing two shots at my feet.

Bam! Bam! Clumps of dirt kicked up on my pant legs. I jumped sideways and rolled to the ground. Victory buzzed over Rawley's head, causing him to fire a wild round into the air before losing his balance and stumbling forward to his knees in front of Ned.

"Hold your fire!" Sheriff Logan shouted.

Jake, thinking I'd been shot by Rawley's gunplay, took aim at him, still wobbling on his knees. Jake's finger began pressing the gray steel of his trigger till Ma moved unknowingly into his line of fire. Angry at not squeezing off a round, Jake charged, carrying his weapon like a bayonet while venting his rage with a battle cry.

Sheriff Logan spun around. "Halt! Halt!" he ordered, raising his rifle.

Rawley stood, twisting toward Jake, raising his pistol at Jake's charge. Pa swung up his weapon and shotgun-butted Rawley in the side of his forehead just as his pistol fired. It knocked Jake off his feet, dropping his rifle as he skidded across the dirt toward them. He lay writhing in pain, his gyrations unnatural. The bullet had plowed a trail near Jake's back.

"Nooo!" Ma screamed. "Help your brother!"

She and Pa joined me as we scampered toward Jake before dropping by his side.

Deputy Smith ran up from his cruiser, his rifle raised at shoulder level.

"Jake...Jake!" I shouted, not able to process the horror.

Jake shook, gazing up at us. Pa had dropped his shotgun and wrapped his arms around Lily, who was frantic.

Deputy Smith stood over Rawley, dazed and bleeding from Pa's shotgun whipping. At that cruel moment, time froze. *Why didn't I get here sooner?* Blood oozed from Jake's side, his face shriveled in pain. Numb, I stared at Jake's loaded rifle lying beside me.

Sheriff Logan gave an order. "Smith, confirm my call for an ambulance and bring the first aid kit!" The deputy ran to his cruiser. My eyes glazed over as my hand caressed the smooth steel barrel of Jake's rifle. Powerful deputy Cowler rose to his feet, wiping blood away from his eyes. He flashed his pistol, stomping his foot on my hand. Rawley's words pierced my soul like a twisting knife: "You're too slow...boy!"

I looked up, feeling more hatred than I'd ever known—for a man I hardly knew. I stared, my hand motionless, fingers feeling crushed on my brother's rifle barrel.

Sheriff Logan faced double trouble. "Billy, that's enough!" he warned. "Leave the rifle! Lower your pistol, Rawley!" Deputy Cowler hunched, still bleeding from his forehead.

I turned, gazing down Sheriff Logan's rifle barrel, my stare cold and vacant, exhaling hope as I shifted my view to a twitching Jake.

"Billy, do what the sheriff says," said Pa, his hands still wrapped around his wailing wife. Obeying, Rawley raised his foot, and I moved my hand off the rifle and placed it on Jake's trembling face. Sheriff Logan picked up Jake's rifle, carrying it away.

Between uneven gasps and muscle spasms, Jake turned his head, looking me in the eyes. He whispered, "It's...up to...you."

Ma's screams deflated into moans. She slumped to the ground groaning words of blame that lodged in my mind: "Why didn't Billy warn us in time?"

I rolled over, lying beside my wounded brother as Deputy Smith rushed in to start first aid to stop his bleeding. Rawley used gauze to wipe away blood from his forehead. I lay exhausted, emotionally devastated, gazing at the upper part of our cabin clearing. That had always been my doorway to the mountain, a passageway to peace and tranquility, now tainted by conflict and hostility. My gaze fell onto the lone figure of my brother Chester as he approached, bent over in pain from a side ache. The closer he came, the more frightened his face appeared. His horrified expression seared itself into my memory as I saw him fall to his knees beside Ma and Pa.

A faint siren from an ambulance grew stronger as it arrived, followed by Tom and Jenny in the Blue Beauty, who had turned around to follow the ambulance.

Medics lifted Jake onto a stretcher and secured him in the ambulance before driving to the Gorman Hospital. Pa, Ma, and Chester hollered for me to join them in the pickup, but I remained grounded by guilt and blame, my body locked down. Tom hollered that he'd get me to the hospital. My folks slammed the pickup doors and took off.

Jenny held me close as I gazed at passing clouds that morphed into a dusky darkness as crickets began grinding at night. Later, Tom and Jenny helped me into the Blue Beauty on our way to the hospital.

CHAPTER 11

Pa's Sentencing in Court

Pa sat beside his court-appointed attorney, waiting for the judge to announce his sentence. In the summer heat, they both wore short-sleeved shirts and striped ties. Ma, Chester, Tom, and I sat in the row behind Pa. Jenny and her cheerleader friend, Darla, sat beside us. Dressed up, the girls looked too sophisticated to me.

Sitting behind us on our side of the court gallery was Pa's former high-school cross country coach, Pop O'Reilly. Pa never talked about him, and I had only seen Pa speak to him twice. I thought it strange. When I'd discovered a copy of Pa's high-school yearbook, I'd asked him about the cross-country team picture. Pa had no comment, and my curiosity spiked.

Pop O'Reilly, now middle-aged, was the most respected man in town. He was the founder and headmaster of Cliffview Boys' Home, a first-rate boarding school that included a wing to house handicapped boys. I had never heard of its equal in the Smokies. During the year, businesses placed posters in their shop windows to raise money for Pop's school. They advertised concerts, dances, and a special auction each year. He received sizeable donations and praise, for students came from all parts of the state and beyond.

Stories of Pop's burn-scarred hands and arms fascinated all. I overheard a kid tell a friend he had fought a fire-breathing dragon. Another said he'd been a fireman. I knew the truth.

The Cowler clan sat behind the prosecuting attorney. It didn't surprise me when Cale Clausen, my cross-country coach and Pa's former teammate, sat with the Cowlers. His pepper-gray military haircut highlighted his authoritative manner, a distinction that matched the reputation of his long-time buddy, Deputy Rawley Cowler.

Clausen shared my glance for a moment before turning to Blimp and making a comment. This brought subdued laughter from Rawley, Cletus, and Gopher, and others who turned their heads in my direction. I knew Coach Clausen was cut from the same cloth as the Cowlers.

"All rise!" said the bailiff. Judge Jasper entered. "Hear ye! Hear ye! Hear ye! Court is now in session—Judge Jasper presiding." I stared at the judge's face, trying to figure out how bad this would be for our family. We watched as the judge cleared his throat and shuffled papers behind the bench.

As we sat, I noticed the courtroom was half full on our side but packed on the Cowler side. I realized that Jake had made few friends since pitching his last baseball game for the Ravens. This court case had gobbled up headlines in the *Rockside Bugle* while heating the editorial page. The articles argued, pro and con, why they placed Jake in the local jail and not at the larger Haybury facility. They also debated issues between the Clausen-Cowler clan and the Clines, which had occupied town gossip for years, dating back to the auction.

"The defendant will please stand," intoned Judge Jasper. Pa rose. "Ned Cline, a jury of your peers has found you guilty of harboring your fugitive son, Jake Cline, and assaulting an officer of the law, Deputy Rawley Cowler. Your son is now rehabilitating from a life-threatening injury, caused by gunplay at his arrest. The jury does not believe you are a danger to our community but must acknowledge your role in disobeying the letter of the law. Therefore, you are sentenced to one year of probation and a fine of $500." The judge pounded his gavel to gasps of appreciation from us Clines and angry groans from the other side. Cletus stomped out of the courtroom after the judge's words had settled.

Pa hugged Ma first and then put his arms around Chester and me. I glanced across the aisle. The Clausen and Cowler stares were thick, like a fog that wouldn't lift.

When we left the courthouse, the Cowlers were waiting for us on the outside steps. Jenny, Tom, and Darla walked together behind me. When I saw the Cowler boys, Jenny squeezed my arm. They looked ready to accost me until a blonde reporter, Lizzy Looper, stepped up and asked Pa a few questions while the Rockside photographer snapped pictures.

Before Pa could respond, Pop O'Reilly stepped between them and extended his arm to shake Pa's hand. The reporter stopped her questioning. The photographer paused, his camera lowered. The crowd hushed and moved back, giving room for Pop. "I pray your sons and your wife recover from this tragedy and grow in forgiveness and peace each day."

I had never seen Pop O'Reilly's burned arms up close until now. His scars were indescribable, revealed by wearing a short-sleeved shirt. Pa's eyes fixed on Pop's disfigured flesh. When a tear came, Pa's reaction confused me.

Perhaps his reaction was relief for the lighter sentence of probation. He was still a free man. Though the fine was stiff, he could keep working. *Will this be Pa's only handshake?* I didn't know, but Pa's eyes locked onto Pop's scars. He couldn't or wouldn't look up at Pop's face. He only glanced once at the Cowlers and Coach Clausen. As Mr. O'Reilly walked away, Pa cleared his throat to answer the reporter's questions, but his efforts failed. He held up his hand to the cameras, shook his head, and walked down the steps.

Cletus and Gopher waved me toward them, and I knew trouble was coming. I motioned for Tom and the girls to move on. I would face the Cowler boys alone.

Cletus wasted no time. "The sheriff suspended our Pa for six months!"

"Without pay!" Gopher added.

"Calling it insubordination!" Cletus said, pointing his finger at my chest.

I looked up to see a group of their buddies standing nearby, hoping for a fight.

"You comparin' that with what happened to Jake?" I said. "My brother may never walk again!" There was a pause before I continued. "If you boys get hungry because of a lack of funds over your Pa's suspension, there's plenty of roadkill on the highway."

Cletus shoved me, but I held him off. With townspeople filing by, no fists flew.

"Oh! You're askin' for it now!" said Cletus. "You're a gutless coward, just like your Pa."

"With a streak of yellow as wide as…as a school bus," Gopher added.

Cletus glanced at his buddies. "We've talked with Jimmy Jack, and he feels the same as us. We ain't keen on you runnin' cross country…and neither is Coach Clausen. If you do, you'd better watch your back!"

"If I do, you'll be watchin' my back!" I said, shoving past Cletus.

Chester saw our pickup window first. The back window had a spider web crack, and in the center of it was a three-inch hole. A baseball rested among the bits of shattered glass in the bed. Chester climbed in, picked it up, and cocked his arm, threatening to throw it at Cletus.

"Whoa! Another speedball freak!" Cletus said. The Cowlers and his buddies laughed.

Nearing the pickup, Ma turned and hollered to the Cowlers, "Throw me some of that heat!" I coaxed Ma into the front seat as Pa circled to the driver's door.

"At least we got a free baseball, hey, Ma?"

"Stay clear o' them Cowlers, son." Pa cocked his head, leaning over. "Goin' up with your friends?" I nodded, glancing at Jenny, Tom, and Darla, all waiting by the Blue Beauty.

Jenny tried to smile as I approached, but I offered no encouragement. She jumped in the backseat with Darla so I could ride shotgun. Tom knew the cliffs would be my choice, a place where I could vent my feelings.

"We're gonna join you," Jenny insisted.

Chapter 12

Billy and Jenny's Romance

We all changed into comfortable clothes for the hike up the mountain: Tom and I chose running gear. Jenny added a backpack. Conversation on the way up was limited—nothing about the sentence, just small talk as we followed the tattered yellow streamers.

At the boulder cliff lookout, the T-Cross was empty, as was the old nest tree. "He must be fishing," Tom said. He stepped into the shelter and pulled out the binoculars. He sat beside Darla, who listened to her transistor radio through earphones while filing her fingernails. Tom surveyed Rockside. "Hey, there's my house," he said as Jenny and I strolled to the cliff's edge.

"Billy, be thankful. Your Pa walked out with no jail time."

"My brother can't walk at all. He may never pitch again."

"Your Pa knows something about heartbreak over a brother."

The pain from Jake's injuries dominated my thinking. I would have shared the weight, but it was mine. I'd been too slow. That's what Rawley Cowler said. And when I tried to refute it, I couldn't. I was with my girlfriend at my favorite spot on earth, yet nothing was right. It encased me in a vacuum, drained me of joy, my strength receding from a lifeless shell. *Oh, Lord!* Jenny put her hand in mine.

We scanned the forested green mountainsides, the subtle color change of leaves to oranges and reds peeking out, the yellows and blues painted across the summer sky, an oasis of nature's serenity. Jenny gave my hand another squeeze when we spotted Victory soaring over the cliffs.

The moment gave me goose bumps. I took in a full breath and slowly felt the warmth of life circulating through the maze of my body, steadily energizing me with a new vigor. I had never experienced such a sudden change in mere moments.

As I gazed at Victory sweeping through the skies, I asked, "What's it like to soar?"

"It must be amazing to view the forest from the clouds. Wouldn't you like to hang glide someday?"

"I doubt I could soar the way Victory does. Bad memories could swell up and ground me."

"Ground you over Jake?"

"Yes, but…also Pa's high school race. Years ago, I read his rendition of that race in his high school writings. He continues to relive that sour moment. I've been training hard to sweeten his memory. If I could win that same race in October, I'd taste a few pleasant drops of success. But if I could win that championship for my Pa and restore his honor in his own mind, the satisfaction would linger a lifetime."

Jenny pointed to Victory. "You risked your life so Victory could soar. Are you convinced that risking all for your Pa would free him, too?"

She released my hand. "Look, my favorite wildflower—a Catawba rhododendron. It smells wonderful!" She took in its aroma before scanning the horizon. She made me see the mountainside as it was, a scenic paradise.

"If only I could soar above the hatred I've seen and felt." Thoughts of Jake's twisted life returned, but I remained eager to sustain my visual flight over reality till ugly doubts surfaced, cutting off my resurgence like the slice of a guillotine. Reeling backward into blame brought failure. Ma's words rang in my head, my heart, my soul—words that could penetrate through reason and logic—*Why didn't Billy warn us?* Emotions swept over me. I was in freefall.

Jenny read me. She placed her hand on my shoulder as I shook, giving me time. I loved that about her. She pulled away, and I observed her walk to the cliff's edge. She let me enjoy her attractiveness, her auburn hair blowing in the wind. As I watched, wonder from her natural beauty filled me. Back at the courthouse, her dolled-up appearance made me uncomfortable, even jealous. She'd appeared too adult—as if she were trying to be somebody she wasn't.

"Jenny, why were you dressed up so fancy in that blue dress?"

"It was the only pretty one I had. Jimmy Jack bought it for me before our second date, before his Pa sent him off for helping your brother Jake."

"Jimmy Jack's got many sides to him, I'll admit that."

"Don't you like the dress?"

"No, not if it's from him. You know I prefer you in pink."

"I like dressin' up. It's who I'd like to be."

"It's who you were when you were with him." We stood still before I asked, "Why are you here...with me?"

"Where would you want me to be?"

"Where your heart tells you to be."

"And where's that?"

"Where it beats true...and isn't full of guilt."

Jenny frowned. "You think that's why I'm with you? To salve a guilty conscience? I've already dealt with Jimmy Jack's lies!" She paused briefly. "Somethin's got a hold of you, Billy."

My lip quivered. "I'm a dream-killer!"

"Billy..."

"I killed Ma's dream of raising a Major League pitcher...and Jake's dream of being one."

"Jake killed his own dream. He was a gambler and a thief, and he broke outta jail. None of that is your fault!"

Tom stood at the sudden change in our tone. But just when we hit this snag, Victory circled us and landed on the T-Cross. How perfect!

Trying to compose myself, I looked up toward Rocky Point Peak. "Jenny, Tom and I need to run up Rocky Point...to get ready."

"Ready? Ready for what? You forgettin' about Coach Clausen? The Cowlers? And Jimmy Jack?"

"Jimmy Jack?"

"He's coming back. He called me from reform school and bragged how much he's trained...that he'll win the championship this October."

"Anything else?"

"That he'll win my heart back, too."

"You mean his blue-sequined dress didn't win it?"

"What do you think? I hung up!"

I pulled back to give her space. "I'm sorry, Jenny. Trusting is a lesson I'm trying to learn. Trust me when I say this: I'm takin' October's cross-country championship. Tom and I will be trainin' hard, runnin' extra workouts before school...past your house."

"Past my house? Nice idea. I get to wave at ya when you run by."

I took off my glasses and handed them to her.

"Not again! Runnin' without glasses!"

"I won't need 'em if Tom and I perfect our communication skills."

Jenny shook her head. "Running half-blind makes you bleed! That's a communication breakdown!"

"It's about me not minding I bleed."

"You seem to think anything's possible. It isn't." She held up her hands. "How many fingers do you see?"

"Uh...eleven?" I answered with a straight face. She paused, broke into a grin, and we laughed as I hugged her. "Be here to patch me up?" I begged, nibbling on her ear, feeling her body move against mine. She grinned and then squirmed. I held on until Tom broke it up.

"Sooner we go, sooner we're back," he said, seeing the sun dropping.

Jenny gave up. "Get goin', then. Take care of him, Tom."

I blew her a kiss and ran as Tom led the way. Darla's wave coincided with Victory's departure from the T-Cross to join us.

"It's the toughest trail on the mountain!" Tom bragged.

"Guide me up, Tom!" We ran past the Rocky Point Trail sign: *Hike at your own risk.*

Tom yelled out warnings on the trail. "Okay, high knees! Left... slow...step up!" I followed every command. "Clear! Pursuit pace!"

We sped up when the trail broke into the clear, free from thick stands of trees and overgrown vegetation. We slowed in dense growth where the trail meandered upward and steepness sapped our strength. I followed the numerical information Tom shouted. Numbers represented degrees or angles on this improbable quest to conquer Rocky Point Peak. Tom's familiar cadence of phrases spoke truth.

"Half-speed! Ninety degrees right…now! Right branch! Hand-up! Duck! Sixty left…now! High step! Slow! Veer left…now! Chuck hole! Thirty right…now! Run my left side! Clear!"

Victory shrieked, his wings flapping over us, his shadow before us, leading us.

Thrilled and motivated, having fallen only two times, I responded with a shout, "Faster! Faster!" As we ran, trees whizzed past us. I kicked into high gear and ran twenty yards ahead of Tom until I tripped and fell hard, scraping my legs, hands, and torso.

"Owww…oooh," I said, struggling to my feet. "All that hurts can heal…I think." I was assuring myself more than Tom.

My tumble and cuts didn't faze Tom since it had become the accepted hazard and its usual result. But, when he saw several wounds oozing blood, he turned me back downhill. I ran off his left shoulder at half speed and didn't argue.

Tom did his best to warn me of obstacles I couldn't see well enough to avoid on my own. It was a typical return. I stumbled several times, accumulating more battle scars on the slopes of this treacherous trail. The damage had come when my exuberance to race ahead took precedence over the logic of following Tom's steady drone of directions.

As we slowed our descent, I pictured Jenny and Darla lying on the boulder lookout, trying to tan in the summer sun. I wanted to hurry to see Jenny, but I knew haste would mean waste—my thrashed body lying along a twisting trail. I followed Tom's commands.

What are Jenny and Darla talking about? I wondered. I remembered Jenny telling me that when she dated Jimmy Jack she'd felt like a trophy on a shelf. She wouldn't settle for that. She said Darla might replace her since she nurtured a crush on Jimmy Jack. Darla agreed she didn't want to be a trophy, either. She preferred being a medal, snuggled around Jimmy Jack's neck.

Shriek! Victory flew in and landed on the T-Cross. As Tom and I lumbered in, Jenny, now wearing a long, pink dress, gasped, noticing my limp and the cuts and scrapes. She scampered to the first aid kit.

"How bad is he?"

"Dunno…he fell three times goin' up but only two times comin' down."

"Thank God for small miracles! Darla, get the canteen and some rags!" She guided me to the boulder and pulled out the medical supplies. Darla, her face scrunched, her eyes half open, poured water over my worst wounds, and with a high-pitched moan, washed away dirt, rock particles, and wood chips.

As Jenny daubed them, I gazed between grimaces. "You're looking pretty in pink…ouch!"

"You're not."

"This is nothin'," I said as Jenny put antiseptic on the cuts. I held my breath, squirming.

"Nothin'?"

"Compared to Glenn Cunningham…that great Kansas runner…" My voice broke, getting louder as I exhaled through the pain. "Ever heard of him?"

"Nope," she said, showing little sympathy.

"Glenn got his legs burned in an early morning school-house fire. Ouch! Easy, Jenny!" She paused, giving me time to recover. "Flames engulfed Glenn and his older brother after someone had replaced kerosene with gasoline in the furnace the night before. The boys ran home in the snow but his brother died."

"Ewww," Jenny said, her mood darkened.

"The doctor considered amputating Glenn's legs. He begged his ma to save 'em."

"Did she?"

"Glenn later ran a world record in the mile. Got a silver in the '36 Berlin Olympics."

"You have an answer for everything."

"That's why you like me."

"Oh, really?" Jenny squeezed around my puncture wound, making it bleed.

"Owww!"

Jenny sensed her opportunity. "It's about me not minding you bleed, remember?"

Tom looked at me, shaking his head. Darla didn't like it either… not one bit.

Jenny dried the skin around the wounds before slapping Band-Aids on the bigger cuts. Tom handed me a canteen so we could toast our efforts.

"Here's to another failed attempt to run up Rocky Point Peak!" I proclaimed.

"Yeah!" Tom shouted as we banged our canteens and guzzled water. If it was whiskey at a western bar, a new record would exist. The girls looked puzzled, trying their best to understand this male display of toughness through pain.

Jenny and Darla picked up the first aid supplies and organized the lookout. I put on sweatpants and a shirt as cool breezes swirled.

Tom glanced at the horizon. "Look, the sun's goin' down. We've gotta get back."

"I can't. I'm visiting Jake at his therapy session and have an appointment with Dr. Chu for my keratoconus. New glasses may be my only option since an operation is out of the question, moneywise. I need to think tonight…up here."

Jenny paused, then looked at Darla and winked. "So, Billy, do you need company while you think?" she asked in a sultry manner.

"I wouldn't be thinking about Jake or my eyes, would I?"

"No, you'd be thinking about me."

Tom and Darla grinned. Jenny paused before taking a few brisk steps away. She whirled to Tom and Darla. "Wait for me at the water-fall, will ya?"

Tom and Darla turned down the trail.

Jenny strolled ahead to the cliff's edge and met my eyes. "Dance with me," she said. Not only did her words surprise me, but her directness canceled any negative answer. Though battered by the run, her boldness filled me with curiosity.

As we danced, I became more vulnerable to share my feelings with her than I had ever been to anyone. "Jenny, I've lost so much, I feel like I'm suffocating. I run up here just to breathe. Jake struggles to breathe. Ma loves him so much."

Jenny lifted her hand to my face. "You love him, too. Jake has always lived on the edge. Honor them and your Pa…and win this championship."

"You believe in me? That I could win?" I saw her nod. "Your beauty, coupled with your faith, makes me want to hold you forever. Your presence is richer than a 'runner's high.'"

"And what is a 'runner's high'?"

I took two breaths, not wanting to break the mood, but I went ahead. I spun her around and held her, looking out together at the forested valley and the glowing sunset. "Running has a rhythm, a pace, a beat. It's musical. Each scene I run by inspires a melody and how I hear it depends on my mood. Each foot strike on a trail, each leap over a log is a dance with nature, and when I hasten the tempo, my heartbeat follows and all I see flies by me, thrilling my soul. When I'm in rhythm with the music, the joy lingers, and it's magical—a runner's high!"

"Are we in rhythm with the music?" Jenny asked with a grin.

"Our rhythm is perfect." I kissed her. Against the colors of dusk at sunset, we danced again on the edge of the cliff. The forested mountainsides and green valleys below became our backdrop. Energized, I imagined how our silhouette played against the dimming sky. Our lengthening shadows swept over the cliffs until Victory lifted off and circled, creating a halo-like form above us. Our romance affirmed, it was a moment in time to treasure.

After the dance, Jenny trekked down the mountain to join Tom and Darla. I found it difficult to think about Jake's future or a potential operation on my eyes. When I relaxed, peace presided over the lookout. A gentle breeze cooled my body, which still glistened from the summer heat. No one was around me but Victory, the one who had endured tougher problems than I had ever experienced. There he was, on his T-Cross, always present.

I grew lonely as I sprawled on the boulder, putting a wet wash-cloth over my eyes. This action created darkness, blocking the sun's disappearing rays until none remained.

Later, while lying in my sleeping bag, I stared out at the vastness of the universe, a canvas of truth, of time and motion, of light and darkness, forever mysterious, forever bold. Stars danced and twinkled, daring me to feel isolated or alone. I felt each flicker was a star saying, "Hi, Billy," or "You'll be okay, Billy." Those stars shone brightly and had life ahead of them. A shooting star, perhaps light-years away, shot over me, flashing brilliantly across the night sky before vanishing to nothing. *Just like Jake.*

I turned over and wiped a tear before falling asleep.

CHAPTER 13

Hospital Shenanigans

Tom and Jenny picked me up at the cabin by mid-morning. *No more explanations.* That's what I had decided. As we pulled into the parking lot at Gorman Hospital, we slowed behind a van of teenagers. On its side was an eagle picture with the words *Cliffview Boys' Home.* Inside, boys were laughing as they sang Rossini's *Figaro* from the *Barber of Seville* along with the soloist on the van's speakers.

"Fi-ga-ro, Fi-ga-ro, Figaro, Figaro, Figaro, Figaro, Figaro—Fi-ga-ro!" they sang at the top of their lungs.

Tom pulled in two parking spots over. "Is that opera they're singing?" he asked, chuckling.

"Italian opera," I confirmed. We could still hear the voices and laughter inside their van.

"How would you know?" said Tom.

Jenny piped in, "Because he saw cartoons with Tom and Jerry and Bugs Bunny and Elmer Fudd. That's where he learned about opera, right, Billy?" I smiled since she was right.

Tom slammed his hand on the steering wheel, "Yeah, now I remember! I saw those, too. So that's Italian opera, huh?"

I sighed as I climbed out. "See you when I'm done."

"We'll be here," Jenny assured me, respecting my wishes to go in alone. I stood motionless, wanting to observe this strange group of teens. *All right, now I'm just stalling. I'm here to see Jake and get my eye test.* Despite my thoughts, curiosity arose as these boys enjoyed themselves with my Pa's old coach.

Pop O'Reilly, the Irish headmaster and founder of Cliffview, was the only person who'd had the guts to shake Pa's hand at the sentencing. I'd never forget that!

"Okay, boys, time for your physicals…and some fun!" Pop said, hopping out of the van. "Bubba, pull Luke out. Andy, grab the bag. Does Pete have his papers? Zack and Zeke, let's go!"

Six students unloaded from the van. Bubba, a huge fellow with a hearing aid looped over one ear, pulled out a wheelchair and lifted a well-built boy out of the van and into it. Luke had been an up-and-coming running back his freshman year at Rockside High until he'd been in a car accident. His injuries had resulted in the amputation of both his legs at mid-thigh. It was nice to know he was still in town. Bubba grabbed a large boom box and carried it in.

In the parking lot, Luke performed spinning stunts from his wheelchair. Every time he spun around, the boys sang "Figaro, Figaro, Figaro, Fi-ga-ro!" *They could charge for tickets.*

Pop hollered to a small, fragile boy, a midget. "Andy, grab the duffle bag, and tell Pete to carry it in."

Andy, after making eye contact with Pete, hollered to him while also using sign language. His nimble hands and expressive wording were smooth and deliberate; he was a veteran of sign language. "Help me carry in the duffel bag," he said as he signed. It was pure mystery but not to Pete, who responded in sign. Pete was tall, slender, and athletic. As he signed, he laughed while Andy struggled to lift the duffel bag out of the van. Pete grabbed it and hoisted it over his shoulders, flexing his muscles, and signed what I assumed was a wisecrack to Andy.

"At least I can sing better than you!" said Andy, as he signed to Pete and took up another rendition of "Figaro."

"Come on, Zack, bring in your twin brother," urged Pop.

Zack could see but Zeke was partially blind. Zack held one end of a three-foot elastic band with a closed loop to guide his brother. Zeke held onto the other looped end. I felt sad to see this boy towed around, and I wondered why he didn't use a cane. But it seemed an efficient way from point A to point B. *How lucky to have a brother who would sacrifice himself.* I realized I was lucky, too, when Tom guided me over treacherous terrain.

Fascinated, I stayed behind them, distracted from the dread of facing Jake. Pop led this odd assortment of teenage boys into the hospital lobby. Turning around at the door, Pop gave a low-five to Andy and a high-five to Bubba. I laughed as the two boys gave each other a five. They seemed unlikely buddies.

Pop stepped to the counter and wrote the six students' names on the appointment ledger. Lining up behind Pop at the receptionist's counter, I noticed that Luke was now out of his wheelchair and like a gymnast, had pressed up into a handstand. He walked on his hands, wearing a pair of modified canvas shoes on each hand. Below eye-level, Luke's exposed stumps flailed in the air, shocking passersby in the lobby. Those seated seemed more puzzled than shocked. Andy sat in Luke's wheelchair and pulled out a realistic-looking papier-mâché head, complete with lifelike shoulders from his duffle bag.

Bubba played "The Twist" from his boombox. "Chubby Checker rocks!" said Bubba as he swung his huge hips back and forth. Pete conducted the music, his arms thrashing like a demented maestro, spurred on by Bubba's moves!

Zeke held his end of the elastic band to circle his sighted twin. Zeke performed dynamic aerial ballet leaps in the center of the lobby. He had those scissor kicks down to an art, even the pointed toes. People lowered their magazines. Little kids stared with their mouths gaping until turning into a grin.

Pop exchanged smiles with an older female attendant who glanced over at the receptionist. She gave Pop a "thumbs-up" as he rang the bell at the desk.

The receptionist, in her late 50s, had shuffled papers into neat piles and was filing them behind the counter. She gave no reaction to the bell. Pop rang a second time, causing her to puff her way to the desk, disturbed by the interruption. She wore a large plastic badge with her name, Sally Grundman, written in huge letters. I noticed her badge matched her oversized beehive hairdo, which spiraled up eight inches. She could barely fit under the sign that read, "Please sign in here," the arrow pointing downward into her hair.

The circus-like atmosphere in the lobby dominated her attention. Mrs. Grundman appeared mesmerized. I glanced at the lady attendant, doubled over, giggling behind a cabinet.

Pop rang the bell a third time since the receptionist had failed to acknowledge his presence. Spying her nametag, he began, "I'm Pop O'Reilly from Cliffview…and you are…Sally Grundman? The new receptionist?"

"Nooo, *no*…" Sally said, releasing air like an over-inflated tire with a leak.

"No, you're not Sally Grundman, or, no, I'm not Pop O'Reilly?"

"*Whooo* are they?" she questioned under her breath, staring owl-like at the boys.

Sally's face froze as she watched Andy climb on a chair and place the dummy head and shoulders over Luke's upside-down stumps. Luke now had two heads, the fake papier-mâché one on top, complete with a torso, and his real head below. Finishing the conversion, Luke continued to walk the lobby upside down.

Pete grunted louder as he conducted Bubba, whose hip movements looked more like a hula hoop demonstration than a dance.

Andy, a student of mime, wandered the lobby imitating an organ-grinder's monkey while singing "Figaro" and scratching his armpits. This brought reactions as visitors laughed and pointed at the performers. Me, too. It felt good to laugh again.

Three ladies, dressed impeccably in office attire, entered the lobby from outside, involved in their conversation. Their fast-paced chatter stalled as Andy distracted them, his monkey mime-walk the epitome of perfection. Crossing in front of the speedy trio, he turned to them with a grimace, calling out, "Ooo-ooo-ooo, ahhh-ahhh-ahhh," all the while scratching like a primate. The ladies made a wide arc around Andy, approaching Luke.

Still walking on his hands, Luke spoke, "Hey, ladies, can you spare a dime?" They looked at his "head" on top, stymied by its lifeless expression. "I'm down here!"

The ladies gasped, then let loose blood-curdling screams that reverberated off the lobby walls. Turning tail, they scurried toward the hospital exit as one lost her high-heeled shoe.

"Cinderella!" Luke shouted.

With bursts of laughter, the lobby patrons clapped their approval as Andy pinched the shoe with two fingers and did his bow-legged monkey-walk to Sally Grundman and offered it to her.

"Does it fit?" asked Luke. He turned as one lady returned for the shoe.

"I'm callin' security!" Sally pounded out the code on the phone. "Security, get up here! My lobby's a circus stage!" She paused. "Describe it?" She glanced at the lobby. "Are you crazy?" She slammed the phone.

"Oh, boys, security's comin'!" warned Pop. In seconds, Andy leaped to a chair, pulled off Luke's papier-mâché head, and with Pete's help, stuffed it into his oversized duffel bag. Luke did a forward roll to the ground.

Bubba lifted Luke into his wheelchair and picked up his boom box. Pete grabbed the duffel bag from Andy and stood statue-like, facing straight ahead beside Zack and Zeke. Pop joined them. The boys' expressions exuded innocence, resembling saints lining up at the pearly gates.

Two security officers in their thirties entered the lobby in a rush. Their serious expressions changed to huge grins when they saw Pop.

"Hey, Dave. Hey, Lionel. How's it goin'?" greeted Pop.

"We're fine, Pop," said Dave. "It's been awhile since we did our routines at Cliffview."

Sally Grundman sputtered as she looked straight at Dave. "I...I want these...these creatures...brought to...to..."

"Your house?" muttered Pop as the boys guffawed.

Dave raised his hand. "Mrs. Grundman, this is just Pop and his boys...havin' some fun. We know where they go."

"I know where they should go, too! To the zoo!"

"Well..." said Dave as several boys mimicked animal sounds that brought chuckles from the lobby visitors. "Uh...we'll take 'em to their appointments."

"Were their routines smooth, Pop?" asked Lionel.

"Like chocolate pie!

Dave and Lionel laughed, leading the boys across the lobby.

Dave shared a memory with the boys as several needed to stop to organize their gear. "When we were with Pop, Lionel and I used to do chocolate pie routines. When party crowds gathered on Valentine's Day, we carried in two large chocolate pies on tin plates. Everybody seemed to believe it was for them, from their sweetheart. Approaching the crowd, both of us sniffed like a dog as if we would release a massive sneeze that caused us to lose our balance with the chocolate pies."

The boys approached the hospital corridor and the automatic doors opened. I stood beside the receptionist's desk, listening for the end of the story, along with everyone else in the lobby.

Dave continued, "We kept sucking in air...then..."

The auto doors closed. All I could hear was three seconds of silence, followed by a muffled outburst of laughter from the boys.

Sally, her hands on her hips, glared at me. "And whatta you want?"

"The punchline?" Several in the lobby chuckled. "Uh, no, I'm here to see my brother, Jake Cline, and to get an eye test from Dr. Chu, the ophthalmologist. I'm Billy Cline."

"Another Cline checking in? Poor boy."

Following Sally Grundman's eyes, I turned, viewing the doors reopen. Ma guided Pa inside and slid him into a lobby chair where he slumped. Pa was drunk and disheveled with bandages on his face. Ma appeared frustrated as she tried to comfort him to no avail. She walked up to Sally Grundman at the receptionist's desk, surprised to see me on time.

I stayed, not knowing what happened to Pa. Ma approached and smacked the bell twice, receiving a cold stare and bitter words from Sally.

"You gonna sign yourself in, too? You know, keep it all in the family?"

"I'm signing my husband out!" Ma said as she jotted on the chart.

"Good riddance to him!" said Sally. "I'm dog-tired, workin' a double shift. At 4:00 a.m., your drunken husband broke Skinny Larson's nose in a fight at the railroad yards! Skinny's my cousin! Your husband got flat-out fired from the railroad!" She said it as if it were a campaign slogan, preparing for a fight of her own.

Ma stepped up to the counter and used a quiet voice. "Sally, a fastball down the pipe would shut you up, but there's more. Your beehive will never hide the fact you are part unicorn."

Sally's face got flushed. "My husband said you Clines were a rowdy bunch. Now get your husband outta my lobby!"

"It's okay to believe your husband but stop believin' your hair-dresser!" Ma glanced at me as she walked back to Pa.

Before I could move, Sally spoke. "And as for you, Billy Cline, your brother, Jake Cline, is in therapy right now. After you help your Ma, Lily Cline, to get your Pa, Ned Cline, out of my lobby, go to room 140 for your eye test with Dr. Chu. Then you can see your brother, Jake Cline, if he's done with rehab. Is that clear, Billy Cline? Probably not!"

It surprised me I held my temper. In a brisk walk across the lobby, I joined Ma, who stood beside Pop O'Reilly to escort Pa out of the hospital. I figured Pop had seen Pa when he'd walked his boys to their check-ups and decided to help him.

Pop and I walked Pa outside and into the pickup so Ma could drive him home.

As Pop and I reentered the lobby, I asked him a question that had nagged me. "Why do your boys do those routines?"

"To celebrate their handicaps. We don't apologize for 'em, we celebrate 'em. We showcase them into a dramatic scene."

I paused, taking it in. "What good does it do them?"

"It gets 'em through their day—hopefully with a smile." Several adults in the lobby nodded. Pop zeroed in on me, "What gets you through your day?" It stunned me and I couldn't answer. We walked through the automatic doors and down the corridor past the nurses' station.

Pop and I stopped outside room 140 where a bench seat and end table had the *Rockside Bugle* and magazines scattered on top. Pop picked up the newspaper. "The *Rockside Bugle* calls you the 'eagle boy.' Says you run mountain trails below a mysterious eagle."

"We don't get the paper…but I'll win the individual cross-country title in October."

Pop offered a handshake, and I took it. "Well done," he said. "Maintain confidence." His hand felt like leather, not skin. "Why stop at an individual title? Go for the team title, too!"

"A team title?" I said. "They don't want me on their team!"

"That didn't stop your Pa. He fought for the opportunity to run."

"All he fights for now is a drink," I said. "I know you coached him. I saw his old yearbook, but I never saw your arms up close until Pa's sentencing. Thanks for…shaking Pa's hand."

"Ned was a decent runner, a late bloomer. I knew he had spirit, but he wouldn't show it to others. He kept it bottled up inside."

"Well, his temper must have flared up—he got in a fight. The receptionist said he got fired off his night-shift railroad job."

Pop looked down. "Your family's facing an uphill battle. Believe me. Go easy on your Pa. At Cliffview, we don't apologize for our struggles or our defeats. We celebrate them, then create a plan to overcome our weaknesses by working together. It's our unity through celebration that gets us through our day."

"That sounds great, but how can I celebrate my brother's day? I was too slow to warn him so he got shot and has nerve damage. How can I celebrate my Pa's day? He got fired!"

I walked into Dr. Chu's office, leaving Pop in the hallway. In ten minutes, they buried my face into a Placido's disk. My eyes engaged swirling concentric circles, somehow measuring the damage keratoconus had done to my cornea. Dr. Chu summed it up: "I can upgrade your glasses again so you can run and navigate the challenges of regular life, but if this test shows your keratoconus is progressing, you may need a corneal transplant to see clearly."

When my appointment concluded, Pop was still waiting for his boys to complete their checkups. Pop joined me as we knocked on the door of the Rehabilitation Room. He opened it for me, then followed me inside. The room had various exercise equipment to strengthen the body and restore independence. A sliding glass door was open to a grassy courtyard outside. I peered into the courtyard as a tall therapist in a white smock shouted, "Shaky Jake! Shake and bake! What a great headpiece!"

"Your very own turtle shell!" said a short therapist, also dressed in a white smock.

Jake's movements were jerky, as if he were fighting himself. He wore an old leather football helmet with "Shaky Jake" written in bold letters.

"One foot in front of the other! Come on, Shaky Jake!" said the tall therapist. It appalled me, not believing what I was seeing and hearing. "Who shot ya, Jake? Ya hate 'em? Gonna get even? They'd be so scared! Oh, no! It's the spastic shell man, and he's comin' after me!" The therapist raised his arms as if mimicking pedestrians in those Godzilla movies. "Stay on your feet!" Jake's face scrunched as he lifted a leg and fell face-first to the grass, groaning.

"He's down at midfield for no gain! Could be a KO...one... two...three..." ridiculed the short therapist.

"Want payback? Then walk!" the tall therapist shouted. "If you hate enough, you'll quit crawlin'!"

"Where's your snap? Your bite? Get up, spastic shell man!" The short therapist moved close to Jake's face, who lay shaking and twitching, fighting back tears.

I rushed onto the patio. "Get away from him!"

"Who're you?" asked the tall therapist.

"His brother! Back off!" The short therapist did. Both men were silent for a moment. Snot, sweat, and grass covered Jake's face. I looked for something to wipe his face, and Pop was there, tossing me a towel.

The short therapist grabbed a phone on the courtyard wall. With a high-pitched voice, he yelled, "Security to Rehab, stat!"

"What ya doin' to him?" I said, kneeling and wiping his face. The tall therapist was not backing down.

"It's called therapy!"

I stood, challenging him. "Hate therapy, you mean! You're both scum!"

"Because we do the dirty work you're too chicken to do? It's his hate we're usin'…to make him learn to walk! He was ready to give up!"

Floored by the words that hit me, I looked at Jake lying defenseless, speechless, in pain and twitching. I never saw Dave and Lionel enter, only Pop who held out his hand like a traffic cop to stop security in their tracks.

I heard Dave's words: "Just get him outta here, Pop."

Pop tugged my arms, guiding me out of the patio, through another room, and out of the hospital. My vision was blurry, my emotions churning, and my outlook grim.

Intermittent raindrops greeted us outside. As I groaned with grief, Pop stood beside me, his scarred hand on my shoulder, comforting me with his authoritative presence and kind words.

"Billy, your Pa and I will figure something out."

Tom drove up as Jenny's expression shown through the window. She knew something was wrong. Pop helped me into the front seat. I tried to thank him, but no words left my lips. *I wonder how many times he's had to deal with tragedy from his students.*

Jenny slid over. I heard the song "I'm Sorry" on the radio while raindrops smacked the front windshield and Tom departed toward my homestead.

"What happened?" Jenny asked. I couldn't respond. All I could hear was Brenda Lee belting out heartbreaking words. Those words stung. *How could anyone forgive me?* I had called in the burglary—Jake got arrested. I was too late warning Jake at the pharmacy and at our cabin. I'd just witnessed his hate therapy. Was I to blame? As I punched the next radio button, Roger Miller sang "Dang Me." *Why would anyone shed a tear for me?*

With my head in my hands, Tom drove across town and up the dirt road to our place.

"Jake is being shamed by 'hate therapy.' It's immoral! His body is messed up. He can't change it. It's hopeless! My eyesight is failing, and without a major operation, I could end up being legally blind for a lifetime!" I leaned back and sighed.

Barreling down the dirt road, Sheriff Logan's cruiser passed us in the opposite direction.

Jenny retaliated. "Tom, this isn't the party I was expecting. The Cline boys are helpless and hopeless? Billy, I know that's not the Cline way you believe in. Your brother may be in a bad situation, but don't be selling me tickets to attend your pity party. I'm not buyin'!"

Tom stomped the pedal of his Blue Beauty, spinning around corners toward the cabin as I turned off the radio and buried my face in my hands.

CHAPTER 14

Fish Feast at the Cabin

Chester threw a rubber baseball toward the plywood backstop as we arrived in the Blue Beauty. His heart wasn't in it. The ball missed the backstop so he ambled into the forest, chasing it down.

Pa stood beside his rocker, his back to us, facing Ma's boarded-up window frame, where the stained-glass had once shined. Strumming his guitar, Pa hummed the Scottish love song "A Red, Red Rose." *He's serenading Ma through the plywood.*

He turned and sat on his rocker, wearing bandages on his face and over one eye from his fight. After a glance our way, he settled in, plucking the strings, looking as though he didn't have a care in the world.

Jenny squeezed my arm before I climbed out. I turned to look at her but had no plan. I walked up to the porch and slumped into the second rocker, still stinging from witnessing Jake's therapy and my problematic prognosis.

Jenny climbed out of the Blue Beauty and followed, staring at me as I rocked beside Pa. *Why won't she leave?*

Pa kept strumming and humming. Jenny sat on the third rocker and hummed in harmony, eliciting a smile on Pa's face. He shrugged in surprise and stopped, adjusting his bandages. He grabbed his jug, held it to his forearm, and took a long slow swig before wiping his face.

"Jenny…you sing?" Pa questioned.

"A little," she answered with a smile.

"How 'bout your daddy? Does he sing?"

"His voice doesn't ring the bell."

Pa smiled and began a verse, this time with the words. Jenny sang with him while grinning at me, proving she knew the song. *Sweetness!*

> My love is like a red, red rose
> That's newly sprung in June.
> My heart is like a melody
> That's sweetly play'd in tune.
> And fair art thou, my bonnie love
> So deep in love am I.
> And I will love thee still, my dear
> Till all the seas run dry.

*****

Pa set his guitar down and reached for his jug. "You're welcome, you know, to stay for a meal." I thought of Ma inside, banging empty pots and pans with no food to cook. But Pa seemed oblivious what being fired from the railroad would do to his family. Enjoying the singing, Jenny rose and motioned Tom to drive off in his Blue Beauty.

"Pick me up at dark!" she shouted, and Tom drove away.

I rose. "Jenny, I need time with Pa." I felt her smile calming me. I knew she was special. My sadness was put on hold.

Pa rose and lifted a porch plank, pulling out a hidden bottle of bourbon lying in a watery ice bucket. He motioned me to pick up the bucket of bait that Ma had recently placed on the porch. I joined him for a walk. I knew what he expected. The kitchen cupboards were bare. We meandered toward the small stream that flowed past our cabin into Ruby Lake.

"Sheriff Logan just paid me a visit. He got a call about you on his radio, about your escapades at the hospital. The report said you were rantin' and ravin' about 'hate therapy.' You caused quite a ruckus. I told Bart that you were a level-headed kid and would calm down."

"Like father, like son?" It took several moments for the joke to sink in since Pa was still wobbly from drinking, but he laughed.

"You know, son, I didn't start that fight last night, but I finished it."

"We Clines must like hospitals, eh, Pa?"

Pa stood stone still. "Ha...ha...ha!" he bellowed in a laugh that made me smile. "Guess I can't argue that!" His laughter must have caused him pain since he straightened his bandage again through a few groans. "Skinny's left came out of right field."

We continued our walk. "Son, what's your news?"

"Dr. Chu may not certify me safe to run. Depends on results from a Placido's disk and new glasses. Just gotta wait." I saw him shake his head. "Ya know, Pa, it ain't right those guys usin' hate therapy on Jake. There's gotta be a better way."

"I wish to God I knew. Ma's inside, crazy with grief over the death of Jake's dream. She ordered me outside, then locked the door!"

I took a quick glance back and pointed at Ma on the porch, now standing next to Jenny.

Pa continued, "Bart warned me with Deputy Cowler suspended and school startin' Monday, those Cowler boys'll be trouble. And Jimmy Jack will back them up. He's returned from reform camp or running camp, whatever you call it."

Arriving at the stream, I placed my hands on my hips, looking up the mountain.

"You ready to face 'em?" Pa asked, as if conflict was as certain as the sun's rising.

"Do I have a choice?"

"Whatta you think? Look at that little fish trying to swim upstream. You'll feel like that."

"So I should chicken out, turn around, and go with the flow?"

"No, you're a man now, Billy. You've gotta find your own way."

I pulled out my washcloth and dipped it in the stream, putting its coolness against my closed eyes. Then I yanked it off. "If I would'a run faster to Jake, none of this would'a happened!" With bait in the bucket, I ran off to Ruby Lake. Pa shook his head again, grabbing another bottle he had placed in the stream to cool.

Ma had told Jenny I would fish, so she joined me by running past Pa and chasing me the two hundred yards to the dock.

I leaped from the dock into our rowboat and manned the oars like a madman. Jenny followed my lead and jumped in with me, nearly knocking me into the water. I was no master oarsman as water splashed over the side from my awkward rowing motions. This only raised my determination to speed up.

I found my rhythm and propelled the boat through the lake water, trying to impress Jenny. After several minutes, exhaustion set in. The rowboat slowed to a standstill. A few droplets from the sky wrinkled the smooth lake waters. I gathered enough strength to look up. A squall moved overhead, shut off the sun's rays, and released torrents of liquid sunshine.

Rain pelted our heads, our backs, everything. Fatigue forced me to lean on the oars as I stared at my feet. I glanced up at Jenny, who wore a peculiar smile. "Listen, Jenny. I'm steamed. These feet have been my trusted means of transportation, yet they're of no use in the middle of a lake! Perhaps Jesus could walk on water, but I'm not in His league! I'm not in the same league as the apostle Peter, either, who'd at least tried to walk on water. I'm no duck, either! Do you see any webbed feet?"

Jenny giggled, causing me to ease up. After a warm glance, we kissed. *I wonder if God Himself understands my humor.* I laughed harder at the absurdity of that thought.

I sat on the wooden seat, feeling small next to the power of nature. After the downpour, dark clouds scattered, the rain ceased, and rays of sunlight flashed bright beams onto the lake, which moments before were polka-dotted by cascading droplets. I looked over at luscious greenery on the shore, the raw beauty of the peaks, and the amazing person sitting across from me. Not caring that water sloshed back and forth in the bottom of the boat, I became lost in myself, not knowing if I should cry or moan until I heard a familiar shriek.

"All right! I see ya!" I shouted. Victory shrieked twice more, circling my rowboat from a distance. "Okay! I'll fish! Quit buggin' me!"

We baited our hooks and cast on the left side of the boat. It surprised me to see Victory so soon, knowing the squall had just blown by.

Victory circled high in the sky before swooping down at great speed, skimming the lake on the right side of the rowboat. He slowed just in time to snatch a fish. He was showing off in front of me, impressing Jenny more than I could. *What nerve!*

"Hey! That's my fish!" I stood in the boat while it teetered. "Did ya come out to cheer me or pick up dinner for yourself?" The rowboat swayed as Jenny and I nearly fell overboard. I re-balanced myself and shouted as Victory soared away. "You're not the only one who knows how to fish, ya know!" I watched as he held his catch firm in his talons and headed to the cliffs.

Jenny had an idea. "Victory caught his fish on the right side of the boat. He knows where the fish are!" We cast on the other side. In no time, we both reeled in fish after fish. My voice changed from vague words of frustration to upbeat words of pure joy. In a moment of silence as we rested, water splashed from fish inside the boat. "If we catch too many fish, Jenny, we'll just watch 'em swim around our feet!"

Listening to what I'd just said made me chuckle. To pass time, we bailed water.

*****

An hour later, we docked the rowboat and collected our catch. Success brightened our mood. I was smiling now as we walked through the final stand of trees to my cabin. My doubts centered on Ma. *What will she do when we return? What will she want me to do?* I knew what Pa would do; he had his jug. What about Chester? What about? I couldn't mention Jake.

We walked into the clearing around the cabin, but nobody saw us. We stopped, taking in the sight of my family. Pa slept on his porch rocker. Ma looked red-eyed from crying. She must have come outside to comfort a hungry and teary-eyed Chester, who rocked on the porch. I figured she was trying to stake her claim as a guiding light in the family.

Chester seemed to accept her efforts until he stood and yanked on Pa's sleeve, trying to wake him. "Pa, we're hungry!"

"Huh?" Pa stirred, holding his head. "Fix somethin'."

"We don't got nothin'!" That's when Chester noticed us in front of the cabin. He sprang up. "What ya got there, Billy?"

"More fish than we can eat."

Chester ran and grabbed hold of the catch. "Look, Ma. We'll eat like kings!"

Ma barked orders. "Take 'em inside, Chester. Get the knife to filet 'em and stoke the fire!" Jenny responded to help Chester. I followed her inside but peeked back. Pa put his arms around Ma as he confessed, "I never understood Jake like you do. Please, forgive me." With arms still wrapped around each other, they joined us inside for a family fish feast.

CHAPTER 15

First Senior Day at Rockside High

The next morning Pa dropped Chester and me off in front of Rockside High for the first day of school. Chester walked to the junior high as I gazed at the high-school billboard and read WELCOME BACK, STUDENTS! Pa and I exchanged nods before he drove off. I expected a test would come soon, and I didn't have to wait long—the Clausen-Cowler crowd had gathered.

Jimmy Jack Clausen was tall and lean with long-flowing reddish hair. He seemed to enjoy his freedom after three months in reform school. He stood behind the Cowler boys, hovering like a high-strung bumblebee. All eyes fell on Jimmy Jack, who signaled his allies. I stepped onto the grassy yard, now filled with Jimmy Jack worshippers. *Talk about steppin' into it!*

Cletus greeted me. "Hey, Billy! Tough luck, your Pa fired from the railroad and all!" *That's one.* I kept walking. "And your Pa, found guilty of harboring your fugitive brother!" *That's two.* "And you Clines, watching Jake get gunned down like a mangy dog on your own property!" During Gopher's obnoxious laugh, I charged Cletus, knocking him flat before twisting over him onto the ground. Gopher and his friends grabbed me before I could bloody him. They jerked me up to face the one boy I had not greeted, Jimmy Jack Clausen. Bloodlust swelled within the crowd in seconds, ready for the first fight of the school year.

"Billy, ain't ya gonna say hi?" Jimmy Jack said with an arrogant smile. Cletus stepped back as Jimmy Jack moved to center stage.

"So the great Jimmy Jack is back!" I said, gazing at him with mock adoration.

Jimmy Jack nodded, then sucker-punched me in the mouth, sending me to the ground. "That's right! The great Jimmy Jack is back...and I'm back to claim what's mine! The conference title in October and my girl, Jenny!" His friends enjoyed a laugh at my expense.

"Back in three months?" I said, standing, held by the Cowlers while spitting blood. "My brother gets jail time, a bullet in the back, and you get a reform-school vacation? Have you seen Jake?"

"Jake's a Cline!" Jimmy Jack shrugged.

"He can't even walk!" Blood dripped from my chin as I struggled free from the Cowlers.

"Look, boys, he's gonna cry!" Jimmy Jack gestured for crowd support. "I'm just a minor. In reform school, I trained hard, like my ol' man said. I'll be runnin' first man!"

"First man? We'll see," I challenged.

"You? See? Ha! I'm just tryin' to educate ya. This is school, isn't it, boys?" The crowd snickered. Jimmy Jack waved his arm to the side, saying, "Shoo! Shoo! Leave!"

Cletus rushed in and shoved me in the back to the ground. "I told ya to watch your back!"

Gopher's laugh didn't last long when a yard lady approached. "What's going on here?" she asked. Students scurried off in all directions like roaches when a light comes on.

Cletus hollered again, "When's your Pa gonna fix that busted pickup window?" Gopher and the others guffawed, congratulating Cletus. I moved toward the flagpole to Jenny.

"There you are," she said. She looked over my shoulder. "Jimmy Jack is back? What was going on over there? Everybody's staring." As I turned, Jimmy Jack sent her a flying kiss. The Cowler group laughed, causing Jenny to stomp her foot. She turned. "He doesn't believe it's over! What'd he say? Billy, your lip's bleeding. What happened?"

"Doesn't matter." I took her hand and felt its warmth, grateful for her friendship and love. Together, we walked up the front steps as the school bell rang.

Students rushed in for their first classes. They mashed us at Jenny's locker when Tom approached. "So it's true? Jimmy Jack is back? What happened to you, Billy?"

"Nothin', just greetings from the Clausen and Cowler kin welcoming committee."

"You still gonna try out?"

"I ain't afraid of Jimmy Jack...or the Roadrunner!"

"That's my Wile E. Coyote," Jenny responded, hands on her hips.

"Workout's gonna rock! See ya!" Tom hustled down the busy hallway as Jenny put her hand on my shoulder before walking into her class.

*****

After school, the cross-country runners met on the bleachers, ready for tryouts on the track. Tom and I arrived early and saw Jimmy Jack celebrated like a rock star returning from a worldwide concert tour. They slapped him on the back, shared jokes, and listened to him brag about reform school until Coach began his welcome speech.

Coach Cale Clausen had a strong build, a military-type haircut, and a determined personality. He wore a whistle that never left his neck. He stood tall on the uppermost bleacher bench, making us turn to look up at him.

"Good afternoon," he began. He eyeballed the group, pointing his index finger at each runner as he counted them under his breath. "For you newer guys, I'm Coach Clausen. Our best runner so far is my son, Jimmy Jack. He runs in Nike's. Steve Prefontaine, America's best distance runner from Oregon, said, 'To give anything less than your best is to sacrifice the gift.' In Rockside, cross-country races are 3.1 miles, a 5K. Today, we race a mile to find our varsity seven. I've coached the last two individual cross-country champions! My third sits at my feet!"

Clausen paused in his speech, giving a split-second glance at his son. Every runner knew he was the chosen one, preordained to repeat as the next champion.

"I don't give a hoot in a haystack for second place! In the 1920s, Paavo Nurmi, the 'Flying Finn,' won nine Olympic gold medals in running. Who was second to Nurmi? Come on!"

Silence reigned.

"Nobody cares who was second!" thundered Clausen.

Tom covered his mouth and leaned over. "Nobody cares that Nurmi won, either."

"Prefontaine said, 'I run to see who has the most guts.'" Clausen marched back and forth on the top bleacher row. "One of you will win the conference championship in late October and defeat those braggarts from Haybury High! Who will it be? You? You? Your teammate?"

He pointed at us in a belittling way. At first, I assumed he thought it would fire us up, but what I saw were counterfeit stares. He believed none of us could rise to challenge Jimmy Jack or the top runners at Haybury. Disbelief hung like a heavy cloud, team-wise. Most glanced down when he pointed at us as if any positive response would be received as a joke.

"Nurmi carried a stopwatch in training. That watch was his rival, hounding his every stride. I'm your personal stopwatch. Now go stretch for the mile time trial!" Clausen waved his arms toward the track and watched as the runners left to warm up for the mile race.

Tom and I stayed as did Coach Clausen. I poured cool water from my canteen onto my washcloth and lay on the bleachers, the coolness easing my eyes and the cloth blocking the sunlight.

"Tom, go stretch!" ordered Clausen. I felt the vibrations as Tom stepped off the bleachers.

"Why are you here? Lookin' for trouble or takin' a nap?" I gave no response, so Clausen went for the jugular. "Don't you know the court allowed Jimmy Jack to return with no penalty?"

I yanked off my washcloth in disbelief, then replaced it.

"Look at me when I'm talkin'!" Clausen said. I chucked the washcloth and listened. "Son, since the dawn of alphabetical seating in grade school, your Pa's been a thorn between my buddy Rawley and me. You runnin' on my team with Rawley's sons would be like… like diggin' up a whole lot of bad history!"

"Are you tellin' me to quit?"

"Just…make the smart decision."

"Well, here it is. I'm takin' that race in October."

Coach Clausen shook his head. After he left, I rose to stretch.

Twelve rookie runners awaited heat two on the sidelines, preparing to watch the race they would soon run themselves. As a senior, I would race in the top group of ten runners.

Jenny and Darla sat near the rookies, staring at Jimmy Jack and me as we toed the line. Darla spoke first. "Decide, Jenny. Which boy do you like best?"

"With Billy, I'm free to be me."

Clausen raised his starter pistol as a gust of wind blew from the west. "Veteran runners! On your mark!" An eagle's shriek broke the silence as everyone gazed skyward. It was Victory. I imitated my best eagle shriek.

"Shut up, buzzard boy!" Cletus shouted. Laughter from the runners seemed to ignite the ire of Coach Clausen. Another eagle shriek resounded, followed by a loud crack and puff of smoke from Clausen's starter pistol.

Wind swept over us as we stormed down the straight and around turn one. On the backstretch, Jimmy Jack powered to a five-yard lead over a pack of four—Cletus inside me, and behind us, Tom inside Gopher. The other runners trailed us by twenty yards, the gap widening.

On turn two, Gopher ran close behind me, breathing down my neck, showing he, too, was a force. He moved to my outside and nudged me hard with an elbow, pushing me off balance into Cletus, who shoved me back into Gopher. The heel of Gopher's left hand hit the back of my right elbow and with a shove, I stumbled, plummeting to the cinder track onto my chest.

Cletus, Gopher, and Tom kept running, still chasing Jimmy Jack. The following pack passed on both sides of me, avoiding a fall. I felt the sting of cinders scrape my forearms and legs. Jumping up, I stormed after them, but I was limping. I relaxed for a while till I got my bearings. I was in last place, but I worked through the limp, my gait becoming smoother and stronger. On the fourth lap, I passed a few more tiring runners and crossed the line.

I wasn't sure if I'd made the top seven. My vision was blurry and my frames were bent, sitting crooked on my nose. A scorekeeper jogged up as I was leaning over, examining scrapes and a deeper cut down my leg. My hands and arms were stinging, and I was breathing hard, struggling to stand.

The scorekeeper's words faded in and out. "Are you okay? Man, you got hammered! I can't believe you finished, but...you got seventh."

That's when I looked up. Tom, my true running buddy, rushed over. "I made varsity! I was fourth. You got seventh? We're in!" Nodding, I raised my hand to salute Tom's accomplishment, but all I could think about was my fall. It hadn't been an accident.

As Tom and I recovered, we saw a crowd gather around Coach Clausen as he lifted Jimmy Jack's hand like a winning prizefighter. Cheers went up from the next heat of runners and the students who cheered on Jimmy Jack.

I took off my glasses and rubbed my eyes while walking inside the track. As I straightened the frames, Tom spoke, "They put you on the ground, didn't they?"

"How did you know?"

"I heard it from the runners on the sidelines."

"It was pure luck I could run at all after that fall."

"It's hard for me to believe," Tom said, "but I was fourth. I never dreamed that could happen. Maybe I could make all-conference, too! But who can beat Jimmy Jack?"

"I can...if you'll guide me! Tom, you're as talented as me. I promise you...if you'll work with me and do all I ask, including morning runs, I'll beat Jimmy Jack, and you'll make all-conference."

"You mean it? You think it's possible?"

"Are you in?"

Tom looked at the other runners, then nodded.

CHAPTER 16

Morning Runs and Dog Alley

The next morning, a thin, low fog hung in the air. Even though Pa was without a steady job, he drove Chester and me into town early on school days so I could do my morning runs with Tom. Pa then could look for work. Along with us and our school supplies, Pa loaded his guitar case and several jugs in the pickup.

"How's a guitar and jugs gonna get you a job?" Ma said.

"Simple. Since Billy and Chester are goin' in early to school, I'll drive 'em and still have time to strum a few tunes while the factories open. I met a friend who'll give me some coin if I can move the genuine shine he's made. That'll cover my gas. Then I'll look for a job. I'm still gonna go to counseling in the evenings to get my job back."

"Sure," Ma said, disappointment etched across her face. "You're under a spell…a spell of the jug."

"I'm sleepy," said Chester.

"Just study your homework," Ma said, "and get to bed earlier tonight."

I, too, had my suspicions of Pa's explanation.

As we neared town, we saw the Blue Beauty parked beside the railroad tracks. "Just drop me off there," I said to Pa. Tom was already stretching. "We'll be runnin' four-milers each morning, except on meet days."

"Four-mile runs?" Pa said. "I thought you'd get a couple miles or three…but four? That couldn't have been Clausen's idea."

"It was mine."

"Can your bodies hold up for his after-school workouts?"

"Got to."

Pa pulled in and stopped. Dressed in running clothes, I climbed out, carrying a backpack and a duffle bag filled with jeans, shirts, and other essentials for the week ahead.

"Hey, I'm here like I promised. You got enough clothes for the week?" Tom asked.

"Yep, glad to see you." I smiled, opened the Beauty's back door, and threw in my backpack and duffel bag.

"Who's gonna drive the Blue Beauty to school?" Pa asked.

"Jenny'll drive it with our stuff. She has a key. If there's a problem, Chester can bring my books to the school office. Right, Chester?"

"Yeah, I guess so."

Pa smiled. "So you've got a plan?"

"We've gotta build endurance before we can get faster. Jimmy Jack ran away from us yesterday, and the Cowler boys are right in the mix with us."

"You're right to increase mileage. Clausen won't do you any favors. Does he know about this?"

"No, but it's not like we can hide it when we run into the gym before school."

As Pa drove off, Chester waved goodbye, his nose pressed against the cracked back window, the hole now covered in black tape.

Tom had filled us in on the logistics. "If I park the Blue Beauty at the tracks, the run is on. If I park at my house, the plan has changed." I hoped Jenny might look out her upstairs window when we started, but she didn't.

About a mile into the run, our route passed a dog kennel. Dog owners filed in and out with their pets. We ran past two large ladies, each holding a leashed Chihuahua. We must have spooked the dogs because they lunged for us, their barks as fierce as hungry wolves. I'll admit our pace quickened. Looking back, I laughed as the ladies held on to their leashes, yelling at their dogs.

As Tom and I neared Rockside High, we saw one of those big, long, yellow buses, nicknamed "cheese wagons," loaded with students, stuck in a line of cars. I knew the traffic light would change soon, and I hated jogging in place, waiting for it.

"Sprint now, Tom!" I yelled. As we sprinted toward the intersection, students on the packed bus looked back and saw us. Several yelled out the window.

"Run, run, run, run, run, run!" The chanting grew louder as more students joined in, rocking the bus.

"Shut up!" the bus driver screamed.

We dashed past the bus, whose nose had entered the intersection as the light turned yellow. The driver applied his brakes. A chorus of "boos" spilled out the bus windows. Tom and I completed most of our sprint through the intersection on the yellow light as cars on our right waited until we high-stepped the curb onto school grounds.

By mid-morning, Tom and I arrived at the vice principal's office to explain that morning's incident to him and our female counselor. The bus driver had written us up, getting our names from several "canaries" on the bus. I took a deep breath and tried to explain.

"Sir, there is nothing illegal about walking or running to school, or roller skating or skateboarding to school, or riding a bicycle or tricycle to school, or riding in a car or hauled in a big yellow cheese wagon to school. Some people think the law states that red means stop, green means go, and yellow means go very fast. But that's not what Tom and I believe, sir. The light turned yellow when we had entered the intersection. We did what the law required by exiting the intersection safely. See…we're here…and we're safe."

The vice principal, Mr. Deeter, glanced toward the counselor who laughed through a choking cough, then turned back. A grin covered his face as he replied, "Thank you for that detailed explanation. Your light in this office has just turned yellow. Please, exit the office and return to class—safely." Tom and I thanked him and walked out of his office, thinking he might be cool.

One day the next week, we arrived at the railroad tracks. Tom was a no-show. "Chester, take my books into the high school office, will ya? I'll pick 'em up there." He nodded. Chester waved goodbye, watching me from the cracked back window. I could tell he and Pa were proud of my commitment.

As I began my run, a light shone from Jenny's upper bedroom window. I ran up her driveway, picked up a small pebble, and dinged it off her window. She looked out and threw me a kiss. She realized Tom wasn't there, and I knew she would exert pressure on him to show up in the future and run when they rode together to school that morning.

The next day was sunny. Pa dropped me off as usual, and this time, Tom was waiting. When I climbed out of our pickup with my books, Chester spun in his seat and turned both thumbs downward as he looked out the back window at Tom.

"Nothing like positive feedback," Tom said in jest. "What'd I do?"

"It's not what you did, but what you didn't do yesterday."

"Not showing up?"

"Yep."

Tom appeared stunned. I believed our friendship gave him a pass. If he missed, he had a reason. When I ran, the energy I put into it was up to me. Why should I expect anything different from Tom? I had to think that way since I needed Tom's eyesight, his friendship, and an ally.

After I threw my books in Tom's car and stretched, we began our run. Again, about seven minutes in, two Scottish terriers got riled up. A man in a tweed vest who smoked a pipe had escorted them into the kennel, but lost his grip.

"What is it about dog owners?" Tom said. We sped up, pushed on by our canine pursuers. The dogs stopped, giving up on us.

As our heart rates returned to normal, I said, "We should call this place 'Dog Alley.'"

Almost three miles into the run, we ran by two junior-high-school boys riding up a slight hill on their Sting Ray, chopper-style, twenty-inch bicycles. It amazed the cyclists to see us pass them and open a gap. They rose off their seats, stomping on their pedals. We picked up the pace, never letting them get close enough to think they could beat us. When they gave up, we smiled.

Another morning run several weeks later was memorable. Rain came down sideways, driven by strong winds. Pa complained, "I ain't lookin' for a job in this weather! I'll be headin' back home after I drop you boys off." I understood since Pa hadn't shaved for two days.

Sitting beside Chester in the pickup, I doubted myself. I wasn't happy about running in a monsoon, either, but I kept my mouth shut. If I didn't show loyalty to my plan, who would?

"Are you gonna run in this downpour?" asked Chester.

"Why not? Three-fourths of the planet is water!" *What a stupid thing to say!*

Chester paused. "You're right...you must swim...I mean... run." Chester laughed. As I got out, I was mad at myself. Tom was a no-show once more.

I left my books with my brother and stretched. As Pa drove off, Chester's nose pressed against the cracked window again, giving me a sympathetic look. I grinned back at him, realizing I couldn't get any wetter.

Near the start, I considered detouring up Jenny's driveway but decided against it. I didn't want the pressure of her trying to talk me out of the run. At two miles, I ran down a short dip on the left side of the road, facing traffic. Three cars hit huge puddles on the lower portion of the road where water always collected. I was awash in a wall of rainwater with nowhere to go.

What stuck in my memory was seeing this old man driving with his wife, holding her hands over her face while a wave of muddy water swept over me. The two cars following behind repeated the same soaking wave. The last driver was laughing.

"Awww!" I groaned, half choking. However, nothing could dampen my spirits that morning. I was getting stronger.

Two weeks later, as I climbed out of the pickup, Chester, with both thumbs in his ears, wiggled his fingers and stuck out his tongue at Tom, who just laughed and said, "Appreciation is so nice."

Down the road at Dog Alley, Tom and I ran past a wiry man with a double leash connected to a pair of Dobermans. They became energized by our fast-paced run, but the man held on to the leashes. Somehow, about thirty seconds later, the two dogs pulled loose, their barks signaling Tom and me to sprint! Chihuahuas and Scottish terriers were a minor problem, but Dobermans were a foe we weren't prepared to handle. Adrenaline pumped through our veins, but it was obvious we were no match for these speedy dogs.

"Jump the fence!" we both yelled. Beside us on the right was the only home on the street with a major fence, a tall chain-link one, like those used at schools. Inside the fence behind some overgrown brush was a large skull and crossbones wooden sign with the following words in blood red: Keep Out! Home of KING, Rockside's giant German shepherd!

The Dobermans had closed in, snapping their jaws, about to bite our backsides when we veered right and leaped high onto the fence webbing, pulling ourselves upward for a higher hold. Both Dobermans missed a chomp on our legs as they crashed against the fence and squealed when repelled backward, still barking savagely, their gnashing teeth protruding from their jutting jaws. Kicking off with our feet, we slung ourselves up and over the fence, then dangled, before landing like cats on the other side.

For a moment, the fence saved us, we thought. I heard a loud huffing noise followed by the unmistakable sound of a thick chain slithering over a wooden porch. We both turned and realized this was the home of King, a legend in Rockside and ready to prove why. The savage beast leaped off the porch and charged our position to defend his turf. The snarling Dobermans, snapping viciously at us on the other side of the fence only raised the ferocity of King's attack. Tom and I stood side by side, backs bent, legs buckling, and our unuttered prayers for mercy ascending to God. After three more enormous strides, King rocketed upward toward us at full speed, his huge paws spread wide to grip our throats.

In a merciful reprieve, King hung in midair, his huge chain reaching maximum length just three feet from our faces. His plunge caused a vicious, throaty growl, as his steel dog collar bent like a hangman's noose from the powerful force of his airborne thrust.

Caught between King and the Dobermans, neither of us were going anywhere. Staring at oversized snapping teeth, I recalled tales of this fierce German shepherd from my earlier school days. The elementary principal had banned their telling in the lower grades because they caused nightmares. But they considered the legends of King a special treat in the upper grades, but only on Halloween.

As King lunged again to seize us, the huge chain stretched taut. I heard the reinforced porch support beams moan as he yanked on the chain, trying to pull out the brackets and nails that anchored it to the old wooden house. The home's wooden structure shivered from King's thrusts as dust rose in the air.

The owner of the Dobermans ran up and grabbed the two leashes, apologizing while tugging the animals away. Tom and I let out a deep breath before climbing the fence to freedom. Slumping on the other side, all we could do was lean over and try to recover from our near-death experience.

As we caught our breath, we heard an old lady call out from her window, "You boys better not trespass here again! King was just playin' with ya!"

Exhausted, we jogged to the Rockside gym. Ambling into the locker room, we sat on the bench beside our lockers, shaking our heads.

"Tom, all in favor of changing our morning running route, say, aye."

"Aye." We both groaned.

CHAPTER 17

Butt Breaker Race

Tom and I sprawled across from each other in the team bus on our way to the sixth cross-country race of the fall. Cletus and Gopher sat a few rows back while Jimmy Jack had stayed in school clothes. *Where's his uniform?* I wondered as I looked at Tom, who read my mind and shrugged. Jimmy Jack had a tote bag beside him, so we figured he'd dress later.

I closed my eyes. My mind spun with memories from five previous races. Jimmy Jack had won them all. From newspaper photos, I'd gotten a glimpse of him raising his arms while breaking the tape, a jubilant Coach Clausen smiling with obvious approval. But I had never witnessed it, being back too far. Last week, though, I'd sighted Jimmy Jack at the finish, as Tom and I gained on him in the last quarter mile. I visualized those pictures plastered in the *Rockside Bugle. How would I feel to live through victory myself?*

Jimmy Jack was still the presumptive favorite for October's Championship 5K. Ace Makowski and other Haybury runners were still in the hunt, along with the Cowler boys, who were putting up strong performances. Thinking over these facts hurt my chance to relax.

The *Rockside Bugle* featured a story about Jimmy Jack each week. Darla was visible in some pictures, holding one end of the finish tape with a look of awe as she stared at him. *Jimmy Jack wouldn't have trouble filling a scrapbook.*

Why didn't Coach Clausen push the team concept? All he talked about was the individual championship. It was as if the team didn't matter. We all knew the team with the lowest combined point total of its top five runners would win. *Wasn't he interested in a team victory?*

Ace Makowski, the top Haybury runner, always bragged about a team championship. "Without Jimmy Jack, we'd skunk ya," he said. "We'd go for fifteen points today. Add 'em up: one plus two, plus three, plus four, plus five equals fifteen. None of your other runners will crack into our top five at the championship!" Then Ace would lead them in their hog routine. It drove me crazy. Tom, the Cowlers, and I had already beaten Haybury's fourth and fifth man at least once. I didn't know what Ace Makowski was smoking, but his head was in a cloud of it.

The Haybury team featured two additional running stars, both as obnoxious as Ace and Jimmy Jack. Their four other runners were strong, which catapulted the Haybury Hogs to the top of the cross-country polls. They always had five runners near the front.

I thought we had a strong five, too. We had a long gap back to our sixth and seventh runners, but our first five were formidable. As usual, though, Jimmy Jack was the only blip on Coach Clausen's radar.

In the early season, my four-mile morning runs tired me for afternoon workouts. Fatigue, caused by lactic acid buildup, seemed to clog my body's veins. My lungs couldn't oxygenate my blood fast enough to restore a balance. Though Tom was running only two or three morning runs each week, he noticed his fatigue, too. But because we persevered, our bodies toughened. We noticed increased strength and endurance. Our times improved each week more than the others.

Jimmy Jack had won our traditional Rockside Invitational, the Haybury Hot Footer, which included hopping over hay bales, Grampa's Gulch Run in Wooster Canyon, the Sweet Lake Circle at Stinky Lake, and the Red Creek Run at Three Hills. Looming on our schedule this morning was the Butt-Breaker Classic at Coal Ridge. I believed my time had arrived.

The ride to the meet became more unsettling when Jimmy Jack tapped me on the shoulder. "Hey, eagle boy, what happened to you? I expected you to challenge me this year."

I looked at my teammates' faces. Their eyes locked onto mine as I replied, "The season's not over, is it?"

Jimmy Jack laughed. "Oh! The season's not over!" Cletus, Gopher, and some others laughed. It was no fun being ridiculed by my own team. Jimmy Jack muttered, "Today's your chance."

"Pipe down!" shouted Coach Clausen. "We've got Haybury today!" The bus stopped below the Butt-Breaker course. I wondered if Coach Clausen would talk about team for a change. "Listen up!" Coach said. "Since Jimmy Jack has won five straight races, I'm savin' him for the championship! You'll take on Haybury today without him. Somebody needs to step up and win it for Jimmy Jack. Now, get out there!"

Was that the pep talk? Was that what Jimmy Jack meant? I might have a chance if he wasn't racing? Why would anybody want to win it for Jimmy Jack?

We filed out. I noticed what little team energy existed had disappeared. Cletus whined to Gopher, "This'll be our last and only chance to get our pictures in the *Rockside Bugle*." I knew they would go for it. Since Deputy Rawley's suspension without pay, they had moved out of their home on the dead-end street and into Deputy Blimp Cowler's smaller house. I knew a win or a top-five finish by either of the Cowler boys would please their Pa.

"What about my picture?" another runner asked.

"Who cares about your picture?" said Gopher, laughing and walking off.

This is no team, only individuals wearing the same uniform. I grew more introspective. *What have I done to promote team victory during this season? Nothing!*

The Haybury Hogs were there in "full snout," as Jake used to describe them. They warmed up in their pink and brown uniforms, finishing with their hog routine to the cheers of their supporters. The routine ended with loud grunts while the "hogs" snorted and ran around in circles. I bristled at their huge egos while holding Jimmy

Jack's challenge foremost in my mind. In our warm-up, I wondered why Coach Clausen held Jimmy Jack out.

We met around Coach just before the race, wearing our red and black uniforms. His concluding words were, "Okay, let's bury Haybury!" We looked at each other but didn't seem so sure. I felt sorry for the new junior varsity runner who'd arrived to fill out our team. The greenhorn walked to the trash can, hovered over it, and lost his lunch before lining up at the starting line. He knew the facts; against these teams, he was roadkill.

Before our last run-out, the top three Haybury runners ran up to Jimmy Jack along with Deucey, Ace's girlfriend. She shoved Jenny out of the way so Ace could approach our team unimpeded. Ace asked, "Hey, Jimmy Jack, did ya break a nail?" Jimmy Jack, with fire in his eyes, raised his fist and pounded his chest in response. The Haybury boys laughed and ignored him. Deucey gave a belittling grin to Jenny, which got me fired up.

Before returning to the starting line from our run-out, I set my plan with Tom. "Start fast, Tom! We'll smoke these porkers from the gun!" We were a threat, and I was determined to beat Ace Makowski, who would have to bleed to beat me!

"Start fast?" Tom questioned. "What about the last mile? I'll die from early speed! And Victory's not here to help."

"I'm gonna run away from 'em at the gun...demoralize 'em. Put such a doubt in Haybury's empty minds that their cocky smiles will vanish to nothing!"

Knowing this race could show our hard work had paid off, Tom nodded, but he didn't appear confident. I knew his last mile would be in jeopardy by starting too fast. I wanted to break out of the shadows into sunlight, to quell doubts I was a legitimate contender for late October's cross-country championship.

I stood between Cletus and Gopher on the front line in our chalk-boxed area. Coach placed Tom and our next three runners behind us in the second row. The Haybury seven laughed.

"They're licking their chops," Tom said. *Bang!*

Cletus shoved me into Gopher, hoping to stall me, but his plan backfired. Tom, on the back row, nicked his heel. Cletus stumbled and fell. I bounced off Gopher and sprinted forward.

Tom and I broke free and powered to the front, ahead of everybody, pulling away from the field of eighty-four runners. "Faster!" I shouted. Tom sped up, keeping a half-stride lead so I could settle in beside him, just a foot off his shoulder.

Standing at the mile marker, the Haybury coach screamed at officials, "Tom is pacing that half-blind Cline kid! DQ 'em both!" The officials looked, but saw no contact between Tom and me, so they ignored his plea. I wore a faint smile, knowing how hard Tom and I had worked on our communication skills.

Making a turn, I glanced back and saw the colors of the top three Haybury runners behind. The Haybury coach began a tirade at the bottom of a steep hill. "What are you doin'? They're for real! Get your butts up there!" For the first time, I saw worried looks on the faces of Haybury fans. Without Jimmy Jack, they still saw two Rockside runners leading Ace and his teammates.

At the 2.5-mile marker, Tom and I still led, but the early speed took its toll. Tom motioned me on before he tripped on a rock and collapsed. All I knew was that my vision was blurrier, my eyes were stinging, and I'd lost my guide.

Fear, like a thief, robbed me of energy. I had entered new territory, a suicidal pace over a challenging course, and I was alone. My eyes watered. I tried to keep from rubbing them. Doubts arose, and I struggled to stave off failure.

I wove, struggling to follow the painted arrows that grew ever more obscure. I needed Victory, but I was too far from his home. Salty sweat flowed into my eyes. I rubbed them and glanced back, a strategic mistake. To runners behind me, I was ringing the dinner bell, announcing myself as the main course.

I made out four runners. Two of the blurry figures wore Rockside colors: the Cowler boys. I suspected the others were Ace and a buddy.

"Come on, Ace! Pass him!" the crowd shouted. I dug deep into my reserves, trying to hold them off. As I neared the finish, the crowd closed in tighter, helping outline the course, keeping me on track. *Where's the finish line?*

I heard footsteps! Panic overwhelmed me. Everything changed to slow motion as my peripheral vision disappeared. White spots appeared. My strides up and down were in a slow, rocking motion. Spectators were a sea of faces like waves off the bow of a battered vessel. Voices reverberated in my head the way screams echo in a tunnel. Driving my arms and legs, my muscles tightened with each stride. I looked left, then right, veering each way, seeing shadowy movement. Two runners on each side inched up, their arms brushing mine. *A few more strides! This must be the finish!* I thrust myself forward as if diving headlong in a final lunge for victory!

The ground was hard! I scrunched into a fetal position as the others swept over me, sprawling past the line, our bodies entangled in a heap of sweating flesh. Spectators gasped! Officials shouted! The Haybury coach screamed for my disqualification!

Two officials lifted me, and a third placed a popsicle stick in my hand, telling my place at the finish. I gripped it and stumbled through the finish chute, collapsing off to the side. Above the din of bedlam was the furious voice of the Haybury coach, shouting at the officials. "DQ him! He's blind as a bat! He's a hazard! DQ Billy Cline!"

Jenny approached as I lay face down on the ground, lungs heaving, eyes closed. "Turn onto your back, Billy!" she shouted. She helped turn me over and placed a cold, dripping washcloth over my eyes, "You did it! First place!"

The officials conferred, concerned with my condition, but made no disqualification.

"I'll file a petition if you don't do something!" the Haybury coach shouted.

Ace Makowski, along with his girlfriend, Deucey, walked to Jenny and me. Deucey wore her own jersey with a huge "2" written on it. Ace had blood dripping down his face from the fall. He stood over me and put his foot on my chest, raising his arms and showing off his biceps like a conqueror. Deucey grinned while Haybury fans laughed, giving partial approval.

"Get your foot off him!" Jenny shouted as she shoved his leg aside. "Look at your face, Ace! You got thumped!" Ace squinted through his swollen cheek and frowned. "And Deucey, your face is Halloween-ready!"

Deucey came to Ace's defense. "My Ace will never lose to your boyfriend who lays there like a scorpion in the dirt. My Ace is number one. You best remember that, Queen Ugly!" Jenny and Deucey exchanged heated glares.

"Pardon me," Ace said, bending over to view my face. "I didn't think you were a serious threat. Next time, I'll run you into the ground before you reach the finish line!"

Jimmy Jack walked up, viewing Ace. "Get used to the runner-up spot, loser!" Ace stared at Jimmy Jack, then shoved him in the chest and walked away. "Come on back!" Jimmy Jack challenged, but Ace wouldn't bite. "That's what I thought!"

I sat up, still dizzy, as Jimmy Jack tapped Jenny on the shoulder. "Hey, Jenny, why don't you come sit with me a spell? Billy's all dirty and sweaty." Jenny didn't budge, so Jimmy Jack walked away.

When I removed the washcloth, everything wound around in a swirling blur. My thoughts moved to Tom's plight. "Where's Tom?" I asked.

"I haven't seen him." Jenny looked at the runners walking through the chute. "Tom hasn't finished."

I lowered my head. In pursuit of winning this race, I had destroyed the race of my best friend and ally, the one who'd pushed the early pace and guided me into the lead because I'd asked him. *What would I say to him? What could I say to him?*

Chapter 18

Eagle Report and Coach's Confrontation

In the science classroom at Rockside, Ms. Fry stood behind the podium as students filed in. "Since some students require help with their reports, you may sit where you like for the next few days."

Tom sat in the front seat of the middle row, with Jenny behind him and me behind her. Darla sat in the back seat of the far row, massaging Jimmy Jack's shoulders. Cletus walked in through the front side door. Moving down our aisle, he bumped into Tom and scowled as he walked behind me and sat beside his girlfriend, Patty.

As soon as Cletus sat, Patty's lips moved. "Cletus, honey, do you like my new sweater? I shopped at three stores and decided on this turquoise one. I got it on sale at…oh, what was the name of that store? It's on that street with the big sign that flashes. You know, uh, oh, yeah, at…"

"Shush!" Cletus said. He seemed angry, and I knew why. I also understood why people called his girlfriend "Chatty Patty."

"Well," she continued, "you could have given me a hint so I knew you were in a…" The tardy bell cut off Patty's words. "Bad mood."

Ms. Fry began class. "Billy Cline will give the first report. Remember, keep to the facts…and be brief. The class may ask relevant questions only. Okay, Billy."

She stepped aside with her gradebook as I worked my way to the podium. I nodded to Tom, who turned on two huge fans placed on the floor. Both fans generated powerful gusts, causing general pandemonium as papers, pens, and cosmetic supplies rolled off school desks. Girls held their hair in place and their dresses down.

"You have just experienced the wind an eagle feels as it soars," I said, motioning for Tom to turn off the fans.

"Glad that's over," said one girl, joining others who gathered their belongings.

"The bald eagle is our national symbol, but also a bird of prey with a wingspan of up to seven feet. A bald eagle can see a fish on the surface of a lake from a mile away and dive a hundred miles per hour to snatch it with its talons."

"You're sayin' they get what they want, right?" Cletus asked.

"Sometimes. An eagle's eye is the size of ours but with four times sharper vision. Its eyelids close during sleep, but an inner clear eyelid blinks…every four seconds."

Jimmy Jack raised his hand for a question. Jenny and the class followed the teacher's eyes and turned around to observe. "When I see a pretty girl, I wink. Isn't a wink like a blink?" Before I could answer, he winked at Jenny. Darla realized the shock on girls' faces so she dropped her hands off his shoulders. During the pause, the class turned to watch Jenny, who stared straight back at Jimmy Jack, eyes wide open, not blinking.

"Only if a pretty girl winks back!" I said. Jenny turned quickly and winked at me. I smiled as many in the class chuckled. Darla pushed her chair back as Jimmy Jack slouched in his seat.

"All right, class," Ms. Fry said with a moan.

"Eagles have a translucent nictitating membrane that slides over the eye, wiping away dust and dirt from the cornea. What do you have, Jimmy Jack?"

"No puffed-out cornea like you, buzzard boy." Snickers erupted, and classmates turned from Jimmy Jack to me.

"That's enough. Questions only."

"Sorry, Ms. Fry," I said. "Bald eagles try to avoid sub-humans like Jimmy Jack who cause them stress, affecting their health, feeding, roosting, nesting, and survival. But, after I saved Victory from that storm five years ago, my eagle now lands on a T-Cross perch that my Pa and I raised near his old nest tree. You all remember that storm—it flattened barns and damaged your homes."

My classmates nodded, recalling that awful day.

"US Fish and Wildlife officers cared for my eagle. They fed him for many weeks, using an eagle puppet to offer pieces of fish to him. This prevented him from being 'imprinted,' which can happen if an eagle depends on humans for food. Imprinting will destroy an eagle's chances of learning to hunt on its own. If that happens, releasing an eagle back into the wild may cause him to die."

The class buzzed with this new information.

An office aide entered the room with a note, handing it to Ms. Fry.

Jimmy Jack raised his hand for another question, gazing at Ms. Fry for approval. She nodded and then skimmed the note.

"So your eagle hangs out with you? I thought there was a fine for messin' with eagles."

"A big fine," I said, "and up to a year in prison for trapping, injuring, annoying, or pursuing a bald eagle."

Ms. Fry conferred with the office aide, so Jimmy Jack continued. "Well, then…why aren't you behind bars…like your big brother, Jake, should be?"

"Jimmy Jack!" Ms. Fry said, her stern eyes peering over her glasses.

I resisted charging him. "It's all right, Ms. Fry," I said, trying to cool off. "I'll answer his question. The reason I'm not behind bars is that I saved my eagle from certain death! Victory pursues me. Do you understand that? Victory is wild, yet he still pursues me!" A pause followed as the class glanced at each of us.

The teacher looked at the clock. "Okay, then. Nice report, Billy, and congratulations are in order. You won a race Saturday? Is that right? You won a medal?" Jenny and a few students clapped as Cletus and Jimmy Jack glared at me.

Cletus suddenly dropped his science book to the floor with a thud. In the silence that followed, Ms. Fry, appearing ready to dish out discipline, looked at him for an explanation.

"Uh, sorry, Ms. Fry," Cletus said, picking up the book. "They held Jimmy Jack out of that race. He's still undefeated. And, those race results…well…they're still in question. Billy may face disqualification."

"Competition can settle a host of problems. Oh, Billy, Coach Clausen wants to see you in his office…right away." Surprised, I took the note Ms. Fry handed me. *Why would Coach want to see me? It wouldn't be for a congratulatory handshake.* Jenny looked puzzled. Jimmy Jack and Cletus smiled.

I walked down the empty hallway with dread. I couldn't imagine any good news coming from this visit.

After knocking, I entered the hallowed shrine of Coach Clausen's office as he hung up the phone. Coach rose and offered me a seat. I gazed at the bear hide covering one wall, the deer head on a second, and the buffalo head mounted on the third wall. The final piece from the overworked taxidermist was a large, black, stuffed raven that sat on a bust of Pallas over his office door. Everyone in school had read the poem "The Raven" by Edgar Allan Poe. Many of my classmates could quote parts.

Behind his desk chair, shelves housed many of his runner's trophies that he kept for safekeeping. I saw his sharpshooter patch from the NRA beside the nameplate on his desk. As I sat, Coach Clausen pushed his chair back so he could stand to circle his office. Was I being stalked? I felt as if I were in a tomb along with those animals, whose severed heads faced me.

"I got off the phone with Dr. Chu, your eye doctor."

"She's my ophthalmologist. Why did you call her?"

"She confirmed that with your present glasses, you are legally blind. Let me see the medal?" He looked down at me from his standing position as I handed it to him.

"What do you mean, legally blind?"

"Doesn't matter. That's unacceptable for my team!" Coach walked the room with gusto. "Let's review your last race, shall we? You and Tom go out blazin' fast, side by side. At 2.5 miles, Tom blows up! You finished like a runnin' drunk! You couldn't stay on course."

He circled again as I twisted in my chair, watching him raise his hands. "Now, the Haybury coach has filed a petition sayin' that Tom paces you! Our whole team could face disqualification! And you know what that means, don't you?"

I shrugged.

"That means that Jimmy Jack's chance for a conference title could be in jeopardy!"

"Since when is runnin' beside a teammate illegal?"

Coach whirled to answer. "Since you're a hazard without him! Somehow, conference officials got copies of your medical file." Clausen cleared his throat. "A select committee from the conference has already met and voted to ban you, as of now, based on that evidence."

"What evidence? Somehow got copies of my medical file? Somehow? A select committee? What select committee?"

"You can appeal, but I'm not riskin' our eligibility for you. And the conference president told me to confiscate this medal and give it to its rightful winner, Ace Makowski."

"My Pa will have somethin' to say!"

No longer pacing, Clausen sat. "I saw your Pa out drinkin' the other night. He's as gutless now as he was in high school."

"What are you sayin' about my Pa?"

"Why don't ya ask him?" Clausen challenged.

"I'll prove what I can do."

"Prove what? That you can't see? I've got the doctor's report right here!" Clausen slammed the report onto his desk. "Somebody sent it here. This report is reality, eagle boy! You think I'm throwin' curves here?"

"I'll hit any pitch you throw!"

Coach Clausen took a deep breath and shrugged. "Oh, Billy... Billy...I thought it was you Clines who threw the beanball pitches."

I was silent, the reference to Jake twisting my insides. I wanted to rip through his barbed-wire rhetoric, but I feared being kicked off the team.

"Okay, I'll let ya up to bat. Cover all my bases...you run. Make one out...you're done."

"Pitch it!"

Clausen rose, leaned over his desk, and fired off his list. "First base: get your eye doctor to certify you fit to run. She hasn't! Second base: prove you can run the course alone. You can't! Third base: get your Pa to sign this liability release. He'll never do it! And, to run Saturday, two-thirds of the coaches must vote you in before race time. Fat chance! You are outta here!" He thrust his right thumb over his ear like an umpire making a call at home plate.

Clausen dropped to his chair as a calloused coldness covered his face. Coach had me by the throat. Though verbally suffocating, I was far from dead. Poetic justice rattled at lightning speed into my never-die mind. For a silent moment with my eyes closed, a scene I envisioned whirled inside my head:

> *"I'll cover your bases! I'm ready to soar!"*
> *I plucked the release and walked to the door.*
> *While grabbing the knob, the paper it tore,*
> *So I spun around nimbly and opened his door.*
> *With neck veins bulging, coach rose with a roar,*
> *His chair bounding airborne, trophies fell to the floor.*
> *Inspired, yet gently, I closed his door,*
> *Below the Raven, saying, "Nevermore."*
> *The school bell rang and the words he swore,*
> *Remained entombed forevermore.*

CHAPTER 19

"Cover My Bases" Speech Played Out

Tom and Jenny joined Ma and me as we entered Rockside's Gorman Hospital. Ma approached the receptionist's counter to sign me in. There was Sally Grundman again, her beehive hairdo spiraling upward, inches below the dangling sign.

"So Ma Cline is back, huh? Gonna check yourself in this time?" said Sally.

"It's Lily Cline," Ma said.

"And Billy will visit the ophthalmologist?"

"You must be psychic." Ma wrote my name on the appointment ledger. "We'll just take a seat until Dr. Chu calls us."

"You'll do no such thing!" Sally said. "You march yourself outta my hospital lobby and use Dr. Chu's waiting room!"

"You'd better watch yourself," Ma said. "I'll turn you upside down and use that beehive of yours like a bottle brush to clean the Rockside Park latrines!"

Sally's face reddened in anger as she grabbed her phone.

Ma continued, "And don't you dare think about callin' security! Those security fellas consider themselves friends of a family!"

Sally slammed the phone down and huffed.

"We're leavin', so don't you worry," Ma said. I couldn't help but smile as we paraded through the lobby with some adults unable to hide their grins.

"Ma, I didn't know the security officers were friends of the family."

"I didn't say what family they were friends of." Ma grinned, and Tom and Jenny laughed.

The ophthalmologist's office was down the hospital hall. I recalled my previous appointment. Tests would determine if my keratoconus had worsened. I thought about the grilling from Coach Clausen. I couldn't believe a select committee could commandeer my medical report without my parents' consent. *Who released it? What did this committee find that killed my opportunity to run for the championship?*

I had confessed to Dr. Chu of eye irritation and that I sometimes rubbed my eyes, making my vision worse. I admitted I didn't see obstacles well, which led me to take more falls than my teammates. So, what? I was here, free from injury. *What if I was clumsy? Would that eliminate my chance to run?* The committee's logic failed.

During my previous appointment, a nurse had ushered me to a device called a Placido's Disk.

"It's marked with concentric circles," she had said. "The lighted rings project onto your cornea, letting us evaluate its curvature." I had followed every instruction, all the while wondering if my dreams, like those concentric circles, were swirling down the drain of lost opportunity. I prepared to receive what I expected would be the devastating results.

The four of us traipsed through the door to Dr. Chu's office and received her greeting. I assured her I wanted my friends here. She pulled out what appeared to be the same report Coach Clausen had plopped onto his desk. *There must be a mole around here.*

"Billy's cornea is thin and cone-shaped," Dr. Chu told Ma. "The irregularities on his cornea cause him irritation and blurring, especially when he rubs his eyes."

What else is new?

"Keratoconus can progress at different rates. Sometimes it will stop progressing. We don't know why. Billy's keratoconus has worsened. He has considerable scarring on the cornea that may be irreversible. Contacts would be painful." During the pause, my heart sank. "Mrs. Cline, your son will need a corneal transplant if he expects to have clear vision."

I jerked up from my chair and spun toward the door, placing both hands on it for support. Jenny and Tom stayed in their chairs, speechless.

"We don't have insurance, Dr. Chu," Ma said. "My husband just lost his job. We can't even pay for new glasses."

Hearing Ma's words pained me. The bills for Jake were piling up, and now the ophthalmologist said I needed surgery. Pa was drinking more than ever. He had picked up a few handyman-type jobs that paid cash, but they only provided enough food to keep our stomachs from grumbling and to support his drinking habit.

I often said a few prayers when Pa drove us to school with a hangover. I hoped he'd sober up enough to drive safely and have enough money for gas.

Standing at the door, I kept hearing her words: *Your son will need a corneal transplant.*

Jenny spoke up: "But, Dr. Chu, can't you give us some good news?" Her buoyancy shocked us all.

"I can," Dr. Chu said. "You know, it's not like I don't read the *Rockside Bugle*. I've been following your races, Billy, hoping you can achieve success before your condition makes it impossible."

"But we can't afford new glasses," Ma said.

"Mrs. Cline, someone already prepaid for a new pair of glasses for Billy." Dr. Chu held up the bill, stamped "Paid in full." We all stared.

"We have changed your prescription enough to clear you for this race. But understand, we can't do it again. You are at the limit. We will have a pair ready by mid-week."

Tom gave a sigh of relief.

"Unbelievable," Jenny said with a smile, "and I'm sure he'll want the same frames he's wearing now. It's cheaper and he's kind of boring about that, Doc!"

"No problem," said Dr. Chu. "You need to thank Pop O'Reilly, a most persuasive man. I signed a statement saying that, in my professional opinion, with these new glasses, you are qualified to race in the cross-country championship this Saturday. Mr. O'Reilly gave me the addresses and I sent my note to each conference coach. Good luck in Saturday's race!"

"But Dr. Chu, my coach said I was out of the race because you said I was 'legally blind.'"

"Yes, Billy, when Coach Clausen called and asked, I said yes, without correction. But as I state in my letter, you are qualified to run. The stipulation is you run with the new glasses."

"Well, well," said Ma. "So you never sent his medical history report to anyone?"

"No, I never received a certified medical request nor would I ever send out his private medical history in such an illegal manner."

Ma twisted in her chair. She pulled a Spalding baseball from her purse and worked it in her hands. "Could someone have gotten access to his file?" Ma demanded.

"No," Dr. Chu said. "I lock my office, except for our cleaning lady. You might know her...Sally Grundman, the new receptionist."

"If that don't beat the drum," muttered Ma. She dug her finger-nails into her baseball.

As Ma walked up to thank Dr. Chu, Jenny gave me a long hug. Tom, gazing at us, said, "Looks like you're on...uh...first base."

*****

On Wednesday afternoon, I stretched beside Tom. This was the day Coach had planned for me to run the course alone. This was also the day my new glasses would arrive.

"Why are you stretching over there?" I said to my teammates. "You can't catch keratoconus." They laughed as Coach Clausen drove his bright red truck to the starting line. There was a gun rack mounted in the back window. Clausen braked to a stop and stepped out, gripping onto his .32-caliber starter's pistol.

"All you sons-of-guns get a break today!" he said. "After you're stretched, take the easy two-mile loop back to school. I want you rested for Saturday's championship!"

Cletus piped in, "Hey, Billy, don't make us send out a search party!" The squad was entertained as Jenny arrived with eyeglasses in hand.

"They were just delivered," she said. I reached for the glasses, noticing the team staring at her.

"His last-chance glasses!" Gopher said. That brought a few chuckles, but I didn't care. I needed clarity to run this course alone. Taking off my old glasses, everything I saw was indistinct. When I put on my new ones, the sharpness of vision improved. Though far from clear, sort of blurry was better than quite fuzzy.

As Coach loaded several blanks into his starter pistol, Jimmy Jack questioned me. "How can you tell which pair is new?"

"By one look through the lenses," I said, glancing at the pistol. *Is a starter pistol necessary for one runner? I wonder if he'll try to DQ me for a false start?* While stepping to the line, I noticed the colors of fall leaves reflecting the sun's rays. Individual leaves now stood out instead of the usual blurry splotches of color. Pent-up anxiety drove my pounding pulse. As I waited for Clausen's remarks, Jimmy Jack put his hand on Jenny's shoulder and whispered in her ear.

Coach gave his ultimatum. "Billy, prove you can run this course alone...without Tom. This is a time trial."

As he raised his pistol skyward, a shriek came from overhead. Victory soared over us. When I gave my rendition of an eagle shriek, the team laughed, directing attention to the annoyed look on Clausen's face.

"Are you kidding me?" Clausen bellowed. He fired his pistol and punched his stopwatch.

No wonder Coach Clausen calls this a trial. He will be the prosecuting attorney, the jury, and the judge all rolled into one.

*****

Sprinting away, I glanced at Coach Clausen, who took a short-cut toward Suicide Plunge. Tom accompanied him as a witness, just as he said he would. I knew Coach would observe my progress from the most useful positions. If I fell or had the least bit of trouble, he could testify of the catastrophic results.

I figured the Rockside team would follow Coach's advice and jog back to school. However, I knew Jenny wouldn't. I suspected that Jimmy Jack wouldn't either. He had a stake in the outcome: to make sure I failed. But his hands were now tied. Success or failure lay in how I managed myself in this unique trial.

Though focusing on the rigorous course, I wondered if Jimmy Jack would try to make a move on Jenny. *What if I fail? What will I do? Will she stay true? Doubts! Dismiss them! Jenny promised to tell me every detail that happened once I finished the trial. And she emphasized that my trial race would succeed. Who could argue with that?*

*****

Jimmy Jack and Jenny stood beside Coach's truck. Jimmy Jack climbed inside and turned the keys, hearing the radio blast a song.

"I wanna dance," Jimmy Jack said. He slid out of the truck into Jenny's arms and danced despite Lesley Gore's words in the song: "You Don't Own Me."

As the song continued, Jimmy Jack smiled, giving Jenny the opportunity to make a better choice—himself. She had decided not to resist him as they danced. Perhaps curiosity drove her to discover how she felt in Jimmy Jack's arms compared to mine. Whatever the reason, Jimmy Jack used his advantage and pressed for Jenny to give him a commitment.

"I'm the emcee this year for the talent show at the Moo Festival." He played off the words of the song without a sliver of embarrassment. Holding her close, he declared, "I could own you, if you let go of your lost cause—that loser running the course now. I would crown you my queen in front of the student body and the entire community. And if you wore the blue-sequined dress I purchased for you, I guarantee you would not only win the singing competition, but also be declared the most beautiful girl in Rockside, along with winning the trophy and the prestige that goes with being the 'Queen of the MOO Festival.'"

As the music and Jimmy Jack heated up, Jenny pushed back. "My heart's my own! It's not for sale!" She dashed away toward the finish line as Jimmy Jack stood silent before turning to jog the short loop back to school.

*****

I ran across the beginning flats and down Suicide Plunge into Death Valley. Victory shrieked, guiding me, sometimes with his body, sometimes with his shadow. I weaved through the lower flats and onto one of three log-planks placed over the rapids, then past the sideless bridge.

As I neared the backside of Death Valley, Victory swept over me, angling his flight pattern to the side above a steep, grassy hill. I glanced over my shoulder to follow his movement. On top of the side hill stood a huge oak tree that grew beside a big, white, wooden cross the town had erected for Easter sunrise services. Victory circled the cross, then landed on the tip of the cross beam. What a sight! I had never seen Victory land on it before. I had mere seconds to enjoy it until my concentration reverted to choosing my foot placement out of Death Valley.

Driving my arms, I forced my knees to lift higher to power up the trail. Reaching the crest, I viewed the three-hundred-yard open field. Victory again soared above. His shadow flashed in front of me before sweeping upward to gain altitude. He was circling for a final pass.

My breathing was rhythmic, my heartbeat steady, but my vision deteriorated as sweat dripped from my forehead into my eyes. I wanted to rub them but resisted, knowing one mistake from a loss of clarity could cause me to twist an ankle or take a fall and, thus, fail to finish. The discomfort sent my thoughts spinning to the negative. Doubts resurfaced.

In my mind, I could hear Ma's pleading cry: *Help your brother.*

Rawley Cowler's stern voice: *You're too slow, boy.*

Jake's lament from his quivering body: *It's…up to…you.*

Ma's gut-wrenching accusation: *Why didn't Billy warn us in time?*

Fatigue swept through me as I dwelt on those memories. My legs grew heavy. The weight of regret bound me in anxiety that weakened my form, forcing my rhythmic strides out of sync.

As I approached the final path between the two rows that marked the course boundary, there stood Jenny, her arms waving, her confidence filling me with belief, fueled by her joy for my efforts.

Victory made a pass above me. I exchanged dark ribbons of doubt for the bright-colored streamers of success that waved over the last hundred yards. I imagined a crowd cheering. Jenny's confidence in me had delivered a sense of worthiness, not only in completing the trial but also of her feelings for me.

"Wooo-eeee!" I yelled, crossing the finish line. Victory shrieked—the final stamp of approval!

Coach Clausen clicked his stopwatch. Jenny ran to him and waited with an expectant look. "He made it, didn't he?"

Clausen's words were emotionless, mechanical. "He passed, with the buzzard's help."

"He's an eagle, sir," Jenny said.

Gasping for air, I knew I had run a fast trial. My thoughts turned to Jake. I remembered running to my big brother when he'd pitched his one-hitter. I imagined him running to congratulate me for conquering the course.

But that could never happen. Not now. Jake couldn't run! Reality struck. Despite my success, sadness for Jake entered my thoughts; the discomfort transferred to my eyes in the form of tears. I tried to rub them away to banish them. However, the blurriness from that act set in motion a painful recovery. The pressure to cross the finish line had drained my physical and mental reserves.

Clausen huffed and looked at Tom. "Give him this non-torn release form."

"He's already got one," Tom said.

Clausen walked to his truck. "Fly Like an Eagle" blasted from the speakers. He turned off the radio in disgust.

Beside Coach's open window, Jenny held out a piece of bubblegum. "Hubba Bubba, Coach?"

Clausen ignored her and fired up the engine, leaving a swirling cloud of dust.

"Well!" Jenny said with an edgy voice. She popped the gum into her mouth, smiled, and strode toward me.

"Two down!" said Tom. "Three days till race day!"

Jenny handed me a wet washcloth. "You're on second base, Billy!"

"Hurry," said Tom. "You're meetin' your Ma at the hospital! Remember?" Jenny and Tom guided me to the Beauty. After climbing in, Tom took off the same way, kicking up dust.

CHAPTER 20

Pa's Confession

Tom and Jenny walked beside me. Jenny's fingers intertwined with mine as we entered the hospital lobby and met Ma. My eyes were itching and red, despite the cool washcloth I had placed over them on the drive here.

Ma stood in the lobby, facing three little girls in red, yellow, and pink polka-dot dresses. The girls stood wide-eyed near a couch, smiling. Ma tossed her rubber baseball three feet into the air with her right hand and waited till the last split-second to twist her left hand and catch it backhanded. She whipped one hand behind her back and slapped the baseball into the other hand. She repeated the move, increasing the speed, much to the delight of the girls. After more dazzling displays of dexterity, I imagined Ma's sassy smile meeting Sally's frown of derision at the lobby counter.

When we approached, Ma tossed me the rubber baseball. I raised my hands to catch it, but it glanced off my fingertips.

"Are you sure you're part of this family?" Ma said, as Tom and Jenny laughed.

"I just finished my time trial," I said, fishing for an excuse.

"I know you made it, 'cause you're a Cline. Am I right?"

"Boy, did he ever make it!" Jenny said.

One of the little girls had run to get the ball and giggled as she returned it to Ma.

"Thank you, dear." As the three of us walked to the counter, I saw Sally Grundman push the security button on the phone, then focused her eyes on me.

"You, boy, look like you fell off a mountain! Did ya lose your other friends?"

I remembered the disabled boys Pop O'Reilly had brought in from Cliffview Boys' Home. "No, ma'am, I don't know them. You know them better than I do from their check-ups."

"Pardon me, then. Are you checking in to join your brother in rehabilitation? Cause you look like you could use it."

"Hey, Sally…Sally Grundman. You ever been in a hospital?" Ma asked, gazing at her oversized name tag.

"As a patient?"

"Yep, as a patient."

"No, only as a receptionist."

"And a cleaning lady for Dr. Chu, right?"

"Well, uh…"

"But, as a receptionist, you know how to receive receptions? Try receiving this one!"

Ma cocked her arm, preparing to fire a fastball with her rubber baseball.

A faint "No!" came from Sally's lips as she dropped behind the counter. I reacted with a shocked look, but it was unnecessary. Ma had already relaxed, uncocked her arm, and winked at the children as we left the registration area.

"I'm just tryin' to smooth out her attitude," Ma muttered with a sheepish smile. "A fastball down the pipe would'a done her some good, though."

I turned back and saw Sally's eyes peeking over the countertop.

"We know this place!" Ma said without looking back.

Dave, one of the security officers, came rushing into the lobby.

Sally hollered to the officer. "Dave, aren't you gonna say somethin' to those Clines?"

Dave looked puzzled and hollered, "Have a nice day!"

Sally slammed the sign-up clipboard onto the counter, glaring at Dave as we left, chuckling.

"I'm thinkin' about quittin' this job and goin' back to beauty school! What do you think about that?"

"Sounds like a wonderful idea," Dave said.

We laughed again, walking through the automatic doors.

When we arrived at Jake's room, Tom and Jenny said their good-byes and left the hospital for their homes. Ma took a deep breath and knocked on the door.

"Come in," Jake said. Ma pushed the door open. "Ma! Billy!" Jake's voice rose. He motioned us to his chair. "It's so good to see you."

Ma bent and kissed his cheek.

"Hi, Jake. You're looking good," I said, giving him a gentle hug.

Ma held out her rubber baseball for Jake. "Maybe this'll bring back good memories." She tried to put the rubber baseball into Jake's hand, but the splint on his thumb prevented him from gripping the ball.

"Sorry…Ma," Jake said. "Can't do much till this splint comes off. I jammed it when I fell in therapy the other day."

"Remember when those scouts were havin' a look-see at your rip-snortin' fastball?"

"I remember, Ma."

"The Hogs were at bat, and that fella came in to pinch run."

"And he lost his shoe when I picked him off!" said Jake with a burst of laughter. "He sat on the first base bag trying to put it back on and then tipped over." We all joined in the laughter, but Ma became quiet.

"I'm so sorry, Jake. Somehow, I thought your hands could… you know…remember the feel of the ball." Ma leaned over Jake, giving a hug while Jake looked at me. For what? Advice? Words abandoned me.

Ma spoke up. "I'll be here for you, Jake. No matter how long it takes. We're family." I knew we were three-fifths of a family now and could unite someday.

After some small talk, Jake raised a hand and pointed to his bedside table and an envelope. He picked up a pen, holding it between his fingers and the splint. He printed with capital letters BLIMP. It looked like second grade printing. Jake struggled, but picked up the letter before handing it to Ma.

"You want me to give this to Blimp?" she asked.

Jake nodded.

"May I read it?"

Jake nodded again.

Ma opened the unsealed letter and saw the same awkward letters printed on the inside page. She read out loud: "To Blimp, I'm sorry. I was wrong to throw at you. I am paying the price. Please forgive me. Jake."

Ma struggled to complete the reading. She turned away and stopped in silence.

"Will you and Pa deliver it?"

Ma hesitated, turned back with a decisive look, and nodded.

*****

On the drive home, Ma and I passed Pop standing beside his school van parked in a turnout a mile from our cabin. Ma honked her horn and Pop waved as we passed. I held on to the liability release that Pa must sign. Ma held onto Jake's note to Blimp. Arriving, Ma parked farther than usual from the cabin. We saw Pa toting two jugs inside. He stood, staring at us from the front door, holding the screen door open with his foot. Five jugs remained on the porch.

"I'm not walkin' in when he's drunk," Ma said. "I asked Pop to come this afternoon. Pa respects him. Go in. Pop'll be here soon."

I stepped out, holding the release form. Pa swung two more jugs inside onto the floor but returned to the porch, still watching us. I figured they'd had words earlier. As I walked up, Pa stared at Ma, who still sat in the pickup. Ma turned away as Pa spat a dark stream into the dirt before moving inside the cabin.

"Been runnin'?" He slurred as I reached for the screen door. He staggered, lifting one of his jugs to open. I walked in, let the screen door slam, and saw an empty jug on its side near the hearth.

"Get over…the light!" Pa commanded, his strident voice punctuating the silence. He put his jug on the hearth and kicked the empty one, watching it slide across the floor. He moved to the window, his back to the glass. I faced Pa and the window behind him. He took my glasses off and pushed my eyelids open with his thumbs.

169

I could smell the foul stench of moonshine as his bloodshot eyes examined mine.

"Worse 'n' ever!" Pa said. When he stepped away from the window to retrieve his jug, I watched Pop's school van in the distance pull up beside our pickup. "How can ya run?" Pa asked as he stomped across the cabin floor toward his chair.

"With new glasses," I said, feeling enthusiastic. "Coach said…"

"Clausen!" Pa interrupted. "Can't believe I let ya run under that lyin' cheat!" Pa stumbled, holding onto his chair for balance. He turned, "He's setting you up to feel the pain I felt in '64 and Matt Centrowitz felt in 1980 before the Olympics! They sabotaged me from winning the 5K in Rockside and denied Centrowitz from competing for the 5,000 meter gold by the Moscow boycott. No championship honor for me and no Olympic honor ever for Matt Centrowitz!" Pa fell back into his chair, reminiscing. "Honor's gone with the shove of an arm or the stroke of a President's pen! I know!" Pa settled, taking a sloppy drink.

"I sat behind Cale Clausen for years…ya know…alphabetical seating. Running as a senior, I ran behind him, but I was getting closer in each race leading to the championship." Pa lifted the rim to his lips and took a swig as I sat on one end of the couch.

"Guess who coached us? Pop O'Reilly! Demanding, no-nonsense! Two races before the championship, Clausen hid in the bushes, cut a short loop off the course, and then lied. Pop considered giving him the boot. Clausen demanded we all quit if Pop punished him! I refused to quit for him over his act of dishonor. Pop held him out of the next race but showed mercy when he confessed. Later, Clausen called me a…a gutless coward."

"They were the gutless ones, Pa."

That memory etched a painful path across Pa's face. Pa snorted another drink when Pop O'Reilly arrived on the porch unseen, outside the screen door. I saw Ma peek in, too, and knew she and Pop could see Pa's hopeless state. Pop raised his hand to knock but hesitated when Pa's words penetrated the core of his heart.

"Months later, the night before New Year's Eve, Pop's house caught fire: an explosion! Flames shot up! His little girl hid in her upstairs closet. Pop fought through those flames! You've seen the scars on his arms! When he found her..." Pa paused, "it burned half her little body! When he carried her down a ladder, flames rose from his own shirt sleeves. He hovered over her...and wailed!" Pa gave a horrendous sigh, gripping his jug for another swig, but it slipped from his fingers and sloshed onto the cabin floor as he cried, "I know!"

My eyes fell onto Pop outside the screen door, grasping the doorframe, his body shaking as brutal memories rushed back to wound him. He placed his hand to his shirt pocket and pulled out a worn photograph. He drew his sleeve across a wet cheek as he gazed at the wrinkled photo.

My eyes swung back to Pa, who yelled, "She died in his arms! Why? Pop couldn't teach! He went around town askin' if he'd wronged anyone...didn't want no guilty conscience...would confess, but...nobody came up with a thing!"

"He come to you?" I asked.

Pa gazed into the fireplace. "He said he was...sorry for not showin' more love...that I had stood behind him. He thanked me, said God would honor me if I honored God. I ain't got no honor! The town got Pop his school! Clausen got to coach! I got this!" Pa struggled to stand but lifted his jug and shattered it into the stone fireplace.

Fire flared out as Pop thrust open the screen door and burst into the cabin. The screen door slammed, and Pa spun around.

"No honor?" Pop shouted, drawing closer. I gazed at Pop's gleaming eyes, the sudden burst of firelight reflecting off them, mocking him like the flames from that horrible night.

Pa turned, "Pop! I saw the two boys who set off fireworks on your porch! When I heard 'em talkin'...how they'd fix you...how they'd hurt Lily...and how they'd burn our Ruby Lake land if I told what they did, I fell mute! And I didn't stop 'em! The flames...why didn't I cry out and warn you? I killed little Rachel!" Pa dropped to his knees.

Pop's lips quivered, his hands shook. He gripped his chest, then leaned on the couch and pulled out a nitroglycerin tablet, placing it under his tongue.

Pa looked up. "You said it was your fault: a frayed cord, a bad heater, gasoline. It wasn't. It was my fault! Those two boys are men you know, and they know I saw 'em that night!"

Pop collapsed onto the couch next to Pa, who was still kneeling. He leaned back on the couch, his chest heaving with broken sobs as Pa continued: "Rawley blames me for losing his election for sheriff… and Clausen…he…"

Pop wiped his face and turned the photo over, looking again at his lost little girl, Rachel, as flames licked the stones behind her picture. In silence, I saw Pop's expression change, altered by recurring memories, born from a living nightmare that fateful night. Gazing into the fury of the fire, Pop faced a new revelation; precious Rachel didn't have to burn. I sensed dark emotions swelling within him, trying to surface. He now had someone else to blame—my Pa.

"I suspected those two, but I couldn't accuse. But this is hard, Ned. You? You could have saved my little Rachel?"

Pop wanted to lunge forward, but the smoke of alcohol-doused logs swept over him as he dug deep, trying to fight off the rage that threatened to expunge forgiveness from his soul and move him toward hatred.

"No!" Pop yelled as he fell back on the couch. "Punishment won't bring her back! Won't change it! Only God can bring new life from her ashes."

Seconds passed by before Pop leaned forward, putting a burn-scarred hand on my Pa's shoulder. "The God I found in my darkest sorrow makes all things new. Ned, you've suffered a lifetime for a youthful mistake. You've confessed. God forgave me. I…forgive you."

Pa looked up, pleading, "I can't live without that." Pa struggled to stand and offered his hand to the calloused one of Pop O'Reilly.

The man with the photo helped lift Pa as both stood facing each other. Pop looked at Pa and uttered three words, "Your new life…" Pop wrapped his burly scarred arms around Pa. Both men shook with sobs, acknowledging the healing touch of forgiveness. Breaking their embrace, their view of each other had changed, forming a renewed and unbreakable bond.

Pop walked to the fire and gazed one more time at the photo. "It's been nineteen years, sweetie. I can look at you now and feel peace, not guilt. It wasn't my fault. Your fire has long since died, but you live on! I'll envision you not as you were, but as you are with a brand-new body!" He kissed the wrinkled photo and tossed it into the fire, watching it curl and disintegrate.

They turned toward me and my own tears flowed. "Pa, I wanna run the championship race Saturday…and show the same guts you showed when you stood up to Clausen and ran in high school." I placed the liability release in front of him.

"That's honor!" Pop said, pointing. "A son who's willing to match the guts of his father!"

Pa looked from Pop's eyes into mine, into the damaged but optimistic eyes of his middle son. He picked up the pen and signed.

The screen door creaked as Ma entered, moving toward Pa with an endearing embrace.

CHAPTER 21

Coaches Vote on Eligibility

The Rockside Cross Country course appeared as if hosting a traveling circus. Teams had erected twenty-four tents over the field, housing the different teams, who prepared to race 3.1 miles against superb competition. There were no high-tops, no giraffes or elephants, and no high-wire acts scheduled, but the mood was festive as pressure mounted for late October's championship 5K race.

A morning mist hung in the valley. Puffs of air from runners' mouths dissipated. A sign read 1983 MOUNTAIN CONFERENCE CROSS COUNTRY CHAMPIONSHIP.

The 168 competitors jogged in groups of seven, their team uniforms ablaze in color. As in the jousting tournaments of old, their colors and mascots identified rivals. Rockside's team wore black with a red horizontal stripe across the chest with RAVENS printed in bold black letters. The Haybury Hogs' uniform was dark brown with pink trim at the neck and armholes. The HOGS lettering, also in pink, was in cursive font. Some claimed if you looked hard, you could make out a tiny curly tail on their backsides. No one could mistake the blue and green plaid colors of the Highlanders or the Scottish military marches their bagpipers played.

Runners who had failed to qualify came to witness the outcome of the championship. On the field, parents, grandparents, neighbors, girlfriends, and classmates carried cameras, preparing to take snapshots for posterity.

Groups of boys wearing school colors ran in packs to invigorate their team's runners and intimidate weak-minded opponents. They waved banners and flags, calling out challenges to other schools' fans. Rockside brought a bugler for the call to the race, mimicking the Kentucky Derby.

Rockside businesses brought booths for selling burgers, corn dogs, funnel cakes, elephant ears, cotton candy, and a wild array of drinks. Others sold T-shirts, hats, and running shoes at a large discount. Sales were booming. The carnival atmosphere was contagious.

One man in a tent tried to sell bogus lakefront property. Sheriff Logan closed him down, offering him temporary jail-cell residency in Rockside.

A disc jockey doubled as the announcer while playing music that reverberated from four huge speakers. He offered continuous commentary between songs while encouraging spectators to buy food and souvenirs.

A huge contingent arrived from the number-one-ranked Haybury Hogs. The disc jockey jacked up the volume. "He's here at last, folks—the Haybury Hogs mascot—the great Hoagie!" Cheers erupted around the Haybury tent as a tractor pulled the flatbed trailer on which lay a sturdy steel cage that housed Haybury's prize-winning hog.

A group of vehicles followed, forming half circles near the Haybury tent. The Haybury coach imitated his outrageous hog call he used to win the state's hog-calling championship. That signaled Ace Makowski and his girlfriend Deucey to lead cheers around the elevated hog. They yelped their own squeals and grunts, which riled up Hoagie, sending him into a hog-wild fit.

The disc jockey, his booth beside Haybury's tent, pushed the microphone through the steel bars. Hoagie's ear-splitting grunts were too country to imitate as he tried to eat the microphone.

Rockside fans pulled beside the Haybury tent in their smaller flatbed trailer, selling "roast pig on a stick" and "pulled-down Haybury pork smothered in Rockside BBQ sauce."

I walked the grassy field with Tom and Jenny, our eyes focused on the officials' tent. Inside, coaches registered their runners and turned in ballots on whether I should compete.

Jenny seemed unnerved by the process. "This reminds me of political conventions. I can't believe you have to win a vote from the coaches before you can run a 5K race!"

We walked toward Pa, who was watching Ma and Chester play catch. Ma raised her index finger to Chester, showing she would throw her fastball. Within earshot were three high-school baseball coaches observing Ma's pitching prowess. They knew where Jake's talent had come from. She double-pumped a windup and threw a knee-high split-fingered fastball with such velocity that the first coach twirled like a spinning top when it smacked Chester's glove. He back-slapped the second coach. "She could start for your team!"

"No doubt," said the third coach, all bursting into laughter.

Ma motioned us together. Jenny handed a sign to Chester. She had drawn a caricature of Billy's face wearing glasses. Surrounding it were the words *See your way to Victory, Billy!*

"I'm very proud of you, Billy," Chester said, glancing at me.

"Make all of us Clines proud, son! Even the one who isn't here."

"I'll do my best." I looked to the sky, scanning the horizon, hoping for inspiration from above. *Where's Victory? Will he show up for the race?*

"I haven't seen him," Jenny said, reading my thoughts.

I glanced at the officials' tent and looked at Tom. "We don't have all day for them to decide. It's time for us to warm up. Jenny. I'll see you at the start. Let's go, Tom."

As we ran across the field, runners pointed at us. We'd been the focus of controversy since the last race. Haybury's coach had filed a petition for my disqualification; a committee had approved it. But, if the coaches accepted Dr. Chu's evaluation, I was a contender.

Someone sent last week's photograph of five runners lying in a heap across the finish line to each area newspaper, including the *Haybury Haymaker*. That picture included an arrow pointing at the fallen figure of Ace Makowski. They'd run a second picture showing Ace wearing a bandage on his face, standing beside Hoagie's mud pit. The caption quoted Ace: "If I can't whup this 'half-blind Cline' kid on Saturday, I'll wallow in Hoagie's mud pit Monday at school!" This quote and picture had set off a firestorm of controversy. And there was a joker in the deck since Jimmy Jack, who was undefeated, would race.

I had covered three of the four bases placed before me. First, the ophthalmologist had approved my new glasses. I could thank Dr. Chu and Pop O'Reilly for that. Second, I had proven to Coach Clausen I could run the course alone. I could thank Victory and Jenny for that. Third, I had turned in the signed liability release from my Pa. I could thank both Pop and my Pa for that. And I thanked God, too. Ma made sure.

The final base to cover was approval by at least sixteen of the twenty-four coaches. I was in my Rockside uniform, lacking only the bib racing number. Coach Clausen had left my name off the team roster but told me to suit up in case they voted me in.

Ben Grundman was not only Sally's husband, but the conference president. His assistant, Miss Harper, whom Ma knew from church, oversaw filling out the paperwork inside the officials' tent. She made sure our family knew what happened that morning.

Grundman chewed a wad of tobacco and spat the juice into a paper cup. Coach Clausen stood near the entrance, opposite the Haybury coach, who hovered over the table where Grundman's hat collected the coaches' votes. The Haybury coach paced back and forth, as if waiting for a new birth or a death sentence.

"You know about piglets, don't ya?" he said with watery eyes. "When born, they can't produce their own heat and need a temperature around ninety degrees, or they...might die. There's a cold... cold breeze this morning. It's an atmosphere more appropriate for a funeral than a race. Ya know, a committee already pronounced this half-blind Cline reject 'dead quick' when I filed my DQ petition! On this chilly morning, let's show mercy, please, and release Billy back to the mountains from whence he came. Otherwise, he'll end up like an orphan piglet, trying to be born again in this cold birthing tent. It just ain't gonna happen!"

Grundman smirked. "You Haybury fellas must know a lot about pigs and hogs."

"I know that Ace Makowski took a nasty fall last week because of Billy!" The Haybury coach turned to Coach Clausen. "And two of your Cowler boys fell, too."

Clausen adjusted his hat. "I don't care which way the vote goes." Miss Harper told us she almost fell out of her chair when she heard those words.

The final two coaches entered and dropped their ballots into the hat. "Okay," Grundman said, "that's twenty-four votes. Count 'em, Miss Harper."

Grundman dumped the ballots from his hat onto a table as Miss Harper counted, placing them in two piles. Grundman appeared shocked by the result. "Billy got...sixteen of twenty-four votes. He runs!"

The Haybury coach rushed to the table. "This appeal's a farce!" he said, slamming his Hog Heaven hat onto the ballots, scattering them. "That boy can run when pigs fly!"

"So, blame my hat!" Grundman hollered back, picking up the Haybury coach's hat by mistake while struggling to put it on. Realizing his mistake, Grundman slammed it to the tent floor. "Where in the..."

"Your language!" yelled Miss Harper, louder than she expected.

"Is my hat! Look!" Grundman said, glaring at the Haybury coach. "He was cleared by an eye doctor and the coaches! Clausen, add Billy Cline to your roster with this form. And, Miss Harper, will you please prepare Billy's bib number so he can run when you receive the form from Coach Clausen! Thank you very much for your... concern."

"You don't have to treat me special, President Grundman. I'm only trying to help with...you know."

Grundman scowled, picked up his hat, and put it on crooked. Leaving the tent, he stepped on the Hog Heaven hat he had discarded. The Haybury coach, grumbling, picked up his smashed hat and chased after Grundman.

Clausen watched them leave, took a few steps to the tent entrance, and nodded to Deputy Rawley Cowler, who walked up with a Rockside junior varsity runner. The runner turned away until Rawley's hand slammed down on his shoulder.

"Not so fast, sonny boy!"

Miss Harper saw them both give her a look that said, *Mind your own business.*

*****

Pop's retelling after that moment had an unusual twist. He had set up his students near a large tree. It was at the end of the open field, at the final turn on the course, where the colorful streamers blew in the wind, about a hundred yards from the finish line.

Pop noticed Luke's agitation as he maneuvered out of his wheelchair. He understood the grief Luke felt over losing both legs in a car accident. Luke hated being isolated. He had been a fierce competitor in football, never backing away from a challenge. Now, he worked out for hours on multiple fitness machines, trying to regain his edge.

Pop stepped to him. "Luke, someday you'll face a challenge that will take you to the limit. I know you'll be up for it. You may never score another touchdown, but I promise to get you in a competition in which you can be proud to take part."

Luke swung himself out of his wheelchair to the top of a large rock. Miscalculating his energetic swing, he slid down the other side, cutting his arm.

Coach Grundman walked by and saw Luke's slide. Grundman's mood was easy to identify by his intense expression, his herky-jerky walk, and the tone of his voice. Spitting tobacco juice and pointing to Luke, Grundman hollered to Pop. "This one of yours?"

"You bet he's one of ours."

"I suppose you want our medical help team to jump up and treat that scrape on his arm?"

"We can take care of it ourselves," Pop said. "But, since you've got an ambulance and plenty of medical personnel standing around, sure, that would be nice."

"Our medical help is for athletes, not this kind."

"He's no different from anyone else. He slipped and got hurt, that's all."

"My feet hurt, too!" Grundman said. "Nobody's comin' to offer me first aid. Why did you bring him here? He could bust another limb!"

"I don't have many limbs left, sir," Luke said, looking down at his missing legs. Grundman just huffed as Luke ignored the scrape and managed his way back into his wheelchair.

"I'll ask again, Pop," said Grundman. "Why are these kind out here?"

"We like to watch the races. Some of my kids can really run!"

"Run? Get serious...handicappers got no business out here. Harness him in...I got a real race comin'!" As Grundman left, he spat tobacco juice, just missing Luke's stumps.

"Hey, mister! Hey!" shouted Luke, as Grundman stomped off. "Never mind, Pop, I'm okay. I'm missing two limbs now, and I might lose another, but I'm not gonna sit around in a boring room all day!" Luke was quiet for a moment and then laughed with Pop at his own words.

Lizzy Looper, the blonde reporter on local TV, wrote articles for the *Rockside Bugle*. She carried a camera and approached Pop while studying the course map.

"Hey, Pop, is this a good spot?"

"Sure, who ya lookin' for?" She held up the *Rockside Bugle* with Pop O'Reilly's Letter to the Editor. Pop's headline read, '*Eagle Boy' To Fly?*'

"Billy Cline," said Lizzy. "You still think Billy can win?"

CHAPTER 22

Billy's Championship Race

October 1983

Grundman spotted me standing beside Tom in the Rockside starting zone, stretching to loosen up. He caught my eye, giving me a thumbs-up gesture.

"I'm runnin'! I'll be joining the front row."

Cletus and Jimmy Jack shook their heads. My competitive instincts were alive. All around us, runners stretched and put on analgesic balm to enhance circulation in their muscles.

Seven Haybury runners jogged by and halted in front of our starting zone. Ace spoke first. "Hey, Billy, did ya bring your cane?"

"Ya four-eyed fool," added the second Haybury runner. My teammates were silent. They looked to Jimmy Jack for a response. None came.

The third Haybury runner followed up. "Tom, you his seeing-eye dog?" All seven runners from Haybury chuckled and yelled, "Woof!" I stayed calm, ready to let my running speak.

"So, ya won your appeal, did ya?" Ace said. "Don't matter. I'm takin' this race!"

Jimmy Jack's anger boiled into words. "Look, you seven chunks of hog slop, I'm number one! Billy and his guide dog are a freak sideshow. Take you and your Haybury hogerinas outta here!"

The Haybury team jeered. Ace responded. "Jimmy Jack, you're the number-one Bozo! Me and my pack of wild hogs are comin' after you!"

"No way!" Jimmy Jack said. "Quoth the Ravens!"

"Nevermore!" shouted the Ravens.

"Sooey!" The shrill sound from the outrageous hog call made my ears tingle. The Haybury coach called to his runners, who mimicked hog grunts as they jogged to their starting zone.

The seventh Haybury Hog gave a thumbs-down gesture to Cletus and then nasaled out "Oink! Oink! Oink!"

"Come back here, Porky!" Cletus shouted.

Tom and I took a fifty-yard run-out to clear the air. "Hey, Billy, remember in the first race when Cletus sneaked an elbow into that Haybury runner's nose?" We laughed, knowing Cletus had bragged about it all the way home on the bus. "That Haybury fella might need a nose job after today's race."

Tom and I stopped our run-out when we saw Jenny standing in the field, holding what looked like my bib number.

"Thanks, Jenny!" I pinned my bib number onto my jersey.

"Miss Harper gave it, Billy. She said you got sixteen of twenty-four votes, but she's nervous, said she was sticking her neck out. There's no name on the bib number Coach Clausen gave her."

"It doesn't matter. I won the vote and my spot. I'll need to cool my eyes in a minute."

Jenny turned and ran back to the starting line. I had something else on my mind.

"Tom, I've got a real problem."

"What problem? You're runnin', man. You made it!"

"These are my old glasses."

"What? The ones you're wearin' now?" I nodded. "Where are your new ones?"

"I don't know. They were missing from my locker after I showered yesterday. My old pair was stashed in an old shoe. I'm using my old glasses with the same frames. Nobody noticed."

"Cletus!" Tom moaned, knowing how far Cletus could go, but knowing how determined I was. Tom shifted his feet, and I knew he was waiting for what I would say next.

I felt like a nagging toothache. If officials knew my glasses were not the approved ones, they could extract me from this race like an impacted molar. "I can't say a word!"

"Neither can Cletus…or he'll condemn himself."

I spun around, gazing skyward, looking for my eagle. All I could see were hazy blue skies.

"This is the championship, Tom. Will ya guide me…one more time?"

Tom kicked at a tuft of grass missed by the mower. "Billy, you promised if I did what you asked, I'd make all-conference. This is my chance. If I go out fast with you, I'll kill my race!"

Frustration sparked between us. "I know…but…" I jogged farther onto the course, stopping at a park bench, to stretch out my hamstrings and calves.

Tom's words were true. I couldn't defend myself. My request to Tom was a death sentence to his own "come from behind" strategy. I had just asked my best friend to sacrifice himself for my glory. *What kind of friend would do that? Shall I go for it without Tom and my new glasses? Shall I quit? What will Jenny say? How will Jenny feel? Where's Victory?*

After all the training runs, all the miles before school, all the sweat, all the falls, the bandages, and the challenges Coach had thrown at me, I couldn't and wouldn't give up now.

When I gazed back a hundred yards, I couldn't single out Tom nor Jenny, just a mass of runners, keeping limber. In minutes, 168 runners would storm off the line in the most important race of my life—a race I had dreamed of winning, just like Pa nineteen years ago. I had only minutes to decide.

Music blasted from the loudspeakers as vibrations created a pulsating beat.

"Okay, gang," the disc jockey announced, "WKRK plays your favorite songs for your favorite team!" Some in the crowd cheered as Ace Makowski and his girlfriend Deucey showboated with the Haybury team to the Dave Clark Five hit "Catch Me If You Can."

Just when the Haybury runners and fans thought they were in hog heaven, Jenny sprinted onto the field, disrupting the dancing circle of Haybury Hogs, and interrupted their performance by pointing to the sky. It was Victory, circling the field! The disc jockey cut the music off as he announced, "Look! Up in the sky! It's Billy's eagle!"

The crowd responded with "oohs" and "aahs." The Hogs had lost their audience and their music. Deucey gave Jenny the "stink eye."

Jenny stood alone in the middle of the field. Victory, after making a wide arc, swept over her and landed beside me on the park bench.

"Well, folks," the disc jockey said, "he ain't called the Eagle Boy for nothin'! But…wait a minute…we may have a race delay. I see a red flag where officials are conferring."

Now that she saw Victory with me, Jenny ran back to the starting line. I looked at Victory, perched on the park bench. His presence lifted my spirits, my doubts replaced by resolve.

"I wish you could understand," I said to Victory. "This is my chance to restore Pa's honor. Keep me on course. I should never have doubted that you'd be here for me." Victory shrieked.

A bugler from Rockside gave the "Call to the Post." A huge cheer erupted.

"Time to soar!" I shouted. I hot-footed my way toward the starting line as Victory lifted off, his powerful wings flapping, propelling him above me in an effortless glide.

"Let's hear it for the eagle!" said the announcer. Townspeople clapped, whooped, and hollered as I sprinted in. "I've seen everything now, folks!"

Many were still clapping as I sprinted toward the line. Jenny approached with tears in her eyes, giving a hug and kissing my cheek. "This is your day, Billy, and the crowd loves it!"

"The race is about to begin," I said as Jenny handed me a cold, dripping washcloth. I laid in front of our starting zone, the soaked cloth covering my eyes, the same eyes that needed to provide my vision through inferior lenses.

"Coach Clausen is angry and won't talk," Jenny said.

Within seconds, the race starter, using the bullhorn, gave his call to clear the course. "Non-competitors, please exit the starting line." I jumped up and tossed the washcloth to Jenny.

Three bagpipers began the drone of a Scottish military march. All family and friends of the participants left the team zones to take places behind the rainbow-colored plastic ribbons. I lined up in the front row of the Rockside zone, between Jimmy Jack and Cletus.

"What a freak stunt!" Jimmy Jack said, gazing at my "no name" bib number.

"Billy, do you like your new glasses?" Cletus taunted from my other side.

I chose silence. Tom tapped me on the shoulder from the back row and took me in front of the starting line for privacy. "Billy, I'll stay with you as long as I can—to the rapids, I hope."

"But that'll wreck your race. I don't want that…"

"It's my decision. I won't let them cheat you like they did your Pa."

I put my hand on his shoulder. "Just get me across those logs, if you can."

Just then, Grundman, Clausen, and the Cowler deputies approached. "Billy, hold on a minute," said Grundman. Rawley and Blimp grabbed my arms and walked me farther onto the course.

The long line of runners stuck their heads over the starting line, staring at us, upset about the delay. They moved from one leg to another, trying to keep their muscles loose. The official starter raised his bullhorn. "Runners, relax a minute. We have a delay." Those words caused groans from spectators and runners.

The disc jockey piped in, "Don't forget our concessions—hot dogs, burgers, chocolate bars, buttered popcorn, pork rinds, cotton candy, and RC Cola!"

Grundman gave me his decision. "Sorry, but your name is not on the official roster. Your bib number is invalid." Grundman yanked off the bib number and scrunched it in his hand.

"I'm not on the roster? I covered all the bases Coach Clausen demanded!"

Grundman led the Cowler deputies who grabbed me, escorting me away from the line. I twisted my body toward Coach Clausen to confirm I had earned my right to run. When our eyes met, Clausen turned his back and signaled the junior varsity replacement runner to our zone. He had the official bib number pinned onto his jersey. Jimmy Jack gave him a high-five, but Cletus shoved him from the front row to the second row, between Gopher and Tom. Gopher grabbed him and shoved him to the third row as Gopher moved up front.

Cletus turned to Tom. "Lose your bark?" Tom stared at the Cowler deputies holding me.

Pop and Lizzy jogged to Grundman, where Pop challenged him for an explanation.

"His coach decided!" argued Grundman. "He struck Billy from his roster!"

Lizzy added, "Your assistant, a Miss Harper, told us an eye doctor approved Billy to run and was voted in by the coaches! Many fans came here just to watch him run!"

"If he's not on the official roster, I can't let him run! We've got our rules! Now, get outta my face!" That was Grundman's speech. The Cowler deputies walked me off to the side.

Pop shook his head and hollered. "A travesty of justice!" Luke sprang out of his wheelchair, walking in circles on his hands as Pop signed to Andy and Pete.

The disc jockey, with speakers in full force, blared out the news. "It seems there is a disqualification. It's Billy Cline! We don't know why, but the Eagle Boy…is out!"

Seven drummers began a drumroll. Intensity built as the crowd, by tradition, hummed a low note played by the bagpipers that crescendoed along with the powerful drum rolls. On a boundary of the course, a mother lifted the colorful plastic ribbons and chased down her giggling little toddler who ran full speed onto the course. She caught him and lifted him up, his feet still running in air, his laughter now turning into cries of frustration as she carried him off the course, behind the barrier.

As I stood, held captive by the Cowlers, I could see Jenny standing nearby, sobbing. She turned to Darla for comfort until she read the sign Darla was holding: "Jimmy Jack don't cut no slack!" Jenny crouched, her hands covering her face. I looked to Pa and saw him holding onto Ma, keeping her from charging onto the field. Chester snapped his sign over his knee.

I glanced at my teammates. Jimmy Jack, Cletus, and Gopher were grinning. The Haybury Hogs were giving the *V* sign. My frustration grew to anger.

In a methodical voice, the starter spoke into his bullhorn. "Gentlemen...you will race 3.1 miles, a 5K. Take one step backward, please!" He waited. The runners retreated one step and checked their positions, making sure they were not impeding anyone. Drumrolls intensified. The crowd's low hum grew to a vibrant roar. A wind swept over the field as the starter continued. "On your marks!" Runners, tense with anticipation, stepped to the line. I was in disbelief.

The gun fired! The crowd roared! Tom sprinted out with Jimmy Jack and three Haybury runners. The vibration from trampling feet resembled a buffalo stampede. The crowd scattered.

I felt the Cowlers' grasp loosen for a split second. I broke free. They tried to grab me, but Blimp lost his balance and stumbled. I sprinted across the open field into last place, twenty yards behind the back of the pack, pushing myself to catch up.

"They're off!" shouted the disc jockey over his public-address system. "Runners from twenty-four schools, giving it their all!" After a pause, he continued, "And...and it looks like Billy Cline is...is back in the race!"

The pack made an arc around both sides of a lone skinny tree. As I was sprinting, I saw a runner nudged, slipping on fallen leaves, his body now wrapped around the tree.

Soaring behind the wild pack of runners, Victory swept over me. Random voices emerged from the runners as they jockeyed for position: "Watch it! Get over! Who farted?"

I raced through the pack, making up for lost time. Feeling like an Indy 500 racer, I worked my way to the front. After a half mile, I closed on the lead runners.

"Billy!" Jimmy Jack yelled. It stunned him when we ran side by side. Jimmy Jack angled toward me, but I burst around the third Haybury runner and glanced back. Jimmy Jack swung an arm, hitting the Haybury boy in the solar plexus. The Haybury runner stayed afoot but collided with another, who tripped and fell, hurdled by one behind him. I kept clear of contact and moved up beside Tom, who seemed reenergized by my appearance.

After another minute, I became one of five runners up front: Ace Makowski, his number-two Haybury teammate, Tom, me, and Jimmy Jack. I knew Cletus and Gopher were not far behind, after passing them. The second Haybury runner was ahead of Tom and me, but he kept looking back. Tom's breathing became labored, caused not only by his fast start but by what I believed was the energy drain from his anger.

"Faster! Faster!" I shouted to Tom. A sign read SUICIDE PLUNGE—RUNNERS USE LOW GEAR! Victory shrieked as we passed the sign and disappeared down the steep bank.

For the extreme downhill speed, we held our arms out to maintain balance. They flailed but kept us upright. I ran a little too close to Tom, nudging him till I corrected my position. The second Haybury runner, fearing the steep decline, dropped back beside Jimmy Jack. Tom located *Lover's Leap* halfway down the grassy hill. It was a wide boulder, half buried on the hill. It ramped up about thirty inches with arrows pointing from both sides to its placement. Sprinting downhill at blazing speed and then up the inclined boulder before leaping airborne into the sky required not only an attitude of reckless abandon, but also the skill of balance to survive the inevitable acrobatic landing, which separated the fearless from the pretenders.

Ace took the leap first. Before Tom and I reached it, Tom gave the verbal command, "*Lover's Leap*—Now!" We flew fifteen feet before landing and keeping our footing. Beside us, the second Haybury runner jumped off with Jimmy Jack—not a wise decision since he nudged the Haybury boy, who had a lucky landing, losing only a few seconds after recovering.

Tom and I pulled up beside Ace just before the rapids. Victory shrieked above, giving us an emotional lift. We scampered across the flat rocks and moved inches into the lead. We prepared to cross one of three parallel log-planks. Set eight feet apart, they extended over a shallow stream. Runners had to cross on one of three log-planks or add about fifteen yards by crossing on the rickety wooden bridge. Tom and I chose the log-plank on the left. I followed him, noticing his energetic gait weakening. Exhaustion forced Tom to slow.

Ace crossed on the middle log-plank but slipped off right at its end. I heard one of his feet splash into soggy grass, followed by a shout of anger. Jimmy Jack passed on the third log-plank.

"I'm tired!" moaned Tom. "Go for it!" I raised my hand to acknowledge him.

Both Ace and Jimmy Jack passed Tom soon after. The squishing sound from one of Ace's shoes spoke louder than the signs his Haybury fans had carried all morning long: THIS RACE BELONGS TO ACE. I thought, *Don't believe everything you read.*

Jimmy Jack put on a burst of speed, making a decisive move past Ace and pulling even with me. I knew he wanted to deflate Ace's hopes and scare me into submission. *Not today.*

Jimmy Jack and I dueled side by side, our arms and elbows smacking each other. I wouldn't give him an inch. If I did, I might never see it again. We were playing bumper cars with our bodies. The battle continued as we drew near the sideless bridge. Victory shrieked overhead.

Bubba, the large student at Pop's school, was fishing off the bridge. An official carrying a red flag was hollering to Bubba—ordering him off while we raced. Holding his fishing pole under one arm, Bubba stood in the middle of the bridge at the edge, clapping as we approached. Jimmy Jack kept nudging me, forcing my path along the edge. If I didn't back off and concede the lead to Jimmy Jack, a head-on with Bubba was inevitable, a collision I would lose. Bubba's eyes bulged; he had no place to go except over the edge into five to six feet of water that pooled below. He took the plunge!

Passing, I heard the cannonball splash. As the official moved to see if Bubba was okay, I shoved my shoulder into Jimmy Jack. He rebounded to the center of the sideless bridge.

With the race official distracted, Jimmy Jack waited for the turn through tall brush to end my race with some aggressive jolts, but our feet became entangled and we both tumbled to the ground. My glasses lay crooked on my nose as our bodies skidded across the dirt. A quick swipe from Jimmy Jack's hand dislodged the glasses for good. As I groped for them, Jimmy Jack rose and stomped them before taking off. I snagged the bent frames, my fingers sliding over the shattered lenses. Ace Makowski passed me and I figured his momentum might position him up with Jimmy Jack. I held my glasses in one hand and gave chase, my thoughts whirling.

It's a blur! It's all a blur! Control your anger! Settle down. You're wasting energy. Sprint to them! Do it now! I sprinted up the trail, their moving figures becoming more distorted as their lead lengthened. My blurred vision demanded I establish contact soon or I would lose them. *They can guide me to the finish line. I'll use whatever fast-twitch muscle fibers that remain to close the gap, to get close enough to hear them breathe. I must attach myself to them.*

Knowing this course well, I engaged my memory. My desperate sprint succeeded. Though burning precious energy, I was behind them, keeping Jimmy Jack and Ace in a close visual blur. They were running side by side, throwing elbows. I ran between their back kicks, having no choice but to stay connected, following them up the rigorous climb out of Death Valley.

Go to sleep. This was a tactic I used when under extreme duress. My eyes were half open to maintain contact, but my running form was economical, spending no extraneous energy. I was running in a trance, gathering strength until I would awaken from my slumber and pounce.

The large white wooden cross and old oak tree loomed beside us at the top of the adjacent hillside. I dared not look since I couldn't see it, anyway. We were running uphill, and the pace slowed. Jimmy Jack and Ace were jostling each other viciously while I was in sleep mode.

I recalled the time trial just days before. Victory had perched on the huge cross, his stately head observing my progress out of Death Valley. I fed off that memory.

Halfway up, I heard Victory shriek above me. Jimmy Jack and Ace collided again, rebounding off each other. I burst between them as if they had opened the door for me. Running by memory and following Victory's blurred motion, I increased the tempo, powering up the climb, emerging from the depths of Death Valley with a lead.

"It's Billy Cline!" shouted fans as I emerged from Death Valley. The crowd spread on both sides of the course as I entered the three-hundred-yard open field.

"Where's his glasses?" said another fan. I didn't know it, but I had a twenty-yard lead on Jimmy Jack and ten more on Ace. I needed to maintain a steady rhythm across the open field until I reached the colorful plastic ribbons marking the home stretch. But my vision betrayed me. Victory shrieked. I was no longer in sleep mode but a mode of desperation. I rubbed my eyes, seeking clarity, but painful irritation resulted. With no glasses, I was nearly blind.

Listen to the crowd! Run between both sides of their movement! I knew one landmark—the large tree where Pop and his handicapped students were staged. Approaching it, I veered toward the tree, knowing the course turned left just before it.

"He's toast!" yelled a fan, the comment to me. "Come on, Jimmy Jack! Get him!"

"Ace! You've got to go now!" screamed another. "Get up there, you Hog!" I knew I still had a lead by the delay of shouts, but I was struggling, and not just with my sight. The breakaway out of Death Valley had sapped my reserves.

Run toward the tree! Trying to run on a patch of uneven ground threw me off balance. I lunged but stayed upright. Staring at the blurry tree in the distance caused an awkward gait.

"Victory..." I uttered, but I couldn't see or hear him. It was chaos. The wind was blowing, the crowd was moving, and I was reeling, not sure when to angle left at the tree.

"Watch out, Billy!" a tense voice shouted at the tree. It was Pop's voice!

Make the turn! Wham! My forehead smacked the tree limb jutting down. Spectators screamed as my feet went out from under me and my body crashed. My back took a major blow. Blood streamed through my eyebrows and down the creases of my face onto my uniform.

"Nooo!" I shouted as I rolled to the side and pounded the earth with my hand. "I can't see!" I tried to get up, but it stunned me. The clicks from Lizzy's camera and the fluctuating sounds of the crowd seemed to echo from a distant world.

Luke yelled my name and tossed me his sweatshirt. I grasped it, wiping the blood, but it smeared across my face.

"Way to go, Jimmy Jack! Win it!" yelled a fan. I heard footsteps as he passed by.

"Come on, Ace! Run a strong finish!" I heard his footsteps, too.

I felt strong arms wrap around me as a kind voice spoke with authority. "Keep it together, son. I've gotcha." It was Pop O'Reilly. I squirmed at first, and Pop loosened his arms. But I realized my race was over. The shattered glasses slid from my grasp into the dirt.

"That took courage," Pop said, trying to renew my spirit.

Victory shrieked, hovering above me. The distinctive clicks from Lizzy's camera froze the moment.

"We have a new leader!" the announcer proclaimed over the loudspeakers. "Jimmy Jack Clausen!"

I could picture Jimmy Jack, arms raised to break the tape beside a jubilant Coach Clausen and a smiling Deputy Rawley Cowler, concluding his undefeated season.

"Clausen wins!" the announcer proclaimed. "Rockside has another individual champion! And, in the runner-up position, it's Haybury's favorite son, Ace Makowski!"

I will not let my family see me lying in the dirt…just like Jake.

Chester was first to appear. He must have run at full speed because I heard him slide to a stop as if I was home plate. Two medics followed. I was still dazed as they wiped my face clean and slathered on ointment before bandaging my forehead.

"Take me to the cliffs, Chester! Take me now!"

Chester helped me stand. I stepped away, but Chester resisted at first, offering me a drink from his canteen. That kept me still until I jerked away with Chester.

One medic spoke out of frustration, "You've got to let us check you out! You've taken a blow!" But Chester succumbed to my order and whisked me into the trees.

"Where is he?" Jenny asked, jogging in with Ma and Pa, who had not seen my fall.

"Chester took him," said Pop. "They took off over there." Jenny turned to follow.

"Jenny! Leave him alone!" Pa demanded. She stopped and turned to Pa, having never heard a harsh tone from him. Pa held onto Ma with both hands and looked her in the eye. "You understand my feelings." Ma looked at him but never opened her mouth.

"What's going on?" Jenny asked. "Why can't I help Billy?"

"It's the Cline way," said Pa.

One medic was losing his patience. "What are we supposed to do when he walks away from our help? He needs to lie down on the stretcher."

"Why don't you take a nap on it!" answered Pa. "He doesn't need a stretcher, does he? He walked away under his own power. I'm his Pa. You fixed his head. He needs no more of your help. All he needs now is to be with his brother. Go help these other kids."

"Well, it's up to you…for now," the medic said, "since he's your son. Okay, pack this stuff up," he announced to other members of his team. "Move to the finish line with the others."

Chester led me into a thick stand of trees before we angled toward the mountain slopes. Everything swirled around me, plus the thought of Jenny not knowing our family ways. One thing was certain, Chester's grip was one that would not break.

CHAPTER 23

Retreat to the Cliffs

When Chester left me on the mountain after Saturday's race, he was grumbling with frustration that I wouldn't return home. I imagined Pa's thoughts. Jake was lying in a hospital bed, I was somewhere on the cliffs, and tradition forced Ma to be a silent spectator. *Will stubbornness destroy us?* Pa must have thought about himself, too, giving in to drink again, jobless, yet holding onto a conviction born from his roots that could lead to the ruin of his middle son. Darkness must have filled the cabin as it did the skies.

*****

Late Sunday afternoon, Chester followed the yellow ribbons and climbed to the cliffs. He wore a backpack and slung a full canteen onto the boulder where I lay curled up.

"Since you're too stubborn to come home, I brought you some food!" Chester unzipped the backpack. "Two pimento cheese sandwiches, some beef jerky, and an apple." He appeared troubled as he offered it. I never twitched a muscle. He glanced at Victory on the T-Cross beside me. Chester just sat as the sun's direct rays vanished. Soon, he sobbed, his shoulders shaking. In between his ragged breathing, a torrent of words rushed out.

"Okay, I know I'm just the little brother, but it's been awful for me, too. After the race, when you and I got to the lookout, I had to go home alone. It was dark when I got back. Ma had turned out the lights before I arrived like she didn't want me there."

I stood and walked a few steps, turning my back to him. I knew what he was talking about. If Ma had turned out the lights, she and Pa were having a major disagreement. She would read her Bible by candlelight, a tear trickling down her cheek. Chester said she hadn't uttered a word. Pa's decision to allow Chester and me to retreat into the forest had threatened family unity.

"And Pa just sat in his chair…." Chester continued to sob. Yeah, Pa would stare at flames, deep in thought. I'm sure the fire would fail to warm the emotional chill sweeping through that room. I'd felt times like that before.

"Nobody said anything, Billy! Nobody cared I was scared! Pa spun around and faced Ma."

It wasn't Chester's voice I heard anymore, but Pa's. "'I've taught him to think for himself! That's the way Grampa raised me. He'll come home when he's ready. It's up to him, Lily!'" Pa's words were a rod-ironed law in our home.

Chester added, "And then, the embers fell, right after Pa spoke! The flames dwindled to a reddish glow."

I could almost hear Ma's reply. "And what's up to you, Ned?"

Chester kept talking. "You know, last night I sat up on my cot and put my bare feet on the cold, cabin floor and looked at the empty bunk beds where you and Jake slept. I pictured the three of us rough-housing…having a pillow fight. Ma and Pa could hear our noisy arguments and we could hear Ma and Pa yell at us to keep quiet. But this morning, how could I answer all the questions at church? 'Where's Billy? Why isn't your Pa at church? Why are your Ma's eyes so red?' Billy, I remember the happy days, when we were all together. I remember the normal days and even the sad days, too. All were better days than now. Please, take this food and come home."

"Stop it!" I said to him. "Pack up the food! Take it home!" I flung those words like a knife. "Don't come back here again!" Chester's face could not hide the pain he felt from my defiance. Slowly, he zipped up the backpack, placed it over his slumped shoulders, and walked downward into the forest, under the dimming skies.

I turned my back to him and within a minute he had vanished. Excuses flowed through my mind. *I'm punishing myself for what?* Soon a severe craving for food swept over me, and I rose and followed his path for thirty seconds. I spotted the sack of food he had left despite my orders. I downed the offering in a hurry. Reminiscing, I sank to the rocky surface and cried. Now, I had failed to thank the little brother I loved. Chester was better than me.

I limped past Victory on his T-Cross and stood on the precipice, gazing at the dark chasm. Short puffs of air spiraled up between my blurry eyes and the full moon. I had no glasses, but I peeled off part of a scab from my forehead. A sickness spread in my stomach. What I'd said to Chester was unforgiveable! My throat tightened. I closed my eyes, stretched out my arms, and felt a cold draft sweep up from below and whistle through my hair and across my face.

"Why can't I fly away with you, Victory?" He shrieked. I paused, lowered my arms, and limped to the T-Cross, slumping off to the side of his perch.

*****

"The Monday morning after your championship race was one of the toughest I ever faced," Pop told me later. He relived it, peeling back the scenes of time, layer by layer.

He had been pacing back and forth in his office at Cliffview Boys' Home. His face was rigid, his manner sullen. He spread a copy of Monday morning's special run of the *Rockside Bugle* over his desk. He leaned to view the front page again, those agonizing moments captured by the pictures, already burned into his memory.

The picture showed me bleeding, holding my glasses—bent frames with shards of useless glass. Pop's arms cradled me. Victory's wings spread wide, hovering over us. The large headline read: "*End of a Dream—'Eagle Boy' Grounded*." A subhead read: "*Technical DQ Called 'Rip Off.'*" The article quoted teammate Tom Pryor. "Billy had the doctor's approval, and the coaches voted him in. Not letting him run legally was a total rip off!"

"*Clausen Takes Championship*." There was one picture of Jimmy Jack's finish, and another of him receiving his winning medal, but just one quote from him: "Jimmy Jack is back!"

The article included most of Coach Clausen's rants, thanks to Lizzy's tape recorder. Pop had heard Clausen's complaints firsthand. He slumped, alone in his office, adding another experience to his list of tragic events.

He re-read Clausen's words. "Jimmy Jack is my third individual champion in three years. He won it last year, also. Since I'm the coach, I decide who runs and who doesn't. That's the way it is. Reporters complain little when basketball coaches replace players in and out of their lineups. Billy Cline got our team disqualified. I don't give a hog's…uh, look, that eye doctor, Chu, I think it is, the one who said Billy can see—she wears glasses herself. She rear-ended one of our teacher's trucks and she don't speak English none too good, either. You don't have to put that in the paper. But let me be clear, I fought for Jimmy Jack to keep his championship medal. You all should thank me for that. I coach winners…and my record proves it. That blind-Cline kid didn't win, did he? He didn't even finish! Case closed."

Another picture told it all—Cale Clausen's hands raised as though he had won a championship fight.

A final headline centered over a team picture of the champions: *Haybury wins conference.* In the picture with the smiling Haybury team was its championship trophy, their hog mascot, Hoagie, and Ace's girlfriend, Deucey.

Pop rose and walked to his window, staring out at the mountain that towered over Rockside. He said he moaned in his spirit for most of the early morning.

Pop didn't react at first to the knock on his door. Another followed.

"Come in."

Andy opened the door for Luke, who rolled to a stop near the headmaster. Pop was motionless, still staring out the window.

"We're sorry to disturb you," Luke said.

Pop didn't respond. It puzzled the boys, and they glanced at each other until Luke saw the newspaper spread across Pop's desk. He rolled to it as Andy joined him, reading the headlines and skimming the stories. Andy shook his head and turned to Luke. "Billy's just like us."

CHAPTER 24

The MOO Festival

As I lay in my sleeping bag that same Monday morning on the cliffs, I knew Tom would drive Jenny to school. I also knew she'd be worried about me. *Why am I lying on the cliffs without a word to Jenny?* I knew today was a special day for her, the day she would sing on the school stage. Here I was, alone and hungry by my own decision. *I'm not worthy of her song.*

Tom later shared with me what happened that morning. I wanted to plug my ears. The Blue Beauty passed beneath the colorful banner that stretched over both sides of the road. It read, "MOO Festival—Celebrating a Month Of Oldies. All-County Talent Show—1:00 p.m. Guest Judge—Tennessee Music Star Braelynn Rogers!" It featured a large drawing of a cow wearing sunglasses, a leather jacket, and a pompadour.

Jenny wore the stunning blue dress with sequins Jimmy Jack had bought her. Tom had heard a mouthful from her as he drove into Rockside High's parking lot.

"Nobody has seen him, or they're not tellin'! Billy promised he'd hear me sing today!"

"Promises mean little to him," Tom said. "He promised I'd make all-conference." After parking, Tom and Jenny walked to the school. Jenny stopped suddenly.

"This is the third day! I need to know what's happened to him. You're his best friend, Tom. Don't you care? He could be in real danger!"

"Okay, I'll go up." Tom shuffled his feet.

"Tell him...just tell him..." Jenny stuttered.

"I will," Tom said.

She shivered, the sequins on her blue dress dancing in the morning light.

"Whisper a prayer I find him," said Tom, as he headed to the Blue Beauty.

"Jenny, I'm here for you." Jenny spun to see Jimmy Jack in his letterman's jacket. His championship medal hung from his neck. He placed his hands over Jenny's shivering arms. "You still look beautiful in my favorite dress, but you're freezing." His gentle voice surprised her as he took off his jacket and placed it over her shoulders.

"Thank you."

"Look, I know you're concerned for Billy, but look at the facts. They disqualified our team because of Billy. It was only because of my dad's prestige I got to keep this championship medal as the individual conference champion. Coach had no choice but to kick Billy off the team."

"You're saying it's Billy's fault? That he's to blame?"

"Coach held him out for his own good. Look what's happened to him since the race. Nobody's seen him. Some think he jumped off a cliff. Face it, Jenny, if he's alive, he's not who you deserve."

Jimmy Jack looked her over again, his eyes scanning her from head to toe as he fingered his shiny medal. He cupped her face in his hands. "A beauty like you belongs with a winner." He drew his face closer. "Since I'm the student emcee for the festival, I'll be onstage to introduce you. I heard you're singing a love song. Sing it for me, Jenny, and I guarantee you'll win."

Jenny stared into his brown eyes, blinking back her tears.

Jimmy Jack backed off. She paused, pulling the jacket tighter before walking away. As she left, Jimmy Jack added, "I'm free tonight. Call me and we'll celebrate your win." With a burst of enthusiasm, he snapped his fingers on both hands and exhaled.

*****

Tom drove the Blue Beauty to our cabin. Once in a hurry, he was unsure what to say to my folks. Later that morning, Tom would give me a blow-by-blow account of their conversation.

Pa gazed at him from his rocker. He wasn't rocking, and Tom noticed his squinting look. After giving up on the coffee cup in his hand, Pa set it down on a barrel, grabbing hold of his head with both hands.

"I've got a headache rolling around like my brains will explode!"

Ma stood on the other end of the porch with a paint brush dipped in a can of white paint. She had painted a white cross on her boarded-up window. Ma knew how to whittle the corners of a strike zone, but the edges of her painted cross looked more like the crooked path from a knuckleball. Splattered paint mimicked the shattered stained-glass Tom knew had laid there.

"Good morning," Tom said. "'The air bites shrewdly. It is bitter cold.'"

"It ain't that cold," replied Pa.

"I'm sorry. That's from Shakespeare's *Hamlet*. A character said it while he was standing on the battlements of a castle."

"Well, this ain't much of a castle, either. You come for Billy?"

"Yes, sir. I imagine he's at the boulder lookout. Do you think he's okay?"

"He's bruised and broken!" Ma said, spinning around.

"What about food?"

"You hungry?" Pa asked.

"No, food for Billy."

Pa held his head and scrunched his face, embarrassed as he stood from his rocker and motioned Tom inside. Ma put her paintbrush down and led Tom into the kitchen.

"This blasted headache!" said Pa. "I hate bein' on the wagon, Lily!"

Ma shook her head and muttered. "Man don't live by whiskey alone… He's trying a little cold turkey."

"Isn't that a drink?" Tom said.

"Just relax, Tom," said Ma. "I'll make sandwiches for Billy." Ma slapped together two peanut butter and jelly sandwiches. While Tom waited, he looked at Ma's family picture, taken when she was a young teen, before she'd married Jacob. Tom saw her dad with her six brothers, all holding bats or wearing gloves. It looked more like a team picture than a family portrait.

"Baseball was our family game," Ma explained, noticing Tom's fascination with the picture. "Pa taught me, and I taught my brothers to pitch, with help from Jacob. That's Jacob there beside me. He bought the stained glass in Italy." Tom noticed her sadness. She glanced at a bucket that held the old fragments of stained glass and an unopened bourbon bottle Ned had rejected.

"Tom, when you find Billy, bring him to our family graveyard at five o'clock, will you? Thanks. It's important."

Tom had nodded before pulling out my new glasses from his pocket. "Speakin' of glass, the vice principal handed me Billy's new glasses this morning."

"Yeah, they're Billy's!" Ma said. "Nobody at Rockside wears lenses that thick. I bet there's a story behind that."

Ma finished packing the sandwiches in a small backpack and threw in a banana.

"Thank you, Mrs. Cline."

Tom set a quick pace up the mountain, the backpack slung over his shoulders. When Tom approached the small waterfall, I lay on a rock in the morning sun beside the natural pool, cooling my eyes as I warmed my body.

An hour before, I was wearing running shorts, having stood below the natural cold-water shower, an experience like the ice baths people from Finland take in the winter. After I dried off, I put on a clean set of clothes and socks, along with my jacket. I had quit shivering as heat from the sun's rays warmed me. The gentle sound of water cascading from the spring was peaceful. Within the pristine atmosphere of the forest, I heard twigs break.

"Who is it?" I shouted.

"Where you been?" Tom walked toward me.

"You scared me half to death! Where do you think I've been? It took forever to locate the waterfall, a place I thought I could find in my sleep. With no glasses, I am more than half blind."

Tom came close. "From what I heard, Billy, you weren't too keen on anybody helpin' you after the race."

"Yeah. Chester got me here. He came back yesterday and sneaked in a meal even though I tried to shoo him away."

"Was it wise to dismiss Chester?"

"No. People need people. I need people."

"You need a shave, too!"

I felt my face. Tom was right. "If Victory hadn't arrived, I don't know what…"

"So how're you doing?"

"I'm hungry. I was walking down…but failed to see some of the streamers."

"You're in luck." Tom took off the backpack and offered me a sandwich. I reached for it, smelling Ma's homemade jelly. It oozed as I bit into the first sandwich. I felt another round of thankfulness for Tom's friendship, but my mouth was so full I couldn't speak.

"Your school counselor asked me about you at church yesterday."

My only response was to take another bite.

"Well, neither of us made All-Conference," said Tom. "But the whole school is talkin' about us. The vice principal says you defaced the track bus since they found your new thick glasses there."

"That vice principal is no Perry Mason!"

"He gave me your glasses to give to you. And, Jenny thinks you forgot about her singin' today—you know—the MOO Festival. Did ya forget? She's really worried about you."

I finished the first sandwich, twirling my tongue to clear the heavy spread of peanut butter off the roof of my mouth. Snatching the second sandwich, I devoured it with the same gusto as the first, appearing like a starving pilgrim. When I finished, I peeled the banana and inhaled it. Tom burst into laughter.

"Will you take a breath?" After the banana had disappeared, Tom spoke again. "Here, take 'em." He handed me my new glasses. I fumbled with them since my hands were still sticky from ravaging my meal.

"Wow! I can see! My vision is superb!" I looked around, enjoying my surroundings. "It's like I have a new set of eyes!" I grabbed the canteen I had filled with spring water and drank and drank. Tom stared in amazement.

After a belch, I spoke: "Tom, I never forgot about Jenny singing in this contest. I wasn't sure I'd find my way. Let's go!"

Tom hollered between turns on the trail. "Jenny's the last singer in the contest! We've got enough time, if we hustle!" We leapt off a rock. "Whoa!" Tom yelled.

On the drive down the dirt road from my cabin, Tom filled me in on what had happened at school and at my cabin that morning. Upon reaching the paved road, we turned and peeled rubber on our way toward town.

*****

The Rockside auditorium would be full, not only with Rockside students, but with members of the community including Pop O'Reilly's students. It was Pop who later told me what we missed.

On the Rockside auditorium stage, Jimmy Jack Clausen, the student emcee, walked in from backstage to wild applause as he stepped to his microphone. He gripped his cross-country medal and then released it, letting it dangle from his neck. Loud music, enhanced by special speakers, blared from a jukebox that energized the audience. The jukebox stood behind him in front of a large painted '50s–'60s backdrop.

"Welcome to this year's rendition of the MOO Festival!" Applause erupted again. "We want to thank Caruso's Diner, who donated the use of their jukebox for us! Let 'em hear your thanks!" Clapping and hoots of appreciation followed. "And a big thanks to students in our art department for the great backdrop that celebrates the '50s and early '60s." Additional applause.

A loud "moo" reverberated over the speakers, bouncing off the auditorium walls. Out came Braelynn Rogers, shoving a large "two-boy cow-costume" onto the stage. The audience laughed at the outrageous design of the costume while others tried to mimic the loud "moos" from the cow. Wearing a glittering crown and a tutu, and with one brown and three white cowboy boots, the awkward cow strutted next to Jimmy Jack, almost knocking him over.

Braelynn Rogers, the head judge, turned her microphone on. "That cow reminds me of our old milk cow when I was a kid. Come on, everybody, let's hear it for "Elsie" the cow!"

Cheers and laughter erupted from the audience as the two boys in the cow costume tried to bow to Braelynn but fell to the stage floor.

"Good one, Braelynn!" Jimmy Jack joked from his microphone. "Let's give a big cheer for our special judge, the amazing Braelynn Rogers!" The cheers grew as the two boys got onto their cow feet and adjusted the costume, recovering all the dignity a lopsided cow deserved. During the applause, Braelynn bowed to Elsie. The crowd settled as Braelynn tugged Elsie backstage.

"And now, our first contestant for the talent show in this year's MOO Festival—the soon-to-be-famous, Dirk Peabody!"

Jimmy Jack exited the stage as a student juggler entered flipping cones, dazzling all.

Pop attended with many of his Cliffview boys and had plenty to say about the talent show. Students applauded as the juggler tossed up three cones that flipped end over end while he spun in a full circle and caught them and then sent them up again. The audience groaned near the end when he missed one of his cones and they all tumbled in disarray. He still received an ovation.

Jimmy Jack returned. "You've heard a month of oldies on the local radio station. Now, to sing 'Over the Rainbow,' here's Wilma Gann, all the way from Rick-a-Saw Corners!" Moderate applause welcomed young Wilma as she entered from stage right.

"Go, Wilma!" a female voice shouted. As she stood facing the microphone at center stage, young Wilma blinked long, fake eye-lashes. Her musical introduction from the band played.

"Some..." Wilma hiccupped into the microphone, missing words on the first line. She was not to be deterred and continued.

"Over the..." She hiccupped again. Wilma fought on.

"Rainbow..." After her third hiccup, she lost all composure and ran off the stage, her hand over her mouth with tears flowing.

The music stopped, and all anyone saw or heard was Gopher Cowler standing and shouting from the front row.

"Willl-maaa! Yaba-daba-dooo!" The student crowd erupted in laughter. Several of Wilma's female friends stood to their feet and smacked laughing boys with their purses.

Farther down the front row, Cletus sat with his girlfriend, chatty Patty. He spotted two teachers marching toward Gopher's position.

"Oh, oh," said Cletus loudly, "it's Battle-Axe Ann and Sergeant Shelly!" The teachers ousted the girls sitting beside Gopher and took up residency on each side of him. Gopher's ears turned red.

*****

After a half hour of spinning around corners, Tom and I entered the school parking lot. Tom skidded to a stop at the side entrance. Tom was beside me as we entered the hallway. Loud clapping blasted over the hallway speakers. *Are we too late?* I knew Jenny's accompaniment would soon play. *I've gotta get to the stage!*

Down the hallway stood Brock Binkerhoff. He wore a black leather jacket and had his long hair slicked straight back in a duck-bill. Several chains looped from his black jeans. He blocked the center of the hallway with his arms folded. Two short freshmen tough-guy wannabes wearing matching black leather jackets and cocky smiles stood on each side of him.

"Hey, Brock! You lettin' us through?" I asked in a husky tone.

Brock spread a wide grin, his hands on his hips, and shook his head. "Not a chance, unless you can double the five bucks Jimmy Jack gave me!" He slipped a five-dollar bill from his jacket pocket and held it up. One wannabe tapped Brock's arm. "Oh, yeah, and some coin for my two buddies—for Twinkies," Brock added. The two wannabes smiled in agreement.

"That's hallway robbery!" I said. Tom and I reached maximum speed in five strides, spearing Brock, driving him backward down the hallway as he crashed against a classroom door and slumped. The two wannabes had lunged to the walls of the hallway and clung like wallpaper.

*****

Tom and I heard Jimmy Jack's announcements from the hallway speakers as we continued around the corner, the $5 bill snatched from Brock's hand by Tom. We dashed down the next hall and entered the lobby outside the auditorium where festive cakes were sold. Seeing a teacher guarding access to the auditorium, Tom bought a whipped cream covered cake with the $5 bill and swallowed some whipped cream. He dove to the floor near the auditorium entrance, faking a wild-eyed, trembling, convulsive fit. Girls screamed, causing the teacher to rush to Tom's aid.

I sneaked around the crowd, pulling open the center doors, and stood unseen at the top of the aisle. Jimmy Jack escorted Jenny to center stage. Indistinct chatter arose when Jimmy Jack leaned over and kissed her hand. That brought "oohs" from the student crowd. "And now," Jimmy Jack said, ready to introduce Jenny as a snare drum rolled, "our last contestant of the day! The beautiful, the elegant, the stunning—and all the way from Scotland, Miss Jenny Hart!" A bass drum pounded, accompanying the snare. Applause mounted to a roar when a bagpipe joined in. "She'll be singing a song entitled 'Loch Lomond' from her native Scotland." Jenny searched the audience as three girls joined her onstage. Jenny nodded, then spoke into her microphone as all musicians began the intro.

"A year ago, I lived near Loch Lomond, a beautiful body of water in the highlands of Scotland. I walked the rugged shoreline, longing to find my true love. I didn't know then I would not find him there or in the Scottish hills, but on the bold rocky cliffs above Rockside." Jenny wiped her tears. "I haven't seen my true love since the cross-country championship." The audience stirred, gazing at Jimmy Jack peeking around the stage curtain. "I was told he may be dead, that my true love and I may never meet again."

I stood frozen in place, realizing she loved me. Her solo voice was intense and full.

> By yon bonnie banks and by yon bonnie braes,
> Where the sun shines bright on Loch Lomond.
> Where me and my true love will never meet again.
> On the bonnie, bonnie banks of Loch Lomond.

The trio joined Jenny on the chorus, bringing sighs from the crowd.

> O ye'll take the high road and I'll take the low road,
> An' I'll be in Scotland before you.
> For me and my true love will never meet again,
> On the bonnie, bonnie banks o' Loch Lomond.

Jenny's next solo was plaintive, the audience silent.

> 'Twas there that we parted in yon shady glen,
> On the steep, steep side o' Ben Lomond.
> Where in the purple hue the Highland hills we view,
> An' the moon comin' out in the gloamin'.

During the next chorus, I walked down the center aisle toward the elevated stage. Jenny's face brightened. Her crystal-clear tone soared through the rafters. The gossip lines had been alive all morning, and teachers and students knew of my trouble. As I passed each row, students gawked with open mouths. She caressed the microphone and strode to the edge of the stage, gazing down at me.

> O ye'll take the high road and I'll take the low road,
> An' I'll be in Scotland before you.
> For me and my true love will never meet again,
> On the bonnie, bonnie banks of Loch Lomond.

Jimmy Jack peeked around the stage curtain, aghast. Cletus and Gopher couldn't stop me because of the teachers. Jenny had won over the hearts of the audience, and they all knew why.

Coach Clausen and the vice principal moved toward me and motioned several teachers to assist, but they waited since Jenny's solo was in full force.

> The wee birdies sing and the wildflowers spring,
> And in sunshine the waters are sleepin'
> But the broken heart it mends in second spring again
> On the bonnie, bonnie banks o' Loch Lomond.

The audience had witnessed a growing love, a love unashamed. In tears, Jenny could not sing with the trio on the final chorus. She ran across the stage, dashing down the stairs to meet me. Suddenly blocked by Coach Clausen and the vice-principal, other teachers helped haul me away.

> O ye'll take the high road and I'll take the low road,
> An' I'll be in Scotland before you.

All the music died down and stopped as Jenny sang alone.

> For me and my true love...will never meet again...

Silence enveloped the auditorium as Jenny collapsed with a moan.

Just then, Elsie entered, trying to distract the audience from the ruckus. A loud "moo" blasted from the speakers, but it was Jimmy Jack who spun the event around. He sprinted across the stage trying to reclaim Jenny for himself. Instead, he slipped and rammed Elsie to the floor while sliding off the stage head-first into the giant bell of the tuba. The crowd "oohed" and "ahhed," his head stuck in the tuba and the costumed boys sprawled onto the stage.

Gopher stood from his front-row seat and yelled, "Cow tipping! Yeah!" Boys roared in laughter when Battle-Axe Ann and Sergeant

Shelly grabbed the back of Gopher's overalls and lifted him, carrying him out of the auditorium as he swam in the air, yelling, "Mercy! Mercy! Mercy!"

Left behind at what should have been a moment of celebration, Jenny held her hands over her face, devastated by my forced removal. Braelynn walked to Jenny and turned the microphone off. "Don't you worry, honey. Your sweetheart will figure a way out of this."

Braelynn then turned the microphone on. "We've got an award to give out. All contestants, file to the stage." Braelynn determined the show would go on. Lizzy Looper rushed up to take pictures.

The contestants lined up. Jimmy Jack was out of action, his head still stuck in the tuba. The senior class president delivered the award box to Braelynn. She stood beside the costumed boys, who had recovered. "And the winner of this year's MOO Festival is..." The loud moo reverberated again over the auditorium speakers. "The winner is...Miss Jenny Hart!" The audience clapped and cheered as Braelynn took the large cow crown and placed it upon Jenny's head. The words "Udderly Fine" in gold letters shone from the lighted crown.

Braelynn continued. "Let's hear it for the MOO Festival mascot!" The audience cheered and laughed again. "Now, come on, Elsie, it's back to the barn for you!"

The audience roared again as Braelynn chased the costumed boys, who waddled off the stage and behind the curtain. A loud crash echoed from backstage. Braelynn glanced back, "Well, that's all folks!" The contestants waved goodbye and Jenny walked off with Braelynn.

"Big Ernest," the huge tuba player, surrounded by band members and his teacher, took three deep breaths, and as his cheeks puffed out, he blasted a note from his tuba. Jimmy Jack's head burst from the tuba and he fell to the floor to cheers from the band members, who congratulated Big Ernest.

CHAPTER 25

Expulsion from Rockside

They brought me into the vice principal's office. I slumped into a chair as Mr. Deeter and Coach Clausen shut the door.

"Billy, I think you know why you're here." He looked at Coach Clausen, who stood at my side. Your behavior concerns your coach and me. I'm in charge of discipline at the high school, so I'm in charge in this room. Understand?"

I nodded.

Mr. Deeter continued, "It concerns your counselor, too—your disappearance over the weekend and the start of school today. And now you pull this stunt!"

Clausen pulled his chair close. "Look, I'll take part of the blame. I knew he was trouble before the season began. After his disqualification, I shouldn't have taken him back."

"Whatta you mean?" I argued. "The officials never disqualified me! It was you, Coach! I earned my way back until that phony petition went around. I did everything you told me…to prove I could run in the championship!" My voice had risen many decibels.

Coach raised the decibels even higher. "I'm the coach, and I decide who runs and who doesn't! I'm not bound by any timetable or list you might conjure up!"

"That's not what he said, Mr. Deeter. He told me certain things I had to do, and I did 'em."

"Did anyone else hear this conversation?" Mr. Deeter asked.

"No, sir, only me."

Coach Clausen rose, a grin on his face. "Ya know, Deet, this boy lives in a make-believe world." Coach turned toward me. "I suppose you and your partner-in-crime, Tom Pryor, didn't run down Brock Binkerhoff in the hallway?"

"Run down Brock Binkerhoff? He's a linebacker! No wonder our team was one and nine!"

"You double-teamed him...and Brock's second string," Mr. Deeter said. "Those other two fellas with Brock testified in writing to what happened. The secretary has signed documents. She said their knees were shakin'! And Brock ain't too pleased about the tear in his leather jacket."

"Give me a hanky!"

"Okay, that's it, mister!" said Mr. Deeter.

"So...what about Gopher in the assembly?" I questioned.

"That doesn't concern you. Quiet."

The verbal assault crushed my resolve. I decided to accept the consequences. I was giving up, which wasn't like me. I had never faced such a blatant attack for telling the truth. They kept up the onslaught, reading the testimonies. But I wasn't listening. Not much, anyway. I was in my world, my own thoughts. *Why should I fight to stay here and get beaten down again next week?*

I leaned back in my chair and grew silent. I looked at a certificate on the wall behind Mr. Deeter's chair as he droned on. It thanked him for his work as an assistant defensive linebacker coach for the football team. *Figures.*

The vice principal continued the barrage. "I tried to call your Pa, to give him an opportunity to come down here and defend you. Is your phone disconnected?"

"Just the ringer."

"Like I said before, his Pa is gutless," added Clausen. "Nothing would be accomplished from talking to him, anyway."

"Okay, Coach, you need to keep those comments to yourself," Mr. Deeter said.

"Sorry. You're right. Sorry there, Billy. He might not be gutless. Who knows?"

Mr. Deeter looked over his glasses and raised his eyebrows at Clausen. "Billy, listen to what you've done. You got our cross-country team disqualified, we found your new glasses in the defaced bus, you cut school this morning, and you interrupted the MOO Festival this afternoon—all in three days. Your light at this school just turned red!"

The principal walked into the office. "Sorry I'm late. We had another altercation. So…what's the verdict with Billy?"

*****

Tom and Jenny sat on a bench outside the school, waiting for me to exit the office. Only a few students waited for their rides. Tom held papers in his hand when I joined them and sat.

"Tom got five days' suspension," Jenny said. I was silent.

Tom stared at his feet as Jenny adjusted her crown. Tom looked up, irritated.

"What's the problem?" Jenny said.

"The shindig's over. You can take off your cow crown now, udders and all."

Jenny reached up and unhooked the crown. She placed it on the bench beside her. "I guess you're right. It's over." She sighed. "What did they do to you, Billy?"

Tom answered for me. "What Coach has wanted to do since the season began."

*****

Tom drove Jenny and me toward the cabin without speaking: no music, no nothing. He turned down a side road that led to our family graveyard. Stepping out of the Blue Beauty, I saw my family standing near Jacob's grave. Asking for silence, my friends had given it. I turned to Jenny and opened her door. She stepped out, and I put my hands on her shoulders and gave her a hug, knowing how hurt she was but not knowing what to say.

"What will you do? What should I do?" Jenny asked.

"You sing…I run."

I leaned over and kissed her on the cheek. *Will this be our last kiss?* I turned and walked away, leaving her standing alone as she climbed into the Beauty. I scrunched the papers I'd received into my pocket. Tom drove away as I moved to join my family. I could still feel Jenny's tear on my cheek. Stopping, I looked back, seeing dust from Tom's tires vanish to nothing.

I trudged toward the grave. Pa had dug a hole two feet by three feet wide and three feet deep beside Jacob's headstone. Ma knelt behind her bucket of stained glass shards. She gave a handful of flowers to Pa and two others to Chester and me. We all stood in silent reverence.

Lily and Pa put her bouquet on Jacob's headstone, and Chester and I followed. Lily dumped her stained-glass shards into the mini-grave. Ned poured in a full bottle of bourbon and dropped the bottle into it. Chester tossed in Jake's fake Honus Wagner card.

I pulled out my expulsion papers and gave them to Pa. He scanned them and dropped them into the mini-grave before tossing in a lighted match afterword. Standing together, arms around each other, we watched it all burn.

CHAPTER 26

Interview at Cliffview Boys' Home

Pa pushed open the office door to Cliffview Boys' Home. The room was not fancy, but tidy. Margaret, Pop's secretary, was the same lady who led the Saturday knitting group Ma often attended. I knew Ma liked her, especially when she held up a bonnet for her grandchild, causing Ma to light up with enthusiasm for its simplistic beauty.

"Good morning. We've been expecting you," Margaret said. She rose to greet us.

Pop appeared and opened the door to a larger conference room. As we entered, I scanned the pictures on the wall. They showed students interacting with each other, their faces full of excitement. *That's different.*

"Let's pull these chairs around the table. This'll be fine," he said. He had a way of making us feel comfortable. Ma let Chester scoot in first. She followed, and I was next. Pa put his hands on my shoulders to show his support before he leaned over and shook Pop's hand before sitting.

"You're familiar with our family, I know," said Pa.

"I sure know you from high school." Pop chuckled. "And Billy and I endured a tough experience at the hospital." He smiled at me and added, "I remember that. What they were doin' to Jake was just...incomprehensible."

Pa responded, "We appreciate you talking with Jake when you bring your students to see their doctors. Thank you."

"It was Billy who exposed Jake's hate therapy and Billy's love for his brother that inspired me to help." Pop looked at me. "Your Pa and

I have put his hate therapy under a spotlight. A healing community is a better way."

Pa explained. "Jake turned positive. After he wrote that letter of apology to Blimp in his own shaky hand, I believed I could change, too." Pa rubbed his mouth as Ma nodded. "I can quit drinkin'."

We all gave approval, having seen how hard it was for Pa. Ma gave Pa's hand a squeeze.

I shared. "On the cliffs, I kept thinking about your students that time in the hospital lobby. They seemed together, like one team. They were crazy, but united like a team should be." I smiled and released a laugh as I reminisced. "Look, I've got great parents here, and a great brother, Chester, and..." I paused, feeling the energy drain over Jake. "I just couldn't run fast enough."

Glancing at Ma, I slid out of my chair, hurrying to the room's end. Against the wall, I faced a picture of Jesus and zeroed in on his rugged yet friendly expression.

Pa spoke first. "Billy, you didn't fail Jake."

"Do you think He blames you?" Pop asked.

I spun around, thinking it was an accusation. Then I thought again, *What if Jake does blame me?* I had never considered that. I gazed at Pop, feeling exposed by the question.

Pop pointed to the picture. "No, do you think He—Jesus—blames you? A person can't live well if he's half buried in guilt. I know that fact."

Now I knew what Pop meant. I turned to view Jesus's face again and shook my head. "No."

Pop rocked back, relaxed. "So what happens on the cliffs, Billy?"

"My eagle gives me a sense of purpose...of acceptance. Victory had it tough when his parents died. But he's free now, and he soars. I want to soar. I want to see the way he sees and run the way he soars. Is that possible?"

Pop rose and joined me across the room. "It is if you'll stretch your wings farther than you ever have before. I'm forming a new running team at Cliffview. If you became captain, could you capture that vision and share it with the team?"

His eyes were letting me in. Pop offered me his burn-scarred hand. That hand held my gaze the same as it had Pa's at the courthouse. I grasped his hand and shook it, tentatively at first, then with a firm grip as my confidence grew and my eyes looked up at his face unafraid.

With a laugh, everyone hugged. Pop seemed to enjoy it as much as we did. Margaret knocked and burst into the room. She stepped over to Ma and hugged her before showing off her new project: a little pink knitted vest for a granddaughter.

"Billy can learn a lot from Pop," Margaret said.

"Hey, everybody!" Pop said. "I know how Billy can meet the guys!"

*****

Pop drove the Cliffview van down the highway as music blasted from the speakers. Pop, Andy, Keith, Bubba, and I were engaged in Luke's story.

"The guy said, 'Why don't ya turn your stumps in for a new set of wheels!'" We burst into laughter as Luke continued. "He was serious!"

"You get this stuff all the time?" I asked.

"We eat it up, don't we, Pop?" Andy said.

"Just don't chew on it forever!"

"Come on, Pop!" Luke said. "I told ya my most embarrassing moment. Tell us yours!"

"Oh, no...I shouldn't...I..."

In unison, we all urged him. "Come on, we wanna hear it! You can't back out now!"

Pop kept his attention on the road, but said, "You sure you wanna hear this?"

"Come on, tell us!"

"Okay. I'd been driving for hours across the desert, and I see this greasy spoon. Pardon my language, but they were advertising 'Hotter-than-hell chili! Get a free ticket if you finish!'"

"A free ticket? To hell?" asked Keith.

"For the chili, man!" said Luke, who flicked Keith's ears.

"So, I stopped…you know, it's like a challenge. I wondered if I could down it all. So I parked…and it was hotter than blazes!"

"So how hot was hell?" joked Keith. We were still laughing.

"Four hours later, I'm in Las Vegas, and I'm not feeling too well. It's pitch-black outside, but in Vegas, it's like daytime…bright lights everywhere. Raised a country boy, I'd never seen this. So I'm drivin' slow, looking at all the sights."

"Something's about to happen," Andy warned.

"From my rearview mirror, I see these flashing lights. A cop pulls me over! I'm thinking, 'Man, I sure wasn't speeding!' He walks up to the window and tells me in a guttural voice, 'Let me see your license.' So I give it to him, and he asks, 'What's your name?' I'm tired, so I answer, 'It's on the license.' As a school headmaster, I'm wondering if the officer knows how to read. He asks again, and I add, 'Read it from the license. Come on, you can do it.'"

"Oh, oh! You're in big trouble now!" Keith said as we chuckled.

"He orders me to step out of the vehicle, put my hands on the hood, spread my legs, and bend over. He's giving me a pat-down! So I'm stretched out after driving four hours, and when he's frisking me at the ankles, this humongous bubble of hot air emerges! I was lifted off my feet!"

The van rocked with laughter.

"That poor cop is gasping for air, then cuffs me and throws me in the back of his buddy's back-up cruiser! I asked, 'What's the crime?'"

"He scrunches his nose and yells, 'For breaking Nevada's pollution laws!'"

We were slap-happy now, trying to recover.

"I asked him, 'How are you gonna explain this to your chief?'"

"One whiff is all he'll need!" He thought about it since the chief was not there and finally let me go with a warning: 'No more chili!'"

As we continued laughing and bonding while engaging in Pop's story, I realized I had found a place where I felt at home—a place I could belong—Cliffview Boys' Home.

I looked out the side window, watching the blur of trees, crops, grass, and small country homes whiz by. I listened to my new friends and their unique voices and observed their varied statures.

Bubba was well over six feet and huge. I asked him about the two fishing poles and supplies in the van. "I take them wherever I go," he said.

Andy was a genuine midget, smart and quick-witted with boundless mental energy. But he had a weak heart. He and Bubba were close friends. I laughed, thinking of the old saying that opposites attract. It worked for them.

Luke pushed himself in everything he did. He made sure he was included in all challenges. I liked his spirit. He, too, was lucky to have Bubba around to load and unload him and his wheelchair without complaint.

Keith was hyperactive, always moving. He liked to argue over comments with his own take on a situation. Keith wouldn't permit a dull moment. *I wonder if he, too, got kicked out of school or sent off.* I didn't know or care. I liked him a lot.

I already knew about Pop. Yet I had learned much more about him firsthand, from seeing him at the hospital and with us in the van.

"Here's the turnoff, Pop," said Andy, holding the map. "Remember, the boy's name is Ethan...Ethan Gorman...and he's rich! Look at that mansion!" Andy gagged as he spoke.

A security gate opened onto a driveway leading to a home in the foothills. We drove between two lines of trees into the park-like setting and stopped. Our mouths gaped.

"Will ya look at that!" I shouted, spying a colorful go-cart parked on the large porch.

"Everybody stay put in the van, except Billy," Pop said. "Come with me. You're new, just like Ethan." Pop and I grinned as I pressed the doorbell chimes at the massive front door. The peephole opened and closed. We heard the locks being unbolted. The door swung open like a bank vault. A thin boy in a three-piece suit stood before us without saying a word. *He looks scared.*

"Good morning. I'm Pop O'Reilly and this is Billy. We're from Cliffview Boys' Home in Rockside."

Still no response. He seemed shy, and I saw his scarred face on one side. When he raised his hand to his face, he tried to cover it, then turned away. *Our school will serve him well.*

"Is Dr. Nicholas Gorman in?" Pop asked.

"He's my grandfather. I'm Ethan. Come in." Ethan opened the door wider.

We entered the lavish interior filled with pictures of go-carts and travel scenes from around the world.

His aunt entered and explained, "Dr. Gorman cannot see you. NASA called him away on business."

"Sorry to hear that," Pop said.

Ethan took over the conversation. "You can see pictures of him, though," Ethan said as he pointed to a gallery of photographs.

We turned to those hanging on the wall and displayed on various shelves and stands. Noticeable were four large pictures of a man I guessed to be Dr. Gorman. One showed him standing next to a railroad car; in another, he was with several NASA employees beside President John F. Kennedy. The third pictured him again with NASA employees beside an unusual go-cart. In the fourth, he was completing a marathon with a friend.

"Wow!" I said. "Your grandfather works for NASA? He met President Kennedy?"

"And President Johnson, too. He helped design the Lunar Roving Vehicle, to explore the moon. My grandfather also co-owns a company called Go-Go Go-Carts and travels a lot for NASA. He's so busy doing important work, he doesn't have time for me." Ethan walked to a desk and turned on a reel-to-reel tape player.

"Grandfather left instructions," Ethan said. His aunt seemed confident that Ethan could handle the conversation as she dusted a bookcase. We waited for the recording.

"Ethan has my permission to attend Cliffview Boys' Home. The envelope includes the tuition check plus $1,000 for miscellaneous expenses. I have signed the release, paid the fees, and expect the school to fulfill its agreement. I want no unnecessary calls. Respectfully, Dr. Nicholas Gorman." Ethan turned off the recording, killed the power, and handed the envelope to Pop.

"Well…quick and to the point," said Pop, scanning the check.

"He's quick on his feet, too. He runs every day, though he has cancer. I hope they find a cure. Since my folks' accident, he's arranged for my care. Grandfather said I didn't fit in at the prep school I went to first. After that he enrolled me in a military school. He had a dispute with the commander, so…you're my third school this year." Ethan picked up a water pitcher.

"Oh, I could use some…" I began. But Ethan watered plants instead, trying to assist his aunt. I was quiet, letting my body dehydrate.

"My luggage is by the door."

"Ethan," Pop said, "I want you to meet Billy. He's also a new student at Cliffview." We shook hands.

"Pleased to meet you. And thank you, Mr. O'Reilly." Ethan smiled.

Pop and I grabbed his luggage and walked onto the porch. Ethan hugged his aunt and said goodbye, then she locked the front door.

On the massive porch, I eyeballed the go-cart. "Wow!" I said as I touched it. Ethan joined me as Pop stayed cool, letting us get acquainted. "You ride?" I asked.

"Some…like I said, Grandfather owns the business."

"Hey, Pop, can you imagine Luke drivin' a set of wheels like this?"

"He would if he could."

We walked to the van, but I kept looking back at the go-cart.

"Did you ever compete in sports?" I asked.

"No, it was too inconvenient for my parents. I like to hike, though," Ethan said. "I've hiked all over these hills." He then pointed to a large tree with an unfinished fort. "See that tree fort? The wooden steps? Grandfather says I 'never finish anything.'"

I paused before speaking. "I know how ya feel."

On the way back to Cliffview, we bonded, treating Ethan like a long-lost brother. Music blasted from the van's speakers and out came the stories of shenanigans Pop encouraged us to perform in public settings!

"All of you pull stunts like that?" Ethan asked.

"Yes," said Bubba. "Pop calls 'em 'routines!' Chubby Checker's my specialty." Bubba tried to show off his moves in the van while everybody laughed and sang along with him.

"Gentlemen!" Pop said. "It's time to design our best group routine yet. Andy? Any ideas?"

"Yes! I've got it! We'll call that cute little chicklette on Channel 2—Lizzy Looper!" The boys whooped and hollered in excitement as the van rolled down the highway. "Ethan, just wait till you see her!"

CHAPTER 27

Ethan Enrolls in Cliffview

Nestled up the mountain near the city park, Pop's school bordered a distant section of the Rockside cross-country course. Additional trails led deeper into the mountains—perfect for the most daring of hikers or runners.

Pa couldn't afford to transport Chester and me to and from school with our different schedules. So, when Pop offered me a scholarship at Cliffview, Ma and Pa agreed. They would have one fewer mouth to feed and could spend time and money on Jake. I could stay involved in activities at Cliffview, complete my campus duties, and earn the right to captain the new cross-country team. If weekends became free, I could visit Jake or home.

Pop placed me in a dorm room with Ethan. We would experience life at Cliffview together. On the first day my schedule listed two PE classes, one during first period and the other last period. Pop and I had agreed to this plan, which included assisting challenged students.

As I entered the gym, I saw a list of names posted on the door, categorized by squad. The first name on squad one was mine, the second Ethan Gorman. Several disabled students filled my morning and afternoon squads, but many had no physical limitations at all.

Students came to Pop's school for an assortment of reasons: social problems, safety issues in their environment, and tragedies in their families, just as Ethan had with the loss of his parents in a car accident. The school was a microcosm of the state's human community.

When the bell rang, everyone grew quiet. Pop walked in front of us and cleared his throat. *What will he say? Will he resemble Coach Clausen in any way?*

"As some of you know," Pop began, "I've transferred some normal duties in the office to my assistant. I'm returning to coaching. I'm still the headmaster and will work to maintain our excellent record in the community. However, I am adding a new emphasis on camaraderie to unite us in our pursuit of excellence.

The gym door flew open. I turned and saw Keith. He ran to the back of my squad and saluted Pop as if a five-star general. Several chuckled. He kept up his antics, wiggling, doing weird stretches and contortions.

"Good morning, Keith," Pop said. "That-a-way, Keith, get the kinks out. I admire Keith's dedication in keeping loose. Most athletes don't stretch as they should. Keith uses his abundance of energy to increase his flexibility."

Keith finished and smiled at Pop, saluting him again.

"Excuse me, Keith, come here." Keith pointed to himself, surprised, then walked to the front of my squad as Pop approached him, whispering in his ear.

"He's thinking, class," Pop said.

"Okay."

"Okay, what?" Pop asked.

"I'll be on time...every day," Keith said before returning to my squad.

"That's what I like in this young man, real commitment! Keith, how many hours in a day?"

"Uh, twenty-four?"

"Correct!" Pop said. "Since you sleep about eight hours at night, that leaves sixteen hours to be awake, does it not?" The class all nodded except for Keith.

"But I only sleep seven and a half hours at night," Keith said with a mischievous grin.

"I'm adding a half hour for dozing off in class," Pop said with a similar grin.

The class laughed along with Keith.

"Are you kidding? Keith asleep? Never!" Andy said, moving his hands in a kind of sign language as he spoke. Pop laughed along with us.

"Spending just one percent of your actual awake time working out is…how much time?"

"Nine minutes and thirty-six seconds!" Andy shouted.

"Nine thirty-six…impressive!" Pop said.

"I can catch rainbow trout that fast!" Bubba said. That brought more chuckles.

"That's true, Bubba, but has anyone here ever run for nine minutes and thirty-six seconds without stopping? Back through history, man ran to hunt food. The fleet-footed caught their prey. The slow faced starvation and possible extinction."

"I sure don't want starvation," Bubba said, "or that 'stinction' thing. I use Right Guard." The class laughed again.

"We all appreciate that, Bubba," Pop said. "Has anyone here ever run for nine minutes and thirty-six seconds?" I raised my hand, and so did Keith and a few others. When Pop stared and raised his eyebrows, only Keith and I kept up our hands.

"Two hands? Mankind's first sport was running. We will be fit, not victims of our push-button culture. If I asked how many sit-ups you do in a typical day, what would you say? One? Half when you get up in the morning, and the other half when you lie down at night?"

"Today, we will become one-percenters!" Pop said.

"Then can I fish?" Bubba asked, raising his hand.

"After you're a one-percenter, Bubba. We work for improvement. We'll develop arm strength for those with arms, leg strength for those with legs…"

"And brain strength for those with brains?" Keith asked.

"Right on, Keith!"

"What about the afternoon disabled class? Will they be forced to do this? Wheelchair guys can't run, the deaf can't hear directions, and the blind can't see where to run."

"We'll develop what we have to overcome what's missing. Wheelchair athletes will get stronger arms to improve mobility. The deaf will learn multiple ways to communicate. Nothing is wrong with a blind runner's legs."

Pop motioned for Ethan and me to step out from our squad. "I want to introduce two new students to you. This is Ethan Gorman—his first day."

"Hi, Ethan," the class said in unison. Ethan raised his hand before stepping back in line.

"The other new student will introduce himself and help answer Keith's question."

I turned to face the class. "My name is Billy Cline...and without glasses, I'm legally blind. But I still led October's championship cross-country race until the last hundred yards."

"The 'eagle boy!'" Bubba shouted. "I caught a rainbow trout during your race!"

"Until you joined him in the creek!" Keith said. Bubba's lower lip dropped.

"Thank you, Billy," Pop said. "I've carried a dream for a long time—to coach a running team that includes those whom the world calls 'handicapped.' This team won't be a perfect fit for everyone. At Cliffview, we create opportunities to improve ourselves. This team is only one opportunity. If you try out and make the top seven—great! If not, but you want to help, join our support group. We'll need your help. Today, we begin, and I've asked Billy to be our captain."

"Okay, I'm ready for a run!" Keith said.

"Yeah? I'm ready for a snack!" Bubba added. We gathered at the starting point in the gym.

"Remember, this is a beginning workout, not a race. One percent!" Pop instructed.

I noticed that Andy was signing again though no deaf students were present.

"Set!" Pop blew the whistle! Keith sprinted, while most ran at a leisurely pace.

*****

When the bell rang for the last physical education class of the day, Pop stood on the outdoor track taking attendance. Most students, like me, had signed up for two PE classes instead of study hall. It was a blustery afternoon, and I tested myself, blazing through a fast warmup. When I joined the group, Pop gave me specific instructions and a warning.

"The mundane times of working with the disabled will test you more than the most difficult run," he said. "Believe me on this. You need to accept these students as official representatives of Cliffview Boys' Home, whether they run or become helpers or not."

I tried to line up those in wheelchairs, on crutches, or who were blind or deaf, but it was chaos until Pop restored order. I sighed with relief since everything I'd tried didn't work.

"Hold it!" Pop yelled as Andy signed. "On the outside, help may fail, but at Cliffview, we help each other. Line 'em up! Wheelchairs outside—lanes six, seven, and eight! Those assigned as guides in four. Blind in five. Three-legged runners in two and three." Everybody reacted. Pop grinned and looked at me. "Put the deaf in lane one, Billy."

"Hey, guys, lane 1!" I shouted. Andy's short legs propelled him to my side.

"You gotta learn to sign, Billy! They're deaf!" I must have turned a few shades of red.

"I'm so sorry."

Andy signed to the six-member deaf group and saw them line up in lane one. "We'll teach you the basics of sign language."

In lane two, Clyde, who had only one leg, held his crutches up against his body and twirled like a spinning top on one foot. It was amazing to see the speed he generated.

"Wow! I'm dizzy!" Clyde said. When his dizziness subsided, he asked, "Pop, why are we called 'three-legged runners'? I do my spinnin' top on one leg."

"The spinnin' top you perform is a thing of beauty," Pop said, "but we're training to cover ground, not act like dizzy jackrabbits on an out-of-control merry-go-round!"

"Someday you may receive an artificial leg, but now your two crutches and one leg give you a leg up on everyone else. Work on smoothing out your gait."

"What about my soreness?" Other crutchers laughed as Clyde rubbed his armpits. "I know I shouldn't support all my weight on the crutch, but I get tired and it rubs me the wrong way!"

"Andy has solved your SAP."

"SAP?"

"Sore armpits, Clyde!" Andy shouted. Andy pulled out two soft rubber-contoured cups from a bag and showed the procedure. "Two bands fit around the neck and chest. I call it the 'SAP Rejuvenator.'" Andy grinned, proud of himself. "You place the rubber cup in each pit, put the short bands around each shoulder, and the middle-sized bands around your neck and chest! Voila! Instant pit relief!" Andy tossed them to the three-legged runners.

They tried to put them on, saying, "Viola! Valla Walla! Voila!" But they needed work.

Pop got serious. "Today, we're practicing on working together as a team. That takes extra time. So, in this class, we're 'three percent' athletes! How much time is that, Andy?"

"Twenty-eight minutes and forty-eight seconds!" Andy said before he signed, "Three percent" to a deaf speedster, Pete, and his buddies.

"That's right!" Pop said. A shriek caused many to lift their heads.

"Wooo-eee! It's Victory!" I yelled. Victory circled the track before landing on a short fence near us.

"Victory will be our inspiration for three percent!" Pop shouted. "Okay! Let's go!"

As I ran beside the blind and their guides, I offered strategies to the twins. Zack held one end of an elastic band while Zeke held the other. A tug here and there and verbal clues kept Zeke aligned on the track. It reminded me of how Tom had done the same for me. I wondered how a more limited blind runner such as Zeke would perform on a dangerous mountain trail.

Luke completed a lap in his wheelchair, his strong arms powering around lane eight. Pete, the lead deaf runner, sprinted fast inside him in lane one.

Andy took notes on a clipboard like an assistant coach. The Cliffview students knew he had restrictions from strenuous activity. They treated him as a teenage inventor. Pop gave him advanced duties. If a student excelled, Pop encouraged Andy to develop ways for him to solve problems, become more proficient, and help his teammates.

I noted the attention Zack and Zeke gave each other. Zack had perfect vision, but Zeke saw objects as shadowy shapes. On a dark night, Zeke had trouble seeing at all. Zack held his elastic band in lane four while his brother held the other end in lane five. I learned that Zeke's name had the letter "e" in the middle for "eye." That's how we knew Zeke as the blind twin.

Luke, Pete, Clyde, and the Z twins, as we called them, led each of their respective groups. As I passed by on a lap, I heard Andy's analysis: "Luke's got the fastest wheels in town! And Pete's deafness doesn't prevent him from running all-out all the time!"

During the run, I sprinted away from Zack and Zeke and caught up to Pete and Luke. After running between them for a lap, I gave the two boys a smile and a thumbs-up sign.

Andy laughed beside Pop, then shouted, "At least you signed to Pete this time!"

Luke was tiring and slowing. I stayed with him as Pete ran ahead. I soon realized that racing a wheelchair could tax even the strongest arms.

Luke veered inward, out of his lane, and dodged wheelchairs he'd lapped, causing him to tip over onto the track. I knew Pop and Andy saw him fall. Pop pointed so I called for Ethan and his blind runner he guided to stop. We hovered over Luke, checking for injuries.

"I'm okay…just scratches," Luke said between heaving breaths. "I got hit harder playing football! But this wheelchair is unstable!" I motioned the others to continue. Ethan helped me right the wheelchair and put Luke back in it. As Luke brushed the dirt from his clothes, he examined the scrapes on his arms.

"Why can't I ride in a wheelchair that's designed for my needs? One that's safe and fast?" Ethan was silent, listening. "And with a sidecar for a friend!"

"Yeah," I said, looking at Ethan. "And motorized with a suspension system to travel dirt trails! Like a super go-cart wheelchair!"

"It must be light and look good, too!" said Luke, to end his rant.

"You're serious?" Ethan said. Neither of us budged. We stared until we got the answer we wanted. "Well, my grandfather owns a company that could make it." Our grins widened.

*****

The next day nine of us gathered in the lounge for an hour of group persuasion tactics. Ethan walked to the hallway phone with some notes in hand. We all followed.

"If you say it like you practiced it, he can't say no!" I said to Ethan.

"Oh, no, no-no-no! I'm not sure about this. You don't know my grandfather."

Keith chipped in. "Ask for it like a Christmas present!"

"Well, I guess I could, but I'm so nervous," said Ethan. "I've seen business owners crumble in front of Grandfather."

I tapped his shoulder. "But you're his grandson. That should make a difference." Ethan placed coins into the pay phone and dialed. Andy tugged on Bubba's arm, so Bubba hoisted Andy over his head and onto his shoulders.

"Shush!" Andy yelled. "Silence!"

Ring! Ring! Ring! "Dr. Gorman speaking."

"Hello, Grandfather! It's me, Ethan."

"Why the call, Ethan? Anything wrong?"

"It's a necessary call. I know you may not believe it, but I've come up with a business idea, a great business idea."

"Really? I assume it has nothing to do with tree forts."

"No tree forts, sir. I got the idea from students here at Cliffview."

"So the students are the ones teaching now? You have one minute."

"One minute?" Ethan panicked, glancing at us. I pointed to his notes, and he began.

"Wheelchair kids have lost the freedom to travel off-road. Luke is one of my good friends. He had a car accident, just like Mom and Dad and I did. They amputated his legs at mid-thigh. He can't dream of going on back trails the way other kids can. His wheelchair lacks a superior suspension system, like the one you developed for our super go-carts. There's a market for advanced wheelchairs you and your engineers could design and manufacture. It would catch on across the country if you promoted it." A long pause occurred. "Grandfather, are you still there?"

"Yes, go on."

"Would you commission your engineers to research and design a rugged prototype off-road wheelchair with sidecar?"

"Off-road wheelchair…with sidecar?" Dr. Gorman questioned.

Ethan threw his script over his head. "Yeah! Giant tires, a huge engine, plush seats, and fancy lights! Wheelchair kids like to have fun with their friends, ya know!"

Andy, still on Bubba's shoulders, was so excited that he smashed his hand down on Pete's "Cat in the Hat" hat. It squished over his face. Everybody laughed.

"Who are those boys I hear?"

"Some you can give hope to…like you did for NASA in the '60s."

"You want a Lunar Roving Vehicle with a sidecar? For the handicapped?"

The boys looked at themselves and nodded. "If it's light enough!" shouted Ethan.

"Now, that's a challenge," Dr. Gorman said. "Let me consider your request."

"You've built relationships with engineers all over this country, Grandfather. Please convince somebody to adapt what you've already invented. My friends need it! And now!"

"I've never heard you speak like this, Ethan."

"I've never been so excited, Grandfather. You won't be sorry. Bye, Grandfather!"

"Dogpile!" Andy shouted. We all dog piled Ethan. Andy slid off Bubba's shoulders onto the top of the heap. He clenched his hands in the air and shouted, "Look, Ma! Top of the world!"

CHAPTER 28

President's Day: 1984 TV Routine

Walking onto the Cliffview track, I saw a TV cameraman filming Lizzy Looper, the reporter Andy had a crush on. Pop stood beside her and a large banner at the track that read, "Cliffview's 15th Annual President's Day Fund-Raiser" in large block letters. *Would Andy's idea of a new routine work?*

"This is Lizzy Looper reporting. Last week, we met Tammy and her tap-dancing parrots. This week, I'm at Cliffview Boys' Home with its founder, Pop O'Reilly. Since 1970, this school has delivered an outstanding education for students who face a wide variety of challenges. But that's only part of what makes this school unique. Today, students will run on foot or will race with crutches or in wheelchairs to raise funds for Cliffview's educational and social needs."

"Welcome, Lizzy! We're proud to have you here," Pop said. "The students at Cliffview believe in having fun while they're raising monetary support." Pop laughed and pointed to one of his younger students, who approached. "This is Gabe. He wants to give you a gift—a drawing he made." Students pressed close for a better view. Gabe stepped in front of Andy and me, giving Lizzy his detailed pencil-sketch drawing of her face.

Lizzy brightened as she scanned it. "I can't believe it—it's me!" Andy signed her words to Gabe, who grinned from ear to ear.

"Gabe is deaf, but he watches your TV specials and drew you," Pop said. Lizzy held the drawing up next to her face for the camera.

"Thank you," she said to Gabe, patting him on the head. "Now, to the track where your students participate in a 'camaraderie workout?'"

"Yes," said Pop. "Our students assist each other on the track, in the classroom, and even on the basketball court. Each one gives to others what they may lack, whether it's sight, hearing, or help with locomotion."

Beside the banner, we filed onto the track. Cliffview students wore hand-lettered T-shirts that read "Deaf Speedster," "King of the Crutch," "Crutch Warrior," "Blinding Speed," "Easy on the Eyes," "Chariot Champ," and "Chariot Chump."

"You race the deaf and blind together with kids on crutches and in wheelchairs? Why did you invent this workout, Pop?"

"To meet their emotional and physical needs. Observe, Lizzy."

Pop blew his whistle. All athletes looked his way except for the deaf. "Andy!" Pop yelled.

Using American Sign Language, Andy signed these words to the six deaf athletes, "Check out the chick." The deaf students turned to Lizzy, grinning and waving. Lizzy waved back.

"Communication takes different forms for different students," Pop said, frowning at Andy.

"They sure are a happy group," Lizzy added.

"No doubt," Pop answered.

As they settled, the cameraman focused on the crutch racers. There was a heightened competitive spirit among the three crutch racers in lane two and the three in lane three. As they eyed one another, Clyde did his spinnin' top routine on one foot, and when he stopped, it was an all-out crutch sword fight among the athletes in both lanes. They supported themselves on one foot with a solid crutch, then slashed at their opponents in the next lane with a lighter one.

"Crutches at your sides…now!" yelled Pop. All spun to attention, their crutches close to their bodies, under control.

The cameraman turned to focus on the blind guides and their blind running partners in lanes four and five. Each partner held on to his respective elastic bands.

"There are several categories of blindness here at our school, Lizzy. We don't have any totally blind students. We have boys who can see movement and shapes only from certain distances, and others who have various degrees of blurry vision." Pop noticed that one blind runner was in the blind-guide lane.

"Whoops!" said Pop. "Billy, we've got a bad case of the blind leading the blind." Some students laughed along with the small crowd. Ethan and I, being guides, reset him.

Out rolled six donated lightweight wheelchairs and their racers, dressed in charioteer garb, two each in lanes six, seven, and eight. Luke led the wheelchairs out, each flashing gold-painted cardboard blades on their wheels. The sparkling blades twirled in the sunlight.

"The athletes are set." Lizzy spoke into her microphone like a golf announcer. "Tension is mounting as Pop O'Reilly prepares his challenged athletes and their helpers for the finals of his 'camaraderie workout.' The looks on their faces are spellbinding!"

The cameraman filmed Pop blowing his whistle.

"And they're off!" shouted Lizzy.

Luke's wheelchair came out blazing fast in lane eight, but his hand slipped, causing him to steer into lane seven. The other wheelchair followed, forcing both lane seven wheelchairs into those in lane six, who cut into the blind, toppling several blind runners, now draped over the wheelchairs. These out-of-control wheelchairs forced the blind guides inside, where they tangled with crutchers in lanes two and three, causing a massive pile-up in lanes one, two, and three as the deaf now toppled over them.

"We've got a massive pile-up!" announced Lizzy. An old air-raid siren blared while Bubba and Keith, with red flashing lights strapped onto their heads, rushed in with a stretcher. The camera caught the athletes laughing and mugging for the camera.

Lizzy, standing beside grounded participants, smiled and leaned in toward the cameraman. "Is it a camaraderie workout or camaraderie comedy? You decide…but I think we got pranked!" She laughed along with the cameraman in the background.

"This is Lizzy Looper reporting, and on behalf of Pop O'Reilly and Cliffview Boys' Home on this President's Day, please support these special boys with your generous donations."

*****

I heard the Clausen-Cowler clan sat watching Lizzy's TV special at Blimp's place. At the end of the broadcast, Blimp placed the note from Jake into its envelope and set it down, turning off the TV and walking to the kitchen.

"What was that?" said Rawley, sitting on the couch beside his sons and Jimmy Jack.

"A fund-raiser for a school of freaks!" said Jimmy Jack.

"So now they're gettin' airtime and sympathy?" Jabbing his finger at Cletus, Rawley shouted, "It's Billy and his buzzard that got you DQed from the championship and me suspended for six months! It's why we got no money. It's why we moved in with Blimp! I thought you two, my own flesh and blood, would take care of him!" Rawley stomped out.

"We'll pay those freaks a visit," said Cletus.

"And put 'em in their place," added Gopher. Jimmy Jack just sat there as the brothers walked into the backyard to iron out the details of a response to their Pa.

I had no illusions of secrecy in the Cowler household. I knew Jimmy Jack would find out about Jake's apology letter for beaning Blimp. It was President's Day that reignited Rawley's anger and set off the Cowler boys in full fury against us.

Jimmy Jack had joined Blimp on his cruiser beat through town. He told Blimp he had sneaked a read of the letter Jake wrote. They both agreed it moved them but didn't know what to do about it. Later that day, Blimp stopped me on a run and shared that he liked the letter and so did Jimmy Jack. It surprised me, but I wasn't sure if that would make any difference how he acted toward us. When he warned me about Rawley's anger toward his Cowler sons, I prepared for the worst.

CHAPTER 29

Fight at Caruso's Diner

On Tuesday evening, Tom promised to bring Jenny to Caruso's Pizza Diner, where I could meet up with her. For now, I was holed up with Luke and Andy, studying in their dorm room, waiting for Bubba, not a fan of Tuesday's dinner menu.

While we were studying, three loud knocks rattled the door. "Guess who?" Andy said.

"He's early," added Luke, wheeling to the door and turning the knob. Another knock rumbled the door open, sending Luke rolling across the room.

"Bubba, a 7.5 on the Richter scale! Take it easy!" said Luke.

"Sorry. Uh…I'm hungry."

"Caruso's?" I suggested.

"Yeah, Caruso's!"

"Best pizza this side of the Leaning Tower of Pisa," added Luke.

"Yeah, yeah, a tower of pizza!" Bubba said, adjusting his hearing aid that gave a screeching sound.

Andy spoke to Luke. "He thinks you're buyin' him a tower of pizza."

"What else is new?" Luke said, shrugging. "It's the least I can do for liftin' me and my wheelchair all over town."

"After you," said Bubba, holding the door. But neither of us could get by Bubba's massive frame.

"First one down the hallway to Caruso's gets two extra pieces!" yelled Luke. Bubba grinned and chugged down the hallway like a runaway locomotive. Andy's short legs pushed the back of Luke's

236

wheelchair, following Bubba. I played the caboose, running from behind. Bubba's foot stomps caused the hallway chandeliers to sway.

"He thinks you said the first one gets two extra pizzas!" Andy yelled in Luke's ear.

"No, man! No!" Luke moaned.

All of us passed by Clyde's door as he hopped into the hallway, shouting, "Buhh-baaaaa!" Clyde's words echoed twister-like as he did his spinnin' top routine.

We walked several blocks to Caruso's, where I saw Tom's car pull in. "Thanks, Tom. Look, Jenny and I will join you for pizza later. We're gonna cross to the park and perhaps study the constellations." I took Jenny's hand and pulled her away.

Tom laughed and pulled out a rolled-up *Rockside Bugle*, walking in behind Luke, Andy, and Bubba. The great tenor opera piece, "Di Quella Pira" by Verdi, blasted from the restaurant speakers via the makeshift turntable on the counter. It was difficult to carry on a conversation.

"They still haven't fixed the jukebox!" said Luke, frustrated, covering his ears.

"Giuseppe Verdi is not so bad—he's Italian," said Andy, reading the record jacket.

Luke frowned, trying to reason with Bubba. "Listen, Bubba, remember that diet expert we read about in the magazine? He said, 'Thin is in.'"

Bubba glanced toward heaven. "Thank you, God!" He strolled to his favorite booth and spread out, taking the entire booth for himself.

"Bubba heard, 'Thin is…sin!'" Andy said.

"If thin is sin, I can't win!" Luke groaned. He followed Andy to the booth across the aisle from Bubba. Andy slid into his seat as Luke positioned his wheelchair in the aisle, tucking in sideways. Contemplating the cost, Luke grabbed his wallet and counted his money at the booth with Andy. "Glad my uncle sent money this month for my birthday."

Tom decided not to sit alone, so approached Luke and Andy at their booth. "Hey, guys, how's Billy doin' at Cliffview?"

"Good," Luke said. "Wanna join us?"

"Thanks, Luke." Tom waited for Luke to back up, then slid in across from Andy. "Have you seen the article about your guys on the sports page?"

*****

Outside Caruso's, Cletus's red Chevy convertible pulled in. Jimmy Jack rode shotgun while Gopher read the *Rockside Bugle* in the backseat.

"Well, if it isn't the little handicappers," said Jimmy Jack, glancing through Caruso's window.

"Definitely freaks of nature," added Cletus.

"Hey! Listen to this!" said Gopher. "Some blind freak, Zeke, thinks their new Cliffview running team can be…powerful!"

"Oooh…powerful!" Jimmy Jack mocked.

Gopher went on: "His twin, Zack, agreed, saying, 'I think we can match up and whip those Rockside High boys and their cross-country team.' It's right here in the paper!"

"Match up with us? Whip us?" said Cletus, snatching the article. "Zack, huh? Boy, is he gonna get it!"

Jimmy Jack spied Tom's Blue Beauty. He looked through the windows into Caruso's. "Look who's braggin' about the article. It's Tom!" They peered inside and saw Tom holding up the newspaper.

"Coach warned him. Tom's a turncoat! That means Billy will be nearby. Let's show these bottom feeders their place on the food chain," Jimmy Jack said, opening his door. Cletus and Gopher joined him, following inside.

The three waited for the hostess, glaring at Tom's table while overpowered by the opera.

"I hate that hoity-toity noise! Verdi is vanquished!" Jimmy Jack said as he stepped behind the counter and shut down the heroic music on the final note.

The young hostess looked at him to object, but the eyes she met were cold and did not debate. She turned away.

Caruso's was now silent. Bubba rose from his booth with an empty jug, leaving behind two half-eaten pizzas. He lumbered toward the soda dispenser. Bubba drew all eyes when he expelled a belch for the ages and stumbled into the jukebox. The power light flickered and stayed on.

"Wipe Out!" by the Surfaris blasted over the jukebox speakers.

"Oh, yeah! All right! He fixed the jukebox!" yelled several Caruso customers, who cheered Bubba.

Bubba spun in a circle, looking proud, saluting them with his empty pitcher. He squinted, saying, "I gotta go!" He hobbled down the aisle in a cramped walk and through a door marked "Men."

Moans rang out as Bubba walked inside carrying the empty pitcher.

Caruso's returned to normal as the crowd grooved to the driving rock beat.

Jimmy Jack and the Cowler boys walked toward Tom's table. Andy looked up, seeing them first. "What are you Cowlers and kin doin' here?"

"We're from the psychiatrist's office, lookin' for morons," said Gopher.

"Look in the mirror," said Andy.

Jimmy Jack held back Gopher and got in Tom's face. "Coach told you not to mingle with freaks!"

"I'm just eating pizza, Jimmy Jack," Tom said, folding his newspaper closed. Tom nodded to Cletus and Gopher, but they didn't respond. The Cowler boys stood like racehorses preparing to burst out of a starting gate.

"We saw you waving the sports page," Jimmy Jack said, grabbing Tom's newspaper and pointing to the story. "Coach said no freaks!"

"You? Callin' me a freak?" challenged Luke from his wheelchair.

Jimmy Jack grabbed Luke's shirt and yanked him above his wheelchair, yelling into his face, "Freak!"

Luke snatched Jimmy Jack's arms with surprising strength, but Jimmy Jack leveraged his body to jerk Luke up higher, exposing his stumps. He twisted Luke to the side and set him onto Bubba's two opened pizzas across the aisle.

239

Tom and Andy tried to get up, but Cletus and Gopher shoved them back into the booth. Gasps and looks of disapproval grew from the patrons as the three departed for their car. Luke was irate from sitting on pizzas. Tom and Andy picked him up and lowered Luke back into his wheelchair.

*****

At the park across from Caruso's, I leaned against a tree and embraced Jenny, gazing into her eyes. Just before our kiss, I said, "If I was Shakespeare, I'd be..."

"Speechless?" said Jenny. "Ahhh...got you."

*****

Tom sprinted through Caruso's and burst out the door. He charged Jimmy Jack, who turned and spun Tom into the passenger door with a thud.

*****

I glanced up, hearing Tom collide into Cletus's car. Tom landed a right cross to Jimmy Jack's jaw, sending him backward. Cletus and Gopher joined in by ramming Tom into the door again, pummeling Tom in his gut until Jimmy Jack added his punches. I sprinted from Jenny to Caruso's parking lot. I saw Jimmy Jack's final punch send Tom slumping to the ground.

Jimmy Jack held his jaw and yelled, "No more teammate!" while staring at Tom on the asphalt. That's when I leaped up and swooped over the convertible, eagle-like, landing on Jimmy Jack, knocking him backward to the ground before I rolled off him.

Gopher and Jimmy Jack dove into the backseat as Cletus roared his engine and peeled out.

Andy ran out of Caruso's and knelt over Tom, yelling, "Somebody call for help!" Several bystanders who had run outside ran back in to call for an ambulance.

Inside, Bubba returned to his table after refilling his pitcher and stood motionless, holding a half-gallon jug of root beer over his squashed meal. "What happened to my pizzas?"

*****

Several days later, Pop called me to his Cliffview office to join him for a meeting. After I arrived, Tom, now on crutches, walked in beside his mother.

Pop started the meeting. "Well, son, what can I do for you?"

Tom fidgeted. "I hate these crutches. The doctor said they're precautionary, and I know my hip's gonna heal in a couple of weeks, but I need to heal in peace. I'm not getting that at Rockside High, and we know the authorities won't do anything to the Cowlers." Tom looked to his mother.

"Mr. O'Reilly, we're shocked Coach Clausen had the gall to defend Jimmy Jack's actions to the principal! We're afraid for Tom's safety. Jimmy Jack showed off his facial bruise and got his way! I'll quote from the principal's letter. 'Tom's running momentum caused him to crash into Cletus's car door, resulting in his hip injury. His bruised ribs and getting the wind knocked out of him were also caused by his own momentum into the car. The disturbance at Caruso's before was a verbal one. It's true someone pushed him into his seat, but only to prevent a fight from happening inside Caruso's. It was Tom's anger and his attack on Jimmy Jack outside that started the physical fight. Therefore, Tom is suspended.' End of quote."

Tom was huffing in anger. "The Cowler boys and Jimmy Jack got nothing!"

Pop raised his hands.

"Tom...Mrs. Pryor...I understand. Know this: I understand. Nineteen years ago, my little Rachel suffered major burns from the flames of a house fire. On that night before New Year's Eve, I couldn't save her in time. I carried her down a ladder, but she died in my arms. In her memory, I help all who come here." Mrs. Pryor nodded as Tom slowed his breathing.

Pop continued, "If any could climb out of their wheelchairs and walk, or throw down their crutches and run, or hear the sound of a waterfall, or see the colors of a rainbow, I'd feel my work here was worthy of my little Rachel."

Tom's mother rose and shook Pop's burn-scarred hand. Signing the admission papers, she kissed Tom on the forehead and left.

I looked at Tom, then Pop. "We've got us a team of seven."

Pop picked up the phone. He looked determined. "Coach Grundman, it's Pop O'Reilly. Yeah, doin' good. How about you? Good. Look, I've assembled a cross-country team here at Cliffview. No, I'm not kidding. I'm asking for permission to join the conference…as equals." A pause followed. "That's right…as equals. The only addendum is the elastic band held by our partially blind twin, Zeke. He'll be guided and run beside his brother Zack."

A longer pause ensued. "A conference vote in three weeks? Sure, that's my birthday! Okay, I'll bring Billy, our team captain, but don't say 'yes' now and then allow them to chew up Billy and spit him out! I want no one tryin' to grill him about the championship race last season." Another pause. "Okay, I know one coach who might start something, but you can quell it, right?" Another pause. "Okay. I'm glad you feel the same way. You know, for years I've wanted to join this conference if I could assemble a team." Another pause. "All right, then." Pop hung up.

The happiness that covered my face disappeared. Pop and Tom's intense stares made me nervous. When our team got together that night back at Cliffview, we shared all that had happened.

CHAPTER 30

Blind Free Throw Contest

Two weeks later, I led our new team on a run along hiking trails over the upper part of Rockside. I set a slow pace as Pop had suggested. This kept our team together for most of the run. The doctor had released Tom, and he grinned as we took it easy for his first major effort. Joining Tom and me were Keith, Pete, and the Z twins. Ethan ran beside us most of the way until dropping off the pace.

Thoughts of attending the conference vote kept churning inside me. "Take 'em home, Tom," I said, pointing. He had seen that look before. With less than a mile to go, I peeled off, sprinting up an overgrown trail into a dense part of the forest.

"Billy! Where ya goin'?" Tom shouted. I didn't respond. Some runners slowed until Tom spoke up: "Keep it together, guys. Billy's just doing his thing."

I had to push this mental wall back—this mind-set of limitation. I had to disintegrate it. Doubt kept rising in front of me, haunting me—an attitude that would block my improvement. *Why not view this negative mind-set as an illusion, a fabrication of the mind? No doubts—no limitations,* I would demand more of myself—whether I felt like it or not.

Driving hard with my arms, I lifted my legs high to avoid jagged rocks while maintaining my balance on the twisting trail. I felt the rough bushes and tree limbs scrape me, but I protected my face, knowing I couldn't afford to lose my glasses.

Victory would not fly here, too dense and dark. I was on my own. I kept hearing Jake's solemn words—*It's up to you.* I ran like a wildman—attacking the terrain, shifting my route to stay afoot, leaping over fallen timber and dodging branches to the top of a rise and over it.

The steep descent on the other side surprised me. My speed increased to a borderline freefall. I had only a split second to choose my foot placement with every stride. The ground grew rocky and sharp, and the trail disappeared. I was out of control. Seeing a limb, I grabbed hold, crashing into it to slow myself before I tumbled to the rocky earth. I felt my shirt rip along with the skin on my legs as I skidded to a stop in the brush near the bottom of the hillside. *What a stupid idea!*

*****

My Cliffview teammates had walked into the gym after their workout when Pop appeared. "Where's Billy?" Pop asked.

"He's still running—not happy with only six percent," said Tom.

"Freelancing, huh? He'll miss this announcement. Gather 'round, boys." As they did, a smile rose on Pop's face. He motioned for Luke to roll to the front. "Ethan, step forward...beside Luke." Exhausted, Ethan joined Luke. "I just got a call. Your grandfather's team has not only started production on the wheelchair—they're halfway finished with it! He said he's proud of your business idea!"

Everyone cheered! Luke gave a high-five to Ethan. It stunned him for a few seconds. Luke rocked back and forth in his wheelchair, drawing laughter.

After the hoopla, most of the boys headed for the lockers. Before Pop left, he spoke to Andy. "Buzz me when Billy gets back."

"Sure, Pop." Luke and Andy stayed behind in the gym, watching Zack shoot hoops. Zeke sat in a chair at the free throw line, waiting his turn.

"Keep your seat, Zeke!" said Zack. "I towed you around for a six-percenter. Give me a break. Aren't you worn out from the workout?"

"You guided me…not towed me," said Zeke. "I'm not tired. Come on, I've heard you swish three in a row! That ties your record. Get off the line."

"Not until I equal your record. You'll get your turn."

*****

I rose from the brush, my shirt shredded and bloody. I glanced at my legs, knees, and body, scraped and bleeding. I limped, taking a shortcut to Cliffview.

*****

A door opened into the Cliffview gym. Cletus and Gopher peeked in. Seeing only the four boys on the basketball court, they slipped inside.

"Can't believe Tom left us for this dump," said Gopher, looking around the gym. They strutted across the basketball court toward Luke.

Luke was sitting in his wheelchair near half court when Cletus sneaked behind him and shoved him. "Hey!" Luke shouted as he rolled toward Andy.

"Watch it!" Andy shouted while stopping Luke's wheelchair. He stood, glaring at the Cowler boys. "You almost knocked me over!"

"You wouldn't have far to fall!" said Gopher. Cletus stared at Andy, then laughed, and sauntered up to the twins at the charity stripe.

Zack held onto his basketball, not budging, just looking at the two intruders.

"What's the matter, brother?" Zeke asked from his chair.

Before Zack could answer, Cletus spoke: "None of your business, bright eyes!" Gopher snickered. Cletus looked at Zack. "Are you Zack?"

"Yeah. Are you Cowlers lost?"

"No, we're from the demolition department, notifying you this gym will be leveled upon our return. It has been declared an 'eyesore,'" said Cletus.

Zeke twisted in his chair. "Look, I'm half blind, so I can't see what you Cowler boys see. But my other senses are highly developed—like identifying the distinct odor of a skunk and a half-dead possum since you entered—creating a 'nose sore.' Which one are you, Cletus?"

Cletus came at Zeke, but Zack stepped between them and took the shove. Zack landed on Zeke, knocking him out of his chair. The boys lay crumpled on the floor.

"If you twins wanna run like you said in the *Bugle*, you gotta learn to stay on your feet!" Cletus smacked his hands together several times as Gopher guffawed.

Zack helped his brother rise and turned to size up Cletus. But Cletus was way ahead of him, grabbing the loose basketball. "Look what I've got!"

"Give it back!" Zack said. Luke wheeled over as Andy followed.

"Wow! You Cowler boys are tough!" Luke said. "Why don't ya shoot for it? Or are you afraid to test your free throw skills against a twin?"

"Why should I?" Cletus said. "I've already got the ball. And who washed the pizza off your backside?"

"The same guy who'll wipe that stupid grin off your chicken face!" Luke said.

Cletus leered back. "Ya know, Luke, after your accident, we felt sorry for you, but now you're all talk and no action."

"It ain't just talk!" Andy said. "Hot air is your specialty! Luke just gave you a challenge! If you can't man up, it'll be all over town that you're the biggest yellow-bellied, chicken-faced Raven in all of Rockside!"

"Watch your mouth, midget man."

Undaunted, Andy continued, "The challenge is ten free throws. You pick the twin."

Gopher laughed again as Cletus confirmed the challenge. "Me...shoot against either twin? Ten free throws?"

Andy nodded, "Visitors first."

"You make the rules?"

"I'm their agent," Andy said.

Cletus shook his head, staring at Zeke. "Were you the first half or the last half of the twin?"

Zack's face reddened as he responded. "Are you gonna shoot the ball or keep yappin'? Your momma must need earplugs."

"I don't have a momma," Cletus said.

"Not surprised. Chickens are hatched!"

"I'll deal with you later," Cletus said, holding back a Zack attack. He spun the basketball in his hands and sank shots one, two, four, seven, and eight. Shots nine and ten rolled off the rim. Angry at missing his last two shots, Cletus one-bounced the ball hard to Zeke, bloodying his lip as it ricocheted off his face.

Andy restrained Zack, standing between them as blood covered Zeke's teeth.

"Just try it!" Cletus challenged.

Gopher got the ball and walked it to Zeke. "Looks like he might have to forfeit." Gopher stuffed the ball hard into Zeke's gut.

"Ugh...You made five baskets," said Zeke.

"How did you know, blind boy?" asked Gopher.

"He listens! You deaf...and a dunce?" Zack said. Cletus now had to restrain Gopher.

Zack walked up and whispered into his brother's ear. "Concentrate...you can do it." Zack positioned Zeke's toes on the line, his feet shoulder width apart, and made sure his head pointed straight at the basket.

"It's like pin the tail on the blind jackass!" Gopher shouted as he gave Cletus a hand-slap. "Why don't ya spin him around?"

Andy moved beneath the basket. He looked up at the hoop to be precise in his position. Zack stood beside Zeke.

"They got the midget rebounding!" Gopher shouted, laughing hysterically.

"Fifteen feet...use some arch," Zack reminded his brother.

"Listen to my voice," Andy said. "I am under the basket."

Zeke bounced the ball three times and shot, hitting the side of the rim. *Clang.* "Eight inches right, a little long," said Zack.

Cletus and Gopher laughed, but the team ignored it.

Andy rebounded and passed to Zack, who handed the ball to Zeke. Andy got into position again and bounced the ball twice. "Find your range," Andy spoke again. "I'm right here."

Zeke's shot hit on the left side of the rim. *Clang.* "Four inches left...distance perfect," said Zack. Andy returned the ball as before.

"Come on, you can do it!" Andy shouted. "Focus!"

"Focus?" Gopher snickered under his breath. Zeke's shot was straight but off the back rim. Clang. "Just long—about four inches," said Zack. The ball was returned as if from a slingshot.

"Concentrate...concentrate," Andy said. Zeke heard his voice and swished the fourth shot.

Zeke shot the next one without a dribble and swished shots five through eight! *Swish, swish, swish, swish.*

Cletus, realizing Zeke was in a shooting zone, plowed into him as he fired his ninth shot. *Clang!* The shot hit off the rim.

Tom, Keith, Pete, and Ethan had gotten word the Cowler boys were there and walked out in street clothes from the locker room. Everyone froze.

That was when I pushed the door open and entered the gym. "What's going on here?"

Luke announced, "It's a free throw contest! It's tied, and they're chicken! Zeke's got one more shot!" Cletus grabbed Luke by the neck.

As I moved forward, all eyes were on my blood-smeared body. Even Cletus and Gopher seemed repulsed by my appearance. "He'll take his last shot," I said.

Tom moved forward, and the others followed. "You wanna take us all on?" Tom said.

"You're a turncoat traitor!" Cletus shouted.

"Let Luke go, and we'll back off," I said. The team retreated as Cletus let go.

Zack lined up his brother again.

"Come on, Zeke," Andy said. "Come on...in the hole!"

Zeke fired. *Swish!* It was in! A collective cheer went up. "Yeah! Zeke's the man! Team! Team! Team!"

Astonished, Cletus and Gopher sauntered toward the door. Nearing the exit, Gopher grabbed the loose basketball that rolled to him. Tucking it under his arm, Gopher prepared a final insult as the exit doors opened behind the clueless Cowler boys. There stood Bubba with his fishing pole.

"Hey, freaks!" Gopher hollered, holding the basketball high in the air to stop the celebration. "Finders keepers!"

Gopher and Cletus turned to leave. However, Bubba's huge frame stopped Gopher, who stood still, gazing at Bubba's feet as he scanned upward to Bubba's face.

Bubba grinned as he shook his finger back and forth. "No, no, no, no, nooo."

"Who are you?" said Gopher.

"Your worst nightmare!" Bubba raised his fishing pole.

Gopher dropped the ball as Andy led in a unison shout: "Losers weepers!" Cletus and Gopher squeezed past Bubba and out the door.

The celebration was back on!

CHAPTER 31

The Vote for Equality

A week later in the afternoon, ten of us approached the old tool shed at Cliffview. Andy and I scanned the area for movement and gave the all-clear sign. Ethan held a rolled-up blueprint in his hand. "You're gonna love it!" he said. I unlocked the large double doors with the key Luke had purloined, and Bubba pushed them open.

Keith flipped on the switch, and a dim light shone as the door was closed. Ethan held up the blueprint like a relay baton.

"I can't wait to see it in real life!" Luke said from his wheelchair.

"Not yet," Ethan responded. "But we're gettin' closer, aren't we, Andy?"

"You bet your bottom dollar!"

Ethan pointed my way. "Just take care of your end of the deal tonight with Pop."

I nodded. It satisfied Andy. "It's the perfect place for the new wheelchair."

"Yeah, but this place stinks!" said Zeke, standing beside his twin.

Bubba agreed. "Smells worse than a swamp…like you're fishin' for alligator bait and critters like that!"

"Perhaps," said Andy, "but from such places great things emerge!"

"Like Godzilla?" joked Keith. The gang laughed.

"Shhh!" said Pete, raising his index finger to his lips with a mischievous grin after sign language from Andy. The gang laughed even louder.

I looked at Tom. "It's been a long road, but after the vote tonight, we'll run as one team that can compete against the Rockside Ravens." We slapped hands. We both had something to prove. "I'm going to the meeting tonight in my running gear. I'll be so stoked, I'll want to blow off steam with a run."

"Don't be late for the party," Tom reminded me.

Andy emphasized, "We need to keep these riding lawn mowers near the front so we can hide the *Eagle 7* in the corner."

Andy moved first, trying hard to push one mower to the front but couldn't budge it. "Hey, Bubba," Andy called, "it's too heavy for me. Someone must have set the brake."

The team laughed at Andy's logic. Bubba hoisted one end up and rolled it past Andy. "Where do you want it?"

"Whoa!" Andy said. "Right there!"

"Shhh!" said Pete and Keith together, with humor. Bubba pushed the second mower beside the first.

Andy wiped his forehead. "Organization is hard work."

Tom looked at his watch. "You're a lucky guy, Billy. It's time for you to head to Pop's place for dinner. We've got enough muscle here to finish," he said, pointing to Andy.

"Okay, everybody, I'm on my way to Pop's, and then to the conference vote. I'll be representing you tonight. Pop's dream will come true on his birthday! Cliffview will be the newest member of the Mountain Conference!"

"Oh, yeah!" everyone shouted.

"Glory!" said Bubba.

"Jenny and her cheerleader friends are decorating the cafeteria to celebrate Pop's birthday after the meeting. As Tom keeps reminding me, don't be late!"

"Cheerleaders and food? Nobody will be late!" said Keith.

*****

Pop and I enjoyed Mrs. O'Reilly's pasta. Pop patted his stomach and winked at her as she carried the dishes away. "Irish luck to marry an Italian cook."

I chuckled. "After the conference vote, will she join us to celebrate your birthday?"

"Not a chance...she's a real homebody." Pop got up and pushed his chair in, motioning for me to join him outside.

He walked to the rail fence at the edge of his backyard and stood there, relaxing. He gazed toward the mountains, viewing an angry sky. Lightning flashed in the distance. "This is where I do a lot of my thinking. I like the calm of enjoying God's creation, even when the storms approach."

"I get that, too, on the cliffs with Victory."

Pop smiled. "I thought so. I've got several tough questions I need to ask you...and some thoughts I want to share before the conference vote tonight." Pop hesitated and took a deep breath. "The boys have been runnin' hard, Billy. Too hard?"

"Too hard? No," I said. "They're tough...well...some...a few of 'em."

"And the grumbling? 'Billy won't ease up. He wants higher percent levels. Billy won't let us quit on a run!'"

"Quitting can become a habit."

"That's true. You run for the prize by completing the workouts for each individual athlete. Each runner trains to bring his body under control with his mind, based on his level of strength, speed, and endurance. Do they know why they train so hard?"

"So they won't live in defeat, day after day after day," said Billy with increasing volume.

"And what is defeat to you, Billy?"

I squirmed with emotion. "Not warning my brother, causin' him to get shot, wreckin' his life!" I knew Pop could sense the searing hole within my soul.

"How many defeats make you a failure?"

I gave Pop a confused stare. "Why are you giving me the third degree?"

Pop answered with silence. Then I realized something as words just popped out of my mouth. "All I know is defeat." I hung my head until Pop motioned me inside to his study.

Pop walked to his desk and turned. "Victory in a race is only one goal in life."

"But, Pop, you said I was a catalyst who could lead this team to compete as equals. I've given you everything I've got to make us winners."

"I never doubted that, Billy, and that's not defeat." Pop pointed at two paintings on his wall. "Two former students painted these. One shows the agony Jesus endured on the cross. The other shows Jesus at His ascension to heaven. Which shows Him giving everything He's got?"

I gazed at the paintings and pointed to Jesus on the cross. "I don't know, Pop, but that's where I live, on the cross, just like Jake!"

"You can't live there. Jesus didn't." Pop left me alone.

*****

The approaching storm had darkened the skies. Inside the shed, a protective mask covered Ethan's face as he used an acetylene torch. Luke, Andy, Keith, Zack, and Bubba watched as he extinguished it. Pulling off his mask, Ethan pointed to the nameplate, EAGLE 7.

"The emblem of a well-produced dream," said Andy.

"Grandfather says he will deliver it tonight after the finale for Pop's birthday party."

*****

Ma and Pa were designated chaperones at the team party while Pop and I were on our way to the conference meeting at Rockside High. Jenny and Darla worked on a banner for Pop's birthday while Ma baked a cake. Pa helped Jenny hang the banner: "Pop's Birthday Dream."

Most of the gang were there, including Chester and Gabe, the young artist. Jenny, Darla, and some other girls kept the boys entertained playing Twister.

A TV announcement warned of record rainfall and severe thunderstorms, old news to us. Rain was pouring, and we had seen flashes of lightning and heard thunder.

Everyone cheered as Jenny and Pa hung the sign: "Mountain Conference—Here We Come!" Suddenly, the swinging doors flew open and everyone spun around to see Bubba, dripping wet, but boldly holding a string of Rainbow trout.

"Pop's dream is comin' true tonight!" Tom shouted to him.

"Pop's been dreamin' of trout?" Bubba said, surprised. Everybody laughed, circling Bubba to view his catch. As usual, Andy signed to Pete as Keith shook his head.

*****

Pop and I arrived at Rockside High in a downpour. As we climbed out of the Cliffview van, Pop grimaced.

"Are you all right?" I asked.

"Just a little indigestion." I put an umbrella over Pop's head as he reached for a nitroglycerin tablet to put under his tongue. He leaned against the school van, letting the pill take effect, though it was hard to stand still in the driving rain. More coaches drove up, but the waves of hello were brief as they scurried inside. "I'm better now," Pop said. We made our way inside.

I noticed an old bearded man take off his trench coat, revealing a Hawaiian shirt underneath as he sat in the back of the auditorium. He wasn't a coach…not anyone I knew. He gave me a curious stare. I thought he looked familiar, but I couldn't place him. Then I spotted Jimmy Jack. He was laughing with three new coaches to something that Coach Clausen was saying. Clausen seemed to honor Jimmy Jack, offering a seat to his conference champion. When my eyes met Jimmy Jack's, I knew the competition between us was alive more than ever.

Ben Grundman, conference president, stood at the podium chewing tobacco. A crack of thunder reverberated through the auditorium, causing all to scan if lightning had struck the building.

"Let's get this meeting underway!" Coach Clausen yelled.

"We can all agree on that! We've got a full house here—all twenty-four coaches, despite the weather. Thank you for coming. Let me introduce three new cross-country coaches for next fall: Tim Barnes of Lincoln, Ron Dunn of Valley, and Tracy Smith of Pierce." All three raised their hands as Coach Clausen slapped their backs.

Pop leaned close. "Acts like he's runnin' for office." I smiled.

"I don't want to miss this opportunity to introduce last year's conference champion, Jimmy Jack Clausen." Jimmy Jack stood and waved. "He went undefeated, folks. Uh, Coach Clausen, is that three champions in a row?" Clausen nodded while raising his hand.

"Also, Pop O'Reilly is our guest from Cliffview Boys' Home. You may have heard of Pop's work there. He's brought his transferred runner and team captain, Billy Cline, known in this town and others as the 'eagle boy.'" The room rocked with another thunder blast.

"Let's get these ballots going!" shouted the Haybury Coach.

"Coach Clausen, if you and your conference champ there, uh, Jimmy Jack, could help us pass these ballots out...please, and thank you. Look, some coaches here have demanded I question Billy and Jimmy Jack about what happened in last season's race. That's why they're here tonight. But I won't do it! It's history! We're here to make an up or down vote on whether Cliffview be accepted into our conference, with one addendum, allowing an elastic band used to guide a partially blind twin runner by his brother. You all got my detailed message. Let's vote up or down on this before we're buildin' arks!"

"So what does a 'yes' vote mean?" asked a new coach. "I missed the memo."

Coach Clausen burst out, "It's easy! Check 'yes' if you want Pop's handicappers in our conference or 'no' if you believe it's legal suicide for our conference!"

Pop stood faster than a jack-in-the-box. "Excuse me! Legal suicide?"

Clausen continued, "Last year, our team got DQed because of the 'eagle boy.' I could'a won my first team championship! It's pure luck...but truly common sense...that the officials awarded Jimmy Jack his individual championship win!"

During the buzz, Pop raised his voice. "I refuse to believe a group of educated people such as yourselves could ever vote to ban a runner cleared by a bona fide medical doctor!"

"Gentlemen! Gentlemen!" urged Grundman from the podium. "We'll do this dramatically! Ah, spittle! Democratically!" Tobacco juice dripped down Grundman's chin as he groped for his paper cup.

The Haybury coach stood. "As the reigning championship coach, I've got a question. Why is Coach Clausen concerned about 'em? His team loses every year!" That brought chuckles, raising Clausen's ire. The Haybury Coach shifted his pants. "Down at Haybury, our championship boys know these handicapped or whatever-you-call-'em runners at Cliffview could be nowhere near our level. What level are they on?"

Jimmy Jack, having passed out the ballots, walked by me and grinned before shouting, "The subterranean level!" The room grew as silent as a cemetery. I leaped from my seat, grabbed Jimmy Jack, and spun him around as we wrestled each other to the floor.

"Boys! Boys!" Grundman shouted from the podium.

Pop did what any red-blooded coach would do. He stepped in to separate us, but in our struggle, we bumped him hard and he collapsed.

Several coaches grabbed Jimmy Jack and me and pulled us apart, but Pop lay sprawled on the floor, holding his heaving chest.

"My pills!" Pop groaned.

"I know where they are!" I shouted as I jerked free and knelt at Pop's side, pulling out his van keys and nitro pills. Stashing the keys in my pocket, I unscrewed the lid of his nitro pills and gave him one. Pop placed it under his tongue, his face gazing into mine, the trickle of a tear running down the side of his face.

The coaches adjusted him into a more comfortable position.

"Call for an ambulance!" Grundman shouted. A coach ran to the office.

"Give him air!" shouted another coach, who pushed me aside and loosened Pop's collar. A third coach grabbed the nitro pills and gave Pop another.

Two coaches escorted me to a seat away from Pop. I held my head in my hands. When I rose, all I saw were glaring looks from coaches. I knew they blamed me. I blamed myself. Wasn't that enough?

The ambulance soon arrived as medical personnel, drenched in rain, brought a stretcher to carry Pop away. Pop gave me his best look of assurance as he left. Grundman announced, "For your information, the vote was fifteen in favor of Cliffview and nine against. Cliffview is one vote short of a two-thirds majority."

I held a long stare with Jimmy Jack until Coach Clausen got in my face. "How many more lives are you gonna ruin? Is this how you'll run your next race?"

I stood and faced him. "Prefontaine said, 'The best race is suicide pace and today looks like a good day to die!'"

A rumble of thunder jarred the building again as I burst across the room and past the old, bearded man who shouted, "Billy!"

Grundman hollered, "Come back here!" I struck the panic bar on the outside door and felt the force of nature's violent tears on my face as I sprinted across the parking lot and through the pouring rain before slipping on the pavement and crashing into the van.

"Pop! I'm sorry! Pop!" I yelled as I put the key in and peeled out, passing "Mr. Hawaii," who ran out waving his arms, trying to stop me. I avoided him and drove over a curb, sliding in the rain as I headed to the cross-country course a half mile away.

Having no driver's license and with blurry vision, I had only one thing on my mind. I would take the course down. Nothing would stop me!

Chapter 32

Billy's Run to Redemption

I whirled Pop's van onto the cross-country course, braking hard and skidding to a stop. I slid out of the seat and ran, hell-bent to the starting line. Oblivious of the storm and the bearded man who followed me, I ignored his Jeep and its beeping horn and began my run.

The old man hurried from his Jeep, trying to cut me off, then opened a large umbrella with a NASA logo, yelling, "Abort the run! Abort the run!" I glanced back as a gust of wind caught his umbrella, turning it inside out, as he fell into the mud. *Is Mr. Hawaii Ethan's grandfather?*

My stride was strong, my demeanor fierce. In the downpour, I sprinted from the start and soon heard the Jeep following me again across the flats before it jerked to a final stop at the top of Suicide Plunge. I ran over the side in a mud-splattering descent. Halfway down, I gave a primal scream, clenching my fists off Lover's Leap. The slippery conditions caused me to skid sideways and roll over and over, slamming into a tree.

With my wind knocked out and my body propped against a tree trunk, I stared at a parade of ants on the bark. I groaned—my lungs locked stiff. Panic rose in a deathly fear, but I willed it away, praying that time would release the vice-like grip on my chest. The tightness eased.

Onward! I stumbled forward, willing my legs and arms to pump amid lightning bolts, thunder claps, and waving tree limbs. My breathing deepened as I sprinted through a rain-soaked clearing.

Ahead were three imbedded log-planks, all submerged below rushing waters.

Trying to cross on the third log, a roar came from upstream. A flash flood of muddy debris swept down the ravine, targeting me. Slapped off the log, I tumbled into the turbulent flow, twisting downstream while spinning in muddy waters. I saw the log ripped from the bank, careening my way. I slammed into a boulder, using my feet to absorb the impact. My hands gripped a crevice in the rock as a small tree branch gouged my back. Wincing, I heard booming thuds and glanced back. The free-flowing log ricocheted off boulders on its course toward me.

Reaching for a higher hold, I pulled myself up as my feet propelled me to the top. The log struck the boulder and split apart, swirling downstream.

I collapsed, motionless on top of the boulder. Recovering, I surveyed my diminishing chance of crossing the raging stream. A crack of thunder spurred me into action. I leapfrogged on larger rocks and lunged through muddy waters, crawling up the other bank.

I staggered along the trail toward the sideless bridge. Sections of the splintered log were pinned below it. Limping over the bridge, I began my ascent from Death Valley. I drew my eyes to the side, up the steep grassy bank that led to the white wooden cross, shimmering amidst flashes that pierced through the darkness. A large red oak stood beside it. The cross mesmerized me as an ugly shame washed over me. *What if Pop dies? What if Coach Clausen is right?*

Exhaustion and guilt brought me down. Falling face-first in the mud, I wept, powerless to stop. Waves of anguish swept over my shattered spirit.

With mud smeared on my face, I raised my head from the mire. My vision of the cross confronted my senses, and I screamed at the top of my lungs, "God! Help me to see!"

I rolled over, my body shaking through groans of remorse. Fierce rain pelted me, washing mud from my face, my glasses, my eyes. I got to my knees, peering at the white wooden cross silhouetted against the lightning-filled sky. For a flashing moment, I *visual-*

ized a figure on the cross. Urgency squeezed my heart. *I want answers! I need answers!*

"God! What do you want from me? You curse me with bad eyes! You strike down Jake! You crush my Pa! You end Ma's dreams! And now you destroy Pop?"

I turned off the course and clawed on all fours up the soggy hillside. "Don't take Pop!" I shouted. "I'm to blame!" Slipping and sliding, I dug my fingers into the soft turf, struggling upward as I fell to my face again and again while rising higher up the slope.

Reaching the summit, I rammed my shoulder into the cross. My arms encircled it, trying to wrench it from the earth. I shinnied up to the crossbeam. Grabbing hold, I pulled myself to a kneeling position on the side beam. Clinging to the center pole, I lifted my knee and stood, grasping the top of the vertical beam. I faced the storm head-on and raised a clenched fist.

"Don't take Pop! Take me!" Sheets of lightning arced across the hillside. Deafening thunder followed shafts of light. A lightning bolt struck the large red oak beside the cross! *Wham!* I fell! Swirls of sparkling embers fluttered down beside the empty cross.

*****

In the school kitchen, Ma placed candles on Pop's birthday cake as Chester chased girls with a squirt gun through the swinging doors. Celebration filled the room.

Jenny and Darla waited inside those doors for Pop and me to walk through and enter like royalty. "That last hour took forever," Jenny told me later. "I thought we were moments away from realizing acceptance into the conference when I heard footsteps and raised my voice, "Here they come, everybody!' I stepped back, preparing to lead in the *Happy Birthday* song for Pop."

The doors swung open to cheers, but the happy voices faded as the doors swung shut.

"I hate to say this," said President Grundman solemnly, "but Pop had a heart attack and your team lost by one vote. Pop's at the hospital." Disbelief filled the room. Grundman continued, "A coach saw Billy drive off in your school van, but not toward the hospital." Grundman disappeared quickly, leaving the "Ker-thump, thump, thump" of the swinging doors behind.

Ma entered from the kitchen and carried a birthday cake filled with dozens of lighted candles. "Happy birthday!" she shouted before pausing in silence.

"Pop had a heart attack," Pa said. Ma sighed and set the cake down.

"We've gotta find Billy," Jenny said. The group was motionless. "The course!"

"You're right! Grab flashlights!" Pa said, waving them into action. "Out to the pickup! Somebody check on Pop!" Everyone jumped into action, except for Gabe, the deaf artist, who couldn't hear the details but knew it was bad. While others ran from the room, Gabe gazed at his birthday gift, a sketch of Pop grinning. In tears, he approached the cake with its multitude of candles. In three bursts of air, he blew out all the candles...save one.

*****

Outside, Pa realized the futility of transporting everyone. Zack hollered, "Zeke and I will get a ride to the hospital with the girls! Go without us!" Pa, Jenny, and Ma climbed in the cab of the pickup. Most of the gang jumped in the pickup bed.

The storm had passed, leaving behind distant flashes of lightning that lit up the eastern sky. The noise in the pickup was deafening—everyone talking at once. Ma opened the dash and gave an extra flashlight to Jenny. The pickup sped to the course, free from the rain.

"Jenny was right! There's the school van!" Ma shouted as Pa pulled up. Ma leaped out her door, shouting, "Billy! Billy!"

Tom was faster and peeked inside the van. "Not here!" But it was too late for Ma. She had slipped and fallen, gashing her leg on a sharp rock.

Everyone kept calling out my name as Pa knelt at Ma's side.

Keith stooped to assess Ma's wound. "A first aid kit's in the van. I'll get it!" he said. Ma bit her lip, gazing down at her leg and then at Pa.

"It's bleeding bad!" Pa said. Keith rushed back and opened the first aid kit. Pa whisked dirt away and did his best to clean her leg. Keith had the bandage ready as Pa dressed her wound.

"That's my grandfather's Jeep at the top of Suicide Plunge!" yelled Ethan. "Where is he?"

"Hold it!" Tom shouted, raising his arms. "Four of us know this course! We'll run it and find Billy!" Tom looked straight at Andy. "Tell Pete!" Wasting no time, Andy signed to Pete, who nodded. With Tom leading, Keith and Pete fell in line.

A panicked look came from Ethan as he kept turning around, looking for his grandfather. "Grandfather must have tried to stop Billy or is following him! Remember, he's a runner himself! I'm going with you!" Before doubts could surface, the four boys with one flashlight to guide them were off across the flats toward Suicide Plunge before they'd descend into the dark, soggy depths of Death Valley.

"Tom! Tom!" Jenny shouted. No use. Tom and his group were sprinting away.

Pa looked directly at Ma. "Lily, we've gotta trust the boys to find him."

Jenny approached Ma and Pa. "I'm gonna cover the course backward…down into Death Valley, the back way! Can anyone help me?"

"Chester! Chester!" Pa yelled. "Help Jenny find your brother! I've gotta stay with Ma."

Chester nodded. Ma gave her flashlight to him. "Billy needs you both," Ma said. Jenny shined her flashlight toward the backside exit of Death Valley and took off with Chester.

"Bubba!" Andy shouted. "Show them the way down to the sideless bridge—to your fishin' spot!" Bubba gave a thumbs-up and joined Jenny and Chester.

Ma returned a thumbs-up to Bubba as he joined the search party. Pa and Andy helped her into the pickup. Sitting on the front seat with the door open, Ma grabbed a baseball from the dash and worked it in her hands. Through grimaces, she spoke: "It's the bottom of the ninth. We're down three—Pop, Billy, and Ethan's grandfather. Time to pray!"

*****

Tom, Keith, Pete, and Ethan did their best to stay upright. As Tom reported later, they often slid down the slopes, their shoes like skis. When their soles gripped the turf, it caught them by surprise, causing them to tumble end over end and roll. Streaked with mud, they nursed sore shoulders and hips. They ran by moonlight and a flashlight until it broke from a fall. Flickers of distant lightning from the departing storm offered sporadic light. Tom said it dumbfounded him when he saw the logs washed away, including the rickety bridge.

They stared at mud oozing downstream. As Tom said, "It looks more like a tar pit."

"Who knows how deep the mud is?" said Keith. "Trying to cross it now with the ground still moving would be like walking into quicksand." Ethan turned and dropped to the ground. Keith rallied with a new comment. "I'm sorry, Ethan, but if Billy or your grandfather got this far, they would have made it across before the mudslide."

Tom took control. "We've gotta get professional help here! Let's turn around and go back!" Tom, Keith, and Pete finally got Ethan to agree.

Retreating backward, Tom's head was down but each step up was a determined one. They needed to hurry so the officers could put fresh rescuers into action. That's when Pete grimaced and blurted out guttural groans while grabbing onto Ethan. Pete dragged Ethan off his feet, past a squashed, muddy hat, and down a grassy slope. Tom and Keith followed, thinking Pete had gone crazy. In seconds, they gazed at an old bearded man passed out in sloshy muddy grass.

Ethan ran to him and tried to turn him over. The others joined in. The old man opened his eyes, coming to consciousness.

"Oh, Grandfather!" said Ethan.

"Help me! I fell hard!"

"We'll get you out!" Ethan promised. The boys watched Ethan hug him again before they raised him. They began the march upward, picking up Dr. Gorman's hat.

Dr. Gorman explained, "I followed Billy, trying to holler for him to stop! He was sprinting all-out, then falling, and running again. I thought he might listen, but he was so fast! When I fell, I must have passed out. I think Billy's in real trouble."

"We'll make it out. Right, Grandfather?"

Dr. Gorman took several painful breaths and nodded. Ethan put Dr. Gorman's arm over his shoulder, as did Pete. They staggered until he could walk under his own power. "It wasn't right what happened to Billy or Pop in that meeting. I was there!"

"We heard Pop was at the hospital," said Ethan.

Once the sheriff and deputy Smith saw them from the cruiser, they shortened their trek by driving over. "Okay," the sheriff ordered, "I'll drive you all to his Jeep. Deputy Smith, you'll drive Dr. Gorman and his son to the hospital and I'll take the others."

*****

Searching the course backward, Bubba asked Jenny to stay at the top of the Death Valley exit so they could holler up to her for help. Jenny wasn't keen on the idea, but when Chester sided with Bubba, she agreed.

"Billy! Billy!" Bubba and Chester hollered as they began the backward descent into Death Valley. Soon they were out of sight, and Jenny realized she couldn't see the pickup near the starting line, anyway. She felt isolated.

"Billy, can you hear me? Billy!" Nothing. An idea popped into her head. Jenny cupped her hands and cut loose the familiar wail Billy used to call Victory.

"Wooo-eee!" she yelled. "Wooo-eee!"

She heard a faint shriek. Again, she yelled, "Wooo-eee!" She was positive the second shriek had come from Victory. For a moment, it puzzled Jenny. I had told her that eagles don't fly in storms. She knew, but the storm had already passed. She perked up and ran along the ridge, following the shriek to the cross.

"Up here!" she yelled to Chester and Bubba. "The big cross!" She never once thought Victory would give her false hope.

On their descent into Death Valley, Bubba and Chester heard Jenny's voice and stopped.

"Come on!" shouted Chester. "Let's get up there!"

Jenny aimed her flashlight toward the cross and ran along the muddy trail to get closer. She hopped over several limbs still smoldering from the lightning strike. There was Victory, perched on the cross. She directed her light downward and saw my body lying below.

"I see him! The big cross!" Jenny hollered. She ran over, gazing at me in the mud.

Propping the flashlight against a rock, she knelt. "Oh, Billy! Billy!"

I heard her and opened my eyes. "It hurts…"

"Billy, we've gotta get you out!"

"I was…tore up inside." I moaned.

"What?"

"I was trapped, a prisoner, feeding on insults, blaming everyone, my family, even God. I punished myself, trying to sweat out the pain."

Jenny fidgeted as I squirmed.

"I felt a lot of…pain."

"Billy…"

"My problem was me…hanging onto hate…spewing blame." Tears flowed. "I let it all go! It's gone! It's on that ugly cross…that beautiful cross. I'm free, Jenny! I'm free of it!"

Jenny reached for me, and I surrendered to her embrace. Victory shrieked above as Jenny shined her flashlight on him, a full moon glowing in the distance. "Victory found you," she said.

"Pop?" I asked, my lip quivering in hope.

"We don't know."

Chester led Bubba up the hill and hovered over us, trying to recover. "Can we move you, Billy?"

"I think so…just take it easy."

"Step aside, y'all," Bubba said. "I'll pretend I'm packin' out a deep-sea marlin!" Bubba placed his arms under me, and, with Chester's help, hoisted me up and over his shoulders in a fireman's carry.

Jenny pulled out a pack of her gum. "Hubba Bubba, Bubba?" Bubba nodded as Jenny slipped a piece into his mouth. What a story to tell!

CHAPTER 33

Eagle 7 Humiliates Cowler Boys

Sheriff Logan drove with his cruiser lights flashing, escorting the Jeep into the emergency entrance of the Gorman Hospital in Rockside. Out stepped three exhausted boys. They gathered around the Jeep as Ethan gave his grandfather another hug.

"Let us help you out," Ethan said. With Pete assisting, Ethan helped his battered grandfather out of the Jeep.

They stared at the glaring hospital emergency sign, their clothes tattered and faces marred, realizing their previous efforts had stiffened them. An orderly pushed an empty wheelchair toward them.

"Please, sir, let's get you inside," he said. Ethan's grandfather, already hunched over, sat, and rode into the emergency entrance with the boys limping behind.

The old man had no trouble verbalizing his thoughts. "You will not check me in till I find out what happened to Billy Cline and Pop O'Reilly! Then you can admit me, fix me up, and put me in my wing."

"Your wing?" the orderly asked.

"The Dr. Nicholas Gorman wing of the hospital," Ethan added.

"You're that…Gorman?"

"Yes, he is, and he's my grandfather."

Weary students and eager parents filled the waiting room for news on the whereabouts of us all. Without fanfare, Tom, Keith, Pete, and Ethan limped in beside Dr. Gorman in his wheelchair.

"They're back!" Jenny shouted. That awakened everybody. Silence ruled as they gazed at the battered boys. Tom limped forward, gazing around the room, counting team members in his head, feeling guilt for being one runner short.

"A mudslide washed away the logs and the bridge! It was insane. We had to turn back!" Tom's emotion was potent. "On the way back…" Tom looked for Ethan to continue.

"We found my grandfather." Ethan turned and gazed at him in the wheelchair with a look of pride, putting his hand on his shoulder. "My grandfather had seen Billy run into Death Valley and searched for him. When the four of us followed, the huge mudslide at the stream forced us to turn back. Coming back, Pete spotted my grandfather's hat in the grass and dragged me down a soggy slope where we found him." Ethan's eyes filled with tears as he looked at Pete. "If we hadn't turned back, Pete never would have seen my grandfather."

Dr. Gorman reached out his hand and squeezed Pete's arm. Pete gave a gentle hug to Dr. Gorman, then signed to Andy.

Andy stood. "Dr. Gorman and Pete are asking, 'What about Billy? What about Pop?'"

In a calm voice, Jenny shared with them. "Billy's injured, but they think he'll be okay. He crossed during the actual mudslide. Washed downstream, he survived by climbing a boulder. He's recovering from several injuries." Andy signed to Pete, who fist-pumped.

"So Billy's okay? Tom sighed with relief from confirmation. "And Pop?"

"Pop is stable," Jenny answered.

Tom squatted onto the carpet, relieved. Keith shouted, "Yes!" Ethan bent and hugged his grandfather while Pete raised his arms with a smile. Students and families comforted them.

Jenny passed a note to a nurse to give to Billy, saying, "Everyone is back and okay."

*****

The next morning, I awakened in my hospital bed with the nurse's note clutched in my hand. My nurse hovered over me. "Good morning. How are you feeling today?"

"Better after reading this note. But I'm sore all over, and my back and head hurt." I sat up but felt woozy. I touched the bandages on my head and felt the heavy dressing taped on my back. "I'm a little dizzy, but nothing hurts too bad. I'll be all right, won't I?"

"They had to stitch up a laceration on your back and bandage cuts on your head, arms, and legs, but the x-rays turned out negative. We're keeping you a few days for observation. You can see your parents and your friends briefly this afternoon.

I nodded, giving me a reason to hope: my folk's support and hearing my friends' stories.

On the second day, the nurse said, "Someone invited you to a meeting. You up for it?"

I shrugged.

"Okay," she said, "let's get you into this wheelchair."

"All right." She helped me into the wheelchair and passed me a note.

"A fellow named Andy asked me to give you that." She scribbled on my chart.

I read Andy's note out loud. "The *Eagle 7* has landed. I've got a plan to get in the conference by using it." I sat there amazed. "What plan?"

After my morning duties, the door opened. "Jake! You're walking great!" I tried to rise from the wheelchair but the pain was real.

"It's not much of a walk," Jake said. "I've been taking longer strolls this week. So now I get to walk beside you while you're in a wheelchair?"

The nurse peeked out, giving us the green light. She took us slowly to a private room.

"Well, Pop, here they are—the Cline boys, as you requested. You boys have ten minutes…and only because Pop's numbers look so good." She glanced at Pop, then at the monitor, smiling.

"You can tell they're brothers by their love of hospitals," Pop joked to the nurse. Jake and I laughed and Jake gave Pop a hug.

Pop shifted positions. "The *Eagle 7* will be a game changer, Billy. But I'm sorry about losing admittance to the conference by one vote. That was a big disappointment."

"I'm dealing with it, Pop. Don't feel bad, though, I got a lot settled two nights ago."

"I'm glad, Billy, real glad. It appears both of you Cline boys are workin' your way back."

"Pop, Andy has developed a plan to get us into the conference using the *Eagle 7.*"

"Ya don't say?" He laughed. "Knowing Andy, you'd better fasten your seatbelts!"

*****

Later that evening, I received a call from Andy. Groggy from pain pills, I merely listened to Andy's rendition of the evening. "Ethan, Luke, and I stood outside the old tool shed tonight. I slipped in the key and unlocked the double doors. Ethan pushed Luke inside. Flipping on the light switch, triangular floodlights shone, revealing a gas-powered, hopped-up wheelchair with sidecar, oversized tires, shocks, chrome pipes, padded seat, and decals! Sound familiar?"

"'Baby, baby, baby!' Luke said, 'I can't wait to test drive that thing!'"

"Wait till you see it, Billy! I can't wait to ride in the sidecar! Ethan then stepped forward and mounted the *Eagle 7* nameplate on the front. It's so cool, Billy."

"Luke's comment topped it off, 'This will make wheelchair history!'"

"'Thanks to my grandfather!' added Ethan. We walked toward the double doors to leave until we heard a noise outside. Ethan flipped off the light switch, and we all held our breath."

"The doorknob squeaked and the double doors opened, revealing a massive figure saying, 'Anybody hungry?'"

"'Bubba!' We all yelled."

I laughed so hard my back hurt!

*****

Two days later, I left the hospital, ready for an easy jog. Tom picked me up, dropping me at the curve on Hedge Road, beside the tall half-mile-long hedge on one side of the road. Out in the country, the road led back to Rockside High. I gasped, gazing at Luke in the driver's seat of the *Eagle 7*. Andy sat in the sidecar, pinching his nose, reading "Smells Great" on a pizza box.

Tom continued, "Luke found out the Cowler boys would run the Hedge Road back to school for workout. Andy's got a plan. See you later." Tom drove off.

Andy took over. "Billy, you've got to stay hidden as you run beside us on the back side of the single hedge row. Believe me, they won't see you, and you'll enjoy our demonstration."

"What did you name the pizza?" I asked.

"Elsie—on whole wheat."

"Elsie?"

"A gift from my neighbor's cow."

"Yuck!" Soon the *Eagle 7* and I slithered through a hedge gap before Cletus and Gopher ran by. Luke fired up the *Eagle 7* and burst out onto the road, burning rubber, doing a wheelie before pulling up on the far side of the Cowler boys. Andy grinned from the sidecar, looking at the Cowler boys and seeing me running, concealed while jogging alongside the far side of the hedge. Andy began his plan. "Hey, look! It's two mental midgets—the Cowler boys! Hey, Gopher, want some pizza?"

"What kind of contraption is that?" Gopher said, his eyes scanning it as he jogged.

"A wheelchair, you cow chipper!"

Cletus and Gopher sprinted toward them, but Luke gunned it, passing them and staying out of their reach. Andy swiveled in his seat.

"Hey, Cletus, did you tell your friends how you got whupped by a blind free throw shooter?"

"Give me the pizza," Cletus ordered, "and I'll guarantee you one day of good health!"

"Why should I?" said Andy. "You're too slow to catch us and too yellow to race us!"

"Who's yellow?" Cletus yelled as they sprinted, reaching for the *Eagle 7*.

Andy yanked out two cans of yellow aerosol paint and sprayed them both. "You are!"

"Oooh! Why youuu!"

I forced myself to silence my laughing spree as I glanced through the hedge, gazing at the Cowlers, now dripping in yellow paint.

The Cowlers sprinted again, trying to grab hold of the *Eagle 7*. Cletus grabbed streamers flowing off the back and knocked one of the spray cans from Andy's hand. It was a stalemate between Cletus trying to slow down the *Eagle 7* and Luke trying to pull away.

Cletus gave the order, "Gimme the pizza, moron!"

"Let him have it!" Luke yelled.

Andy stuffed Elsie's pizza in Cletus's face! Cletus released the *Eagle 7* in a rage, wiping slimy manure from his face with his shirt.

"It comes with moist towelettes!" Andy yelled as the *Eagle 7* roared down the road.

I stopped as Gopher caught Cletus and fanned the air from the stench, saying, "You stink!" Seconds later, Cletus was retching.

*****

Being a former Rockside Raven, I ran another route to their after-workout meeting place and sneaked through some hillside trees to overhear their conversation.

Ten minutes later, Cletus and Gopher returned to the Rockside team, yellow, with Cletus pasted in manure. I knew the Ravens' team would tell anybody who had ears what happened. Some would be glad the Cowlers got punished—but from a midget? That would sell the story schoolwide!

Jimmy Jack saw the Cowlers first. "Whoa! It's yellow men!" The Rockside team struggled to suppress their laughter.

"Coach! Coach! I've had it! I've thrown up three times!" Cletus yelled in fury. The Rockside runners stepped to the side, giving Cletus more room. "Those handicapped freaks!" Cletus picked up a teammate's workout shirt and wiped his face.

Gopher spoke up: "They had this weird machine. Said we're too yellow to race 'em! We're not…." A long pause followed as his team saw yellow paint drip from Gopher's chin.

"Come on, Jimmy Jack, let's go get 'em!" yelled Cletus.

Coach Clausen stepped forward, his finger pointing at Cletus, anger oozing through his words. "Nobody will get anybody!" Coach commanded. "Not yet! I'm not lettin' you get kicked out of school. I mean it!"

"But they gotta pay!"

"I know what they want," Jimmy Jack offered in a calm voice. "A race…a showdown race against us, to prove they belong." The team grew hyper, considering Jimmy Jack's plan. "Let's give it to 'em. The course…plus Rocky Point Trail."

"A team match race?" said Clausen.

"Yeah, for payback."

"We gotta do this, Coach!" said Gopher. "They'll pay big time!" Gopher spat as he spoke. "We'll…give 'em a taste…of their own… medicine!"

Clausen realized the team had bought into Jimmy Jack's plan. "Okay, but under the following conditions: a secret match race, us against them, the last Saturday in May. Nothing happens till then. We keep our mouths shut. Wired shut! Jimmy Jack, you set it up with Billy."

"We'll need bait," Jimmy Jack said. "Coach, they missed joining the conference by one vote. If they race us, can I tell 'em you'll switch your vote…and vote 'em in…as equals?"

"Equals?" Clausen said, his face red with frustration. The Rockside runners stared at him. "That course is eight miles," Clausen said. "I'll vote 'em in if they can beat us. But, get this, an unsanctioned race on those hiking trails means…no rules!"

Gopher raised his hands and shouted, "No rules? No more Cliffview!"

Jimmy Jack led the charge. "Quoth the Ravens?"

"Nevermore!" the team shouted.

The Rockside team roared as Cletus tossed the dirty shirt back to his ungrateful teammate. Jimmy Jack declined a Cletus high-five as they walked in to clean up.

*****

I didn't know what events were coming. I only knew I felt better, body and soul, when I was released from the hospital and witnessed the Cowlers' humiliation. Ethan had told me his version of his grandfather's rescue and the attempt to find me. In days, my world had changed.

Three days later I jogged toward the Rockside cross country course. My thoughts shifted to the last time I'd been there—the storm. Things were different now, I hoped. But were they?

Victory circled above me as I ran through the parking lot. Jimmy Jack was leaning against Cletus's '57 red Chevy Bel Air convertible, ready for our meeting. As I slowed, I saw a "For Sale" sign taped onto the window. Below it were the words *Make Offer*.

"Didn't think you'd show," Jimmy Jack said as I slowed to a stop.

Victory swooped downward toward Jimmy Jack's head, causing him to drop to the asphalt on all fours. I smiled. "Where's your white flag?"

"Who does he think he is?" Jimmy Jack said in a huff.

"He knows he's an eagle."

Jimmy Jack turned to Victory, who had landed on a fence post. He gazed at the eagle. Victory returned his gaze.

"I ain't talkin' to you with those eagle eyes starin' at me," said Jimmy Jack.

"Like he's lookin' straight through ya? He does that," I added. "He doesn't change."

"When I look into his eyes, there's no end to 'em." Jimmy Jack turned. "I'll tell ya straight. We're gonna give you a match race. No media, no leaks, totally secret. Only our teams, yours against mine, the last Saturday in May, high noon."

"Over the course?"

"And the back woods. And over the peak, including the cliffs along Rocky Point Trail."

"That's…eight miles," I said. "Rocky Point's for serious climbers. Nobody would sanction a race over terrain like that!"

"No one will know! If you leak it, you forfeit! Do you get it, eagle boy? When the dying oxygen-starved carcasses of your handicapped freaks stagger to the finish line, we'll be dining on T-Bone steaks with our girlfriends! But, if you can beat us, Clausen said he'll change his vote and put you in the conference."

"As equals?" I asked.

"As equals. But, if you lose, or better yet, when you lose, your team is banished from our conference forever. Take it or leave it."

I pondered my choices. This was Pop's dream. I had to make it happen. Then I saw a potential solution to help Jake. "Wait a minute, Jimmy Jack. I've heard Blimp might drop his own personal charges against Jake. Is that true?"

Jimmy Jack grinned. "So that's what you want, eh? A bargaining chip? I'll say this, if you race us, I might convince him to drop his charges. He has been acting different since Jake's apology letter. Oh, yeah, I read his chicken scratch. But don't kid yourself, Jake'll still get slammer time for breakin' out of jail! And who knows if Jake will ever pitch again with the same skill he showed before tangling with my cousins." Jimmy Jack swaggered into the red convertible and fired it up.

"Take my advice," he said. "If you choose to race us, you'd better wear a crash helmet like your pitiful brother Jake did." He grinned and drove off, honking his horn and squealing his tires.

CHAPTER 34

A Sniper's Shot

On a pleasant spring Saturday morning, Jenny was waiting at the Rockside course parking lot when the Cliffview van and the *Eagle 7* arrived. Luke honked the *Eagle 7* air horn as our team exited the school van, driven by Mr. Spraker, a substitute teacher who wanted to help us.

Pa and Ma arrived, honking the pickup horn with Pop in the back seat. Dr. Gorman followed in his Jeep, beeping his horn, too.

"Pop and Ethan's grandfather are back from the hospital!" yelled Tom, as they drove up beside the team. Bubba lifted Andy out of the sidecar and onto his shoulders as we boys and Jenny surrounded Bubba and Andy in celebration.

We began a rhythmic chant while bobbing up and down from our toes: "Pizza boy—he delivers! Andy is his name! Pizza boy—he delivers! Yes, he's got an aim! Pizza boy—he delivers! Elsie is to blame! Pizza boy—he delivers! Oh, what a shame!"

We all roared in hilarity as Pop laughed, standing tall beside the pickup. "Ned busted me out of the hospital! The doctors think I'm home for bed rest! But the truth is…"

"You're here for workout!" yelled the team with laughter and cheers.

"Yes!" said Pop. "You all motivate me for life!"

Dr. Gorman approached them, carrying a large box. "In honor of Pop's birthday!"

"New jerseys!" said Ethan, grabbing the box as Bubba lowered Andy and ripped the box open, giving Jenny the first one. The team cheered as Jenny took hers and ran to the school van to put it on.

Ma took one from the box and held it up to the team. The front showed a beautiful eagle flying in the clouds with "Soaring Eagles" inscribed on it. The back had a mountain image and, over it, the words "Soar to the Top!" Brilliant blue and gold outlined the jersey.

Jenny returned, and I summed up the team's feelings. "My, that is one fine-looking jersey!" The team laughed, and I never got a reprimand, just a sideways frown from Ma.

Pop O'Reilly and Dr. Gorman grabbed their jerseys next and stepped aside, conversing while Ethan and Andy passed out new jerseys for everyone to replace their old ones.

During their sharing Dr. Gorman asked, "Coach, how are you doing?"

"Fine, as long as my ticker holds out." Pop glanced toward his team, enjoying their excitement. "I think your gift of new jerseys is a hit! And the *Eagle 7* is beyond words. Thank you."

"I've never seen Ethan so excited," said Dr. Gorman. "That awful day of years ago remains seared in my mind—how my grandson was at the point of death from my son's car accident. I couldn't believe Ethan survived. Those Rockside doctors brought him back from death. And now, you've brought his spirit back... and mine, too. You've shown us all a better way."

"I know how hard it is to lose a daughter. I'm sorry about your son and daughter-in-law."

Dr. Gorman sighed. "So many times, I've wished I hadn't left town...because..."

Pop saw him struggling and added, "Well, NASA and the man-in-the-moon are sure glad you provided transportation for our astronauts—up there."

"Ha! That's a good one." Dr. Gorman chuckled. "But I can't help wishing that if I had stayed, my son might not have made that... that drive...and my grandson might not have suffered as he has."

"We all have regrets," Pop said. "But for you and me now...it's about how we finish."

A gust of wind brought Victory soaring overhead followed by a shriek. Luke's eyes got big as Victory descended. The team spread out to give room as Victory opened his wings and landed on the roll bar of the *Eagle 7*. "What a bold move!" said Luke.

"Let me get a picture!" Dr. Gorman said. Mr. Spraker offered to take the picture to include Ethan's grandfather. The camera captured a great signature shot of our team and support group with Victory and the Eagle 7.

Ma and Pa left, smiling, walking alongside Dr. Gorman back to their vehicles. The team turned to Pop for workout.

"We will train twice a day, six days a week. This morning, we launch a three-pronged set of training strategies: German interval training, Swedish fartlek, and American LSD."

Keith raised his hand. "I know about interval training, but LSD? Fartlek? You mean we'll be psychedelic runners with gas?" The team and Pop laughed.

"Fartlek means 'speed-play' in Swedish: run as you feel, vary the speed! LSD means long, slow distance. This morning, everybody will load up on LSD. Run the course twice. Luke and Andy will serve you Gatorade when you pass by the first loop."

"Take LSD with Gatorade?" Keith said, grinning. Andy splashed Keith with a stream of Gatorade from the sidecar, as Luke hot-dogged in the *Eagle 7*, raising their spirits.

"All right, Billy. Lead 'em out!" Pop hollered.

The morning sun crossed the sky. It seemed the world was smiling.

*****

During the late afternoon workout, the team stretched at the Death Valley exit. I held a handful of purple wildflowers I had picked for Jenny. The team couldn't wait to see her reaction.

Jenny was blushing with surprise. "Catawba rhododendrons!" She winked at me.

"Awww…how sweet," the team said. Pop cleared his throat and got our attention.

"Long intervals now—from the sideless bridge to right here, the Death Valley exit. Bubba's fishin' off the bridge and has water. Ninety-seconds rest at the bridge. How much rest?"

"Ninety seconds!" we all shouted. Some team members gave me a questioning look.

"Pop," I said, "that's a half-mile—uphill. How many will we run?"

"How many wildflowers did you pick for Jenny?"

"Eight."

"Do eight repeats."

The team reacted. "Awww! Billy! Take some back!"

Jenny responded, "Sorry, boys…no way!" The team laughed as Jenny held the flowers to her nose and sniffed their fragrance. The team jogged the back way into Death Valley.

Bubba was sitting in the *Eagle 7* at the sideless bridge, having already collected a string of trout. He and Luke had water in each runner's tin cup waiting for us. We drank as Tom timed ninety seconds of rest. I grabbed my washcloth, doused it with cool water, and placed it over my eyes.

When Tom completed the countdown, he and I led the team charge up the backside of Death Valley. At the top, Tom and I were together, with Victory soaring overhead, our inspiration from the sky. Keith and Pete were also together, back about thirty yards. They weaved a pattern to crisscross each other without getting their legs entangled.

Pop commented, "Keith, you and Pete are making me dizzy with that zigzag pattern."

"We call it our 'Double-X' routine," said Keith.

"Let's not turn it into a collision routine!" Pop cautioned.

Finishing in the third group were the Z twins and Ethan. Ethan struggled to stay with the twins, dropping back near the Death Valley exit on each repeat. On the jog back down, Ethan was ahead of the Z twins every time since Zack insisted on caution for Zeke downhill. Jenny cheered for each of us, knowing our efforts were genuine. The afternoon sun faded to dusk.

Three mornings later, the team pulled up to the course in the van and the *Eagle 7*. We climbed out and stretched in a half circle as Pop explained the workout.

"Fartlek is the order of the morning. Really blow it out! Back and forth! Pursuit pace, then normal striding. Pursuit pace, then normal striding. It's a technique like 'surging.'"

I held up my hand.

"Billy, you've got a suggestion?"

"Yes, I know you're right to start us together and keep us together for as long as possible, and we're committed to catching up on the striding sections if we get strung out. Right, team?"

"Yeah," they said.

"But when we get exhausted and it's impossible for us all to stay together, let us reorganize into smaller groups."

"It's true about staying together," Pop said. "You see that strategy used in bicycle racing, like the Tour de France. If we're scattered, we can't help each other. So, start together in one 'pack attack!' Catch up on the striding sections but run as one united team. When extreme fatigue hits, do what Billy suggested. Go to your three 'pack attack' units. Keep those units together! You'll energize each other!"

As we ran along the flats, I shouted, "Pursuit pace!" All seven of us picked up the pace together, our strides smooth and strong. Victory soared above, challenging us with his shrieks. I shouted, "Stride!" We slowed to a manageable pace, keeping together, moving across the canyons, the forest trails, and the climbs.

Later, when we struggled to stay together, I yelled, "Pack attack units!" The twins and Ethan slowed, losing contact with us, yet keeping up a respectable pace by staying together. The same tactics worked later for Keith and Pete when they dropped back from Tom and me. Nobody was alone, hung out to "flap in the wind" as Pop would say. We kept together until the "run for home," as Pop called it.

I assessed the mental toughness of our team, figuring how fast we could run the pursuit pace, how long we could hold it before slowing, and how long to continue the slower striding pace. Our goal was to stay together for as long as possible. It was a work in progress, and we worked it for weeks, improving as we became more resilient.

On one afternoon workout, we were running interval repeats at the sideless bridge. Luke had driven Pop down in the sidecar of the *Eagle 7* to observe. After we finished our jog down, Bubba held up a huge string of fish while cooling off, standing near the bank in waist-deep water below the bridge.

"Guess what's for dinner?" Bubba shouted, his enthusiasm bubbling over. As we gazed, Keith complained, "Not fish again! I'm growin' gills!"

*****

It was late May, and the secret match race lurked days away. Pop stared out his office window at the mountain, contemplating his next move. He had canceled morning workouts for two days. A clock clicked to 3:00 p.m. The school bell rang at Cliffview Boys' Home.

*****

At the course, I yelled, "Wooo-eee!" Victory shrieked above in a radiant blue sky as we gathered for Pop's instructions. We had hydrated, and Luke had the *Eagle 7* ready for any emergency.

"Today is our last run before the match race. We've spent months building up our endurance. Today, show me you can conquer Rocky Point Trail—all the way to the peak—as one team—in one big pack attack!"

I looked at my teammates' faces—each one confident.

"We've done it by sections," Pop continued, "but today, we'll put it all together. I'm giving three days' rest before the match race—just stretching and a jog. The hay's in the barn!"

"Three days off?" said Keith. "All right!"

"Billy, as captain, do you have anything to add?"

"Yes, the key to this race is steadiness up the steep climb to the peak. But an immediate speedy descent must follow along those narrow cliff trails and across the open field to the finish. We must switch to a faster pace on the downhill section to win! They've been runnin' sprints in track. They'll fade on the way up. We won't!"

"Billy, during the race, you'll determine when to split into pack attack units. The timing will be critical! When they fade, we'll pounce! What's it called?"

"Pack attack! Pack attack! Pack attack!" we shouted. With our practices working, belief flowed from Pop. "To the top, Zack! Keep holdin' on, Zeke!"

"I'll keep a strong grip!" Zeke said.

Ethan pitched in. "It's a match made in heaven!"

"It's true!" Zeke said. "When we were born, I was hanging onto Zack's umbilical cord!"

All seven of us ran a 2–2–3 controlled pattern across the flats, up a short hill, and down Suicide Plunge into Death Valley. We scattered only to cross the implanted log-planks, then reorganized and passed over the sideless bridge in formation. As we ran upward, I gazed at the big white cross at the top of the hill to our side and shouted, "We've conquered Death Valley!"

We turned into the backwoods to make our way up Rocky Point Trail. Though not at a blistering pace, we ran our patterns with drill team precision.

Rocky Point Trail offered a host of challenges. Staying together was the toughest. Nobody liked the switchbacks, but we persevered. We slipped and slid but helped each other, making a slow but continuous rise toward the peak.

*****

In the long, rising canyon far below the peak, a watchman sneaked around trees, brush, and rocks. He saw a man who leaped from his truck and secured a dog carrier, a rifle, and a thick blanket onto a large four-wheeled dolly. The watchman knew the man with the rifle and continued to stay undetected, watching him push the large-wheeled dolly along the valley floor, rising somewhat along the contours of the canyon.

*****

On the climb to the peak, our biggest problem came from the Z twins running the steep trail while holding the elastic band. When Zack slipped, Zeke went down. When Zeke slipped, Zack stopped, so he didn't drag Zeke over the rocks. Our biggest asset was Victory soaring above, inspiring us. He kept our minds on the goal of conquering Rocky Point Trail to the peak.

*****

In the canyon below, the watchman observed the man complete his push of the dolly and untie the green dog carrier from it. The watchman saw the man he knew pick up his rifle and lay it across a protruding tree branch at shoulder level. The watchman saw the man gaze through the rifle scope, its barrel aimed toward the peak.

*****

On the climb, we gritted our teeth and kept at it with relentless determination. Our breathing resembled the sound I imagined from seven miniature locomotives, each trying to move forward. The higher we climbed, the more rapid our breathing became. Victory shrieked above, and we glanced up, renewing our fervor.

"Billy, I can see the peak!" Tom shouted.

"One final assault!" I confirmed.

We reached the summit, raising our hands to the sky. We moved to the summit's edge and viewed the canyon and forest below, putting perspective on our team's amazing accomplishment.

*****

In the canyon, the watchman crept closer beside rocky terrain to the man with the rifle. The watchman saw the man he knew adjust the scope and place his finger on the trigger.

*****

From the peak, the sun dipped to the horizon. A golden hue painted the skies. Our smiles looked tame, since we had little energy left to express it, but joy surged through our veins. When Victory circled over us, I cried out to him, the same cry I had shouted years before.

"Wooo-eee! Victory!" In one joint gaze over the canyon, our team saw Victory circle and shriek.

"Wooo-eee! Victory!" The team shouted the same call and Victory shrieked again.

A bang! An echo!

*****

The watchman, Jimmy Jack Clausen, flinched from the sound of the rifle shot and its echo as he stared around a boulder at the shooter, at the man he knew, at his own Pa, Coach Cale Clausen.

*****

From the peak, I gasped in horror, seeing Victory spiral downward in a chaotic fluttering of wings to the unseen rocky crags below.

"Nooo!" I cried, my voice echoing off canyon walls. Slumped to my knees, I gazed at a lone feather twisting into the abyss. My teammates were beside me. We felt abandoned.

Moments before, we reveled in our achievement, gazing at the brilliance of the afternoon glow, spurred by the diversity of nature's splendor, and dazzled by its beauty. But the sky was now empty, our spirits crushed.

My teammates collapsed as Victory disappeared between a lower hillside and a thick stand of trees. The effort of the climb itself could send us to the ground, exhausted, but the shock of witnessing Victory's fluttering descent sapped us of all remaining energy and hope.

*****

Jimmy Jack ran out and shouted, "Did you kill the eagle?"

"What are you doing following me here, son?" There was an uneasy silence. "Yes, I shot him," Clausen admitted. "We both knew the freaks were going for the Rocky Point summit today. I hope he's dead. It's about time you prove you're a Clausen first and a part-time Cowler after that! No Clausen will ever lose to a Cline. We both proved that when I whipped Ned and you whipped Billy in our races. Now help me move this eagle into the cage. I've got a plan, and it includes you! And you'd better be ready to help!"

It didn't take long for Coach Clausen and Jimmy Jack to find the eagle.

"How much help do you need, Pa? There he is! He's not dead. You just clipped his wing. How are you going to get him into this cage? He doesn't look too pleased."

"Leave that to me."

Coach Clausen took a large blanket to cover Victory. He flipped the eagle over with his rifle barrel, using the blanket to sandwich him. He then dragged the bird into the cage. That was a big mistake. Victory's talons ripped through the blanket and the long-sleeved shirt Coach Clausen wore, gashing his forearms. As Clausen struggled to get the cage shut, talons cut him again, and he voiced a mouthful of expletives.

"Pa, this green dog carrier belongs to the Clines. It's got their name on it."

"Shut up and strap it to the dolly! You'll pull the dolly back to where I parked my truck." Clausen moaned between breaths. "We'll take him alive to the Ruby Lake dock."

When they reached the truck, they lifted the green dog carrier onto the bed. Victory jerked from under the blanket. Clausen, bleeding and in pain, drove to the Ruby Lake dock as Jimmy Jack pondered the situation.

Arriving, Jimmy Jack gazed at his Pa's bloody shirt sleeves. "That eagle showed a lot of fight, Pa."

"He's gonna pay with his own blood!" said Clausen. Stepping out of his truck with Jimmy Jack, Clausen released the back latch. They lifted the cage from the truck to the dock. Clausen reached in and yanked out two of Victory's white tail feathers, creating shrieks and spots of blood.

"How does that feel?" Clausen yelled at Victory. He grew angrier by the minute. "Here's a feather trophy for you and one for me," he said, handing over a white tail feather. "Dump him and the Cline's cage into Ruby Lake after I drive off! We'll pin this on Ned, Rawley will put him in jail, and we'll get the Ruby Lake land for taxes. Payback is our way, boy, and you'd better be all in!" Clausen slipped his white tail feather into his truck's visor and drove off. Jimmy Jack gazed into Ruby Lake and placed the feather in his shirt pocket before scooting the cage to the edge of the dock.

*****

A full moon glistened through passing clouds in the canyon. Nature's gentle voice filled our shocked silence. Firelight flickered on ten faces of grief and a makeshift cross. Pop and the team's helpers had arrived after Tom ran to a local neighbor who brought Pop, Andy, and Bubba. They found us by following the glow from the fire, encircled by stones we had made from matches Tom brought from the neighbor.

Silence reigned as we glared from the fire to the makeshift grave: raised earth, stones, and a wooden cross we had formed.

I held a bloodied wing feather in my hand and broke the silence. "One brown wing feather? That's all? If Victory's dead, where's his body?"

"Footprints don't lie!" said Keith, pointing to the ground. "They'll strip him of his feathers for the money! I hate 'em for this! It's payback time."

Pete twisted to his knees as words of agony burst out, "Ooouuuweeeaaaooo! Ooouuuweeeaaaooo!" Pete's deep, guttural groans were unrecognizable words for an indescribable action. We collapsed, distraught by his cries, broken in spirit.

I lay on the ground, holding the feather, tears flowing.

Time passed until Pop spoke, holding a two-foot long stick he kept poking into the fire. "Hatred is easy at first. Then it festers, infects, makes you sick, unable to heal. Payback through hatred is poison to healing! You swallow it, you die! You shrink to oblivion, a tainted smear on the garbage dump of life! I know!"

"So you want us to forgive and forget?" I asked.

"No!" Pop answered before calming. "You won't forget, but you can forgive. Forgiveness lifts the weight off your shoulders. True forgiveness…kills revenge." Smoke from dying embers drifted upward. Firelight flashed higher onto the trees.

After midnight, we had returned to Cliffview. Three days later, the darkened sky we had lived through brightened to the noonday sun—race day Saturday.

CHAPTER 35

The Match Race

May 1984

On the last Saturday in May, the city clock tower neared the noon hour. Customers inside Buster's Barber Shop were reading the *Rockside Bugle*. The main headline stood out in huge letters: "Eagle Shot—Shooter Unknown." Another headline on the front page read, "'Eagle Boy' Silent." A third read, "Where is the Eagle?" As soon as customers saw the Rockside athletic bus pass by, they canceled their haircuts and exited the building.

A hardware store owner across the street placed a "Closed" sign on his door and followed the crowd that walked by.

A beautician glanced out her window. Below her, Sally Grundman sat in the chair, her hair coiled straight up into an eight-inch twist, her face encased in a mud facial, and her eyes covered with cucumber slices. The beautician heard the rhythm of a gentle snore. She locked the register, turned off the lights, and walked out, pulling on the front door until it clicked shut.

The twelve gongs rang. Kids on bicycles, roller skates, and skateboards sped down the streets and sidewalks, all following the bus.

President Grundman sat in Caruso's Diner with several conference coaches. Newspapers covered the tables. Grundman nodded toward Deputies Blimp and Rawley Cowler, who were finishing their lunch. When the bus passed, the coaches and deputies wiped their mouths, dropped coin onto the table, and headed for the door. The final gong tolled.

I sat beside Jenny and Darla on a park bench at the cross-country course. The match race loomed before me.

Keith and Tom argued a few feet away. I knew why. My teammates were lining up, choosing sides of an argument I had started. I leaned forward on the bench, elbows to my knees, my hands clasped.

Darla broke the quiet. "Jenny, all of us cheerleaders put up the finish chute at Rocky Point Park last evening, just like you asked. Brock helped me. He's so strong."

"Thanks," Jenny said, nodding, but she focused her attention on me. Jenny placed her hand in mine, gazing at the eagle feather I had pinned onto my jersey.

"Is it wise to wear that?"

"It's all I have left of him, Jenny. I'm numb. I don't know."

"What do you mean you don't know? You do know. You gave a report on eagles, remember?" I sat upright, shaking my head.

Darla stared at the course entrance. "Look at all the people! Patty told me and my friends this was a secret match race."

Jenny and I turned as the Rockside bus pulled into the parking lot. A caravan of trucks, cars, bicyclists, skaters, and people on foot followed.

Darla blocked our view, saying, "Brock told me last night he might come, too. Oh, there's Chuck. He's dreamy. I gotta go."

I rose from the bench as Keith shouted at Tom, "Whatta you mean, it's illegal?"

Tom spun around, pointing at me. "It's illegal for Billy to display or possess an eagle feather! And he knows it!" Pop approached as I joined my team.

"That feather is our battle symbol!" Keith shouted.

Pop intervened. "That feather is a memory of madness!" The team was silent. "We will not allow that despicable act to alter our goal." We remained still as Pop stared at each of us, ending with me. "Billy, that feather may weigh little pinned on your jersey, but it weighs a ton if it's worn for revenge." Pop looked at the team, then stared straight into my eyes, his voice calming, but his look penetrating. "To soar like eagles…take off the weight of unforgiveness."

My shield of resistance came crashing down. Glancing at my teammates, I stroked the eagle feather, taking ragged breaths before unpinning it, handing it over. "I'm sorry, Pop."

Keith vented, "But, Pop, we've got feelings we can't ignore! Don't deny us justice!"

"We don't deny justice, Keith. We embrace mercy. Nobody can steal our love of Victory from here!" Pop pounded his heart and walked away.

"My eagle…our eagle might be gone. But we will soar in his place, above anger, above revenge, above our physical challenges, to victory."

My eyes locked with theirs. I reached my hand into the center of our circle, staring at Keith. Hand joined hand, one at a time. Keith's hand completed our seven and sealed our vow. I shouted, "What's it called?"

"Team!" we shouted.

*****

As we found out later, our team wasn't the only one facing dissension. Coach Clausen parked the Raven bus and reopened his *Rockside Bugle*. He slammed it on the dash. He motioned Jimmy Jack forward for a private talk.

"Anyone see you dump the eagle in the lake?"

Jimmy Jack mouthed, "No."

Inside, Gopher stood in the aisle, his eyes sweeping over the growing crowd. "So much for the secret match race! Chatty Patty blabbed again! Town gossip!"

Cletus rose in defense of his girlfriend and slugged his brother Gopher hard on the shoulder, shocking his teammates. Gopher slumped to his seat.

"Shut up, everybody!" Coach Clausen yelled. "Quiet!" The bus was already graveyard still. Cletus sat, still fuming, as Clausen rose from the driver's seat. He stepped forward and pointed a finger in Cletus's face. In a staccato voice, he spat out the words. "Do…

your…assignment!" He stared as Cletus nodded and sat, gazing at the bus floor.

Clausen paused and smiled, trying to relieve the tension. "I've got a big surprise for the freaks today. When it happens, keep quiet because I know what I'm doing. Is that clear?" Clausen scanned the bus for dissenters and found none. He continued, lively and arrogant. "I don't care if the whole town's here. Give these freak handicappers a donut stretch!"

Gopher stood in the aisle, rubbed his shoulder, and yelled, "Yeah! They'll be nothin' but a big zero in the middle of our donut!"

*****

I led the Soaring Eagles team toward the Rockside bus. We lined up side by side, seven across, with a determined glare on our faces. Coach Clausen led Jimmy Jack and his charge of twenty Raven runners from the bus onto the field of battle.

Cletus challenged us as he walked out: "What are you freaks lookin' at?" No response.

Gopher tried his luck, staring at our new jerseys. "Soaring Eagles? I think not!"

"You can read?" Keith said. Our team laughed.

Jimmy Jack led the Ravens off to stretch while Coach Clausen saw the press and motioned for Pop to join him a few yards away. I followed Pop since I was captain. Clausen seemed annoyed I was there but went ahead, extending his recently bandaged hand to Pop with a big grin, a pure show for the townspeople. A reporter snapped a picture for the *Bugle*.

"How's your heart?" Clausen asked.

"It's beating strong. How's yours?"

Clausen struggled to pull his bandaged-hand grip from Pop, who held on and squeezed before releasing it. Clausen grimaced at Pop's show of force. "Heard Billy's got an eagle feather," Clausen said, walking toward Jimmy Jack, leaving Pop unsure how to respond.

"We'll let our feet do the talking, Pop," I said.

"Okay. Get 'em stretched."

We formed a circle of seven, sitting in the grass, stretching our legs. Soon, twenty Ravens surrounded us, standing above, hovering over us, trying to intimidate us in a "doughnut stretch."

"You're surrounded! It's a massacre!" Gopher shouted.

Our team faced a circular wall of twenty Raven runners as they leaned over us. Deputies Rawley and Blimp Cowler rode up on their motorcycles, revving their engines. Jimmy Jack signaled for the Ravens to back off, so I led our team out of encirclement.

"Sound the retreat! Fall back!" Gopher shouted, mocking us.

I led our team twenty yards from the Ravens. We weren't about to hide or wilt away. We had to cast off their ploy to try to make us feel outnumbered and outclassed.

"We belong here," I said. "They're scared. We're confident."

To my amazement, our pickup arrived with Ma, Pa, and Jake! What an incredible surprise! Following them was Dr. Gorman in his Jeep. Ethan and I grinned. They parked close to where both teams stretched.

The Ravens and the deputies noticed them, too. Ethan and I wanted to greet them, but preparation for the race came first. As we stretched, we watched Jake swing his legs out of the pickup and rise. Ma stood beside him with Pa and Dr. Gorman. Jake took his first steps outside the hospital compound. They were small and tentative, but he was taking them under his own power. Ma was ready to assist, but she stayed clear. Jake paused, nodding to Jimmy Jack, offering a smile while showing no spirit of anger. Astonishment shown on the Ravens' faces. Jimmy Jack stood like a statue, not knowing how to respond.

Jake gave me a nod, and I returned it. Cletus's mocking words fell on Jimmy Jack's ears: "They let Jake out on time served in a hospital?"

Where is Jake going? He moved half step by half step toward the deputies, who stood beside their motorcycles, sandwiched between our two teams. Jake stopped in front of Blimp.

"I meant what I said in the letter. Thanks for dropping your charges," Jake said.

Rawley laughed. "In your dreams, boy."

Blimp leaned to his older brother. "I dropped my charges, Rawley, and Pop posted bail on the other charges. That's why he's out."

"Am I hallucinating?" Rawley asked. "That's how you do your kin?"

"Jake hurt me, not my kin," Blimp said. "It's my decision."

Ma nodded kindly to Blimp before facing Rawley with a fierce look. "How about we bring charges on you, Rawley, over Pop's little Rachel!" Rawley shrunk and walked to Coach Clausen.

"Take a run-out!" Jimmy Jack hollered to his team. The Ravens, minus Jimmy Jack, ran fifty yards down the course. Jimmy Jack stayed where he was as Pop walked to Blimp. *Why didn't Jimmy Jack lead his team out? That's what captains do.* But he stayed and watched Pop hand my brown, blood-stained eagle wing feather to Deputy Blimp Cowler. When Blimp received it, he sighed as he slid the feather into his shirt pocket.

I tried to focus on my team, but everything was happening at once. At the pickup, Pa walked straight toward a pair of angry men, Coach Clausen and Deputy Rawley Cowler. I jogged toward Pa, who turned and signaled me to stop. Thinking Pa was settling old business, I moved close enough to listen but kept them at a distance.

"Got something to say, ex-teammate?" Clausen said.

"I don't know...you changed?"

Clausen spat before speaking. "You haven't—still a gutless coward."

Pa stared at him and I knew his temper could flare up faster than a hornet's nest struck with a baseball bat. But that temper had grown mute for a long time when it concerned a face-to-face confrontation with Coach Clausen and Rawley Cowler.

"Turn around and be on your way," Deputy Rawley said, playing the lawman.

Pa paused for a moment and then walked away toward Jake and Ma. It surprised me, knowing Pa didn't back down from direct confrontation. I had gleaned that as fact after Pa stood up to the lawmen and their gunplay at the cabin.

"He's still gutless," Rawley said to Clausen, trying to stir up Pa.

I couldn't wait any longer. I joined my folks at Jake's side. Before I could speak, Jake shushed me, turning toward Rawley and Coach Clausen.

"Look there," Jake said. I saw the same two tough-guy wannabes from the MOO Festival standing beside Clausen in their leather jackets. They stuffed something green he gave them into their pockets, then walked down the backside into Death Valley. *Was that a payoff?*

"Those guys are gonna take ya out!" Jake said. "They've just been bought."

"I've seen 'em before," I said, starting a jog back to my Cliffview team, but Tom had already led them in a run-out. When I passed near Jimmy Jack, the Raven team was returning from its run-out. Cletus ran to Jimmy Jack, and both were oblivious to my presence.

"Some kid told me he knows who shot Billy's eagle!" That stopped me. Cletus saw the look on Jimmy Jack's face, but I saw the surprised look on Cletus's face when he uttered, "You know?"

Jimmy Jack turned from Cletus and his team and jogged to Blimp. I jogged behind the crowd and got close without being noticed. Jimmy Jack took out a white eagle tail feather and handed it over to Blimp, who now held two illegal feathers.

"Now you've got my tail feather and Billy's wing feather. You know who's got the third. Are you a lawman or not, Uncle Blimp?" Jimmy Jack said, raising his voice.

It surprised Blimp. He pinched the eagle tail feather and slid it into his shirt pocket. Blimp nodded and stepped away, pulling out his radio to make a call.

Jimmy Jack spun around. He stared at me and must have known I had heard. I returned his stare with equal intensity as we moved toward each other. When he pointed down the course between both sides of the crowd, the challenge was on. We sprinted side by side in our own run-out competition. After fifty yards, we slowed and turned around, racing back just as fast.

The huge crowd observed our competitive fire and cheered, dividing into two lines, forming a gauntlet as we raced between both teams' fans. We stopped and faced each other in the ultimate stare down: chests heaving, legs running in place, and knees driving higher and higher as we thrust out our arms like boxers.

The huge crowd had swelled, buzzing with anticipation. Townspeople had deserted most streets, making Rockside look more like a ghost town than a mountain village in the Smokies.

Conference President Ben Grundman raised his bullhorn. "Race time! Runners to the starting line!"

As everyone moved into position, Jimmy Jack got my attention. "Victory's alive. I saved him." Jimmy Jack sprinted off to join his team for a last-minute build-up.

It stunned me, and I told my team what Jimmy Jack had said.

"He's tryin' to get into your head," Tom said.

Ace Makowski, absent from this mess, stepped out from the trees with his girlfriend Deucey. He jogged to the line wearing his Haybury Hog jersey.

"What's he doin' here?" Gopher asked, sneering. Jimmy Jack said nothing.

"You'll find out," Clausen said.

Grundman looked at Ace. "We're about to start a race here."

"I want to run in it," said Ace.

"What? Are you nuts?" said Grundman.

Clausen interrupted. "President Grundman, this is not an official race, and it's none of your business if Ace runs or not. This is a public park. I've scheduled an eight-mile 'freewill' workout, that's all."

"*Freewill* workout?" said Grundman. "Few kids I know would run this course of their own free will! What I heard was if Cliffview wins, you'll switch your vote…and Cliffview will get into the conference. If that's true, this race is my business, since I'm conference president."

"Do I look worried? You're overreacting. Chill, will ya?" Clausen replied.

"Chill, huh? I'm gonna add up the top five places from each team…low score wins. That's what I've done in the past…and that's what I'll do here. Miss Harper!" Grundman shouted, "Have you got your clipboard?" She held it high. "Please record the scores and places for this... 'freewill' workout."

"Yes, sir," Miss Harper said.

Ace stepped up. "I choose, of my own free will, to race for the Ravens."

"You're nuttier than a fruitcake," Grundman said. "The Ravens are your rivals!"

"You're a Raven for a day," said Coach Clausen, tossing Ace a Raven jersey.

"Ace will be number one!" Deucey said, smiling at Jenny while flaunting her own big number "2" Haybury Hog jersey.

"Make sure I get it back, washed," added Clausen.

"Sure," he said, staring at me while putting it on over his Haybury jersey. "As long as I race Billy. That's what I want."

"And we've got a hog to fry!" shouted Keith, stepping toward Ace. "We know you're a hog underneath that jersey!" Pete grabbed hold of Keith and held him back.

Jimmy Jack, Cletus, and Gopher walked off by themselves. I could tell they were angry that Coach Clausen had added their arch enemy, Ace Makowski, to the Raven lineup, even if it was for this one freewill race.

At the line, our two teams fidgeted, trying to stay loose. Now it was twenty-one against seven. The town's spectators had scrunched in close, feeling the competitive angst in the air.

Tom shook his head. "This must worry them to death, bringing in a ringer like Ace."

Pop gathered the team in a circle. "Keith, I heard good advice from your captain. Billy, tell Keith and the team what you told me."

"That we'll let our feet do the talking?"

"Yes, and that's what I want you all to do," said Pop. "Calm your emotions. Use your head first by staying alert, then use your feet next by running the plan we've practiced."

The team turned to Billy. "When we rise over that peak today, remember what happened there. Remember what we lost. Remember how we lost it. Take...it...back! Look at your teammates. We've

gained—a united team. Bring back Victory's spirit. Bring back...
victory!"

Billy turned to Pop, who thrust out both his burn-scarred leath-
ery hands. We clasped them, joining Pop in a moment of serious
anticipation.

"What are the rules of this non-race?" asked Grundman to
Coach Clausen.

"There are no rules. If you want to make it like a race, be my
guest. I brought my starter pistol."

"And an Ace up your sleeve," added Grundman, who raised the
bullhorn. "For all of you from town, this so-called freewill workout
is not sanctioned by anyone. I want to be clear about that. Everyone
who runs is running of his own free will. The race will finish on the
cliffside section of Rocky Point Park! You must circle around to see
the finish!" Grundman nodded to Pop and to Coach Clausen, who
raised his starter pistol in the air. Grundman continued, "Runners...
to your mark! Set..."

CHAPTER 36

Sabotage Setup

Bang! Coach Clausen fired his starter pistol. Twenty-one Raven runners sprinted ahead of us. The crowd moved for better vantage points as we circled the course on the beginning flats. Townsfolk edged toward the top of Suicide Plunge, watching us loop around the field before storming over the side for the wild descent into Death Valley.

Some locals jumped in their vehicles and drove for better views, stopping to cheer out their windows before following the park road to the cliff side. I knew Ma and Pa, for Jake's sake, would be among the first to gather at the finish line.

Our team ran in one pack: Tom and I were up front, followed by Keith and Pete, with Zack, Zeke, and Ethan in the third row.

"Keep together—tight and compact!" I yelled to my teammates. "Stay relaxed! They'll come back to us!" Pop expected that seeing all twenty-one of their runners ahead of us could erode confidence and drain our strength, so he wanted me to assure the team of our plan.

Each runner in the rows behind ran offset between the back kicks of those in front. We knew a steady pace would help Zack as he ran beside Zeke, guiding him with the elastic band.

We had practiced this controlled formation for two months. Zeke had much of the early course memorized since Zack had given commentary at key points. With a tug and a reminder of where they were, Zeke learned to respond. That knowledge had come at a high price. Zeke had taken several nasty falls, but he and his brother focused not on the mistakes but how to overcome them. That's what Tom and I had experienced, and the Z twins had learned from us.

Because we had trained as a team, Tom and I learned to position our formation to offer the best footing. However, the switchbacks and the long climb up to Rocky Point were difficult to maneuver, even for sighted runners. The steep climb had portions of uneven ground, far from runner-friendly.

As we ran, a grin spread across my face. I recalled telling the team to slide into the slipstream Tom and I would generate. "We might not match the slipstream of the Indy 500 racecars," I had said, "since Tom and I don't have legs that can ramp up hundreds of horse-power. But we are a team of runners committed to each other and to reaching the goals we've set."

As we approached Suicide Plunge, we gained on some slower runners. Disappearing over the top, I missed hearing Victory's shriek. Tom and I sped down the grassy hillside to pass two runners. Over Lover's Leap, we kept our footing, though Pete ran up my backside, putting a hand on my shoulder, forcing me to speed up. Near the bottom, we strode past three more runners.

"Five down, sixteen to go!" I shouted.

As we ran through the depths of Death Valley, I kept my wits about me, suspecting mischief ahead. *When will our opponents strike? And how?* I knew it would be sooner than later. But, at present, we had to focus on the three log-planks. The city park crew had cleaned up the area and replaced the logs and the old rickety bridge after the storm. We had practiced crossing it, and I knew if we stayed true to our training, we would be okay. Gazing up, I saw the Ravens splitting up, crossing on all three logs. Nothing seemed amiss until a freshman runner stopped halfway on the log we would cross. He turned, and with a mischievous smile, tried to block us.

Seeing this, Keith sprinted by me to the front, and stepped first onto the third log as the rest of us followed in single file. Keith sprinted across, growling like an unleashed wildebeest and screamed, "Ramming speed!" With Keith charging, we chugged toward the freshman like a powerful locomotive. The young rival glanced at the stream below, tucked tail and sprinted, till he lost his balance and his smile, falling face-first into the mud beside the shallow stream. We followed the trail on the opposite side of the bank toward the sideless bridge.

*****

As I learned later, Andy had discovered key information about the race. He had overheard a young kid revealing the Ravens' dastardly plan, so he ran to warn Luke and Bubba, who were sitting in the *Eagle 7*. "Two guys in black leather jackets want to knock our runners off the sideless bridge!"

"Bubba, that's your fishin' hole!" Luke said.

"Fire it up!" said Bubba. Andy leaped into the cramped sidecar with Bubba as Luke roared the engine and took off in a cloud of dust. To Luke, the *Eagle 7* was an extension of himself when he was a star tailback. He drove it the same way he'd rushed down the field, stiff-arming would-be tacklers to break free for a touchdown. He was highly skilled but borderline reckless.

Traveling at high speed down the backside of Death Valley, the *Eagle 7* soared airborne over the rise, zooming toward the sideless bridge. I could only imagine how Andy and Bubba felt. This had to be the ultimate joyride! But the weight of two boys in the sidecar at high speed created an imbalance, and Luke struggled to maintain control.

Leaning onto Luke's shoulder from the sidecar, Andy tried to re-distribute the weight. Andy's presence half-blinded Luke. Bubba, in the side car, detached his two fishing poles.

He stood, bracing himself against the back of the padded roll bar, holding the fishing poles forward as lances. They neared the sideless bridge like a rocket on wheels. The two wannabes were waiting in the middle of the bridge near its edge. Startled by the roar, they whirled around.

"Whoooah!" cried all three in the *Eagle 7* as they zipped onto the bridge. The saboteurs, fearing a spearing, stood at the edge as Luke zeroed in with Bubba's fishing poles aimed at the villains. Luke stomped on the brake, but the skidding tires were no match for the momentum of the speeding vehicle.

The wannabes leaped off the sideless bridge into the five-foot-deep pooled creek, followed by Bubba, who flew doing a front-flip cannonball, creating a huge splash. Andy had dropped to the floor as the Eagle 7 skidded to a stop. Andy then rose, standing on the sidecar seat, gazing over the bridge. The wannabes waddled toward the bank below, their leather coats looking more like straight-jackets.

Bubba stood in the water, giving Luke and Andy a "thumbs-up." Feeling something strange, he reached into the large front pouch of his windbreaker, pulling out a wiggling trout. He raised it to his mouth, clenched it with his teeth, and waved his fists in triumph!

"All right, Bubba!" Luke and Andy shouted. "Way to go!"

That was when the first Raven runners appeared, crossing the sideless bridge.

Andy yelled to them. "Anybody want a pizza?" Andy told me later the Ravens veered away from the Eagle 7, depressed by the sight of their thug-friends trudging out of the water. The Ravens were scattered with time gaps between them.

When we approached the Eagle 7, we noticed Luke and Andy's gaze down at Bubba. "He's okay!" said Andy. "He caught a trout in his windbreaker pocket!"

"Hurry, Bubba!" Luke said. "We've got to get the Eagle 7 to the finish line!"

"Let's go, Eagles!" I shouted. We chugged up the backside of Death Valley as we had practiced many times before. Halfway up, we made the dreaded turn to the switchbacks that led up and around the mountain toward Rocky Point Peak.

"Surge!" I bellowed. We ramped up our effort, but our speed stayed the same on the steeper grade. We passed two Ravens who were walking.

"Eight down! LSD pace for thirty," I said. We went into a recovery jog to rest since the trail flattened out for a brief stretch.

"That hill got me," Ethan said.

"I slipped! Zeke, keep holdin' on!" said Zack.

"I'm better. Pick it up!" Ethan's bravado surprised me.

"Okay, surge!" I shouted. We did, sweeping past three more Ravens who were slowing.

"Eleven down!" Keith shouted.

"Look up the switchbacks!" Tom warned. I gazed at blurry figures.

"Three more up there! There's five more…and these two!" Tom shouted.

"We'll catch 'em!" I said.

"I'm hurtin'," Ethan admitted.

"Dig in, Ethan, right beside my brother! We keep together," Zack said.

"Keep holdin' on!" Zeke repeated.

"Gut check!" I shouted. "Three surges!"

During the first surge, we passed one runner before slowing. We got another on the second, but Ethan slowed, drifting behind.

"Keep us steady, Tom! I'll help Ethan!" I slowed and swung wide, allowing Keith and Pete to pass me first, followed by the Z twins. "You can do it!" I said to Ethan. Behind us, the two Ravens we had passed now walked. "Let yourself recover! Relax." Ethan and I were about ten yards behind the pack attack. Doubts emerged as time stalled in this zone of pain.

Tom shouted to the team, "Surge three! Go!"

"Pretend I'm towing you!" I said to Ethan, who gritted his teeth for the effort of another surge. Though weakened, our main pack attack group topped a slight rise before slowing. Ethan and I kept up the slower surge pace until we caught up. I could see this Herculean effort left Ethan at the edge of survival mode.

"LSD pace!" I shouted. We kept moving, but it seemed like slow motion. We crossed a plateau and kept the slower pace. I could see movement of runners ahead.

"Three miles to get the last eight of 'em!" I shouted.

Tom yelled out, "I see five scattered…not far ahead!"

"I almost lost it," said Zack.

"Keep holdin' on!" Zeke responded.

Tom glanced at me, catching my attention. His face showed the strain of concern.

"I read you, Tom. Okay, team! Tom and I must…pass these scattered five…and get in position to strike their top three. Pack attack units! Keith and Pete, get these five! No matter what!" I caught my breath again as Keith held out five fingers to Pete, who nodded. "Zack...you and your brother...and Ethan—get somebody!"

"I won't score! I won't count because I can't finish," Ethan said.

"Yes, we can—we all count!" said Zeke.

"We're Soaring Eagles!" I shouted.

Tom and I sped off, along with Keith and Pete. But, we soon separated from them, pulling ahead. Zack, Zeke, and Ethan continued the slower pace, trying to recover.

"We'll reel in somebody—patience!" Zack said to Zeke and Ethan.

*****

As captain, I felt responsible for all members of my team. Our goal was to defeat the Ravens and do it safely. Now that Tom and I were clear of Keith and Pete's mini pack, I had to believe in their desire to persevere. Keith had learned to communicate well with Pete. Though deaf, Pete was instinctive. He could read Keith's mood and had learned his awkward signing. I had to have faith in them. Another concern involved the Z twins and Ethan. Without one of them finishing, we couldn't win. A team score required five runners to finish.

I decided to face the situation, concentrating on Tom and me. Anything more, and I would waste energy in worry for something I had no power to control.

"Let's gun it, Tom, and make up time!" I said. We did, and much to our surprise, we saw Cletus thirty yards ahead, laboring up the steep trail.

"Why's he back here?" Tom seemed suspicious, and I had no clue.

"LSD pace," I said. We slowed to a jog for a minute and then made a wide turn on a switchback. Fifteen yards ahead, we saw Cletus, walking. "Go," I said to Tom. We swung around and passed him without incident. I expected a comeback, but Cletus never reacted.

As we pulled away, I knew his muscular frame didn't suit him for an uphill climb, and uphill was what we faced. But it shocked me that Cletus had fallen this far behind.

The switchbacks were a meandering, rocky climb, with the percentage of grade seeming to rise with each stride. In ten minutes, we picked off four more runners, one at a time, who had run by their lonesome in the rugged climb. As we passed, they put up no resistance. Two were walking. A look of dread covered their faces from the unrelenting toll of the ascent. Our forced jog, slow as it was, kept us pulling away and gaining on their final three.

It was tough enough to keep my eyes fixed on a steep, uneven trail and maintain footing. It was tougher yet to focus blurry eyes farther up the trail and keep from tripping over rocks and debris. I didn't do well, but Tom was alert. Though we were slipping and sliding, Tom cricked his neck and caught a flash of three Ravens on a higher switchback.

"There's Jimmy Jack!" Tom said. "And two behind him—Ace and Gopher!"

I called to Tom, "Believe with me! Win with me!"

*****

Keith and Pete were also on a mission. They reported to us later that as they chugged up Rocky Point Trail, they saw Cletus walking in front. Puzzled, they passed him and kept the hammer down to complete separation.

Closing in on two more, they backed off to recover before surging again. As they approached the runners, they saw them stop, one right after the other. Keith and Pete looked back and saw them sit on a rock. They told me later it was like the Ravens were taking a coffee break. They had knocked off three of the five. Pete held up two fingers, sporting a weary but determined look. Two more to go.

******

The twins and Ethan used a variation of the fartlek strategy, surging to gain on the first two of the five Ravens they had seen. Whenever they surged to a faster run, moderate as it was, they cut valuable yards between them and the two Ravens. When they slowed to a jog, the distance between them remained the same.

Zeke, though blind, heard Ethan stagger, even before he tumbled over. "Stop, Zack, for Ethan! I knew it! I could hear his footsteps—faltering!"

"Help me lift him!" Zack said. The Z twins reached over and pulled Ethan to his feet. But keeping him upright was like carrying dead weight. Ethan had entered a fatigue zone he had never experienced.

"Can you walk?" asked Zack.

"I'll just slow you down," Ethan complained.

"Zeke and I will stay with you."

"No!" Ethan pleaded. "One of us…has to score…as fifth man…or it's over!" Ethan struggled to breathe and then tried to hide his pain by running again, but his strides lasted only about ten seconds before he stopped. "Finish it for Pop! Please! One of us…has to finish!"

"Pop taught us to stay in groups…not to leave a single runner behind!" Zack said.

"Pop taught us…to fight for what we believed! I'm with you in spirit. Take my spirit with you! Now, go!" Ethan said. "I'll finish! I promise, and I'll get a second wind on the downhill!"

Zack tugged on the elastic band, and the twins surged. "He is a good downhill runner."

*****

Tom and I were no longer running. We were mountain climbing. For fifty yards, we often dropped onto all fours by the incline and sliding debris. We both had cuts and scrapes on our knees, legs, and hands, but that wasn't our focus. Speed was. We had three to catch, and time was running short.

We arrived at the turn where the trail rose to the peak. In our final practice with Victory, his inspiring shrieks had taken us to the top, where our team celebration ended with the saddest scene of all, Victory fluttering into the canyon from a rifle shot. As we continued striding to the summit, we remembered. Oh, how we remembered!

I can't explain the emotion. I scanned the sky, wishing for just one more glimpse of him, but all I saw were clouds—no eagle. "Let's go, Tom!" I shouted.

A shriek! Instead of sprinting downward, Tom and I spun around as Victory himself soared low over us before circling and giving another shriek.

"It's Victory!" I yelled. "I don't understand how or why, but he's here! He's returned! Let's change the outcome and follow his wings to victory!"

We were no longer grinding up the mountain. We were on the backside, descending at high speed, letting the downgrade propel us. It may have been fraught with peril, but we dismissed negativity. Our bodies ran free. The treachery of this twisting trail could defeat the most gifted runner, but not us, not today. To Coach Clausen that would guarantee our failure. But to us, it would be our defining moment.

CHAPTER 37

Betrayal

Tom and I bolted with blazing speed down the backside of Rocky Point Peak, fearlessly facing the narrow trails along the cliffs. A misstep could lead to a crash onto rugged rocks, or a high-flying freefall over the precipice. Neither appealed to us.

Tom led, and I stayed slightly behind him, feeding off his foot placements. Rugged boulders hung over the cliff walls. I stumbled over one, my foot strike dislodging it and other debris that ricocheted downward. That was my only close call. I had never known Tom to be as aggressive and precise in his decisions as he was on that stretch of trail.

After the cliffs, we worked our way down to the more forested area. The trail entered through the pines and evergreens leading to the upper flats, a treeless plateau.

Tom shouted, "There they are! Jimmy Jack, Ace, and Gopher!"

"Now is no time to be timid!" I said. "Cut the distance before they see us!"

We surged, taking them by surprise. Gopher looked back and saw us charging with Victory soaring above. "Eagles attacking!" he yelled, but we were in full flight, down by forty yards.

*****

For a few moments, I wondered about Keith and Pete. Had I been a true eagle, I could have seen them push the pace up the mountain and descending as we did.

When I thought about the Z twins, reality hit. We needed one more finisher, and that might be one of them. I had observed a mastery of teamwork from them. *If they can stay on their feet, they have a chance.*

I had no clue where Ethan was, but since he was my roommate, I knew what he wanted. I'd felt his pain when we'd first met, and I had witnessed his gradual transformation at Pop's school. Ethan wanted to please his grandfather, who said Ethan never finished anything. However, the joy he showed from completion of the *Eagle 7* project was evidence of his newfound determination.

My thoughts returned to my present struggle. This trail led to the upper flats just above Rocky Point Park. We had now closed within ten yards of Gopher and twenty yards of Ace, a testimony to Pop's training strategies. Jimmy Jack was leading, mere yards ahead of Ace. We eased off for a moment to regather our strength for another surge.

Many spectators had bet money on the match race and desired to observe their hopes of financial winnings. Spying from a distance, some cheered while the Raven bettors pointed at Victory, shocked by his appearance, our rapid approach, and Victory's shrieks of inspiration. These Raven fans, once overconfident, now panicked, running toward the finish line to cancel their bets, while others gave up, seeking relief in the porta potties.

"Ready to soar?" I yelled to Tom. We surged again on Gopher, who sped up. That brought the three of us beside Ace and cut Jimmy Jack's lead to ten yards. The four of us ran abreast, racing like a tidal wave through the park, sweeping up to Jimmy Jack as we turned and entered the final hundred-yard sprint. Townspeople cheered this climactic match race, lining both sides of the narrowing chute, outlined by the multicolored ribbons.

Gopher and Ace were struggling to maintain form. Jimmy Jack looked over his left shoulder and saw me first, then glanced around to his right and saw Tom back farther. His decision made, Jimmy Jack shifted to his left to block me from passing.

"Come on, Tom!" I shouted. Jimmy Jack was now leading by only two strides. The crowd's voices rang in my ears. With sixty yards to go, Gopher, behind and to my right, threw an elbow at Tom, which had no effect. Gopher's stride broke and he slowed, followed by Ace, who had nothing left and coasted. But Tom and I ran with purpose.

"Go!" I shouted. I darted behind Jimmy Jack and cut to his right side. The tactic was perfect. When he looked to his left again, I wasn't there. I sprinted by him on his right for a two-yard victory! A demoralized Jimmy Jack, late by looking to his right, now missed Tom's fierce charge to his left.

Tom dove airborne, inches ahead of Jimmy Jack at the finish line. The crowd gasped as Tom skidded past the line, face down in the grass.

"Billy Cline, first! Tom Pryor, second!" Grundman shouted through his bullhorn while hunched over the finish line to make the call.

"It's a double steal!" Ma shouted, kicking up her heels.

"Yes!" shouted Pa, who moved close.

Coach Clausen slammed his clipboard to the ground as Rawley and Blimp groaned.

As I slowed, Jimmy Jack held onto my shoulders to prevent me from falling. He muttered, "Great race."

"You, too," I answered. Jimmy Jack collapsed beside a tree. I lurched forward, trying to balance myself.

Ace followed Jimmy Jack across the line in fourth. Gopher, slowing to a mere jog, crossed the line as number five. Seeing Tom still sprawled face down across the finish line, Gopher veered and stomped him on the back as he passed. Moans rose from Tom and the crowd as Tom twisted in pain.

Jenny ran to greet me, giving me a quick hug despite my sweaty body.

Pa stepped up and I shouted, "We did it, Pa! This race was for you and Victory!" I wondered as we embraced if years of frustration would erase his bad memories and replace them with the joy of victory nineteen years later. Jake, too, limped up, beaming, but fell before he could greet me. The pride from his eyes told me everything as Ma helped him up.

Chester grinned when he marked the team places on the poster: Soaring Eagles: 1+2, Ravens: 3+4+5.

Tom lay curled on the grass. Pop hovered over him with a first aid kit, but several other coaches took the kit from Pop and cleaned Tom's scrapes. Pop looked surprised and proud, watching his fellow coaches treat him and his runner with respect he had long desired. In a quick glance, I saw a huge smile covering Tom's face. It overshadowed his grimaces of pain. And I knew why. He had reached his goal of defeating Jimmy Jack.

Deucey bolted to Ace, who leaned against a tree. "You said you'd be number one!" she shouted. "You were fourth!" She stomped her foot and turned to Jenny. "My Ace would have been number one if he'd been wearin' only his hog jersey!"

Jenny mused, "You might be right, Deucey. He was fourth today, but you'll always be number 2." Deucey raised her eyebrows, looked down at her jersey, and turned to comfort Ace.

Darla frowned as she looked down at Jimmy Jack, propped against a tree. She stepped toward Tom, knelt, and flashed a toothy smile, crooning, "Oh, Tommy!"

*****

I heard shouts that Keith and Pete were not far behind the Ravens' fourth and fifth runners as they crossed the flats and neared the rows of fans for the final stretch.

The Raven runners made the turn and ran side by side to make it easier to block a pass attempt. Pete crossed his arms in an "X" on the homestretch and I knew what it meant.

Pete and Keith widened between themselves, pulling up behind the Ravens, causing them to widen while looking over their outside shoulders.

"Double X!" Keith shouted and signed. With forty yards to go, Keith sprinted from left to right and Pete sprinted from right to left, making the "X" behind them. The Ravens both moved inside to block the pass but collided with each other. Keith and Pete sprinted by them on their outsides.

Grundman studied Chester's poster again and used his bull-horn. "Remember, the lowest score wins! Four have scored for the Soaring Eagles, 1+2+6+7, which equals sixteen points. The Ravens have completed their five scorers, 3+4+5+8+9, which equals twen-ty-nine points! Wait! Here are two more Ravens coming in. They are a non-scoring tenth and eleventh place.

As the crowd watched and cheered, Chester marked their non-scoring places on the poster.

Holding his bullhorn, Grundman studied the poster and announced: "The next runner to cross the finish line will determine the winning team!"

*****

During our training runs, the Z twins had learned to apply a specific skill. They had practiced it not only to scale Rocky Point Peak but also on many downhill trails over the past month. Zeke would run behind Zack and to his right. If Zeke fell behind, he would feel the tug from Zack's elastic band and speed up. If he was running too fast or too close, Zeke would raise his left hand to Zack's shoulder to realign himself. It had worked to perfection. It had to, or else.

When Zack told us later what he saw, he experienced a shiver through his body at that decisive moment. It was that event that spun the race in a new direction, on the narrow trail beside the cliffs.

"It's Cletus, waitin' for us!" shouted Zack.

"We can do it! We need one more…to score," said Zeke. Zack tugged on his blind brother's elastic band, passing Cletus on the nar-row trail, not knowing Cletus had been ordered to ambush them. Cletus let them pass, then sprinted, grabbing hold of Zack's shoulders from behind. He shoved Zack, which jerked blind Zeke to follow toward the jagged terrain along the cliff's edge. The Z twins tripped, losing their grip on the elastic band as they braced for the tumble. However, Cletus lost his balance, too, toppling over a boulder.

Zeke groped for his sighted brother, who lay in pain. "Zack, where are you? Zack!"

"Oh! My leg! I think it's broken!" Zack shouted through his pain.

"What'll I do? I can't leave you!"

"You can't help me by stayin'! Run toward the crowd noise! Get help! Go!"

Blind Zeke rose and stumbled to the trail. "Now, where?"

"Left! You've got a narrow trail for a couple of hundred yards! Keep away from the cliffs. When the downhill ends, you'll be in the pine trees. Veer right of them and you'll be in the upper flats. You can follow the crowd noise through the open field to the finish chute!"

Zeke limped downward in a shuffling jog. He could barely see the outline of the cliffs.

Zack groaned, pulling himself up to observe his brother. "Keep your hands in front!"

Zeke's foot grazed the root of a tree. He fell but got up and stepped over it. His acute hearing, his experience, and what little sight he had, told him which way to go.

Zack heard a groan from the side of the boulder and the sound of loose rocks tumbling over the cliff. He crawled over and glared at Cletus, bleeding, semiconscious, inches from the sheer cliff drop-off. Though in excruciating pain himself, Zack slid on his belly and grabbed a sapling in one hand and Cletus's shirt in the other.

Cletus awakened. In his confused state, he wrestled Zack. During the struggle, Cletus rolled off the ledge, dangling over the cliff wall, hanging only by the strength of Zack's grip.

"Keep holdin' on!" Cletus yelled, realizing he was about to go airborne over the cliff wall as he gazed down at tree tops fifty feet below. Cletus struggled to maintain his grip on Zack's hand as his feet banged along the cliff walls, searching for a foothold. More loose rocks broke free and plummeted.

Zack's grip sustained Cletus as he pulled himself up and grabbed a root along the cliff with his free hand. Cletus found a better foothold and pushed up, still held by Zack's firm grip. As he worked his way up and over the ledge, the thin limb from the sapling that Zack held tore loose from the main branch, sending Zack teetering off balance and over the edge.

"Whoah!" Zack yelled, staring at his grip on Cletus's hand. His body slammed onto the cliff walls, punctuating his terror. Cletus slumped to his chest on the ledge and grimaced, using all his strength to hold on to Zack.

"I've got ya!" Cletus said.

"Keep holdin' on!" yelled Zack, who felt his sweating hand slip.

Cletus saw a larger sapling protruding from the cliff wall below.

"Trust me!" he said as he slid Zack along the edge, his own arm getting a deep cut as it scraped the rocky edge. When their grips slipped, Zack fell six feet onto a sturdier sapling.

"Oww! I got it!" Zack said, as his body lay draped over the sapling.

"I'll get help! This is not what I wanted!" said Cletus, bleeding from his arm, his legs, and his head as he limped from the ledge onto the trail down toward the pine forest and upper flats.

*****

Zeke had cleared the pine trees and increased his pace across the upper flats into the open field. The townspeople could now see him. His foot landed in a chuckhole, and he tumbled over, spraining his ankle. He bounded back up but had a serious limp.

Cletus entered the open field with an awkward gait, but was fresher, gaining on Zeke.

Zeke heard voices trying to direct him as he turned for the final hundred-yard straightaway between the two rows of fans. Voices seemed to come from all directions, confusing him.

Zeke shouted, "They hurt my brother on the cliffs!" He brushed left against the crowd, but noise overwhelmed his gasping words. He veered right, brushing against the other row, now resembling a bumper car. Rebounding off the crowd, he moved forward toward the finish line.

Cletus entered the hundred-yard final stretch gaining on Zeke as he pointed toward the Rocky Point cliffs, trying to share Zack's danger, but the crowd did not understand.

"He's dead meat, Cletus!" yelled Coach Clausen. "Destroy him!"

Pop ran along outside the energetic crowd, yelling, "Where's Zack?" But Zeke couldn't hear him as he grimaced from his sprained ankle.

Twenty yards from the finish, Cletus collided with Zeke, both falling in a heap. Screaming fans barked orders, pointing to the finish line.

Coach Clausen shoved between two fathers and lifted the ribbon boundary. He stormed onto the course, hovering over Cletus.

"Get up! Get up, you fool! Beat him!"

Cletus, lying on his back, bleeding, and blinded by the glaring sunlight on his face, tried to sit up, but couldn't. He rolled to his side and pointed toward the Rocky Point cliffs.

"Rocky Point...ahhhh!" Cletus said as he lay injured, turning from the sun's glare. I heard his words, and so did Jimmy Jack.

"Beat these freaks!" Clausen screamed. "You're a disgrace!"

"Get away from me!" Cletus shouted. Clausen raised his foot, but the two fathers rushed up, grabbed hold of Clausen, and shoved him off the course.

"You're the disgrace!" said one father. Jimmy Jack, still sprawled on the ground near the finish line, lowered his head.

The crowd erupted again, shouting at Zeke and Cletus, both writhing in pain. One of the new coaches screamed, "If you touch them or help them, it will disqualify their team!" This caused do-gooders in the crowd to freeze.

Pop and Grundman ignored his comment and stepped onto the course to assist the boys. That was when a host of spectators hollered, pointing back toward the top of the colorful hundred-yard straightaway. Everyone turned, staring at a boy who ran between the two rows of colorful ribbons toward the finish line. He slowed as he approached the two fallen runners.

Dr. Gorman shouted, "It's Ethan!" as a sliver of hope spread across his face.

Ethan stopped, gazing down at Zeke and Cletus. Everyone was screaming, shouting out commands. But Ethan just stood there—in limbo!

"Cross the finish line, and you win!" one fan demanded.

"Win it for yourself!" said another.

Ethan's weary eyes turned first to his grandfather, seeing the strain on his face, and then at the strong presence of Pop O'Reilly beside him. Ethan knelt and pulled Zeke and Cletus up, putting their arms around each of his shoulders. The crowd hushed at first, confused, before applause and shouts of praise grew to an astounding roar as spectators sensed something special happening. Ethan struggled, but Pop and Grundman backed off as Ethan escorted both boys across the finish line, keeping them on their feet before all three collapsed past the line.

Grundman pointed to Ethan, whose torso crossed first, then shouted in his bullhorn: "Soaring Eagles win!" Cheers erupted as Chester marked the poster beside the words that read LOW SCORE WINS!

SOARING EAGLES: 1+2+6+7+12 = 28. ROCKSIDE RAVENS: 3+4+5+8+9 = 29.

Beside them, the two wannabes in black leather jackets arrived, waddling like penguins, unable to bend their stiff arms under their jackets. Clyde did his spinnin' top routine, clipping them on the chin, dropping them to the turf as he apologized. Others waved their crutches in joy. Wheelchair kids spun in circles till they were dizzy.

Ma leaped up. "It's like winnin' the pennant!"

Luke and Andy rocked in the *Eagle 7* with its hydraulics, which tossed Andy a foot in the air. Keith and Pete, with both hands crossed, gave a leaping double high-five salute.

Dr. Gorman hugged Ethan, shouting, "You finished! You did it! I'm so proud!"

Bubba did the twist beside Lizzy Looper, who twirled like a ballerina. Rawley and Blimp, standing nearby, shook their heads in disbelief. A US Fish and Wildlife truck arrived off to the side behind Sheriff Logan and his cruiser.

Tom tried to rise for the celebration, his back spotted with blood. Darla held him, stroking Tom's hair. Keith and Pete rushed over to check on Tom as Jenny shouted, "Something has happened to Zack! I'll find out!"

Jimmy Jack followed me toward Zeke. "Where's his brother?"

315

"I'm not sure. Victory will know!" I said.

Pop was already kneeling at Zeke's side when Victory soared over us, flapping his wings and shrieking. That brought another roar of astonishment from Rockside citizens.

"Look! The eagle is back!" yelled one man.

"Where's Zack?" Pop asked his twin brother.

"The cliffs! Zack broke his leg! Victory knows where they are!" said Zeke in panic-mode.

"I'm not seein' so well," I said to Jimmy Jack. "Will ya help me?"

"I'll guide ya to the cliffs! Come on!" Our sprint away was awkward since stiffness had set in. Victory circled the crowd, then followed us as cheers rose from the people.

Pop turned to Jenny. "Get the boys at the *Eagle 7* to help Zack at the cliffs!"

CHAPTER 38

Life or Death Rescue

As Jimmy Jack and I ran toward the cliffs, he yelled out, "That's my Pa jogging into that grove of pine trees ahead." He, too, was angling toward the cliffs.

I glanced back to the starting line. But with blurry eyes, I could only imagine Pa, Ma, and Chester helping Jake into our pickup to follow us.

I knew Jenny would tell Luke, Andy, and Bubba at the *Eagle 7* that Zack's got a broken leg at the cliffs!

I wasn't surprised when told later what happened. Bubba said, "Fire it up!"

Luke started the engine as Bubba pulled out the large trout from his windbreaker pouch and tossed it to Lizzy. The fish flopped around as she juggled it in her hands.

"All aboard!" Luke shouted. Luke, Bubba, Andy, and Jenny piled into the *Eagle 7*. In a flash, Luke left with three passengers—realizing he'd increased the danger of a wild ride.

"Jimmy Jack is leading Billy to the cliffs!" Jenny shouted from the sidecar.

"You trust Jimmy Jack?" Luke questioned.

"I trust Victory," Jenny said. "Zeke told us that Victory knows where Zack is."

"Stop the *Eagle*, Luke!" Andy yelled. Luke stopped beside a line of plastic ribbons. "Bubba, pull out the ribbon line! Haul 'em aboard! We might need 'em." Bubba stepped out and yanked the ribbons off the poles. Hopping back in, he pulled the ribbon line into the sidecar as they raced forward again.

"I'm reelin' in another marlin!" said Bubba as yards of colored ribbons dragged along the forest trail behind the *Eagle 7*.

*****

Jimmy Jack and I saw Coach Clausen waving his arms to talk with us beside a grove of pine trees. We stopped when we reached him. Coach Clausen stared at me. "Your freak show ruined everything!"

"Help us, Pa! We think one of the twins got hurt on the cliffs!" Jimmy Jack pleaded.

Clausen stood still. "Why should I? Or you? You helpin' 'em proves they don't belong here!"

"No! What happened in this race proves you don't belong!" Jimmy Jack shouted. "What did you tell Cletus to do?"

"That's my business!"

"Pa, please help us find him!" Jimmy Jack pleaded again. Clausen never moved. "What's wrong with you, Pa? I don't even know you anymore!" Jimmy Jack ran off, and Billy joined him, running again toward the cliffs.

Minutes later, the roar of the *Eagle 7* grew louder, passing Coach Clausen at the pine trees.

Pa drove the family pickup, making his own trail as he weaved through the trees. Ma and Jake held on in the front seat while Chester bounced in the bed as if on a trampoline. Pa spotted Coach Clausen and skidded to a stop. He leaped out and confronted him.

"You are a disgrace!" Pa shouted.

"Ned, your handicapped freaks have ruined the traditions of Rockside. But one thing never changes. You are a gutless coward!"

"No more!" shouted Pa. He rushed Clausen, who drew his starter pistol and emptied two rounds into Ned before absorbing the collision and falling to the ground. The pistol sounds echoed through the trees as both men fell in a heap.

Sheriff Logan, joining two US Fish and Wildlife officers in their truck, skidded to a stop. They slammed their truck doors and sprinted to Clausen, spinning him against a pine tree, his arms raised and his feet spread. Sheriff Logan confiscated the starter pistol while one of the US Fish and Wildlife officers checked on Ned, who turned over, his hand feeling his stomach.

"Blanks! Ouch!" said Pa.

Chester rose in the pickup bed, "Look, Ma, the sheriff's got him spread-eagled!"

Ma, Jake, and Chester sighed with relief when Pa gave the okay sign to the family. Ma climbed out of the pickup and spun a baseball in her hand. "There's a meetin' on the mound!" said Ma. "If I was the manager, I'd take him out!"

A Fish and Wildlife officer held up a white eagle tail feather while Sheriff Logan rolled up Clausen's shirt sleeves. Sheriff Logan explained, "We found this white eagle feather in the visor of your truck! Who placed it there and where did you get these talon scratches on your arms?"

Clausen yanked free and ran by Lily. Sheriff Logan drew his sidearm and yelled, "Stop right there! Halt!"

Chester and Jake yelled, "Zing it, Ma!"

Lily's fastball nailed Coach Clausen in the back of the head. He fell and slid on pine needles face first, dazed.

Sheriff Logan ran up, grabbed the baseball, and tossed it to Lily, who flipped it to Chester, who dropped it in the bed as if it was a hot potato. Logan handcuffed Coach Clausen who groaned, "Oh, my head! What happened!"

Pulling him up, Logan pointed to the ground at Clausen's feet. "Pine cones. Big, bad pine cones!" Coach Clausen, confused, saw them, then looked at pine treetops above him, spying Victory, who shrieked before circling back to the cliffs.

Chester spoke, "Ma, Victory must have heard the shots and knew it meant danger back when Jake took a bullet."

Ned had shaken off the blanks by now and thanked Bart and the two officers. Ned never gloated. He nodded to the defeated man before sprinting toward the cliffs.

*****

Jimmy Jack and I had run upward along the most dangerous section of the Rocky Point Cliffs. We looked for signs of struggle to help us locate where Zack might be until we heard Victory's shriek.

"Wooo-eee!" I yelled in response. Victory soared in and shrieked about thirty yards farther up the trail. We sprinted and Jimmy Jack spotted the elastic band lying on the ground.

"Zack! Zack! Can you hear me?" I shouted.

We moved to a section of higher ground that curled above the ledge and jutted out. "There he is!" shouted Jimmy Jack. Zack lay draped over a sapling growing out of the cliff wall. Jimmy Jack climbed down as close as he could and lay on a rock, lowering the elastic band, but it fell short of Zack's grasp.

"Hurry! It's giving way!" shouted Zack in a weakened voice. The sapling sagged.

Just then, I heard the *Eagle 7*. "Keep holdin' on, Zack! Help is here! We've gotta find a smooth surface for the *Eagle 7*." Jimmy Jack found a patch of ground free of major boulders.

"My leg is hurtin'!" Zack said, groaning as the *Eagle 7* skidded to a stop. All but Luke piled out.

"Smart idea!" I saw the line of the plastic ribbons wrapped around Bubba and trailing the vehicle. "Bubba! Unwind yourself so we can collect the line and tie it to the *Eagle 7*!"

He did. "Rugged terrain shredded this line!" Andy said. "It won't handle the weight!"

Bubba held up another section. "This line's cut in half!"

"Join the best ones together! Make them double or triple strength! We're out of time!" I yelled.

Luke roared the *Eagle 7*, trying to get it closer to the cliff's edge, but the ground was too rocky. He spun the *Eagle 7* around and shouted, "Yank out some of these rocks so I can get closer!" We did our best before reaching a huge immoveable boulder.

Jenny looked over the edge. "The sapling is giving way! Hurry!"

I looked at Luke and made one of the toughest calls of my life. "You're the only one light enough yet strong enough to pull him up."

"Hook me up!" Luke said. He swung his stubs out of the driver's seat and flipped into the sidecar. Jimmy Jack found three good lines and untangled them, making it triple strength. I tied one of the joined ends to Luke's belt. Jimmy Jack tied the other end to the back of the *Eagle 7*. Luke walked partway on his hands to the ledge while Andy leaped into the driver's seat. From a standing position, Jimmy Jack, Bubba, and I lowered Luke upside down over the side of the cliff wall, hand over hand till the line grew taut beside Zack's sapling.

The sapling bent downward, and Zack's hand slipped to the end of the branch.

"Hurry!" he yelled.

"Keep holdin' on!" Luke shouted from his upside-down rescue descent. He reached out and bear-hugged Zack under his arms, holding on to him for dear life.

"Pull! Now, Andy!" I yelled.

Andy pressed the accelerator, moving the *Eagle 7* forward till the line was taut. Luke and Zack rose from the cliff walls as we three pulled on the line to help raise him. Soon, it was a stalemate.

"Something has snagged the line!" I said.

"The tires are spinning!" shouted Andy. "I've lost traction!"

"Back up, Andy! Give us some slack!" I yelled, hoping to undo the snag in the line. Andy backed up the *Eagle 7*, which caused Luke and Zack to descend again.

"Keep holdin' on!" Bubba shouted. With only that warning, Bubba let go of the line and ran upward to the *Eagle 7*. Jimmy Jack and I fell from our feet onto our bellies, sliding to the cliff's edge, our arms draped over the side, our hands still clenching the line.

Jenny grabbed my ankle with one hand and Jimmy Jack's with the other. She dug her feet into a rocky crevice to stop us from sliding over the cliff.

Above, Bubba leaped into the sidecar. "I've got traction!" Andy yelled from the *Eagle 7* as it began once again to move forward.

Luke and Zack rose as Jenny's grip let go. Jimmy Jack and I re-gripped the line to help pull them upward while Jenny recovered.

As Luke and Zack rose close to the ledge, I felt a jerking sensation.

Jenny peered over the side. "The plastic is tearing!"

I released my line, hoping it would hold while I dove to the edge and grabbed Luke's shirt. Jimmy Jack picked up the discarded elastic band and scrambled to the ledge, lowering it to Zack, who gripped it. Then the line snapped.

With Andy still gunning the accelerator of the *Eagle 7*, the vehicle lunged forward and hit a rock, popping Bubba high into the air as Andy skidded the *Eagle 7* between some rocks.

"Eeeowww!" Bubba squealed, his cry booming along the cliffs.

Jenny grabbed our ankles again but had little strength remaining. Jimmy Jack and I bent halfway over the edge, still sliding down, fearing a potential free fall into the canyon.

Out of nowhere, Pa sprinted toward us and dove, grabbing Jimmy Jack's leg and one of my own as Jenny's grip gave way. Another stalemate occurred until Luke, now with a free hand, used it to climb over me before flipping onto the ledge, safe but exhausted. I spun to the side and helped Jimmy Jack and my Pa pull Zack up onto the ledge.

Each of us lay grounded, gasping for air while smiling at each other and breaking into spontaneous laughs of relief. Even Zack, in pain with a broken leg, chuckled through his ordeal. When Pa stood to check on Andy and Bubba, Jimmy Jack's expression changed from doubt to trust, watching my Pa, the man who saved his life and mine, walk up to check on the *Eagle 7*.

Zack gave Jimmy Jack a sober look. "You saved my life and risked your own."

"Your team showed me a better way," Jimmy Jack said, looking at Zack and then at me.

Jenny smiled at Jimmy Jack. "Billy said you had many sides."

Everyone grew silent, realizing Jimmy Jack was not with his own team. He was now with ours.

I wonder about the guts he displayed when he disagreed with his father and joined us in the rescue.

Words came from Jimmy Jack, who was now "speakin' from the liver," as Grampa Cline used to say when moments of truth came to light.

"My Pa taught us to hate you Clines. You gotta be careful what one generation teaches the next. Hate seeps into your soul—blinding you to see only your side of an argument. I watched how your team helps each other and how we don't. Peace prospers when both sides unite to forgive and learn from each other."

Zack gripped Jimmy Jack's hand, and we all followed their lead by joining our hands to theirs. Solid unity. I had experienced nothing like it before.

CHAPTER 39

Double Celebration

Pop drove the Cliffview van, loaded with his team and students toward the cliffs. Darla, Lizzy, Cletus, and Gopher were also aboard. They had witnessed Sheriff Logan and the Fish and Wildlife officers arrest Coach Clausen, now seated in the backseat of the truck with his hands handcuffed to reinforced metal hooks.

*****

The Cliffview van approached near the cliffs, followed by a slow-moving mountain rescue vehicle with its crew inside. Both emptied as the medics gathered supplies and two stretchers. Our group helped them carry necessary items up the trail on foot to the rescue site.

When they arrived, Cletus limped up to Jimmy Jack, hollering, "Sheriff Logan and those Fish and Wildlife officers arrested Coach!" Jimmy Jack nodded.

"Where's Zack?" asked Pop.

"Over here! I'll show you," Jenny answered, as everyone, including Cletus, followed her.

Resting beside me, Jimmy Jack spoke: "My Pa's got a lot more to explain."

"Jimmy Jack, what you said before the race…did you save Victory?"

"Yes. The Fish and Wildlife officers believe he'll be able to fly again. We know they're right. He already has. It was my Pa who shot your eagle."

I stood still but thrilled to know Victory was okay.

"Thanks for grabbin' hold," Jimmy Jack added. "I was goin' over the side for sure."

"It was a team effort," I said with a smile. As we joined the others, I pointed to Luke and motioned for Jimmy Jack to help me. We lifted Luke high in the air.

"A hero for the day!" I shouted. The small crowd cheered, and Lizzy snapped pictures of Jimmy Jack and me honoring Luke.

"It's better than scoring a touchdown!" yelled Luke.

Zack called out, "Thank you, Luke!" The other boys circled Zack as he was resting, sprawled on a boulder beside two medics who were treating him. Cletus limped up, apologizing to Zack.

"Eeeeowww!" cried Bubba beside the other two medics.

"He came down on his fish hooks after popping up in the air!" said Andy. Bubba was lying on his tummy, "butt up" over a small boulder as medics pulled out fish hooks one by one from his posterior. "Hey, Bubba, how many fish hooks did ya get?"

"Eeeeowww!" cried Bubba again.

"Never mind!" said Andy.

Tom and Darla joined us. "Welcome back," Tom said.

Jimmy Jack smiled at Darla and answered, "I am back…Jimmy Jack is back."

Pop, with a giant smile, joined us, too. "Jenny told me what happened! What they used to call 'handicapped' has now become a badge of honor! You're a gift from God!" Pop put both hands on my shoulders—a royal connection.

I glanced at Jimmy Jack and then at Pop. "We're all on the same team, Pop. Thanks for showin' us a better way…the only way. Your daughter would be proud."

Pop basked in the joy of his long-held dream finally come true.

*****

Ten weeks later, I stood in the clearing in front of our cabin porch, gazing at Pa. He was sitting on a stool, playing a spunky tune on his guitar. I admit my toes were tappin' to the beat. Behind him was Ma's new stained-glass window, depicting the Ascension of Jesus. Pa wasn't alone. His musician friends were playing a variety of instruments: a banjo, dog house bass, fiddle, mandolin, accordion, sax, flute, guitar, and a set of drums. They were jammin' big time!

Pa wore a brand-spankin' new pair of railroad overalls. He had completed a required set of counseling sessions and was re-hired. He had returned from night shift a few hours earlier and couldn't wait to pluck the strings he loved to play. Beside Pa was the old water barrel. On top of it was an opened soft drink, a new taste Pa was working hard to acquire.

Pa grinned, enjoying the music while watching Jake throw a soft pitch with a rubber baseball to Chester. Like clockwork, Chester threw it to Ma, who stood beside Jake and handed it back to him.

Between a set of songs, Jake spoke up with a loud voice: "I want you all to know I'm ready. I'm ready to serve my time…starting tomorrow! If Pa can earn his way back to the railroad, I can do my time and get back to pitching! Thanks for your support!"

"That's the spirit!" said the banjo player.

Jake threw another slow pitch to Chester.

"That pitch was a strike, Jake!" said Chester.

"Yeah, a perfect pitch to hit out of the stadium!" Jake said as everyone chuckled.

"Today, they might hit it out, but tomorrow? Who knows?" Chester responded.

"Keep practicin', Jake! You're gettin' better every day," Ma said.

"He is…we all are," said Pa, glancing at the musicians. I knew at that moment we were a complete family.

I looked at my watch. "When will they get here?"

I heard the familiar sound of Tom's Blue Beauty on the dirt road leading to our cabin. Following Tom were a half dozen more vehicles, including Pop's van and Dr. Gorman's Jeep.

I guess they're all gonna show. The musicians began another song. Jenny leaped from the Beauty and dashed into my arms.

"You're lookin' great without glasses!" she said.

"So I don't look handsome with glasses?"

"Stop, Billy, I'd never say that." She grinned.

Pop and the team enjoyed the music and ate sandwiches, snacks, and Ma's homemade cookies. They gathered around, wanting to inspect me.

"So these are your new eyes?" asked Bubba.

"Sort of, but more like improved eyes—a corneal transplant! Thanks to Dr. Gorman!" I gave Ethan a high-five. Dr. Gorman waved and smiled. The bongo player gave him a bongo roll. "He also covered the expenses for my lessons and this party!" More bongo rolls.

After another round of refreshments, I announced to the group, "My hang-gliding equipment is in place at the boulder cliff lookout. I've had seven lessons from these two great instructors. One's going up with me to make sure I follow procedures. The other will check on my skills down from the cliff lookout. See you on the shore! Don't be late!"

"I brought my fishin' poles!" exclaimed Bubba. "Can I fish?"

"Sure," I said. "Use the rowboat. I'm sure we'd all love fresh fish a little later! Right, Keith?" All cheered, except Keith, who shook his head, smiling.

Jenny walked close to me. "Okay, you've got your helmet up there, your water vest, your whistle, your rope, and your new eyes! What are you missing?"

"Just you," I said.

"Oh, no, you don't! Heights scare me!"

After those words, the hang-gliding instructor accompanied me upward through the forest toward my lookout as the band played on.

*****

At my cliff lookout, I could still hear the music in my mind. Even when the hang-gliding instructor buckled me into the outfit, memory of the tunes energized me.

An eagle shrieked!

"Shhh! Listen!" I said to the instructor. We looked up in the sky. Victory shrieked again and circled, spreading his wings to slow, landing on the T-Cross.

"Look at that! Victory's back!" I cried. Gazing at Victory, I voiced another challenge. "I'm gonna mount up on wings and soar like an eagle! Wanna join me?"

I looked to the instructor, and after surveying the wind, he gave me the okay. I ran a few steps and launched myself from the cliff. "Wooo-eee!" I shouted. Victory took off from his T-Cross and soared over me in a brilliant blue sky.

The wind whistled over my body, and the music continued to play in my mind. My vision was clear and bright, my flight blended with nature's delights! *Oh, the beauty of majestic mountainsides—of God's creation! I'm soaring! Soaring with Victory!*

*****

I swept along the shorelines of Ruby Lake with Victory, my mind relishing the great and challenging experiences I had endured. Approaching our dock, I saw Bubba in the rowboat, fishing. Another fantastic musical arrangement wafted over the lake as the musicians had shifted to the dock. The clamor of cheering teammates, students, and family standing nearby created the most unique musical atmosphere I had ever witnessed.

While Bubba fished from the rowboat, a sudden down-draft whipped my hang glider lower, putting me on a potential collision course with Bubba, who stood in the rowboat. He smiled, holding up his catch of fish for me to see, until his eyes got huge, realizing I was soaring straight at him. "Abandon ship! Abandon ship!" I yelled.

Bubba dove overboard, losing his fish as I adjusted the craft and swept over the rowboat, landing on the shore. Victory opened his wings and gripped his talons on the top of the Ruby Lake sign post. Many leapt off the dock and joined Bubba in the shallow end of the lake. He laughed along with us since he'd have a great reason to fish again. Keith sighed with relief.

The instructor got me unhitched, and I was free. Darla stood between Jimmy Jack and Tom, her arms around both boys. Jake tossed a slow pitch to Chester as Ma signaled approval. Pop and Pa gave a high-five to each other. I walked to Jenny and embraced her. We turned together as another toe-tapper mirrored the joy across the Ruby Lake dock and its surroundings.

I shouted, "What a ride! What a team! What a time to be alive!" All cheered in response. Looking at Jenny, I asked, "What's up for next year?"

Jenny faced me with a big smile and winked.

ABOUT THE AUTHOR

Wes Folsom, born and raised in Los Angeles, now lives with his wife in Kentucky. A Northern League mile champ in Los Angeles, he has run the hundred-mile week that avid runners often brag about. An educator and coach, he took sixteen track and field and cross-country athletes to the top pedestal of a state championship in Kentucky. *Soaring Eagles* is his first novel.

Author's Race Against Bob Schul, the 5,000-meter Olympic Champ of 1964

I raced Bob Schul in a summer two-mile all-comers race at East Los Angeles Junior College in 1965, early in high school. The announcement he would run astonished me. I weaseled into the second row, gazing at the muscular legs of an Olympic Champion.

My ego blossomed: *Bob might have been the 'cat's meow' last summer in Tokyo, taking down the world's best distance runners, but he's never faced me in the City of Angels!*

The gun fired and twenty-five runners sprinted away. I let Bob go, believing he was tired finishing a tough workout with this race. *Laps later, I might reel him in like a trout.*

Soon Bob Schul disappeared. *Where did he go? He couldn't fear my reputation. I had none!* Deep into oxygen debt in LA-LA land, I tried to salvage the race with a strong kick.

Storming down the homestretch, I saw two girls stretch out a finish tape and a reporter preparing to snap a picture of the gold medalist sprinting to victory. Hearing Bob Schul behind me tearing up the cinders like a wild stallion, I downshifted into "cheetah" mode.

My legs churned like a blender grinding a smoothie! But Bob flashed past me, winning by inches! THEN I FINISHED MY LAST LAP! I had ruined the reporter's photo.

I reminded Bob of the comical incident in Eugene at the 2016 Olympic Trials where he was honored. Both are moments I'll never forget!